Nunslinger:

The Complete Series

Stark Holborn

HODDER

First published in Great Britain in 2014 by Hodder & Stoughton
An Hachette UK company

1

A CIP catalogue record for this title is available from the British Library

Paperback ISBN 978 1 444 78923 2

Typeset in Plantin Light by Hewer Text UK Ltd, Edinburgh

Printed and bound by Clays Ltd, St Ives plc

Hodder & Stoughton policy is to use papers that are natural, renewable
and recyclable products and made from wood grown in sustainable forests.
The logging and manufacturing processes are expected to conform to
the environmental regulations of the country of origin.

Hodder & Stoughton Ltd
338 Euston Road
London NW1 3BH

www.hodder.co.uk

For my sister

Nunslinger: Book 1

The True Tale of how Sister Thomas Josephine of St. Louis, Missouri, began to cross the Overland Trail to Sacramento, California with the help of one Abraham C. Muir

I

The searcher of hearts and reins

Of the wagon train there was nothing left. That is what I first recall.

When I came to, with the sun blazing through my eyelids and the dryness of the plain within my throat, I wondered at how I could be alive. Then I saw him, and I was sure I lived not. He leaned over me, eyes blue as a paper flower and the wind of the plains pushing at his hair; I was both terrified and elated for I thought he was the Lord himself.

Since I happen to be a Bride of Christ, this presented itself as no small matter.

Before he could lay his healing hands on me, there were other hands, used for nothing but their own selfish pleasure. They lifted me roughly and I managed one beseeching look toward my Lord. His pistols caught the light as he smiled. In his hand was a pair of dead man's boots.

2

Their cities thou hast destroyed

They had attacked at dawn, slaughtered the men and stolen the horses, burned all ten wagons. Hours later, the air remained bitter with smoke. Scraps of charred canvas drifted across the dust, evidence of the losses suffered by all. We had been traveling the most desolate stretch of land since our journey began, having left behind Nebraska for the wilds of the plains north of Denver.

There were eight of us together, survivors of that journey. Four were officers' wives on their way to their husbands at distant forts. They kept to themselves, and cried, wailing that their fine stitched shawls and strings of pearls should now be hanging round the necks of red-skinned brats. Fifth was another woman, traveling alone. A butcher's widow, only recently joined at Julesburg, aiming for her sister's home in Salt Lake City.

Sixth was a child, a boy small enough still to be excused from the slaughter. I had seen him during the raid, cowering behind the wheel of a wagon until the fire had flushed him out.

A man, scarred with the tattle-tale marks of a prospector, made up the seventh. His leg had been close to split by a tomahawk strike from behind.

I was the eighth. My head was bruised, but in truth my hurts were slight. I do not believe that I was the target of the blow that knocked me to the ground, and in my heart I forgave the man that dealt it.

The prospector with the shattered leg awoke – his consciousness came and went with the winds. Now the breezes dropped, and the sun burned. The shade cast by our canvas shelter had shrunk to a tiny square. Soon, there would not be room for us all.

Returning my rosary to my belt, I stood. The heat, and the pain in my head made my ears ring and my eyes flood, but it soon passed. I called the young boy to me and we began to move the wounded man further into the shade. As we slid him over the dust, the boy stole a glance my way.

'Do you know your prayers, child?'

His eyes went wide. They were a different color each – lake blue and forest brown – and he nodded.

'Then I would ask you to say one for this man.'

I stepped out into the high noon heat then. The air was like chalk in my lungs and I blessed the wisdom of the habit, for the brown cloth shielded my skin as effectively as a parasol. Through the haze I crossed to a larger tent, canvas like ours but with three enclosed sides. Horses stood passively in its shadow; my fellow survivors had commandeered their customary shelter.

Two soldiers were on guard, leaning on rifles. Their blue uniforms were dull and stripped of color, white lines fanning their eyes from constant squinting.

One of them spoke. 'Best get back to the shade, Sister. A mule couldn't stand in this heat.'

'Forgive my interruption,' I sought out eyes under the hat's brim. 'There is a man yonder who suffers. I believe a few drops of some substance to numb his pain would be a mercy.'

'Can't waste supplies on a torn-up old scratch. Won't be no replacing them 'til we reach Fort Laramie.'

'How far might the fort be?'

'Four days' march, if we stick to the trail. Like as not he'll be long gone by then. Save your breath, Sister.'

'Sergeant.' The voice came from behind us.

The wrinkles in the soldier's uniform seemed to flatten as he pulled himself to attention. In the entrance was the man I had believed to be my Lord. His hair was the color of pale oak wood above his shoulders, and on his hands were broad-cuffed gloves that – despite the ever-present dirt – were clean and creamy as the belly of a calf. I counseled myself to remain calm, but the memory of my earlier mistake continued to agitate me.

'Fetch the medicine chest,' he said to the man I had been addressing. 'You'll see a bottle marked "ether". Bring it to me with one of the cloths that you find there.'

His voice was quick and intelligent; something that gave me hope in that land which was otherwise a wilderness. He turned to me then and pulled the wide hat from his head.

'Sister, I offer my apologies for the idleness of my men. Truly, it is no excuse, but we have had a hard march. They begin to lose their shine the longer we stay from home.'

He lowered his vivid blue eyes, which seemed the only spot of pure color in an inhospitable territory.

'First Lieutenant Theodore F. Carthy, at your service.'

3

For there is no one in death,
that is mindful of thee

The bodies lay before me in a row, stretched out on the dust. Eight in all, the driver and muleskinners, the guide and guards who had been our traveling companions since we left St. Louis. Now their faces were still, ravaged by wounds or blistered by the heat. It had been the best part of a day before the soldiers had seen the smoke of burning wagons and come to our aid. By then, the sun had already begun its work upon the dead. The plain was keen to claim its own.

There was no time for a proper burial, but Lieutenant Carthy spared two men to aid me in restoring some dignity to the dead. The soldiers had dragged the bodies into a line without a word, wiped their brows on their sleeves and had not shuddered at what they touched.

I was told to mind the sun, for it was now well past its peak and the company would soon be riding to less exposed ground. I could see the men saddling horses and stowing packs. Although no one came to press me, I knew for whom they waited.

I took up a palmful of dust and closed my eyes. It ran through my fingers onto the feet of the first man. I prayed, anointing each body with the earth of the plain. This was as much of a burial as they would receive, these men who were soon to be white bones. *Somebody's darling*, the soldiers had said. They were mine, and the Lord's.

A cry from the camp and I crossed myself, thinking my time alone was nearly over. I was too far away to recognize the warning.

'You just stay mighty still, Sister. Ain't got cause to harm you, if you do as I say.'

There was the sound of a pistol being cocked. How the man had managed to draw so close, so silently, I had no notion. Slowly, I raised my arms and crossed them into my sleeves. Riders were galloping from the camp, a cloud of dust spreading behind them like great wings. At their head was Lieutenant Carthy.

I waited. The riders stopped at twenty paces. Six, all armed, their buttons and belts sparking fire.

'Lower your pistol, stranger. Or we will shoot you where you stand.'

There was a kind of wheeze from the man behind me that might have been a laugh.

'Who's to say you'll hit me, Ted? You always seem to miss, and it's beginnin' to be something of a disappointment.'

Carthy's face was as pale as his gloves, two spots of red appearing high on his cheeks at the stranger's words.

'Without your filthy Indian tricks you'd have long been kicking wood, Abraham C.'

'Then I ain't got much of a mind to leave them off.'

Carthy's eyes dropped to mine. He pulled himself straighter in the saddle, smoothed down the snarl upon his face. His voice, ordinarily so light and courteous, took on a commanding edge.

'You release this lady now, Muir. I do not expect it to mean much to an outlaw, but she is a Bride of Christ and under my protection.'

The man's horse drew closer behind me. I could feel the heat of its skin, the breath from its nose on my face. I sensed the muzzle of the pistol mere inches from my temple, but remained as stone, my eyes fixed ahead.

'Well that's the thing,' drawled Muir. 'Maybe I have a mind to repent. Until that time, this lady is to be my insurance.'

I felt a hand grasp my arm. No gloves, fingers, dark and scarred.

'Climb up, Sister.'

I stared into the blue of Carthy's eyes, trying to see some instruction there. Perhaps it was the glare of the lowering sun,

8

but I could read nothing. It did not matter, for his silence was instruction enough. Another pile of dead, more bones for the plain to whip clean.

I set my foot in the empty stirrup. The man Mr Carthy had called an outlaw kept the pistol trained on me. Not an easy task, as I hauled myself awkwardly onto the packs. Once settled, I found my eyes level with Mr Carthy, his gaze fixed upon me, cold and clear.

4

. . . and who shall confess to thee in hell?

'Set me down here.'

The man continued to urge the horse up the hill. My request could have been a louse crawling at his ear, for the attention he paid it.

I raised my hand from the saddle for as long as I dared to attract his attention. I had never ridden behind a man before, especially not in such close quarters. Where Carthy was neat and straight, this man seemed broad and lean, like something that belonged in the wild. I had yet to get a good look at his face. It seemed to shift beneath the shade of his hat until I could not tell what was the crease of an eye, or a deep line filled with shadow.

Yet his scent reached me, strongest of all: raw leather and sweat and something sharp, like the embers of a fire.

The hide jacket was stiff under my fingers. Although I tried to keep a distance, my hold upon his waist was the only thing that prevented me from tumbling down the slope and shattering many a bone in the process. Beneath my arm I could feel his torso, hard muscle and the heat of skin through the calico shirt. I longed to break that contact, for it troubled me. Instead, my eyes found what looked like a necklace beneath his collar, a string of beads the color of old bone. I tore my gaze away and looked resolutely ahead.

'I ask you to set me down here, sir. We are far beyond range of Mr Carthy's guns. Set me down or I shall dismount myself.'

Some expression quirked his ears. It tried the very depths of my composure when I realized that it was a smile.

'Mighty long roll back down that hill, Sister. Like it or not you'd be in pieces by the bottom. I'd be no man if I were to treat my insurance thusly.'

'Why you've been no man at all, *thusly*.'

I bit my lip in self-rebuke, for it was beneath me to speak to him so. Though I did not like it, he was correct. The slope we climbed was close to sheer, a channel scored deep into the hill by some ancient water flow. The passage was at times so narrow that it left lines of pale dust upon the hem of my habit, the toes of my boots.

'No need to fret, Sister,' he grunted. 'I'll do you no harm. There's them below that'd like me dead, wouldn't scruple on sneaking up in the night to do it neither. Like as not they'll think twice on that if they might catch a lady up in the fire. Insurance is what you'll be 'til I feel safe from them.'

He sounded reluctant to speak, voice pitched so low it was almost a rumble. Yet I heard in it a vague warmth, an accent that reminded me of my own childhood; of the half-remembered tones that had been mine, before the years at the convent had washed them away.

I made to answer, but the horse skittered upon the loose stones and I felt sure its hooves would fail, that we would be sent plunging to the floor of the plain far below.

'Up on, Rattle, easy there, up on boy,' the man urged.

We were nearing a summit. The horse's steps began to slow and shudder.

'Forward!' he shouted.

For one terrible moment I saw air beneath the front hooves and we slipped back. I chanced a look over my shoulder. Below, tiny as baubles, were Carthy's troops, their canvas shelter little more than a handkerchief spread on the ground. I commended myself to the Lord.

'Lean forward, damn you!'

I realized he was shouting at me. There was a hand grasping my arm, fingers digging hard into the flesh as I was pulled bodily forward. His own neck was at a level with the horse's, streams of sweat matching one against the other. He landed a last kick on its flanks.

With a cry, the horse surged upward and staggered onto level ground. Shaking from the shock and rough treatment, I near fell from the saddle. As I dismounted, my rosary caught on a buckle. I could do nothing but watch as the chain broke and beads cascaded like rain to the dry earth.

5

Visited by night,
thou hast tried me by fire

'What does the "C" stand for?'

'What's that you say?'

'The gentleman back there, Lieutenant Carthy. He called you "Abraham C."'

The man sniffed deep and spat into the embers of the fire. The charcoaling wood hissed for a second.

'The "C" stands for nothing.'

'I beg your pardon?'

'It stands for no man. Woman neither. Even them Indians in the hills, they got their gods for the earth and the sky and the plateau, but they know they cain't control what's beyond them.'

He must have felt pity for my confusion, for he barked a laugh, the expression scudding across his face like a strip of sun caught between shadows.

'It's "Sea", ma'am,' he allowed me, the end of a smile in his teeth. 'Abraham Sea Muir, like the wide ocean. Not "c" for "cat".'

The cold of the night after the constant slap of heat during the day must have made me stupid, for I could not comprehend him. My fear at being taken hostage had dulled somewhat to wariness as the hours wore on, but I continued to sit as far as possible from the man. Muir did not seem to notice my discomfort, nor even inclined to notice anything. He was banking the fire, dimming it so that it provided warmth but little light.

'If 't weren't for a lady present I'd snuff it out,' he mumbled. 'Still, rocks should do to shield us from any that's down there.'

'You mean Lieutenant Carthy.'

'I mean any that might not wish me well in the night, and that amounts to a greater number than I care for.'

'Lieutenant Carthy is a gentleman.'

The words were from my mouth before I could consider their wisdom, and I felt a tremor of unease. I did not wish to anger this man.

Exhausted and cold though I was, I knew I must find my way back to Carthy and his men. I could make my own escape in the night, but I had seen the dangers of the plain. My thin boots would last all of a day on the cruel shale of the canyon edge, so it seemed my best chance lay in persuading Muir to give me up.

He was watching me from across the fire, face a jumble of dark and light. Some emotion fidgeted below the surface.

'There are no words in your book, Sister, that'll touch a man like Carthy, were you to pray night and day for the salvation of his soul. Some are ventured too far to return.'

His expression then, darker than I'd yet seen, made me fear that he was right. Not about Carthy, but about himself. That there were hard edges to this world I had never imagined; a world of unbound wounds and blood on the earth and shattered teeth, where a man like Muir lived alone.

A shudder ran across my skin and I broke the gaze. I had gathered what was left of the rosary up from the dust, placed the beads in a pouch at my belt. Muir's eyes followed my fingers as I pulled out the remainder of a section.

'No man is beyond salvation, Mr Muir,' I said, as I touched the beads. 'I shall pray for both your souls.'

'Wouldn't wish my name joined to his by any man,' he mumbled. 'Even in prayer.'

The dark look was gone. He pulled off his boots, packed them against the saddle at his head and dragged the blanket from his shoulders.

'Don't lay too near the fire,' he told me, rolling on his side. 'Holy garb burns just as well as any other cloth.'

6

For they shall shortly
wither away as grass

Before dawn I woke, as was my custom. The sky was heavy as a flagstone, but I sensed a gradual freshening of the air, telling me that the sun would not be found too far away. I rose from the blanket into the chill air and extended stiff limbs. It was not so different to winter in my cell in St. Louis. The thought of the convent, with more than ten years' worth of my tread on its floors, filled me again with purpose, reminded me of my duty.

Muir still slept; I could see the crown of his head emerging from the blankets, hair ruffled. I thought about creeping away then, trying to slide my way back down to the plain before he woke, but it did not seem right. I was neither a prisoner nor a criminal. I had considered long and hard before I slept, and determined that the attack on the wagon train and my presence with Mr Muir was the Lord's will, His first tests of me in the west.

Quietly, I made away from the camp. I did not know what I was searching for until I saw it. A long, low stone the color of honey, tall enough for me to rest my hands against and exactly fit for my purpose. I knelt and lowered my head to begin my morning devotions.

The familiar words flowed out like a song, and I forgot all else. When I felt the first light of the sun warming my back it was like life itself, and tears of joy began to gather in my eyes.

'Mourning, Sister?'

Muir's voice cut through my reverie. I was back on the hilltop, knees all needles and pins in the dust. I crossed myself carefully and wiped my eyes.

'Not mourning, Mr Muir, praying. A prayer of thanks to the Lord.'

'Seems to me you got precious little to thank him for. But like as not you're a favorite, an' he won't take offense to you kneeling at a Sioux altar.'

'Is this an Indian place? You shall tell me that they sacrifice goats upon it, Mr Muir.'

'Would you kill a fine and healthy goat, Sister? Only blood here's what they spill from their own flesh. Look down yonder edge.'

I did. On the far side of the rock were brown stains, streaking to the ground, dried into dust.

'Do they mourn here, Mr Muir?'

'They do. They spill blood and tears both at the pain of being alive and not able to follow them they love into the sky. They heal soon enough.'

There was a whistling from the direction of the fire, and he began to trudge back toward our camp.

'Coffee looks to be done. Better step lively, Sister, if you want something hot in your belly. Any case, this is Oglala Territory. Indians won't look too favorable on a white heathen in their holy place.'

7

Some trust in chariots
and some in horses

We made for an awkward pair at first, riding double on Muir's horse. Unaccustomed as I was to human contact, riding behind Muir caused me anxiety. I had held myself apart, yet time and again I was forced to steady myself upon his shoulder, feel the muscles tense as my fingers gripped the travel-worn hide of his coat.

I do not believe his poor beast was used to the extra weight, for at intervals he would slow and peer with one eye at the creatures upon his back in a manner that could only be described as accusatory.

He was a spare thing, all muscle and sinew, but Muir said that was on account of his nervy and capricious nature.

'Found him last spring at an auction in Denver,' he rumbled, directing his conversation out into the sky that spread unrelentingly over the plateau. 'About to be sold for glue, I reckon. Everyone said he were crow bait. I'd had some luck at cards that night. 'f weren't for a drop too much of the who-hit-John he'd be papering a saloon now.'

He slapped the horse's neck affectionately. The beast responded by stopping dead. After a fair amount of clucking we were on the move again.

'Like I said, he's a capricious fellow. But he were worth a week or two's poor eating. You see a horse ever face down a snake, Sister?'

I had not, and did not feel it particularly necessary to say so. Muir took my silence and ploughed on.

'Terrified is what they are. Well, second day out of town and camping by a creek, I hear this sound, like dry beans in a tin. I look up and there he is, Star Chief of the rattlesnakes, and he's quivering and hissing an' ready to strike in an instant. Then this chap, quiet as a schoolma'am, comes on over and stomps it right into the ground. Fangs and all! Looked like a bowl of sofkee time he'd finished. So I called him Rattle.'

Rattle responded by stopping again to urinate loudly.

'If he's taking a break, we may as well,' Muir chuckled.

He turned to help me down, but I was already scrambling from the horse. As I landed, the muscles in my back jarred sharply, and although I tried my best not to let my discomfort show, Muir must have seen something in my face. All his talk disappeared; a flush creeping up his neck like a schoolboy caught stealing eggs.

'If you've need to relieve yourself, Sister, there's some rocks yonder. Just have care to check the ground underfoot.'

I did so, and for a time stood away at the edge of the plateau, contemplating the stretch of plain before me. Under the cloudless sky it looked smooth, like a bolt of linen had been rolled out and out until it covered all with dun – no life – just endless rock and dead, brittle scrub. Far below was a spark, like sun on water. I squinted to make out what looked to be a line of people marching, and although it was difficult to discern anything in the heat, I felt certain it must be Carthy and his men.

I turned to address Muir again with a request to be allowed back down to the plain, but came eye to eye with Rattle. He held my gaze for a long moment, then turned away, back toward his master.

8

Moreover, my reins have corrected me even till night

Dusk found us camped by a small pond, which was just as well, for Muir's canteens had been dry since noon and thirst claimed my throat. Although I had counseled myself to accept the feeling of dust within my lungs, of dehydration and dryness in every pore, I could not deny the relief I felt at the sight of water.

Muir stared at the pool for a while, then he took up his rifle and plunged the wooden butt in, swirling it like broth.

'Nothing dead in there,' he pronounced after a time. 'Fine to drink, like as not.'

He freed Rattle of bridle and pack, and the horse headed straight for the water. Muir let him drink for a time before hauling him back.

'There's proof, Sister, if you needed it. Best fetch the canteens.'

The water was full of silt, gritty on the tongue but clean enough. A haze had fallen on the evening, as if someone had swiped a wet cloth over the landscape's colors, made them bleed and run. This suited us, Muir said, for it meant the smoke from our fire would not be so evident.

He refused still to answer my questions about when I should be reunited with the wagon train, or indeed, why they hunted him so, for we were clearly being followed. In the heat of the afternoon we had overtaken Carthy and his men, but from our high vantage, I had made out several flecks of blue and brown scouting the foot of the plateau for a path.

'Nothing to see, Sister. Ain't another way up nor down for miles.'

It was only the second time he had acknowledged the

Bluecoats' proximity. Press him as I might, he would say nothing further. Instead, he set about unpacking the evening meal. I watched carefully, and calculated. There were few provisions left.

'Fine meal tonight,' he called. 'Beans and salt pork and all the dust you can eat.'

He upended a sack into his pot, shook out the crumbs. There was barely enough for a child.

'Mr Muir, we have bypassed Carthy and his men. How much longer do you propose to detain me as your "insurance"?'

As before, he made no answer, but continued to clatter about with his spoon. I set my feet more firmly.

'Very well, a simpler question. How will half a heel of salt pork and a few canisters of silt last two persons any longer than a day before they starve in this wasteland? I am no fool, Mr Muir. There is a trading post or a station that cannot be more than half a day's ride from this place and you intend to call there.'

A muscle was twitching beneath the line of his jaw. My mind warned me to take care, yet I was flushed with anger and stubbornly continued.

'Whatever this place is, post or stable or telegraph stop, there you shall leave me, sir, and be on your way. That way I shall cost you no more misery, and can re-join Lieutenant Carthy.'

'Good God, woman!'

Muir was on his feet, eyes dark as mahogany just inches from my own. His face was pale with rage.

'I had thought to escort you as far as Rock Creek, five days hence – five days out of my way I should add – so that you would be spared the risk of encountering that hard-case. Yet you're yearnin' for him like a cat in heat. Well, I shall leave you at the trade post as you desire, though I won't prepare you for the sort of men you will encounter there. It seems you are set on engaging with the worst of them.'

Muir's good humor thus evaporated, he strode off across the plateau, leaving me alone in the gathering gloom. I felt the kind of heat that precedes tears, and gulped them back. I confess I was shocked. It had been a long time since I had been spoken to thus. Muir had never before raised his voice.

If it was his intention to escort me across the plains, I had just abandoned the safety of a guide for a remote post. Yet I could not reconcile his words in relation to Mr Carthy. I could not help but think that such anger might stem from jealousy or intolerance rather than truth.

I sighed and climbed to my feet. My own conduct had been unseemly and I determined to rectify matters before Mr Muir and I parted company. But he was back, before I could move a step, his face calm. He held his hat under one arm and squinted off into the distance. I noted for the first time several streaks of gray in his nut-brown hair, though he could not have been any more than thirty.

'I raised my voice to you, Sister Thomas Josephine and for that I am sorry. I'm not accustomed to company out here, least that of a woman. I brought you from the wagon trail for my own ends, an' so I'll not refuse to leave you safe.'

He sounded like one of the children at the convent school, reading an apology by rote. Speech done, he looked me in the eye.

'You're a damn fool if you choose to remain at the post, but I won't hold you against your will, Sister.'

I smiled then, for here was the man I had grown accustomed to.

'I accept your apology, Mr Muir.'

He nodded, knelt by the fire, and set about trying to salvage his pot of beans.

'Allow me.'

Gently, I took the pot and spoon from his grip.

'You ever tried beans and molasses, Mr Muir?' I asked, realizing as I spoke that I was mimicking his drawl in my own, long forgotten southern accent.

His cigar-end smile was slow to emerge, but when it did he turned it upon me in full.

'Can't say I have, Sister. But I reckon you'll be wanting what's left of the sugar.'

21

9

Strike all my adversaries without cause:
break the teeth of sinners

Before noon the following day we saw a thread of smoke on the horizon and heard the distant clang of metal that announced a trading post. It was a makeshift affair. With the plateau behind and the plain stretching at our feet, it looked like a tiny wooden craft with the mighty weight of the ocean ready to crash upon the deck.

Two horses were tethered out front, and a cart; I shot a glance at Muir – Abe as he insisted I call him – but was reluctant to break our newfound truce with more questions.

'Jus' civilians,' he murmured, catching my look. 'Reckon we should have half a day's lead on the Bluecoats.'

He had told me of his intention to ride due west, and south, until he reached the mountains. There, he said, he could make a living on hunting and skinning, for the Union Army was thinly stretched, and would have little cause to go bothering a trapper. I knew there was more to his story, yet so far he had steadfastly avoided any talk that might give me some further clue.

At the post we were met by a short, barrel-chested man in a striped silk waistcoat that would have looked more at home in a saloon than on the high plains of Laramie.

'Abe!' he announced. 'Well now! Din't expect to see you back here so soon. I heard you was fixing to head north.'

'Who told you that then, Enroy?'

Muir had busied himself with handing me down and tying Rattle to the hitching post.

'Why, you did yourself, Abe, can't have been three weeks back.'

'Must be true, then.'

Muir pushed past the other man without further ceremony and jerked his head for me to follow. Inside the shack wares were laid out on boxes, hung along the walls on nails. Muir prowled the room, selecting goods as he went. I waited for him to make an introduction, but when none came, I stepped forward and nodded at Mr Enroy.

'Sir,' I began.

'Been escorting the Sister over the plateau,' broke in Muir, sniffing at a twist of jerky before adding it to his pile. 'She'll be waiting here for a wagon train to arrive, should be no later than tomorrow morn. You'll see to her well-bein' or I'll know of it.'

Enroy melted into a smile.

'I have been expecting a wagon train from Julesburg. Of course it will be my honor and pleasure to play host to the good Sister. It is too long since the hand of the Lord touched such a place as this. Perhaps we might say a prayer together this evening?'

I inclined my head toward him, unwilling to make any promises until I had the measure of his character. Mr Enroy looked as though he would say more, but Muir dumped his armful of purchases on the counter.

'I'll take these,' he grunted. 'What've you to eat?'

'I've some fine jackrabbit stew in the pot, fresh cornbread, salt pork, salt beef, a new jar of eggs open. And,' he bowed his head to me respectfully. 'Should the lady deem it acceptable, a small quantity of preserved pears, all the way from Denver.'

'We'll take the cornbread, pork and pears. Bring it on out, then we'll settle up. I got some twists of tobacco should be to your taste.'

Outside we seated ourselves on a long bench that ran the length of the porch. There was only one other person about, a stranger swathed in hide, his hat tipped down over his face, sound asleep or steadfastly silent, not ten feet away. Flies clustered around the grease on his empty plate. Occasionally the wind would pick up, blowing from the direction of the outhouse. Thankfully, it was some distance away, for in the heat the stench would surely have been enough to make me gag.

After several minutes Enroy appeared again, wearing a canvas apron stiff with stains over his waistcoat. The cornbread was several days old and pocked with fat, the pork gray, but the pears – though thin and watery – were an unexpected treat after days of beans. I looked at the plate and murmured a silent prayer for all those who were without such sustenance, on the battlefield or in besieged cities. I did not hesitate further, but loaded the bread with the tough meat and ate heartily.

I was down to my final slice of pear when I realized Muir had stopped eating and was regarding me thoughtfully.

'Hadn't thought to see you so keen for week-old bread and salt horse,' he observed, hiding a smile.

'You forget, Mr Muir, I am from a convent. Our repasts are sparse by their nature. I eat when I can. A lesson learned young by too many, I fear.'

He wiped the plate with his last piece of cornbread and dropped it quivering into his mouth.

'Orphan?' he chewed. I followed suit.

'The opposite,' I said. 'A large family with a great many mouths to feed. Too many for one couple. We were abandoned, orphans in fact if not in law, I suppose. I was moved from poor-house to orphanage for a while; the convent took me in when I was twelve. I had no one else, so two years later I became a novice. It has been my home for more than ten years now.'

'So you had no choice,' he filled in, picking a stray piece of pork from his teeth. 'The street or the cloth.'

I smiled patiently. It is a mistake that many make when they see a young woman in a habit.

'There is always a choice, Abe. To take holy orders and follow this life was my own wish. The convent prepared me well to be a nurse, should I have desired to leave. It was my decision to stay. Being a Visitandine Sister is my greatest joy in this world.'

'Amen,' a voice broke in. 'So good to hear words of sincerity and holiness in this wasteland of virtue. Abe, I have reckoned your bill if you'd care to settle up?' Enroy called from within.

'Directly, Enroy.'

24

Muir stooped to collect the plates, bringing his mouth level with my ear.

'Word to the wise about Enroy, Sister. He hates Catholics about as much as he hates Indians, even more than drifters like me. Lucky he's a businessman first and foremost. I'll make it worth his while to stay sweet while you wait.'

With that, he stumped into the building, leaving me to ponder his warning. Since the stranger beside me was still insensible, I stood up and wandered over to Rattle, a strange feeling of apprehension heavy in my chest. The horse, satiated with fresh water and oats, stood in a kind of stupor, flicking at insects with his ears. When I reached him, he turned and butted me softly in the chest. I smoothed the dusty coat of his neck, marveling at the strength of such a gentle beast. Was his master such a one? Spare and silent, but eager for a friendly word, the hand of another in companionship?

I was never to reach a conclusion, for a shot cracked across the camp, then another. The two mangy buzzards who guarded the ridge leaped into the air in protest. Fear began to fill my stomach as I started running toward the building, but before I could take more than a step, the door crashed from its hinges. There were two bodies atop it, and one was Muir's.

The sleeping stranger stood to attention on the porch, a rifle in his hands. Beneath the hide jacket I caught a flash of blue, a Union garment. Without pause, he fired, sending wood splinters flying. Muir had rolled off Enroy and was staggering away from the building.

Enroy lurched after him, a shotgun raised. I must have called out then, for he swung around to face me, his gun leveled at my chest. The man in blue knocked it aside.

'You fool, you can't shoot a nun!' he cried.

The next moment he was on the ground, a bullet from Muir's pistol sending a shock of blood exploding from where his throat had been.

'Rattle!' Muir yelled. The horse was rearing, eyes rolling at the noise and the smell of blood. I ran to free him from the post. A bullet whistled past my head, but I forced myself to remain calm, digging my fingers into the leather knot, wrenching it loose. The horse leaped to his master. Muir grappled with the reins and hauled himself up, firing another shot over the saddle.

Enroy was holed up in a corner of the porch, blood streaming into his eye from a scalp wound. For one terrible moment I was consumed by fear, and thought that Muir would plunge off onto the plain and leave me. But then his hand was at my wrist, wrenching me up. I barely had a grip on his jacket before we were away, tearing out of the line of fire.

10

I am like a broken vessel

For the first mile, I was too terrified to open my eyes or look around. My ears strained for the slightest sound of pursuit, though it was only Rattle's hooves that echoed back from the canyon walls.

Another mile and I was able to raise a calm eye to my surroundings. What I saw was not welcome. Barren gutters of land, sides dropping away steeply only to rise again.

'Where are we?' I managed to ask Muir at last. My voice was dry as a husk, subdued by the silence of the place.

'Badlands,' he coughed. 'Runs for miles. Nothing but rock a'tween here and the plain.'

It was then that I saw it, a slow bloom on the shoulder of his jacket, spreading in a dark patch where my hand had rested until a moment before. I looked at my fingertips. They were sticky with blood.

'Abe?'

'I know, Sister.'

'We must stop.'

'Another mile. We ain't safe yet.'

But it was only a half-mile, less even, before the wind started up and drove us from the path. It roared down the length of the canyon, whipping the dust around us in stinging tongues until I could neither hear nor keep my eyes open. I felt Muir slip then, and reached around to take the reins myself, guiding Rattle toward the lee of a great stone. Here was some shelter, and I breathed a prayer of thanks as I pulled Abe from the saddle.

Once he was settled, I checked the state of our provisions. It did not take long. The canteen of silty water, grown stale in the

27

sun; one square of hard tack; a chunk of salt pork. It would not last us a day.

Muir was watching me with his shrewd, dark gaze, his arm hanging limply at his side. He seemed barely to notice the blood that had begun to drip from his wrist onto the earth below. I closed my eyes for a moment and tried to pray. But I was afraid. I did not want to die in such a lonely place, with none to mourn or remember the woman who was flesh above scattered, bleached bones.

I fought my way through a simple prayer, one from childhood. By the time I had finished, strength filled my limbs and my head was clear once more. I looked to the man at my side.

With some persuasion, he drank first from the canteen. I followed suit, a few sips only to moisten my throat, although I made show of swallowing mouthfuls. An honest deception, I hoped. Next, I eased off the hide jacket. His face flashed white but he did not cry out. Neither did he vomit from the pain and lose the precious few mouthfuls of water, for which I was grateful.

At last I could see the wound. A hole the size of a nickel, its edges ragged.

'I shall have to remove your shirt, Mr Muir. If I might borrow your knife?'

'Why, this is my best shirt, Sister. You'll leave me with naught but a burlap sack to cover my decency when we get to town.' He attempted a grin and I smiled in return, although I could not help but notice the way his mouth shook.

The nurse in me took over then. I searched through the packs until I had what I needed; laying out the knife, tin of matches and, after some hesitation, the box of bullets. Carefully, I cut away the fabric and used a spare cloth to sop up some of the blood. My jaw clenched; the bullet could not be seen. Neither had it passed through the flesh on the other side.

'I know it's in there, Sister. Can feel it like a tooth stuck in deep.' Muir turned his head awkwardly and swore. 'Enroy did not intend to take me alive.'

I had heard of the techniques for treating bullet wounds from a group of Benedictines who ran a hospital boat on the

Mississippi. They talked of amputations, of survival rates being high – if treated with proper care. In St. Louis I might have been able to retrieve the bullet and stitch the wound, bathe it in clean water and dress with cotton, but here I was as helpless as a child. I pushed away the anger that threatened my composure and thought hard.

'Mr Muir, I am going to search for the bullet. I shall need you to stay awake. Can you do that?'

A laugh cracked in his throat. 'Sure can.'

His head lolled against mine as I probed the skin of his back. His neck was tanned to a deep, bark brown, the muscles in his shoulders lighter, like two different wood grains, running together. Yet I was not prepared for what I saw below: from shoulder blade to waist the skin was scored with shiny pink scars, raised like the stripes on Enroy's waistcoat. I knew the marks of a flogging when I saw them, but held my tongue.

I could feel the bullet, hard beneath the surface of his skin, which was hot to the touch. With a breath, I drew the tip of the blade over the flesh in a narrow cut. Muir bucked for a moment and bit down on the leather sheath I had given him.

With the tip of the knife I explored the wound. Metal scraped on metal – it was not deep enough yet. It was needful that I work quickly, before the pain became too great. In one movement I pushed the knife tip in deeper, levered it back. Metal came into sight; I levered again and it was out.

Muir was groaning now, the hair at the nape of his neck soaked with sweat. Of what came next I had no experience, and even less confidence. I had read of the practice, but out here, with only the roughest of supplies, what I intended to do seemed barbaric.

'My Lord, grant me the grace to perform this action with you and through love of you. I offer you in advance all the good that I may do and accept all the pain and trouble that I may meet as coming from your fatherly hand.'

I reached for the box of bullets. Muir stiffened; I am sure he guessed for what purpose I needed them.

'Sister, please, you can't . . .' his voice was thick with pain.

'Abraham Muir. I ask you to trust me. The Lord will help me in my work. I shall not let you die here.'

I would not let him speak further, but ripped the shell from the casing with my teeth. Inside was the black powder. I tipped it into the cavity of the wound, as much as it would hold. My hands trembled. I could barely shake out a match in order to strike one on the rock. Before I could think better of what I did, the flame touched the powder in Muir's flesh.

The crack that followed stunned me, throwing me back. Muir screamed in the same instant, then slumped forward. There were scorch marks on my hands, and one cuff of my habit smoldered. I took the knife and hacked off my sleeve at the elbow.

The wound was horrific, blackened and oozing sluggishly. I began to fold strips of the torn habit, binding his shoulder. I tied the final knot and sat back on my heels. My body betrayed me then. I turned and retched from the nerves and the blood and the smell of burned flesh. It was quite some time before I felt composed enough to check up on my patient. He was slumped where I had left him, face slack with pain. Although he shook violently, his eyes were open.

'Sister,' he was motioning weakly toward his blanket roll.

I unbuckled it. A grubby bottle tumbled out into the dust. I did not hesitate, but pulled the cork, held it to his lips. He drank as much as his mouth would hold.

'Bend an elbow, Sister,' he wheezed. 'I won't tell.'

For the first time in my life, I felt the sear of whiskey in my dry throat and I thanked God.

30

I I

For he who requires blood, remembers

'I deserve it.'

Muir's voice was low, so low I barely heard it over the hissing of the fire. I had scavenged scraps of brushwood, and although it smoked like anything, it did serve to keep away the cold that came with the empty sky. Through the haze, I could not tell whether his eyes were open, or if it was merely a fretful dream.

'I deserve this death, Sister.'

'Mr Muir?'

'I am only telling you so that when I pass you will not feel too bad.'

I said that I did not understand, but I had heard that tone of voice before, many times over the years. This was to be a confession. From the marks of a flogging and what I was sure now was a bounty on his head, I was afraid of what he would tell me; not least because I had begun to suspect that – despite appearances – Abraham Muir was a good man.

'Burns like hellfire,' he murmured, shifting the bandage on his shoulder. 'They never tell you, when you join, Sister, that a rifle kicks like a mule when you pull the trigger. First time I fired on a body, damn thing near knocked a tooth out. Not that I was green, mind. Had them pistols since I was fourteen. But a rifle . . . thing can tear a hole in a man's stomach size of a fist at close quarters.

'Took the blue during the fall draft. Should 'a run, skipped town while they slept, I see that now. It were a livestock town in Kansas, not more 'an twenty of us young men together, bare enough to keep the whores in business, so I figured they had us pegged, names and all.

31

'"Ninety days war", they called it. We thought a few months of tramping round the Border States eating cornbread and bacon grease wouldn't be so hard. But we hadn't been more than an hour in uniform 'fore they sent us west. Wrong direction for the secesh, but I didn't bother my head much.

'We garrisoned at Fort Drinkwater. Marching squares all day and sleeping in real beds weren't a bad life for a small-time grifter from Arkansas. Then came the rains, the frost, and still we marched. We marched into the wild, and any infant who can reckon his numbers on one hand could have told you we didn't have enough supplies.

'At first we could drown the weevils from the hard tack in our coffee. Then there was no coffee to be spared and we had to pick 'em out with pins, or just eat them like they was raisins.

'Lad from Wichita way fell ill with the flux and he were the first to die. Time we reached Fort Lyon we weren't no better than beasts. Weeks on half rations, some with no boots, some couldn't walk twenty paces without fouling themselves from the state of their guts.

'We were told to attack a camp of Indian braves. They'd killed some men of the fort, needed controlling. By that time we would've attacked each other if we thought there was a better blanket to get from it.

'Was barely light when we charged the camp. I saw straight away that it were wrong, there was no sentry, too many wigwams, too wide a space, but the cavalry was at our back, forcing us on, firing over our heads. It was hell, and there were fire, we were scattered and had no orders, other than "kill the hostiles". The screams, Sister; they weren't of warriors but of women, children. Saw a man I'd bunked with slit a woman's throat as she ran. A babe fell from her arms, but I didn't see where it went.

'There were a spark, like metal from the edge of my eye and I fired afore I could even tell I had done it.'

Muir's eyes were fixed on me. They were too bright, his skin flushed to a pink that I might have called delicate, were it not for the fact it made my stomach fall. I should have stopped him then, before he agitated himself further, but I could not. He was speaking again, so soft I was obliged to move in close.

'A boy, Sister. A child, not even a hair 'pon his chin. He lay there like a deer, staring at me as he died with my lead in his stomach. I saw then the metal in his hand; it were a silver coin with a picture of Lincoln on it.'

Thou hast brought me down into the dust of death

Dawn spread in a slow wave across the valley, red sky to red earth, and for a moment it was like being encircled by flame. The light did not bring comfort. Muir's condition was worse; by mid-morning he lay almost unconscious, mumbling in delirium. I had succeeded in forcing some slivers of salt pork into his mouth, as much water as he could sip, but he was failing rapidly.

As I had feared in the night, a fever had set in. Infection spread around the wound. I cooled the skin with a damp cloth, but in truth there was little I could do. While he slept, I clutched at what remained of my rosary beads so hard that they left marks on my hands. I tried to reconcile Muir's death with mysteries of life, with God's plan, but I found no solace, no comfort in these thoughts.

In the afternoon he woke, called for water. I dripped some onto his lips. They were cracked, and bled as he spoke.

'Sister . . . I remembered . . .'

He was struggling hard against the fever. I laid my hand to his forehead to calm him, but he squirmed away.

'No, 'fore I forget . . . in the belt, for you . . .' The effort of gesturing sent him slumping back. I unbuckled the holster from around his waist, the one that contained his pistols.

Muir's words were coming fast and breathy now; I could barely make them out. One word, repeated over and again.

'Forgive.'

When he was still again, I opened the belt and drew out one of the guns. It felt heavy in my hand, but smooth and cool. In this land of few possessions, I wondered what they meant to Muir, that he should give them away to me. I drew out the other.

There was something tangled about the muzzle, white and clinking.

It was a necklace, the one I had seen round Muir's neck, hidden beneath jacket and shirt. I ran it through my fingers. It looked Indian. Carved bone, flecked and white, fashioned into rough beads. I reached the end of the string. Attached there by a shining new clasp was a small wooden cross, the marks of fresh carving still upon it. A bloody fingerprint had soaked into the young wood. Muir had been making a rosary. He must have been holding it in the trading post at the moment of the attack.

Sorrow threatened to overwhelm me then, and I found I no longer had the strength to fight. No moisture remained in my body for tears, but dry sobs rose in my throat and soon my head was spinning.

There was no more water. Muir would die, Rattle would die and soon, I would follow them. I pressed the bone rosary to my lips and imagined myself back to the cool corridors of St. Louis.

'God grant that we meet again in heaven, dear Sisters.'

13

Let them become as dust
before the wind

Dusk fell. By then, my eyes were near scorched shut; when I tried to swallow it was as though all the dust of the plain had crept into my mouth as I slept. Abe lay still and I crawled over to him, terrified at what I might find.

He lived, but barely. His breath was too light, too uneven, his skin burning with fever though the heat of the day had been lost into the sky. There was a haze lying over the landscape, and I feared my vision was beginning to fail. The sky began to look akin to smoke, curling upward like a ribbon, twisting . . .

I blinked hard then, tried to clear my eyes, but there it remained, a thin streak of gray from beyond the ridge.

'Smoke,' I rasped, 'Abe, there's smoke . . .'

He did not respond, but I laid my hand against his face, hoping he would feel my words even if he could not hear them.

'We will not die here.'

I made it to my feet, though my head pounded with such bursts as I have never known. The pistols were still in my lap. Twice they fell from my weakened grip as I scrambled upward, until sense made me stow them in my belt. They rested at my waist then, alongside the rosary.

The slope was near vertical, loose stone and grit baked in the sun's glare. It slid beneath my feet, and so I crawled. The rough ground grazed my palms, but I pushed my suffering aside.

Eventually, I reached the peak of the canyon. Below stretched the plain, vast and brown save for a single straight track cutting through. It was the wagon train. Not only canvas, I could see blue, figures moving. Carthy.

My hands shook as I tried to arm the guns. I had never held

a firearm, let alone shot one, and I prayed that Muir had left them loaded. Finally, I felt a click, then another. I set my feet against the narrow ridge and raised one pistol to the sky.

The sound cracked across the plain like thunder.

14

Who is the man that desireth life?

Two days later I alighted at Fort Laramie. It was a rough place; a wooden stockade and stone buildings, a parade ground baked hard. Yet it was shelter from the unforgiving plain. There were beds, fresh water. For the most part I was left to myself, along with the other survivors – my former companions on the wagon train, a lifetime ago.

I had made myself something of a pariah. My appearance did not recommend me, sunburned and ragged as I was; yet it was my opinion of Mr Muir that set me against the fort's superiors.

I could barely recall the details of our rescue, although I'd been conscious enough to insist on his safe passage to the fort. How long my protection would last now that we had made our destination, I did not know.

'Sister Josephine,' Lieutenant Carthy began, as he steered me with a gentle hand toward the washhouse. 'Your concern for the man does you credit. However, I would ask that you also look to your own well-being, if only for a moment.'

Beneath his clear gaze I became painfully aware of the dirt beneath my fingernails, the dust that clung to my habit, my cracked lips. I had to incline my head away to hide the flush that heated my cheeks.

Once alone, I unfastened the veil from my head. It was gray from traveling, my habit in worse state, but I washed them as best I could and spread the cloth to dry while I attended to myself. I scrubbed all over with cold water and hard soap, as I had done at the convent. Afterwards, I felt renewed, like walking from meditation into the first light of day.

My hair had grown since I left St. Louis. Among the soaps and basins I found a pair of shears. Clumsily, I hacked the pale locks from my head. I felt an old pang, when I saw the blonde curls on the wooden floor. Another woman's glory, perhaps.

When I emerged, the fort was quiet. From the position of the sun in the sky, the smell of fat in the air, I judged it to be suppertime. No one prevented me when I crossed the parade ground. It did not take me long to locate the infirmary.

The air in the large room was close, darkened by shutters. Many beds were empty; the faces I did see were pale, pocked with scars. Muir was not among them. I found the surgeon taking his meal in what looked to be a storeroom. The shelves were bare save for a few rolls of cotton and bottles of ether.

'Thought you'd be by,' the surgeon announced before I could speak. He was pulling fat from a stringy cut of meat with his fingers, setting it aside. When he looked up, his eyes were those of a man who worked too much, with too little. 'You're the one scorched a hole in that deserter's shoulder.'

'I cauterized it, yes.' There was barely space for me to edge into the room in order to inspect the shelves. 'How does Mr Muir?'

'You may've stemmed the bleeding, but the wound festers.' The surgeon shrugged and returned his attention to his meal. 'With due care he might keep the arm.'

'May I know where he is? I should like to check the wound myself.'

The surgeon stood. His hands trembled as he collected the strips of fat together.

'I see you do not understand. Desertion in the Union carries a penalty of death. Lieutenant Carthy has held back thus far out of respect for you. There is no doubt that once you continue on your way, Muir will be shot.'

He tipped the fat into a pot that hung over the fire, stirred up the embers beneath it.

'You have seen the stores. Would you suggest I use what supplies I have on a dead man?' He ladled some of the fat and broth into a dented tin bowl and extended it to me, a thin note of compassion in his eyes.

'Here. They will not have fed him well, if at all. He is in the cells.'

Who liveth to see good days?

Muir lay on his side on a straw mattress. He had no blanket, and I chided myself for not having thought to bring one. The surgeon was right, I could see where the bandage was discolored and crusted to the wound. Quietly, I set down the dish and drew a roll of cotton from my sleeve. It was not stealing, I told myself. The bandages belonged to those who needed them. In the corner of the cell was a jug of water. I moistened the old bandage and began to work it loose.

'Might just as well leave it, sir.' Muir's voice was a rasp, but it comforted me to hear him speak. 'You know as well as I where I'm headed. If it kills me 'fore then, so much the better.'

'The future is in God's hands, Mr Muir. We cannot know His plan.'

His whole body tensed at the sound of my voice. I saw the knuckles gripping his arm turn white.

'What do you do here?'

'I am come to tend your wound, Mr Muir, as the surgeon is occupied.'

'Didn't take you for a liar, Sister.'

His tone near froze me to the stone floor. When I spoke, my voice was that of a child.

'I . . . do not know what you mean.'

'You said you'd not let me die there. I would have forgiven you if you had, God knows I blessed you for trying.'

He turned to face me then, wincing from the pain of his wound. In the shadow of the cell his eyes were like liquid silver, over-bright from the fever, from hatred. Bruises bloomed beneath them, purple-blue, yellow on his sunken cheeks. His lip was split. He had been beaten.

'You've brought me back to the hell I been running from. You delivered me to their hands, so that I must die, beaten and mocked by murderers. Any kindness you pretend comes too late.'

The pain I saw in his face was great, and I reached out to touch the bruises, but he flinched away.

'Who has done this?'

'It don't matter.'

'You shall not be treated in this way. I will speak to Lieutenant Carthy, and—'

Muir lunged then, his hand gripping my habit as if he would pull it forward. The roll of cotton tumbled from my fingers.

'That bastard is a murderer,' he hissed, his voice breaking. 'I seen him kill in cold blood and call it honor, something vile beneath that fancy gold on his shoulders . . .'

Muir was working himself into a frenzy; chest ripping with coughs. His grip on my habit loosened, until finally he was still.

'Don't you trust him, Sister,' he whispered. 'Might be you've sentenced me to death, but I'll not wish the same on you. He's a man beyond salvation.'

I reached for the fallen bandages then, covered his rough hand with my own.

'No one is beyond salvation, Abraham Muir.'

16

I am poured out like water

'Will you say grace, Sister?'

It took me a moment to understand the words, but I smiled in agreement to Mr Carthy's request. The prayer I gave was a simple one, and quiet. Perhaps it should have been longer, but weariness dragged at me, and I found that my thoughts were little better than a jumble.

One of Carthy's men had found me outside the cells and extended an invitation to join his superior for supper. My absence during dinner had been noted – surely I was hungry?

In truth, a meal was the very last thing I wanted. The hour I had passed with Mr Muir had left me exhausted, and yet it would be churlish to refuse Mr Carthy's hospitality. At the last moment, I remembered Muir's rosary, and tucked it about my neck out of sight. It hung against my bare skin, light and cool; something that belonged to the plain, not for show in a lieutenant's parlor.

When I had finished the prayer, Carthy began to serve me. I was both discomfited and moved to see what care had been taken with our meal. It was clear that here was the best food the fort could provide, no doubt a far cry from what the men were eating.

'Mr Carthy,' I exclaimed, as he poured me a cup of wine. 'I am grateful for your generosity, but it is not needful. I am more than accustomed to simple fare.'

His smile then was the most unguarded that I had seen, as he poured wine into his own cup.

'Sister, I confess that there is more than a little self-interest in my motives. It is rare that I have the chance to dine with anyone other than the cavalry and they do not make for enlightened company. You will not begrudge me one meal where I may talk of something other than the dried bean supply?'

I laughed then, and after a few sips of wine, was surprised to find myself at ease. Mr Carthy was agreeable company. He had been educated in Boston, before being called out west, and was acquainted with several theologians there, a few whose work was known to myself. He enquired after my previous life in St. Louis, my current mission, the order to which I belonged.

Only once was I reminded of Muir's warning. We had removed from the table to the window, in order to catch the cool evening breeze. From somewhere nearby came a snatch of music, not song exactly, but a keening sort of chant, eerily similar to my own evening litanies. Carthy registered my listening face and his expression hardened.

'Pay no heed, Sister. An Indian captive only. If his noise troubles you I shall send someone to silence him.'

I assured him I was not troubled, but curious as to what the song meant. His eyes settled on me then, half alert and half amused. In the warm light of the oil lamps, his irises were clear pools of perfect blue. All at once, I became aware of the space between us, that I had moved closer without intending to.

There came a knock at the door then, and we stood apart. A rider had come, we were told, with an urgent message for the lieutenant.

'Your pardon, Sister. Please make yourself comfortable.' He bowed and walked smartly from the room.

I did not sit, but paced the room slowly, hands in my sleeves, examining the curios that Mr Carthy displayed. Several animal skulls that might have been wild dogs, a large map of the frontier, marked with the town of Denver and the mountains, and a daguerreotype of a young woman dressed in a fine gown. I could not tell the color of her hair from the inks, and wondered who she was, sister or sweetheart. A bundle of letters rested upon the shelf. I left those alone, and examined the books instead: a collection of sermons, several pamphlets relating to military affairs, a worn but finely bound bible.

44

I smiled, finding an old friend in this most distant of places. The leather was warm and supple beneath my hands and I flicked it open to a page at random, certain to find wisdom. Instead I found a lock of hair, gently pressed between pages. Perhaps the likeness did show Mr Carthy's sweetheart. The hair was a pale curl; I ran it through my fingers and felt the ends freshly cut. A jolt ran through me as I raised the strands to the light. The hair was my own.

A noise at the door alerted me, and I wedged the bible hurriedly onto the shelf.

'Good news, Sister,' Carthy announced, as he entered, a piece of paper crumpled in his hand. 'The general and his company are not two days hence. With speed, they will reach here the day after tomorrow.'

I gave what I hoped was a calm smile, though my heart was pounding.

'They will escort those formerly of the wagon train as far as Salt Lake City. Unless of course, you choose a different path. This is but a poor fort on the furthest edges of the civilized world . . .' His voice trailed off for a moment as he approached the shelf. 'But you would be more than welcome to remain here for a time.'

He was standing close. I could almost see myself reflected in the polished buttons of his collar.

'Thank you for supper, Mr Carthy,' I managed. 'I fear I am wearied now, and have my evening prayers to make. God grant you a good night's rest.'

His eyes followed me as I left the study.

A prayer took my breath as I murmured it, all the way through the dark halls until I knelt steadfastly before my camp bed: 'Through you, Jesus, in you, for you, with you. By your love, with your love, for your love . . .'

45

17

Their right hand is filled with gifts

The general and his men did not come the following day, nor the one after that. The talk around the fort was that they had been detained by rumors of an Indian settlement somewhere north of the plain, although there had been no sightings.

I did not know whether I welcomed or dreaded their arrival. The lock of my hair in Carthy's possession troubled me greatly. Perhaps, I told myself, he thought it belonged to another woman, one of the soldier's wives from the train? Or did it remind him of the lady in the photograph, *his* lady, who waited somewhere, heartsick for his return?

I imposed onto myself strict penalties for dwelling on such thoughts. Long hours of prayer, work in the infirmary, fasts during daylight hours. I refused Mr Carthy's next invitation to supper, pleading fatigue, only to find one of his men waiting for me outside my room with a package. I did not open it until I was safely in the shade of the washhouse. A square of folded black fabric, a note informing me that this item had once belonged to his mother, and that since, he noticed, I no longer carried one, I should treat it as my own.

Inside was a rosary, perfectly matched pearl beads above an ivory cross, its edges touched with gold. For a moment, my hands lingered over the smooth globes. Then I recalled Muir's gift to me: rough bone and wood, lying against my skin.

'It will be today,' the surgeon told me later, as we wound bandages in the storeroom. I believed he'd come to respect my abilities in the infirmary, so we had reached a truce, of sorts.

'What shall?'

'Muir and that Indian traitor will be sentenced by nightfall, mark me.'

My hands froze at his words. 'How do you know this?'

'The general's on his way. Sighted this morning off Far Ridge. He's the only one can order executions within the fort.'

'You said sentenced, not executed, sir.'

'Amounts to the same thing, Sister. I did tell you not to hold out too strong a hope.'

I threw the pile of bandages down then, save one.

'Hope is the only thing we can hold out in this place,' I snapped, seizing the tin dish and some broth. 'I shall speak to Mr Carthy personally, if it comes to it, and he will intervene with the general.'

'Open your eyes, Sister!' the surgeon called, as I hurried away. 'It's Carthy wants him dead. But for you Muir would have a bullet in his skull already!'

Something inside me simmered as I made my way to the cells. I needed wisdom and guidance, but I was alone, and unable to control the anger that seized me. The tin bowl fell before Muir with a clatter.

'Why should Carthy want you dead?'

Muir looked at me, that terrible resignation in his eyes, and reached for the spoon. I kicked the plate away further.

'Why, Mr Muir? If you do not tell me, I cannot help.'

He sighed then, as if my words were weights that brought pain to his chest.

'There's no help now, Sister.'

'I should like to know.'

'Can I eat?'

I pushed the bowl back toward him. He took a clumsy spoonful and grimaced.

'You should'a seen what they gave me yesterday. Bread with mold so thick it looked like lawn.'

He continued to work at his meal.

'Carthy don't need a reason to hate. But I s'pose he wants me dead because I told him "no", made him look a fool. And 'cos I know what lurks behind that soft hair and fancy uniform. He tell you I was part-raised by the Sioux?'

I shook my head. The bone beads at my neck swayed with the movement.

'How?'

'Got taken in an attack as a hostage. Few other little ones, older girls as well. Four years I stayed in a Santee village. Soldiers "rescued" us when I were twelve or so, but most would rather have stayed, tell truth. I was an orphan anyhow, and they was something of a family there.

'One of the white women had married a brave; they took her back nonetheless, dragged her off, though she had a half-breed infant in the camp and another on the way.'

He finished the broth, but continued to run the spoon through the grease riming the bowl.

'Told you of the attack on the Indian village. Might well have been the same tribe that raised me. It were Lieutenant Carthy led that charge. When he found naught but slaughtered women and children, he went into a mighty panic. Right too; civilian deaths, even savages, means demotion if Washington gets wind of it.

'Don't know how, but he heard I spent time with the Sioux. Ordered me to ride into a second village, put them off-guard so the army could attack, collect some warrior scalps. I said no. He had me flogged for a day and a night to change my mind. Left one of his fool sergeants to mind me. Worked one of my hands loose enough to get a good grip on the man's throat. After that I ran.'

My expression must have been one of horror and disbelief, but he looked undaunted into my face.

'I am not an innocent man, Sister.'

48

18

Who teacheth my hands to war

The hours that followed passed in a blur. I remember not whether I sat and prayed or paced the fort like a woman with a demon at her heels. It was not my place to intervene in the carriage of justice, I told myself over and over, until the words became confused with the litany I recited.

Muir had killed – the Indian child, the sergeant, and the stranger at the trading post – were they not also Christian souls who deserved an answer? Carthy too: were the innocent lives he ordered taken present on his conscience or was he merely a pawn of duty? Muir had said he reveled in the deaths, but Muir could lie.

Sundown dropped silently and swiftly upon the fort. With every moment the general drew nearer. Finally, I could withstand my anxiety no further and resolved to pit my conviction against the truth. I was so consumed by my thoughts, that I paid no heed to the time, or indeed the routines of others. It was only when I knocked at Mr Carthy's parlor door and was told that he was occupied with dressing that I realized the unsociable hour of my call.

I made a swift apology and retreated, mortified by my self-indulgence and preoccupation.

'Sister?' Carthy's voice rang out down the hallway. 'Please do come in, I am decent, if not wholly presentable.'

Cheeks burning, I entered the room. A private was dispatched for a jug of water. If Mr Carthy was as embarrassed as I, he made no show of it. He sat at his desk before a half-written letter and a large pile of goods. He was jacketless, gloveless, and it struck me that I had never before seen his hands bare. They seemed peculiarly white against the tanned skin of his neck and face.

'To what do I owe your call, Sister?' he smiled, buttoning his cuffs. 'I am afraid that I cannot be entirely at your disposal. As you know, the general is expected.'

'Mr Carthy, it is I who should apologize. I came to ask . . .' My voice trailed off as I saw what was piled on his desk.

Through a jumble of reins I saw familiar inlaid wood; Muir's pistols. The sight of them was like a recrimination and set my heart pounding. I could not ask for Muir's pardon, it was not my place. It was my calling to see the Lord's presence in the world at every turn, not to cry and whine if I did not like what I saw.

'Sister?'

I remembered the pearl rosary in my pocket, clasped the excuse it gave me gratefully, and extended it to him.

'I am touched by your generosity, Mr Carthy, but I cannot accept such a gift. It is not appropriate for a humble servant of God as myself. I would return it to you before I leave.'

I laid the beads gently on the desk. Carthy's smile seemed sad.

'I should have known that would be your wish. I had hoped you would bear away some piece of this place with you when you left, close to your heart.'

In the small room the scent of his clothes, his skin, was overpowering. I clasped my hands before me so that he might not see their trembling. But his eyes seemed to take in all. Again, I thought of flowers, impossible blue paper roses that I had seen as a child.

He was speaking. I had to force my attention back to his words.

'It would, however, please me greatly to see you wear it once. It has not been worn since my mother passed. She would appreciate its continued use.'

It has not seen much use at all, a small part of my mind hissed, *or the gold would be worn away.* I pushed aside such ill-natured thoughts and assented.

'My thanks, Sister,' he said, his smile warm.

He held up the rosary. The pearls gleamed in the falling dusk, and for a moment I thought of the faces in the infirmary, pale moons in a row of beds. I reached out my hand, but Carthy shook his head.

'Allow me.'

He came close enough for his sleeve to brush against my cheek as he lowered the string. For a long moment, his hands lingered. I could not hold that gaze any longer, so closed my eyes to begin my prayer.

'*Credo in Deum Patrem omnipotentem, Creatorem caeli et terrae . . .*'

But the words, ordinarily of great comfort to me, were only words; I could not make them mean anything. Carthy's presence was strong. I heard a whisper of cloth and fingertips touched my cheek. The prayer faltered. I opened my eyes then and was little better than stone as his lips moved to meet mine.

Then I saw it. Upon his palm were marks, angry and red, peppering the skin like a hundred tiny bites. Most would have dismissed it as a rash; leather chafing from long days spent holding reins. Yet I was a nurse and had seen the marks of syphilis before, long advanced.

My recoil was instant. Carthy still held my gaze. I glanced away, quickly, near ripped the rosary from my neck in haste to be rid of it.

'I must go now,' my voice shook as I turned and dropped the beads onto the desk. 'I shall take up no more of your time.'

I had not even heard him move, but the sound of the key turning in the lock was audible enough.

'Yet you enjoyed our talks so much. I am hurt that you would leave with such little gratitude for your host.'

The blood began to pound in my ears. The fort buildings would be empty, company, staff, all assembling on the parade ground to welcome the general. I could hear the commotion beginning to filter through the window. I spun toward the glass, reached for the latch, but Carthy's hand closed about my wrist. I could feel the infection hot against my skin.

His other hand was tugging at my veil. I fought him off as best I could.

'You will not touch me, I am a Bride of Christ.'

'You are a woman. You are no more than a woman.'

His hand had caught on Muir's rosary and it swung out into the open. It was enough to deflect his attention for a moment as he laughed.

'You prefer his pagan trinkets to mine. What of *my* crimes, Sister? Shall I not be forgiven?'

He pushed me backward and I struck out, my nails catching him across the lip. A scratch only, but enough to break his hold. I lunged for the desk, for Muir's pistols there, pulled one free from the pile.

'Not loaded, Sister.'

Carthy was coming toward me, one hand to his bleeding mouth. There was a box of bullets on the table, I snatched them up as I backed away, but my hands shook so much that I spilled all but two. I had only a moment before Carthy reached me again. This time, I raised the pistol.

'Unchristian of you,' he smiled. 'This violence does not become you, Thomas Josephine.'

There was a cry from outside then, many voices, the scream of a horn; the general had arrived. I armed the gun, in one move.

'A full pardon for Mr Muir.' That knife-hard voice was mine. 'Safe passage to the next state. Or the general shall know of your vile intentions.'

'The general will not treat you with such care as I have done.' Carthy's smile was curling into a snarl. He placed his hand over the muzzle of the pistol.

'He will take you without qualm and without recrimination. What other man could order the slaughter of three hundred innocents, and not a word from Washington? Death is needed where law demands it. Muir shall die. It is God's will and it is mine.'

I caught the sound of boots, marching in formation and knew

my time had run out. Clenching my teeth, I looked him dead in the eye.

'You presume to know God's will, Mr Carthy, but you cannot know mine.'

I pulled the trigger.

Nunslinger: Book 2

The Good, the Bad and the Penitent

The True Tale of how Sister Thomas Josephine of St. Louis, Missouri, came to be Wanted for Murder and faced the Gallows in Carson City, the New State of Nevada

One woe is past; and, behold,
there come two more hereafter

The devil was at Fort Laramie last week when a notorious desperado broke free of confinement on the eve of execution, aided in his escape by a RENEGADE Catholic sister.

The outlaw, named as one Abraham C. Muir, is sought by the Union Army on a charge of cowardice and desertion, as well as MURDER and KIDNAPPING by the Colorado Territory. He was due to answer for his crimes and meet his maker at the hands of the firing squad when he was sprung from detention by a woman – thought previously to have been his hostage – one Sister Thomas Josephine, formerly of St. Louis, Missouri.

"She were like a demon," says Sergeant Bill Purlington, one of the ten men wounded in the bloody affray, "came walking into the cells with these two old pistols raised. All bloodied 'cross the face she was, had this plumb crazy look in her eye. Course I ain't never had cause to raise a weapon to a woman, so I tried to take her guns by force but she fires one of them an' it gets me in the leg. Next thing I know she got the other one at my head. I'm bleeding like a stuck pig but she just takes the keys and tells me to keep a hand on the wound if I'd a mind to live."

Reputedly, the Sister freed not only the outlaw Muir, but also a captive Injun brave. On a brace of horses they made their desperate bid for freedom, beneath the noses of the assembled company, under the command of First Lieutenant Theodore F. Carthy, who was also wounded in the confusion.

There has been no further news of the fugitives, owing to their sudden disappearance into hostile Santee territory.

The paper jerked in the breeze, threatening to fly from my fingers into the valley below. It was from a cheap publication, worn to a scrap by much handling. At that moment, I hoped that the wind would take it from me, bear it away, and with it the memory of my sin.

Yet it could not be forgotten. Slowly, I re-folded the article, falling all to pieces, and returned it to the saddlebag. I gazed instead at the town below. There was no mention of a settlement in these hills, yet here was one, rising from the dirt. Rough cabins were tucked into a fold of the valley, hiding like fleas in the crease of a garment.

The sky pressed heavy as I clucked Rattle into movement. Night was falling, and in that darkness the ridge we traveled seemed the back of a half-starved animal, pale stripes criss-crossing its flesh like the marks of a flaying. I knew those marks, had seen them scarring the land from the end of the South Pass down into the foothills. I had even caught glimpses sometimes of the men who toiled themselves ragged, pulling lumps of rock from the earth in search of riches.

At any other time I should not have stopped in a prospector town. Yet even if I could have gone on and accepted hunger my due, a horse knows nothing of penance and must have oats.

A track led down toward the buildings. There were about forty in all, wooden roofed and walled, held together by stolen nails and hope turned sour. A few larger structures had brick in their make-up and set themselves on either side of a dirt road, but the rest straggled up the hill, in search of level ground. The smell of the air changed as I drew closer to habitation: dust, iron and human detritus.

Stillwater.

The words had been carefully painted in black upon a board, but it lay fallen in the scrub, fixtures stolen. A *yip* sounded nearby and I watched a dog drag scraps of something from a ditch.

She were like a demon. The words returned unbidden, the way they had many times before. I saw myself then through the eyes of another, felt the pressure of a man's hand on the end of the pistol, felt the blood spray hit my cheek, and the cry that broke forth in the thunder of the gunshot . . .

I dragged Rattle from the road so sharply that he stumbled, into a stand of brushwood. My fingers were trembling as I searched for Muir's rosary. The bone beads were cool against my lips, but still that cry echoed in my mind. I tried to imagine the organ at the convent instead, one note, ringing pure. My thoughts slowed into familiar prayer.

When I opened my eyes, dusk had fallen. The barren stumps surrounding me were not dead trees, I realized then. They were loose crosses, secured by threads of leather. Rattle's hooves shifted upon a graveyard.

Lost in contemplation, I did not hear the cracking of dry branches, the slow footsteps until they were at my very elbow. I spun in the saddle, one hand flying to the pistol. The other shot out to connect with flesh.

A small figure twisted and spat, wrist clenched in my hand. I brought out the gun and leveled it as steadily as I could.

'Stay still now, you hear? I have no cause to shoot if you tell me your purpose.'

'Ain't doing nothing! Lemme go or I'll holler for Paxton.'

I near dropped the hand in shock. It was a voice I had not thought to hear in the wilderness: that of a girl child.

She was bundled in a cloak made out of an old carpet, hanging from her sides like broken wings. Her nails and lips were blue beneath the filth. There was a bucket nearby and a few scraps of firewood.

She stared at me with the deliberately blank gaze of one often in trouble, although I would not have put her at more than twelve years of age.

'What is your name, child?'

Her mouth worked for a moment, as if trying to decipher the correct words.

'Nettie,' she pronounced clearly, wiping her nose on the back of her hand. 'Draper, I think, but don't know how that's spelled.'

'Do you live in this place?'

She nodded, jerked a thumb toward the edge of the town, where shacks trailed away into the hills.

'I am looking for a place to rest, and for supplies. Would you run an errand for me?'

Sensing a deal, her look sharpened and she tried a smile along with the nod.

'Can rest up at the cabin, ma'am. We got a fire, and a basin. It's a tin one. Could fix you up right enough. *If* you had the money.'

I reached for the saddle packs, a smile rising to my lips for the first time in a long month of solitary travel.

'Very well, Nettie. I accept. But first we shall need some food.'

2

Strange children have faded away, and have halted from their paths

The girl scraped at the meat in the pan, smiling as if it had performed some jest. The money I had taken from the fort was dwindling, but it had been enough to buy us two small rabbits. To me, they looked old and wizened, but Nettie's face told me how precious fresh meat was in that wilderness. I added on top of these a handful of potatoes, and a small pot of grits. When I told her that it was more than enough to feed two, she looked ready to cry.

When the flesh was sizzling, releasing scant juices, I schooled myself to quiet and looked about, to see if I could work any good there. Despite the poverty of that place, to be within four walls again, in the company of a child after the vast, lonely danger of the trail, was a blessed relief.

The cabin was sparse. Aside from the table at which I sat there were a few old crates, which served as chairs, a rope bed with a wool-stuffed mattress upon it and a selection of hunting equipment in the corner; broken harnesses and an old rifle. Oil lamps spat out their cheap light in two corners. Aside from a faded eiderdown, there was nothing to suggest a woman's touch.

'Nettie? Where is your mother?'

The child was staring at the droplets of fat as if they were gold.

'Dead,' she pronounced, still smiling, 'or gone. Pa said I were three when she went but I don't remember nothin'. Don't reckon on her coming back 'cos that were ten year ago now.'

'Your father, he lives here?'

'Out in the hills.' She threw a potato into the fat and it hissed, spattering her with droplets. She wiped them off hungrily. 'This is Wade's cabin.'

'Wade?'

'My guardian, "godfather", as Pa calls it, though I don't know what he has to do with the faith.' She pointed the spoon at me. 'Is you one of them black caps?'

I told her that I had not heard that name before, but that I was a Bride of Christ.

'Wade don't like it,' she blushed, suddenly shy, poking at the meat. 'Heard about some like you ministering to the hurt in the fighting, called 'em "damn Papists".'

She must have seen my face then, for she looked mortified, busied herself in gathering up two chipped bowls with great concentration.

'Do I look damned to you, Nettie?'

She shook her head, hair covering her face, but would not meet my gaze. I lifted her chin until she had no choice but to look.

'I know there are some who bear an ill will toward my order, but I am here for no other purpose than to work good. Do you understand?'

She nodded, eyes fixed on the bead rosary around my neck.

'Very well. Now, that rabbit looks to be done. Shall we eat?'

The girl did not know any prayers, save for a half-remembered hymn. She watched me curiously while I said a prayer for the sinners of this world, mouthed 'amen' along with me.

It shames me to say that we both fell upon the food. There was no talk while we filled our mouths with meat and corn. Finally, the note of urgency departed. With the weight of a warm meal in my stomach, the cabin seemed almost a haven, the scent of roasted meat and lamp oil in the air. Nettie leaned forward, all eagerness, sucking the grease from her fingers.

'What did you do bad to get made a blackcap?'

I couldn't help but smile at her, as I laid down my spoon.

'This life was my choice. We that take the cloth do so willingly, and with joy.'

An expression flickered across her face. Sadness, almost.

'The way you spoke of sinners, thought you must'a been one. Or known a fair few.'

Muir's face, and another's, came to mind in an instant. I pushed them away, though the heat rose to my cheeks.

'We are all of us sinners, Nettie. Yet the Lord forgives, for we are his children, though many of us stray.'

The girl's face grew red and tight around the eyes. She fidgeted in her seat and I noticed, not for the first time, the way she held her arms wrapped tight around herself beneath the loose, shapeless garment.

'Sinners get punished, ma'am,' she insisted. 'Preacher say so when he talks out in the street. Sinners go to hell and burn in fires there forever.'

I assured her that no one was beyond salvation, if they repented of their sins and prayed to be forgiven.

'Don't know how to repent,' she whispered, and the tears began then, washing the old-too-early look from her face. 'Don't know how, so I'll burn.'

She would not say more. I laid an arm around her thin shoulder, and she clung to me, as if she were afraid the floor might open that minute and demons appear to drag her into the fires. She buried her face into my habit, and it was then I felt it. With one hand I pushed her garment aside, although she tried to stop me.

Her stomach was swollen, taught and round upon her small frame. I felt a hollow anger creep upon me when I realized the cause of her fear. She was with child.

63

3

Thou hast made my arms
like a brazen bow

The coming life in the girl's flesh fluttered beneath my hands. She was thirteen and slender, not yet fully grown. I pushed back a wave of repulsion for the man who had wrought such a thing upon an innocent child, yet attempted to smile, for Nettie watched me close.

I told her the life in her was strong, that she might have two months or more to wait before she was delivered.

'Nettie, where is your father?'

The girl dragged the rug back over her head, grimacing at the catch of the rough fabric.

'Told you, out on the plains. Weren't no place for me so he left me with Wade.'

'And it was he . . .?'

The girl nodded, avoiding my eyes as she set about gathering together the grease-rimed bowls. 'You better get soon, Sister,' she told me quietly, 'he's due back any time, an' he don't like strangers none.'

Rather than preparing to leave, I allowed the rosary to run through my fingers one bead at a time. Worn smooth by the years spent about Muir's neck, their familiarity lent me assurance. Nettie must have guessed what I was thinking, for her eyes flicked to the door and back as I drew out Muir's pistols.

'What you doing?'

'Pray with me, child.'

Face the color of watered milk, she watched me reach into the saddlebags for the box of bullets. I opened the cylinders, began pushing the bullets in one by one, the way I had seen Muir do.

'*Ave Maria, gratia plena, Dominus tecum.* Hail Mary, full of grace. The Lord is with thee. Blessed art thou among women, and blessed is the fruit of thy womb.'

Her lip trembled along with the words. The cylinder of the first gun took me longer than it should have, but nonetheless I finished, got to work on the empty spaces of the second.

'You can't . . .' The voice was weak in her throat.

'Holy Mary, Mother of God, pray for us sinners . . .'

'He'll hurt you, be mad as hell if he sees you here!'

She tugged at me, but still my hands continued their movement.

'. . . now and at the hour of our death.'

'Sister, please!'

The cylinder closed. I laid the loaded pistols upon my lap, side by side. There was a noise outside, growing louder, hooves and the jingle of reins beneath the wind.

'I will not let him touch you anymore, Nettie. Now say "Amen".'

The girl stood frozen, eyes fixed upon the doorframe.

'He'll be mad as hell,' she whispered, backing up. 'He'll be mad as hell. Amen.'

The alkaline wind of the valley blew in first, laden with dust, and a figure followed in leather and skins, a rifle rising like bones from his back. He dropped a sack to the wooden floor and stared about blindly, eyes not yet adjusted from the dark.

'Where'd the hell you get money for meat?' he grunted, snuffing the air as he knelt to remove the wrapping from his boots.

'From me.'

At the sound of my voice Wade spun. He was a slight man and lean, a raked-out beard concealing most of his face. The flesh over his cheeks was slack with want, eyes buried in the sockets. I suppressed a tremor, for I had seen his like before. Men who had been drawn out west by a lure, only to find themselves caught fast and torn without even realizing.

'Net,' he growled, taking a step forward, 'what goes on here?'

The girl's mouth was clamped shut but sobs heaved her shoulders.

'You,' his hand edged toward the knife hanging at his belt. 'What's your business?'

I tightened my grip upon the pistols, hidden in the cloth of my robe.

'You are the girl's godfather?'

'Aye. Don't see what interest that is to you.'

'She is with child.'

His face paled as he stared first at Nettie, then back at me.

'She goes whoring herself 'bout town, there's nothin' I can do.'

'It is *your* doing. Do you deny it?'

His mouth tightened, and I saw his grip on the knife belt grow white.

'Ain't nothin' to nobody,' he spluttered. There was a wildness in his face that seemed to grow with every pulse of blood through the vein in his temple, yet in his eyes, I read fear. 'Get outta here you damn—'

I pulled the pistols from concealment and leveled them at his head, though a tremor took my muscles.

'You will find the girl a suitable home,' I told him, 'and never touch her again. You will kneel and repent, or the Lord knows you will be damned.'

I had been the object of hatred before, yet not in such close quarters.

'Kneel,' I repeated, arming one of the guns.

His lip curled over missing teeth as he began to squat low to the wooden floor. Nettie let out a whimper from the corner, and for a moment, my eye strayed toward her.

He was on me before I could blink, full weight crashing forward and driving the air from my lungs. I must have fired in alarm, for there was thunder and the scent of gunpowder. One pistol fell from my grip and I had no breath to cry out as he knocked the other from my hand, as easily as if I were a child.

I did not know where my limbs were nor how to stop the onslaught. The knife flashed, Nettie screamed and I kicked out, connecting with soft flesh. Wade grunted and I heard the blade clatter to the floor, but then his hands were at my throat, sealing off the air. Panic took me. I could see myself reflected in his eyes: pale with terror, soon to die.

Thy will be done, was all I could think as the air started clouding black. *Thy will be done.*

A glint of metal behind him, a dark mouth of fire and I knew what would happen too late. I tried to meet her gaze, but Nettie's face was wild as her thin arms raised the shotgun.

Thy will be done.

I closed my eyes.

4

I am turned in my anguish, whilst the thorn is fastened

The silence roared into my head, heavy and stifling. All was red and thunderous, and for a long moment I could not fathom what had occurred. Something was broken, like a bowl smashed upon flagstones. But this was more, this was life: flesh and blood and what made up a man, scattered uselessly before my feet . . .

I opened my eyes then; the sight will haunt me for the rest of my days. Wade no longer, but a body, missing half a face and skull, life spilling out, blood and tissue spattered guiltily upon me, upon my eyes and nose so that I breathed him into my very soul.

The rough floor swam before my eyes as I vomited, trying to crawl away from that hideous sight, still warm from life. Something struck me in the side and I lashed out. It was a foot, and for one moment I thought that the Lord had forsaken me; that the body on the floor was mine and that this was hell.

Then I remembered Nettie. She had fallen in a dark corner. I clawed my way toward her. She lay upon her back, the shotgun thrown behind her and a red welt rising from cheekbone to temple from the impact. I reached out and recoiled from my own hand, slick with flesh and blood.

I tried to rid myself of the gore, but there was no clean cloth to wipe it away. My habit, my sleeves, were slick with blood. Hysteria began to bubble within my chest as I scrabbled with more desperation. Then my finger caught upon something. My rosary swung into the open. I clutched at it then, for it remained white, the dull bone shining against my bloody fist.

The sight of it gave me strength, cleared some of the haze from my mind. The Lord would help me. Horror remained, but there was Nettie to care for. I shook her, hard, for something must be done. Slowly, she came to. Her shrieks matched mine when she saw the body, but I wrapped my arms around her, forcing her head away until her cries subsided into terrified gasps.

We clung to each other. My blood-slicked hands left dark smears upon her hair. I knew that I should try to whisper some words of absolution over the body, some salvation, but the thought brought bile to my throat.

Slowly, I became aware that Nettie was tugging at my arm, urging me away.

'Got to get,' I heard her say through the ringing, 'we got to get 'fore they come . . .' Her face was stained where she had touched me, tears making fresh the drying blood upon her cheek. 'They'll hang me! Won't wait 'til I'm delivered neither, say I'm a murderer . . .'

'We cannot.'

She continued to tug at me, but my limbs were lifeless.

'You don't know them, he—'

A change in the light outside made her silent. Orange sparks began to show through the cracks in the door. Boots, crunching in the dirt, spurs on leather, weapons being armed.

'It's the sheriff.'

'Sheriff?'

Her face was swollen and feverish.

'Sheriff Paxton,' she said.

One pair of feet approached the house alone. Nettie was transfixed.

'Paxton . . . he's Wade's brother.'

5

No peace for my bones,
because of my sins

Nettie shivered beside me in the cell. Her nose was bloodied where Paxton had struck out before anyone could stop him. No one had touched me. The crowd of men who surrounded the cabin had stared, but none had met my gaze. Finally, one of them gathered the courage to point his rifle at me, shove me into a walk.

I went without fight, for I had nothing within me then, no words, no mind or voice to argue. Only the sight of that ruined body, the smell of it upon me.

'Sister?'

Nettie's voice was a whisper, barely that, and she repeated the word several times before I realized it was I to whom she spoke. I dragged my eyes down. She sat in the corner of the stone cell, shivering on the packed dirt floor. She seemed younger than ever then, small and cold and frightened.

'Am I going to die?'

Her knees were drawn up, her arms, as always, clutched fast around her stomach. The knowledge that here two lives were at stake dragged me to consciousness, though darkness waited a hair's breadth away in my mind.

'No, Nettie,' my voice sounded distant, and old. 'No, I told you, they will not hurt you anymore.'

I closed my eyes, searching in vain for a prayer, for guidance that might help us. I was adrift in a land of death and vengeance.

But my mercy I will not take away: nor will I suffer my truth to fail.

'No one is beyond salvation,' I murmured, yet the words seemed hollow. What of men such as Wade? Who caused pain and misery to the world and remained unrepentant? Why should they have mercy, the breath of my prayers, when they spared none for an innocent child?

Neither will I profane my covenant: and the words that proceed from my mouth I will not make void.

I pressed my hands into my eyes. One thought was creeping upon me, quiet at first, yet becoming as loud and insistent as bells in the still air. Was this penance for the harm I had inflicted upon the men at the fort? An instruction from the Lord to make reparation? If it was His will then I would not fail in my devotion.

I raised my head to compose myself, for I knew what action must be taken. I beckoned Nettie over to me, told her to listen carefully and not to speak, but to follow what I said. She looked at me with trust. It was enough to secure my resolve.

When the door once again creaked open, I was ready. One by one, men slouched into the single room of the jailhouse. Through the crude iron bars I surveyed them, so that I might judge what I was to face. All of them seemed desperate in some measure, wounded by the war or running from it. Scars, like puckered leather, ran across faces and limbs. Some gazed at me, eyes lit by the fires that had burned farm and homestead; I saw many such wounds far deeper than flesh. I felt their hunger again, their anger, lapping at my face.

This was true of Paxton most of all. He came forward on the balls of his feet, poised to strike. A small man, slim shouldered like a woman, with the hard, narrowed eyes of one who has stared at the sun for too long. I stood, so that he might face me directly. We were of a height; he seemed to take this as an act of insult.

He cursed me as I stood before him, spat upon my face. I had not been allowed to wash, and the flesh of my cheek was still stiff with the blood of his kin.

I raised my sleeve and wiped it away.

'Have mercy, O God, on those who do not know You. Bring them out of darkness into Your light . . .'

In rage, he struck the bars with his fists. Another man came forward to restrain him, but was shaken off.

71

'Think your God's going to keep you safe woman? I'll see you hanged.'

'Take the girl for now,' one of the other men told him, placating. 'Court'll condemn her for this quick enough, she ain't no nun.'

The man who had spoken stepped forward, keys jingling against a set of irons in his hands. I silently begged the Lord for strength and placed myself in their path.

'The girl is innocent. You are aware she is with child?'

The men before me stopped and shifted uneasily.

'Little whore,' Paxton snarled.

'She has been used most grievously and will be released. She has committed no wrong today.'

'*She* has not?' he moved along the bars, eyes lurid. 'Someone done blew my brother's brains out, Sister.'

The sight of the body came to me again, and I swallowed the nausea that rose in my throat. *Make my heart as of iron*, I prayed, *make my will as of stone*. I could not lie, but I could make them believe.

'He was a sinner. Through mortal sin he condemned himself to hell.'

'And you sent him there?'

I looked into the eyes of each man, placed the full conviction of my faith into the words, so they might strike hard into each heart. 'I told him to repent. He did not.'

Paxton leaned into the bars with a grunt that was almost of pleasure, bringing his face within scant inches of mine. It took all my strength not to recoil.

'Let the kid go,' he snarled.

As soon as the door was opened, Nettie scrambled through, ducking past the bodies and out into the night like a rabbit from the jaws of a hound. Relieved though I was, I could not help the tremor of fear that came from facing Paxton alone.

'. . . send a messenger over to Carson,' he was ordering, 'tell the marshal to get over here quick. She's as good as confessed. We got us a murderer to hang.'

6

With deceitful lips, and with
a double heart have they spoken

The long night wore on and I was left alone, save for a jailer who was ill at ease in my company.

I could make out lights beyond the smeared glass of the windows, oil lamps from cabins that appeared only scratches in the darkness. Last night, I had been out there still, journeying alone. After the events at Fort Laramie everything had seemed so clear. The path to California would be a hard one to make alone, that I knew, yet I resolved that the poverty and hunger of the trail should be sacred, the long days of silence dedicated to reflection. It would have separated me from the world as effectively as four stone walls: by the time I reached my new home, I would have had time to atone for my sins.

Yet that had been taken from me. All too easily my thoughts strayed, and I found myself remembering another night, which had begun with a man's blood upon my hands. A night where the hands of the clock faded into the fabric of the world, where time was not marked by minutes but by the scrape of owls' claws on wood and the hiss of wind across the grasses.

I had sat up with him that long night, nursed him under the foreign gaze of a Santee tribe. Muir knew their ways, stayed conscious long enough to speak to the brave who I had freed from Fort Laramie. It was this man who guided us through a maze of dark foothills to a village, who took Abe from me when my arms could no longer bear his dead weight.

The infection from the bullet wound had seethed beneath Abe's skin; I could see it, gnawing deep at muscle and bone. Muir struggled. I longed to pray for him, to whisper blessed words of solace, yet my voice seemed left behind in the uproar of the fort. The

Lord's presence was shadowy, as if he stood apart, to let another through. I sat with Abe, as did a priest of their kind, who smoked a pipe and brought out herbs to treat the wound. Between us we worked at the crossroads of the living and the dead. One foot in the blood of the past and the other in the dew of a new morning, we waited together, for the redemption of the rising sun.

At dawn his eyes found mine, black as old blood. I told him to sleep, and did not wait for him to wake again before I took my leave, bruised and weary to my soul. My steps in that world were not the same as his: my suffering a burden that could not be shared.

Now I was alone, guilt upon my cheek and in my heart. If I was meant to die, then it was not for me to question His plan. Perhaps I had already seen too much.

'What in the hell?'

The guard's grunt pulled me from my contemplations. He was staring out into the darkness, a half-rolled cigarette forgotten in his hand. The paper fluttered to the ground as he dragged out his revolver.

'Watch where you point that thing, boy,' an amused voice warned, 'you might hit something.'

A woman was smirking in the doorway, one hand resting on the frame. Weapon or no, she seemed to take the jailor's silence as permission to enter, and sauntered in. She was followed by a crowd, four other women, then six, all jostling and laughing as if at a fair, brightly dyed calico bodices pulled tight in an attempt to produce curves from their thin frames.

The air changed instantly, thick with the scent of sweat and laughter and cheap perfume. My head began to spin from the noise and the smell. The woman who had entered first smiled, a cruel curl of the lips, and placed herself before the guardsman.

'Heard you boys got yourself a murderess down here,' the woman said, tattered lace gloves on her hips. 'Had to come and have a peep, now, din't we?'

'Shouldn't be here, June, y'all know that. Ain't you got men to see to?'

She shrugged, the movement sending the shoulder of her thin gown sliding.

'Slow night.'

Her companions crowded close around the man, draping him with their shawls, stroking his collar and cuffs and clamoring for tales of my capture. June alone approached me. She stopped before the bars, fingers resting precisely where Paxton's had. I watched her from my seat on the bench and waited.

'Well now,' she breathed and her voice seemed just for me, beneath the noise of the others. 'One of the Lord's doves, all soiled. Come to town to judge us, did you, Sister?'

She had strong features and her face was dull beneath its rouge, too thin, like most in that town. Yet disdain hung heavy in the air between us. In reply I stood, though every inch of me ached. I had encountered her kind before, nursed them even at the convent, when their diseases became too great and they succumbed to the sins made manifest in their flesh.

'I do not judge. I merely pray for those who are lost, who might be redeemed through the Lord's grace . . .'

Her smile then, as if we shared a joke, made my heart clench for an instant; once, I had had such smiles from my fellow sisters at the convent.

'"Lost" is as may be found, but I ain't the one been bathing in men's blood.' She rested her forehead against the bars, and I found myself staring into her eyes, gray as my own. She could not have been older than a handful of years past twenty, yet lines creased her mouth. 'Wanted to see for myself what one of you gone bad looked like. Can't say it were worth it.'

From the pocket of her dress she drew out a rough pipe, its mouthpiece worn from use, and a twist of tobacco.

'You just like us, far as I sees it,' she told me, fingernails scraping at the strands and packing them into the bowl. 'All men bein' equal, and women too – all of us God's children. Hey,' she demanded over her shoulder, 'you got matches?'

Busy relating his tale, my jailer extracted a battered tin box from his belt and tossed it over without a glance.

June took her time in selecting one. Eyes on me, she struck it on the bars, sparks following toward her mouth, as she lit her pipe. She sucked on the stem; it sounded like the wind, hissing over the grasses of the prairie, and to my shame I felt the chill hand of despair threaten me. For in that sorry place, the smell reminded me of companionship, of a journey, of life. She caught me looking.

'Smoke, Sister?'

Before I could answer she laughed her friendly sound and whirled away, gathering the girls, all shrieks and elbows. Then they were gone, nothing left to remind me of their presence but the scent of burning tobacco and old flowers. Casting a decidedly guilty look my way, the jailer resumed his seat at the desk and set about polishing his revolver with great vigor.

I too returned to my post, resolved to pass the long night by praying for the sinners of this world. I was not one verse through when something tugged me back to the earthly plane.

At first I thought it was the scent of June's pipe, still lingering in the air of the cell. But this was a different kind of smoke, sharp and acrid. Then I saw it. Behind the jailer an oil lamp was alight, the guard removed and the flame licking high. Above it, the wall was festooned floor to ceiling with wanted posters and warrants. A tongue of fire was rapidly consuming first one scrap of paper, then blazing through another, and another.

I watched, mesmerized, as feathers of burning paper fluttered to the ground and began to smoke in the dry straw that covered the floor before I approached the bars.

'Sir,' I called, 'your jailhouse is on fire.'

7

They are bound,
and have fallen

Was this the death intended for me by the Lord, a strange form of mercy to save me from the gallows? The heat of the flames scorched through my eyelids, the way the sun had on the plain before *he* had appeared; a sinner with the face of my Lord . . .

There was a figure in the doorway, silhouetted, one hand raised as if in blessing. For a moment, I thought I saw the flash of an eye through the smoke, impossibly blue, but then it was gone. The jailer hurried forward, iron in his hands, a key for the lock extended.

His hands fumbled with the mechanism, swinging the door open just in time. A crack from overhead and the ceiling began to split. Instinct took over and I dived from the building, fleeing into the air.

Outside, there was great confusion. Many cabins and stores were made from rough wood, dry from a summer's blasting heat. The fire had already spread onto the roof of another building and was threatening its neighbor. Smoke plumed into a sky made orange, a hellfire in the darkness. Bodies jostled past me, voices lost in a sea of panic, calling for water to quench the flames. I expected to be apprehended again, but the jailor had disappeared.

Rushing feet had kicked up the dust into a miasma. I stumbled, could not see what lay left or right, for the flames had etched themselves onto my vision, blinding me.

A hand, cold and slick with sweat clamped over my face. My screams were muffled as the grip squeezed tighter. Other hands were on me, tight around my limbs, and fear was a feral cry in my mind. I fought with nail and fist but was being dragged backward, skidding in the dust. The heat and noise of the fire faded as I was pulled from the main street, around a corner. The wall of a building loomed, the heels of my boots caught as I was hauled across the threshold into darkness. I did not stop struggling, for I knew what must come next.

The door was shoved closed and barred. Yellow light flared sharply from a lamp. Shadowed eyes smiled, lace was raised to red lips, bidding me hush.

I was released and staggered away until the wall was at my back. Around me were four figures, rescuers, I realized then. Three I recognized as women from the jailhouse. The fourth was smaller than the rest. Triumph was in her eyes.

'Done worked,' Nettie whispered to the others, a smile shaking her mouth. 'Done worked, like I told you.'

8

The reproach of men,
and the outcast of the people

Slowly, the water around me became tinged with pink, like the sky at dawn. I scrubbed and scrubbed every inch of my skin, ridding it of the dried blood. I had sat there for more than an hour, the bath water growing cold around me, but I could not yet bring myself to leave the tub.

The act of washing had renewed me, recalled to mind the presence of the Lord and his healing power. Slowly, I drew the washcloth from fingertip to elbow, praying that my sins might thus be stripped from me. Eyes were watching my lips, the soundless pattern they made.

The women were ranged around like birds, perched on every surface, gazes fixed upon me. All the brothel's residents, save for June. She I had not seen. Nettie had been given a spare bed for the time being, and had fallen asleep almost as soon as a blanket had been settled over her.

The need to wash had been paramount in my mind. Face coloring, I lowered the cloth with a splash. My request for privacy, peace, for a bowl of cold water only, had been overridden, and now I sat before them, an exhibition in a tin tub.

'Might there be soap?' I managed to ask, with as much dignity as I could muster. There was a great scramble then, as one, then another, produced chunks of hard soap. Some were perfumed with violets, worn to slivers, but I chose the most humble, rough and homemade, such as we might have produced at the convent. I turned my body away from them as best I could and scrubbed at my hair until my fingers were sore.

I did not realize that the room had fallen silent until I sluiced the last of it from my scalp and looked up. June stood in the doorway, her face as unreadable as it had been in the jail. I wondered how long she had been watching me. Deliberately, her eyes lingered over my body, head and face, my ribs, showing through my skin. I closed my arms over my chest, wishing for some shield from the scrutiny.

'Paxton were here,' she announced, as if bored. 'Wanted to search the outbuildings. I don't believe he suspects nothing, but he'll be back; he ain't a total ass.' Her address took in the rest of the women then, ranged about the room. 'She's got one day. At dawn tomorrow she's out, hear?'

A murmur of assent ran through the room. Then she was gone, the door swinging behind her.

'Don't mind her, she din't want none to do with it,' one of the younger girls said in a burst, coming forward with a sheet. 'Said it were too dangerous but rest of us were for it.'

I took the cloth gratefully, and rose from the water, wrapping myself shoulder to ankle. The women crowded around, their powder and perfume surrounding me. I had not been wholly secluded from the world in St. Louis, and had sometimes seen women of the night on the streets there, but never to speak to outside of a hospital wing.

Now, their loose dresses, corsets and bared flesh were enough to make me blush, so I looked instead into their faces. Beneath the rouge and shadow I was relieved to find eyes that could have belonged to any woman, curiosity and good humor in their expressions.

'Nettie raised the alarm,' a woman I remembered was called Sarah told me, gathering up my habit. 'Scratchin' at the back door like a stray cat. Said we were the only ones to speak to her . . . after. Course we knew she were with child. Whole town knew.'

'Wade, he beat on one of the girls, 'bout a year back,' whispered the youngest woman, dark eyes wide. 'Beat her so bad her head ain't right now. June wouldn't let him in after that, so guess he started getting his fix on the kid.'

'Not one person in this town sorry to see him gone.' Sarah's

80

voice was like flint, and the other women fell silent. 'Not one, save for Paxton. Don't matter none who killed him.'

One by one, they began to drift away, for the night had run on into the early hours of the morning. Several stayed behind, the youngest mostly, pressing me for details of Wade's death, of my journey west. Yet I was long past conversation, and soon, disappointed, they too bid me goodnight.

Finally, I was left alone. It could not have been far from dawn, then. In the convent, I might have been rising from my bed, making my way to the chapel in order to say Lauds, in readiness to greet the Lord and a new day.

I knelt to pray, staring at the threadbare rug beneath my knees. The room must have belonged to one of the girls, for it was decorated with scraps of dyed cotton and lace, paper flowers in a vase. I was drawn to the bouquet, and examined the stiff leaves and petals; at the center of the arrangement was a blue rose.

Even in the dim light its color drew me in, petals like jewels, brighter than any flower that could grow on earth. A memory of the cold, of blooms in the snow, and of eyes . . .

I snatched my hand away. Fatigue was pressing heavily, so I lay on the bed. My prayers came halting, and every time I began to drift into sleep the sight of Wade's ruined face assailed me. I rubbed at my arms, for even the touch of eiderdown seemed cold and damp, like flesh.

Come to town to judge us, June had accused. Who was I to judge, who had lied, had hurt and walked a path of death? I did not deserve comfort, even of a narrow bed.

It was only when I lay myself upon the cold, bare boards of the floor that Wade's face sank in my thoughts and sleep claimed me at last.

9

He shall pluck my feet
out of the snare

I had never thought my journey would see me incarcerated in a jailhouse, even less that it would find me seeking sanctuary in a brothel. The women had granted me temporary shelter. That long first day I sat, while men prowled the streets outside, a carnival of hungry wolves.

The time passed slowly. The girls came to visit occasionally, bored after washing or eating, to try and wheedle stories from me, information about my life. They laundered my habit, for which I was grateful. In exchange, several of them made a game of trying it on, striking mock solemn poses before the mirror and exclaiming over the shapes of their faces.

More than once I almost lost my temper, but I held my tongue, for they were my protectors. By and by, they grew tired of the game and gave me needle and cotton, some scraps of calico so I could set about mending the garment. My wimple was in a sorry state; despite the girls' best efforts the bloodstains remained, rust-dark upon the white band. I turned it inside out, for even the gray of travel was better than a mark of violence.

Beyond that, I paced and prayed and paced again. Night would fall. How was I to escape? The girls had promised to aid me as much as they were able. Some were contriving a plan to sneak me out of the whorehouse to the place where Rattle was being stabled. Beyond that, they told me I should ride for the mountains, for the law did not hold the same power in the wilds.

And what of June? She had said nothing to me since my arrival, yet it was clear she did not want me there. Would she betray the wishes of her sisters, should the time arise?

Darkness came after an age but all too soon. Sarah came to

warn me that customers were beginning to arrive in the saloon downstairs, and to prepare myself to leave in short order. The scratch of a fiddle drifted through the building's rough wooden heart, stumbling and falsely cheery. I did not light candle or lamp, but waited, invisible in the darkness.

The night was growing raucous when I heard it: three horses, four, a noise like carriage wheels grinding in the dirt outside. Voices raised in anger. The clank of metal. My skin, already chilled, grew colder as I peered through the dirty window onto the street.

Paxton was holding June by the arm. He was flanked by two men, a badge flashing silver on the chest of one. Behind them was a carriage, bars inset into the one tiny window.

I realized my breath was ragged, and I could not calm it. Words were in my head but they were not of scripture. They came from the mouth of a man dressed in the clothes of justice, face twisted before the barrel of a gun. *Death is needed where law demands it.*

Before I knew what I was doing I had the vase of flowers in my hand. I dragged a blanket from the bed, wrapped the vase and stamped down hard upon the bundle. It cracked and I scrabbled through the pieces of pottery for one that would serve as a weapon: four inches long, curved, the sharp edge tapering to a point. Below, June's voice was raised, calling after the men as they entered the building. Gripping the shard in my hand, I let myself out.

The corridor was quiet, but from below came the crash of a table being upturned. Boots began hammering up the narrow stairs. I darted for the nearest window, desperate for a means of escape, yet it was jammed fast. I pounded at the catch with my fist, a splinter tearing my skin. At any second, they would find me. Not knowing what else to do, I lunged for the nearest door and slipped inside.

It was a small room, dimly lit by a lamp that smoked and spat. The air was heavy with oil and lilac water. Two girls stood before a bed, garments pulled from their shoulders, displaying themselves for their customer.

The voices outside grew and I had nowhere to hide as the room's occupants spun to look at me.

'Sister!' one of them burst out, and I saw it was Sarah. Her eyes strayed to the shard in my hand, blood welling around it from my palm. Her client was shoving her aside, dragging free a revolver from the pants he'd looped over the bedstead. He pointed it at my head before I could even cry out.

Eyes, dark as mahogany found me from the other side of the weapon. The shard slipped from my fingers and all words left me save for one:

'Abe?'

The cleanness of my hands
before his eyes

'Sister?'

Gaze to gaze we stood, separated by a weapon. For a moment, it was as if the walls did not exist, and we were once more travelers upon the plain, sharing fire, sharing hope. Yet without were my hunters, and within . . . I felt the heat rise to my cheeks as I recalled the bare chests of Muir's companions.

'Sister,' repeated Sarah, 'we were told you was locked away.'

'Paxton is here,' I stooped to retrieve my makeshift weapon, relieved to be free of Muir's eyes. 'There is a marshal with him; they are searching the building.'

'We got to get you hid,' she told me, pulling up her dress. 'They'll come for sure—'

'What in God's name are you doing here?'

Abe's words dropped into the room like a blade slicing fat. Even in the half-light I could see there was a flush upon his face. I fought to regain my composure, but could not dull the edge of my voice.

'I might have asked you the same, should I care to dwell upon the answer.'

He opened his mouth indignantly, but any reply was cut off by a shout from outside, the shadow of feet beneath the frame. I found myself being pushed against the wall, out of sight behind the door. Muir too was being hustled away.

'Stay quiet now, you hear, stay real quiet,' hissed Sarah.

The door flew open, but she was ready.

'What is the meaning of this?' she demanded, hands on hips. 'We are entertaining, as well you know.'

The light from the corridor fell upon the scanty gown, barely covering her shoulders. There was something of a pause as more than one man groped around for his voice.

'Got an order to search this place. Looking for a fugitive, dressed like a nun, as may be.'

I heard someone take a few steps into the room. I noticed then the drops of blood from my hand had stained the rough floor, marking a trail that led straight to me. I was barely able to hold my breath steady, but the man seemed to have stopped at the sight of the bed.

Abe was sprawled in only his shirttails, the second girl spread languorously across his lap. For a moment his mouth hung open, staring at me in my place of concealment. Despite the shock and the fear I almost laughed.

'Got two girls,' Muir announced loudly to the room in general. 'Two of 'em, for twice the . . . doings.'

'As y'all heard, we been engaged,' the girl continued, drawing closer to the door. 'But if you boys care to return later, we'd sure like the company.'

'Taking the coach straight to Carson,' coughed the marshal, retreating. 'Y'all watch yourselves and tell us if you see anything. 'S a murderer we're after.'

Then he was gone, the door shut, a chair wedged hurriedly beneath the handle.

I felt Muir's eyes upon me.

'A murderer,' he repeated slowly. 'Something to tell me, Sister?'

Because thou wilt not
leave my soul in hell

'I can explain,' I began reluctantly, averting my eyes.

Muir was wrestling his way back into his trousers, fastening the buttons as if they had angered him.

'You better have some story,' he growled. 'Last I remember we were riding like hellfire out of Laramie. Then I wake up, days gone past, in a goddam Indian camp with a hole in my shoulder and no horse. How the hell—'

He broke off as Sarah delivered a cuff to the side of his head.

'Quiet! You want them to hear? And you watch your tongue around ladies, 'specially ones of God.'

Abe opened his mouth to answer, but I interrupted before he could speak.

'I promise, I shall explain in time. But I must escape this place.' I glanced down at the shard in my hand, my only weapon against a force of violence and arms. 'I do not expect you to involve yourself.'

'You ain't going nowhere, with your hand bleeding all over like that,' he grunted.

The next minutes passed in a blur. There was talk of stables and watchmen and distances beyond the town. One moment stood out clear among the rest; the brush of Abe's fingers, rough against my hand as he fixed a strip of cloth in a tight knot around my palm. His familiar scent found me, filling me at once with comfort and fear.

Then, I found myself being dragged from a window to crawl over the gutter of the whorehouse roof, my bandaged hand throbbing and my heartbeat loud in my ears. The chill October wind tore at my veil. Nearby, an owl screamed in the darkness.

My courage flickered, but I held firm. Summoning my strength, I pulled myself upward. Hands, strong and scarred were on my arms, hauling me to the roof's apex. I shrugged off his touch as soon as I was able. *A man,* I told myself, *like any man.*

'Ain't no time to be sore at me, Sister,' Muir mumbled under the wind. 'We got to work a pair on this one, or there won't be no chance.'

'I assure you, Mr Muir, my feelings are—'

'There you go, "Mr Muir". I were Abe to you before.' Gingerly, we climbed over the peak of the roof. 'Can't be that you was expecting better of me, then, than to go calling on whores.'

'I expect nothing, Abraham Muir. Least of all your aid.'

We clung, shivering, to the ledge, night falling away beneath us.

'Life for a life,' he muttered. 'Ain't that what your book tells?'

A door banged below, the sound of soles on dirt, crunching past. Muir waited until they had faded before scrabbling in his jacket.

'Got to move,' he growled. ''Fore they come back. Help me with this goddam thing, would you?'

A bonnet was clutched in his fist, sprigs of false flowers protruding at all angles.

'Mr Muir, I hardly have more experience than you in these matters.'

He jammed the thing onto his head and even I could see it was the wrong way around. I helped him adjust it, and the sight of the worn satin ribbons secured in a bow beneath his beard was enough to draw a smile, even in such desolate circumstances.

'Glad you can smile,' he said, eyes squinting down below. 'Remember, you follow the minute I free my horse, no sooner. Keep an ear open an' whistle if you hear a body coming close.'

Then he was gone, sliding down the roof and off into the darkness. The ground was lower on this side, but I heard him grunt in pain as he landed. As quietly as I could, I followed, though the fabric of my habit caught and snagged upon the rough beams. Reaching the ledge from which I must jump, I leaned out, but could hear nothing more than the faint shifting of hooves, the muffled clink of reins.

I ran through our plan again in my head. In truth, it did not show any great genius. Muir was to retrieve his horse under disguise of a cloak and bonnet. I was to follow; we would find Rattle and ride for cover of the hills before anyone was the wiser.

'You havin' trouble with that horse, ma'am?' The voice carried up from below, close by. Muir had been seen. I leaned out as far as I dared. The horse still remained tethered, and dark though it was, the disguise would fool no one within ten paces.

I was moving before I could think better of it, pushing away and jumping from the ledge. I landed heavily next to Muir and managed to cast him one fleeting look, trying to make him understand my plan: that I could distract them, draw them away to give him time.

'That's her!'

Feet pounded behind me as I stumbled into the darkness. My pursuers were fast but the Lord gave me strength as I ran out onto the main street, boots slipping in the grit. A prayer was in my mind with every drumming footstep, yet it was not God's name that I called.

'Abe!'

Hooves, thundering hooves and a horse and rider burst from the buildings not ten feet behind. Astride the beast was Muir, urging it forward. I saw him lean from the saddle, dangerously low. He wrapped the reins about one wrist and stretched out the other hand. I threw myself forward, six paces, five ... I could smell the sweat of the horse, taste the dust on my tongue as I gasped for air.

One final step: our hands clasped for an instant, but a shot rang out. I felt hot fire graze my arm and I was down, tumbling in the road. The dust was almost blinding, but from the ground I could see Muir. He was clinging to the side of the bolting horse like a spider in a gale, not looking back but riding, on and away into the night.

. . . and the firmament declareth the work
of his hands

The light of a new day grew and with it the passing landscape rose from obscurity. Beyond the bars of the carriage window I saw the vast, waveless desert, empty save for twisted greasewood and sagebrush, rimed with ash.

The wind howled us on our way to Carson. I longed to drink it in like a draught, for my throat was close and sticky with thirst. They had manacled me, fixed me by a long chain to the bench on which I sat. I had neither horse nor weapon, and so there seemed little reason to explore the security of my confinement.

Muir had fled. I understood the sense in his flight from the town, yet could not repress the strange twisting in my chest at the memory of him, leaving me behind without a backward glance.

I allowed my head to fall back against the carriage's swaying side. We had been traveling toward Carson City most of the night. I had not been injured badly – the bullet had merely grazed the skin of my arm – but rough treatment, thirst and fear made a fine recipe for fatigue. When next I looked outside, it was all forgotten as the breath died in my lungs.

Mountains reared before my eyes like great walls, grander than mortal endeavor or imagining. The humans I had encountered on the plains seemed to fade into mere sparks of being. My life too seemed of little consequence in comparison to such majesty. The sun flashed first from one peak, then another, jumping crag to crag. Snow clung like talons upon the rocky shoulders.

I drew as close to the barred window as my chains would allow. Here was God's hand, a brushstroke of his creation. Awe took me and I praised him, the sight a salve to my wounded soul.

Then the coach turned and the mountains were gone, obscured by jutting wood, one building running into another. We had reached Carson City. The carriage jolted on a road rutted with filth and potholes. The word 'city' had led me to hope for some measure of domesticity, some proof that here at least, wildness had been overcome by a civilizing influence.

I had been raised along the banks of the Mississippi, with its brick-storied buildings and steam-filled waterfronts. In comparison, Carson City looked a lumber-yard, frame stores huddling one against the other, as if in fear of the mighty landscape beyond. The plain winds howled through; tearing at the shingle roofs and canvas signs advertising bearskins and horse auctions, rattling the rough plank sidewalk, as if men were trapped beneath and desperate for freedom.

Seeing the marshal's coach, inhabitants stepped from their porches to stare, eager to catch a glimpse of the newest law-breaker. I bore their stares, their open-mouthed exclamations and studied them in return. They had the look of many in those parts, worn down by war and by frontier-life. Men wore coats cobbled from oilskin cloths, skins and table linens. Women too, dressed in skirts and jackets patched from salvaged goods: old silk sleeves on a cotton bodice, dust in their hair, loose for lack of pins.

A group of boys, too young for service, too old for the stoop, were idling. A handful of muck clattered in through the bars, spattering my face, then another as they began to jeer. We pulled into a square. In the center rose the gallows. Beyond, the mountains towered: their presence a silent, eternal roar.

13

They have numbered all my bones

The cells of the jailhouse had fallen quiet for once, a rare blessing. I had waited for them to come: had looked for them through the short, gray days, listened for them when the light failed. I should have realized they would arrive in that quiet hour, when the world as one came to face itself.

I heard the clicking of beads and flew to the door, desperate to see my sisters. I longed for their clear, calm eyes to behold me, to witness my soul in its nakedness with every sin and scar made bare.

Instead there was a man, staring in through the bars, hatred emanating from him like a cannon blast. He raised his eyes to look at me. The irises were blue, unnaturally pure. Yet I had seen their depths and within was rot, and corruption.

My prayers failed beneath that gaze. He entered the room, uniform stained from traveling, the gold braid of his cuff soaked bronze with blood. I could do nothing as he extended one mangled hand toward me . . . .

I awoke, as though someone had shouted in my ear. All was still. My whole body ached on the hard bench. Slowly, I eased my trembling muscles out. I had sought answers in prayer, in meditation, in sleep, yet found none, only dreams of blood and fire that drained me to my core.

There were noises in the corridor.

'Stand back.' The guard grunted, shouldering open the door, 'Got them that wants a look at you.'

I had only been in the jail two days, yet in that time had become something of an attraction. Here were three men. Two, I was not surprised to see, had the sewn-on patch distinguishing them as peacekeepers in the employ of the marshal. One was younger, doubtless learning the trade. He had a painful sore, red and angry, on the side of his mouth, and flushed when he saw me looking.

I rose from the bench to greet them, though they jeered and laughed for me to stay lying down, where I might be of some use. I faced them, clear-eyed, the Lord at my back.

'She don't look like no killer,' ventured one, rubbing at his chin. 'That tick from Stillwater, Paxton, said she done blown his brother's brain clean out.'

'Sure, she got that crazy look. Lemme see again.'

There was a paper between them, cheap and much thumbed. They studied it like children at an almanac, referring to it, then back to my person.

'Her, no doubt,' the youngest one agreed, voice eager. 'Though she don't look so fine in the likeness.'

The men howled at this, and the boy's face, already red, near turned purple.

'"Fine," he says! Done think him a crazy blackcap's "fine"! You better get him a girl, Frank.'

'Might I see that?'

They stared at me when I spoke, as if I were an animal that had gained the power of speech. I repeated my question, but none of them appeared willing to move. At last the jailer thrust the paper in my direction, muttering that there weren't no harm in it.

Like the scrap of newspaper I had found, it was an announcement from weeks ago, published during my solitary month's journey from Laramie. A drawing dominated the page. The workmanship was crude, but I could not deny it, the face was my own. The detail in it chilled me. It captured the line of my jaw, the curve of my brow, even a mole, high up on my cheek that was unnoticeable to most.

'Where did this come from?'

'Came on the mail coach from east of Salt Lake City. 'S you, ain't it? Look there, "Sister Thomas Josephine, wanted for sundry crimes across the Unified States".'

I managed a nod, thanked them as I handed the paper back.

'Ain't you wanting to know your bounty?' the boy demanded. 'It's up to fifty dollars! Who you done anger? Can't be the state, they only offers twenty-five for capture.'

I knew who sought me then, the only person who could have mapped my face so perfectly for the pencil of another; a man with the face of a saint and the marks of sin upon his hands.

I asked the men to leave me. Seemingly they'd had their fill of entertainment, for they assented, shuffling from the door. I took the rosary in my hand as the lock was once more secured, and though my head was in a fog from what had passed, the Lord saw fit to show me the good I might work.

'If I may?'

The men halted in the corridor. I sought out the eyes of the youngest.

'Witch hazel,' I told him gently, as his hand flew to the sore. 'Works as well as a doctor's cure, more times than not.'

14

Thou hast made his soul
to waste away like a spider

'Battle of Johnsonville! List of the killed! Sherman in Atlanta! List of the wounded!'

The cry of the evening special filtered into my cell. I had been contemplating the wall, the evening light upon it. It danced to the voice's news; the glory and the suffering of the world, woven inextricably together.

Keys clanged against my door. More spectators, no doubt, paying their coin to come and stare upon the renegade Catholic, the 'Papist Murderess', as I heard the papers were calling me.

Wearily, I turned, only for a palm to strike me across the face. Blood filled my mouth and I coughed it free, but a cruel hand found my chin, was dragging it upward.

Eyes, yellow-rimmed, pushed close to mine. Paxton.

'You going to pay,' he spat. There was dirt beneath his nails, in the sweat of his wrists. 'Done buried him yesterday, buried what you left.'

I groped along the floor for something to defend myself with, but he saw, kicked my hand away.

'You going to suffer worse than he did,' his other hand was at my throat, in the place his brother's had been. 'You an' that little whore when I can get at her—'

'Enough o' that, get out of there now.'

The jailer had appeared, hand resting upon the revolver at his hip. Paxton stared me down for a heartbeat, and then another. Finally, he spat and released me, stalked from the cell.

The jailer's apprentice found me later, trying to cool my throbbing face against the stone wall. Carefully, he opened the door, pushed a bowl of water and a cloth toward me.

'We shouldn't 'a let him in, that one,' he mumbled. 'Knew he meant no good.'

I said nothing, but rinsed my mouth, soaked the cloth with a trembling hand and laid it to my cheek. My silence seemed to give the boy some heart, for he crouched at the open frame, elbows on knees, like a small child.

'D'you truly kill his brother?' he asked, eyes shining. 'Papers say you done take his head clean off in one shot, then jus' stood there, soaked in blood and laughin' to God.'

I turned the cloth to its cold side.

'I must thank you for this. It is a comfort.'

'Ain't nothing.' The boy scraped at the wood with a fingernail. 'He shouldn't 'a hit you.'

He knelt still, turning something in his mind.

'There were another man,' he told me slowly, as if afraid of his own words. 'Last night. Heard him asking after you, where you was being held, when the sentence may hap to be passed. Seemed mighty interested. You done anger him too?'

I missed the water bowl and it spun, clattering upon its side.

'Did you see him?' I demanded. 'What was he, this man? Army or . . .?'

'Nah, looked a drifter to me. Darkish. Horse like a rag on a thorn bush.'

The image of Rattle was so exact it nearly brought tears to my eyes.

'This man, is he still in town?'

The boy shrugged. 'Last I heard.'

Hope: a match's spark in the darkness.

'Your name is Jacob, is it not?' I asked.

The boy nodded uneasily, stood as if ready to leave. I mirrored him.

'Jacob, will you do something for me? Will you take a message to this man?'

He looked as though he might refuse me, but only for a moment. His fingers lingered over the healing skin at the corner of his mouth.

'Can't see the harm in it,' he mumbled.

'Listen carefully. Tell him that there is a priest at Grass Valley, that he must ride and beg for clemency. Can you remember that?'

The boy repeated my words.

'Jacob!' I called, through the bars. 'Tell him I sent you. His name is Muir, Abraham Muir.'

15

Whilst they say to me daily:
where is thy God?

October slipped into November. The days of confinement became a week and deprivation began to take its toll. Food was scarce, made scarcer by the waning season and was not likely to be spared for a prisoner. On more than one day my only food came from Jacob, who boiled together plate scrapings with water into a thin gruel.

Hunger had ever been my companion, yet combined with the chill of the cell, it had succeeded in robbing my strength, already weakened from weeks in the saddle. If I had never left the convent, I should have borne the days of silent contemplation as one of my order must: with quiet dignity, acceptance and grace.

Yet I had stepped from that world, had ridden through night and fire as prisoner and liberator, had sent lead flying from my hand and spilt blood upon the earth. I had felt the thrill and the terror of the plains, seen the endless stars and learned a thousand ways to perish.

And I had learned of men too. I had seen truth within the lines of their faces, seen civilization hanging from them as loosely as clothes on a paper doll, humanity at the reach of endurance.

Why had the Lord shown me these things if His intent was for me to die in this place? Surely, the very hands that most itched to place the noose around my neck were the ones I should take in mine, teach the error of hatred and the blessing of forgiveness? Daily, I prayed. For Nettie, for Paxton, even for Carthy – whose name I struggled to mention in my thoughts, whose face was chief among my doubts and fears.

From Muir there came no word, only an endless stream of contradictory reports regarding my sentence: the governor would pass the measure, and it should be tomorrow, the marshal had no power to press the case, the governor was out of town . . .

My status as a Visitandine nun should have afforded me the protection of the church, yet out here, at the very edge of the new world, it counted for little. I had heard of a priest, often visited by a bishop who had set up a mission in these parts. It was to him I had sent Muir, and I prayed he would find some hope there.

The hours of waiting were worse than all the taunts I had withstood, for they made me nervous, made me wake time and again from meditation, the rosary slipping in my fingers, red and stiff with chilblains. Whenever I heard a tread upon the stones I raced for the bars, waiting for Jacob's face to fill the window.

'Nothing, ma'am,' he whispered to me, when four days had passed. 'No one seen hide nor hair of Muir since he bolted. They're all gathered at the town hall today, though, since the governor returned. Like as not fixing on whether it's to be a hanging.'

I thanked him for the news, told him not to worry himself, that all was in the Lord's hands. Sure enough, that evening there was a great commotion in the cells. I rose and prepared, made my face calm, though my heart thundered like a herd of deer upon the plain. Finally, the wait would be over. I would discover my sentence, how many days I might have left to live.

But the voices were many and something was wrong; I could hear sounds of a struggle, boots kicking, grunts of restraint. I could not help but peer out. I could just see the jailers, dragging a man between them through the front doors. He was badly beaten, but fought still, a black eye and twin trails of blood drying stiff beneath his nose. Hope died within my breast.

'Abe!' The cry was from my mouth before I could bite it back.

'Sister!' One good eye was searching for the source of my voice through the tangle of arms. He twisted and spun like a snake, until with a monumental effort he wrenched free of his captors and raced toward me. Instinctively I reached out a hand through the bars.

'Sister, I tried—' he started, but the jailers caught up, cutting off his air with a fist to the stomach.

'Told you it were him,' the marshal said, renewing his grip on Muir's arms. 'Knew that glue-shop horse soon as I saw it.'

'Wouldn't get too close, Sister,' the other guard mocked, hauling him back. 'Got a hatred for your kind, it seems. Warrant on him for assault on a priest, couple of towns over, struck him square in the face with a statue of St Anthony.'

'He wouldn't help,' Abe spat, 'bastard said you should hang, he—'

Another blow knocked the words from his mouth. Blood spattered the floor and hands were on him again. It took another two men to bear him away from me into the depths of the jail, for he fought like one possessed, shouting my name until the walls took his voice.

I remained at the door for a long while, one hand through the bars. I was still thus when Jacob returned.

'Ma'am?' he murmured, and brushed my palm to rouse me. 'News from the hall.'

He told me the details, though he needn't have spared breath. I had known the verdict as soon as I had seen Muir's face.

16

Let their eyes be darkened
that they see not

'*Confiteor Deo omnipotenti, istis Sanctis et omnibus Sanctis. . . quia peccavi in cogitatione, in locutione, in opera . . .* I have sinned. *Meâ culpâ*: I pray that you pray for me.'

At the end of the rosary was the telltale cross, stained by those I had encountered. Muir, his thumbprint deepest, forever etched upon the wood. Carthy, painting the edges, Wade: a dark veneer that would not be rinsed free.

With a shard of stone from the wall I scratched at the skin of my palms until they bled. I let the beads gather, welling crimson and clean against my sullied hands. Then I pressed them together, in the attitude of prayer, closing the cross between them. The wood drank it in. My blood, their blood, mortal flesh.

I heard myself call for Jacob, bid him fetch a pair of shears and a woman to wield them. My manner must have greatly changed, for he turned pale whenever I spoke and would not look me in the eye.

They sent the barber's wife, a timorous woman who sobbed as she cut free every last curl, grown again since that day at Fort Laramie, a lifetime ago, when I'd shorn them myself. She wept as though I might spring up in rage and tear her to shreds at any moment. Yet she finished her work. I heard some guards whisper later that my hair was selling for a dollar a lock, that folk were pinning it to their jackets in preparation for the hanging.

It mattered little. During that last day I neither spoke word nor ate, readying my soul to meet the Lord, my husband eternal, who would wash me of my sins. Night fell and I knelt upon the cold stone floor. When I rose again, it would be to greet death.

Who knows how many hours passed before the voices came. Hunger and weariness had caused my thoughts to grow slow.

'There was a time when I thought *I* was dead for sure,' someone was saying. 'But then I looked up, and I swear, I will remember that sight even when I have forgot my own name. Sister Thomas Josephine, come to my aid, her pistols raised in a blessing, blood like a promise across her fine face.'

The speaker drew closer and with him came a scent, intensely familiar: sweat, leather, embers and ash. I looked up through the bars into Muir's face. He smiled his cigar-end smile and stood back as Jacob opened the door.

Abe's movements were stiff as he entered and knelt before me, so that we were eye to eye.

'Been cleared of my charges,' he told me, showing me his unchained wrists, 'this afternoon. None'll tell me who done it or why. Maybe that priest had a change of heart.'

I saw him glance back at Jacob, who remained in the doorway, before leaning forward. I knew what he would say. He would tell me that we could overpower the boy, that we could make our escape while there was just one guard . . .

Before he spoke I raised my hand, icy though it was, and laid the tips of my fingers against his lips. I had sworn not to speak another word, but I tried to make him see that I had made peace with God's choice.

I felt his jaw tighten. One eye was bruised and swollen near shut, but the other grew bright.

'Boy,' he called over his shoulder, breaking from me. 'You got what I gave you?'

Jacob handed him a small, grubby bottle. Muir turned it in his hands, like a child with a gift.

''S not much, all I had the money for, but they told me I might have five minutes with you, to say goodbye.'

Wiping his nose on his wrist, he pulled the cork. The sting of whiskey reached me, rough and harsh. I shook my head, for I had refused all food, but the look on his face wounded me with its desperation.

'Bend an elbow, Sister,' he whispered. 'I will not tell.'

The ghost of a smile found my mouth as I took the whiskey and drank, one last toast to the life of my friend. The bottle lowered, I found his expression changed, eyes hard and alert.

I frowned in question, but my sight blurred. The liquor was strong. Nausea swept over me and words uncoupled in my mind. I could remain kneeling no more, and felt Abe catch me, his cheek hot against mine.

Laudanum, my wandering mind whispered, picking up the familiar scent from the bottle.

'I'm sorry, Sister,' Abe whispered in my ear, his voice thick with emotion. 'Couldn't do nothing else for you, save this . . .'

Behind him a shadow was looming, blocking out the light from the doorway. I raised my eyes, though I could barely see through the mist. Paxton entered the cell, shoving Muir aside.

I felt the wall behind my head and tried to cry out, yet no sound escaped but a whimper as I began to lose consciousness. Paxton reached forward: I looked beyond him to Abe, to his mouth as the door swung closed.

'Forgive me,' he said.

Nunslinger: Book 3

A Pilgrim and a Stranger

The True Tale of how the Wanted Fugitives Sister Thomas Josephine of St. Louis, Missouri and the Outlaw Abraham C. Muir came to be Hunted for Bounty and fled across the Sierra Nevadas for Sacramento, California

I

. . . and behold, the third
woe cometh quickly

Coffee. It came drifting to me like the first chord of a church organ. Coffee . . .

At the back of my mind were flashes: a merciless face too close to mine, a door sealing me into darkness. But here was light through branches, slipping across my face. Yellow leaves drifting down upon me like the words of God falling to earth. For a moment, I felt the holy breath upon my cheek, fanning troubled sleep from my eyes.

But no – the light was fading and I smelled it again. Coffee, real and bitter. Leaf mulch and smoke and something much nearer. I raised a hand to my pounding head and connected with bare flesh, shorn tufts of hair where my veil should be.

A strong grip caught my arms as I desperately searched the ground for the habit that had become like my second skin: nausea burned my throat as I fought back to no avail, for my strength was utterly taken.

'Easy, easy,' I knew the voice, yet my lungs were empty and I struggled for breath. Finally, hands found my face, warm and rough but no less gentle for it.

'Sister, easy, breathe now. Be still, damn it . . .'

Deep brown eyes and a face, wind-toughened and crooked but young, for all that. I tried to speak, but nothing came out. Instead, sickness took me. I turned aside and sobbed and shuddered until the nausea passed. Mud and leaves swam in and out of view.

'Ain't nothing to come up,' Abe soothed, hands steadying my shoulders. 'Knocked you out bad, that stuff. Easy now, like as not you'll be weak as a kitten.'

He propped me up against a tree, and fetched coffee from the fire. He made me take the hot, thick liquid in small sips, as if I were a child with a fever. After a moment, my panic began to ebb.

'What have you done to me? Where is my habit?'

Muir barked his scratchy laugh as he refilled the cup.

'Saved from the gallows and the first thing she asks is "where's my habit?"'

He must have seen my face, for he lowered the drink.

'Don't look like that. It were necessary, Sister. I couldn't rightly drag you out into the night unclothed.' He indicated my garb, and shrugged as if that explained it, though I noticed that his face was more than a little guarded.

I swallowed another wave of panic as I surveyed my shaking limbs. I was dressed in men's clothes. Rough trousers hatched with stains, a dark shirt, a jacket of leather and hide that came down past my knees. Their smell reached me, sour and unwashed. I picked at a button, wondering where I had seen the garments before.

Realization was a blow to the stomach.

'Paxton's clothes?' I whispered. 'How . . .?'

'Don't fret,' he told me brusquely, kicking dirt over the flames. 'He won't need them any more. Neither will you. Can't have you wandering about in some filthy dead man's leavings forever.'

He plucked appraisingly at the leather collar of Paxton's coat.

'Jacket we'll keep,' he sniffed. 'See what I can manage for the rest.' His finger floated in front of my face. 'Don't you move,' he warned. 'Got to stay hid. Rattle'll keep watch on you, eh boy?'

The horse looked up from a doze to cast a disdainful look at his master.

'You come here and keep the Sister warm. I will be back before long.'

'Wait—'

Then he was crashing away through the leaves and brush, leaving me alone.

'Paxton's dead?' I whispered.

2

For the sake of the words
of thy lips

It was beginning to grow dark by the time Muir returned. I had swaddled myself in a blanket, and as he approached, I used a stick to push the garments that had covered my limbs further into the fire.

He swore when he saw what I was doing and pulled the jacket free, trying to smother the flames and smoke.

'I believe you *wish* to be caught,' he stormed. 'We're not even ten mile from Carson City yet. "Don't move", I say, but you —'

'What happened to Leroy Paxton?'

My voice halted his bustling. He hovered for a moment.

'Dead.'

'How did I come to be wearing his clothes?'

Abe ignored me, sorting through some saddlebags. I hitched the blanket around my shoulders a little higher. A hazy memory came upon me again: heavy breath, hands reaching.

'Did he,' I began, face flushing, 'Mr Muir, was there any case of . . .?'

'No.' Muir stood still, eyes serious. 'Bastard never touched you.'

'Did you kill him?'

In that half-light he seemed a stranger. Yet I was a stranger to myself at that moment, for I did not know how I wished him to answer. My nature, my training should have instructed me to hope that Abe had shown mercy, and yet . . .

'Weren't me that kicked the horse from under him.'

A vision came to me then, of a body, swinging from a gibbet, jerking slowly in suffocation. A figure in a plain brown habit.

'Dear God, forgive me.'

109

I was shaking again and Abe came to my side, yet he did not touch me, even when tears began to mingle with the cold sweat that sprang from my skin. *Death,* my thoughts repeated, throat contracting, *death and its scent upon me. The taking of a life, forever upon my soul.*

I looked up to find Abe's eyes inches from mine.

'You are going to listen to me,' he whispered, lips pale. 'This was not your death. *I* was the one knocked him out, dressed him as you. It was me bribed Jacob to put the bag over his head, when they took him to be hanged. His blood is on *my* hands.'

'He died in my place.'

'Wasn't your place to die. Knew you wouldn't let it be, so I made the choice for you. Surely your God can show you that.'

He was digging something from his pocket. He dropped the rosary, bone pale and bloody, into my hands.

'Your God too, Abe.' I whispered.

He snorted and walked away.

'Doubt he got time for me,' he said, rummaging through a sack some yards away. 'You, on the other hand, I always said you was a favorite.' He threw an armful of cloth in my direction. 'Try these. Like as not he'll forgive you for them.'

My heart sank as I picked through the pile of clothing. There was a shirt, worn gray and thin with use, a pair of loose brown calico trousers, sun-bleached in the creases, a red kerchief balled into knots.

'Got 'em off a lad in the stables,' Abe called, 'weren't too keen on having to part with his Sunday best, but I made him see that it weren't in his interest to refuse.'

'I cannot wear these,' I told him softly. 'Even the most basic gown would—'

'No gowns.' He was sifting through a bundle, acquisitions from the afternoon, I assumed. 'We got a long way to go. Won't take folk in Carson City long to realize they been had, and there's the poster of your likeness from all that business at Laramie doin' the rounds at every staging post from here to San Francisco. I ain't taking to the road with you in a *gown.*'

I began to protest, before his words struck me.

'A long way? What do you mean?'

'Mexico,' he said bluntly, adding a belt to the pile, 'only thing for it. Thought I might be safe in California, but now they got wind of me again, they'll be out for blood. They got no power 'cross the border. You want to be safe, you better come along.'

'No.'

I stood, autumn's chill creeping across my exposed skin. The blanket bared my knees and I longed to hide them away but held firm.

'Sister,' he rubbed his head, as if pained by a petulant child. 'The State's after you, and seems that a certain lieutenant in the army's bearing a grudge—'

I flushed as I recalled what I had done to provoke Carthy's desire for retribution.

'I must head for Sacramento regardless,' I told Muir firmly, to cover my confusion. 'There is a mission there.' I followed him as he circled Rattle, tugged at the saddle's straps. 'The priest, Father Laverman, is expecting me. He will give me shelter, help to clear my name.'

'Won't work,' Muir said, chin tucked into his chest, as if expecting a storm. 'You wouldn't get more than a day or two by road, without me.'

'I could pay you to accompany me. As my guide and my guard.'

He had been fretting with a belt buckle as we spoke. Now his hand stilled.

'The Church has land,' I continued, trying to keep my voice level, 'bought up for the missions. Plots, all over California. Were you to see me safe to Sacramento it would be a fair exchange.'

'Expect me to believe that?'

'I am no liar.'

His fingers beat out a thoughtful tattoo on the worn leather.

'What kind of land? Like as not some rocky waste.'

'Grasslands, for the most part, and some for farming. At least that is what I have heard. There is a new bishop, you see. He is most keen to encourage the faithful to settle in the west.'

Abe's silence lengthened.

'Rattle'd never make it over the mountain passes,' he muttered, finally.

As if in response, the horse moved solemnly to my side. Muir glared at us.

'Sacramento,' he scowled, scooping the clothing from the clearing floor and shoving it back into my arms. 'But you best keep your word. And I mean it: no gowns.'

3

They are bound,
and have fallen

We traveled the entirety of the next day. Abe insisted on keeping away from the roads, taking little used trails, meaning that by the time we drew near the town of Genoa it was past dark. We could not have missed our destination, for lights blazed, not only from the buildings but also the hills. They led upwards in a rough trail, reminding me of the fireflies that would congregate in the courtyard of the convent on hot summer evenings.

The memory made me pause for a long moment. When I questioned Muir, he only grunted, told me that the armies might be swallowing oil by the gallon, but the only things folk here had in abundance were stupidity, and pine.

'Burn it year long, eat it if they could,' he sniffed. 'Saw a man licking pitch from the bark, once, for hunger.'

Muir had been restless all day. He bid me dismount, and led us off the trail, into a group of trees, stunted and ugly from the wind that howled from the mountains.

'You remember,' he told me, voice low, as though we were being watched. 'Let me do the talking. Keep your head down. We find you a mount, then we get. No fuss, no questions. Hear?'

I nodded, trying to find his eyes in the darkness. All I could make out were his teeth, glistening in a grin.

'Alright, Sister,' he motioned, 'time we see what kinda man you are.'

I had known this moment would come; had spent the day preparing for it but still I was unnerved. I had reluctantly donned the clothes Muir had procured for me, but could not feel comfortable in them, and had kept the blanket wrapped firmly around my shoulders since. The first time I felt my legs within the loose trousers I had blushed for shame, especially sitting behind Muir, astride Rattle.

I felt more keenly every place we touched, knee to thigh, the hide of my cuff brushing against the leather of his collar as I gripped his shoulder. I do not believe I had ever spent so much time close to a person, and by the time we dismounted, I felt I would be able to plot a map of every mole and freckle on his neck, from the edge of his beard, one side to another.

It was one thing to ride with my new clothes thus concealed. It would be quite another to stroll into a town so clearly brimming with desperadoes. I would be entirely open to scrutiny, and I was not sure I could withstand it.

My fingers slipped on the knot of a large kerchief that I had secured around my head. Here was another battle: I had not worn my hair exposed since I was girl beginning my training as a novice. It felt wholly wrong. Even in the darkness I could see Muir's eyes on me as I pushed the kerchief down around my neck and ran a tentative hand across my close-cropped curls. Without a word, he removed his own hat and dropped it upon my head.

It was warm from his skin, leather supple and dark from the sweat of his brow. His scent was strong upon it. I peered out from under the brim.

'Can't be looking at no one like that,' he said brusquely, stooping to the ground. 'Them big eyes give you away.' He scooped up a handful of dusty earth and held it up to me. 'You're too clean by half, as well. I been in places such as this,' he told me sternly when I balked at smearing the cold dirt upon my cheeks. 'They don't bathe none too often.'

I took the dirt from his hand and rubbed it across my face, then stood back for his inspection. Paxton's bulky hide jacket did much to conceal my shape, and I was glad for its warmth, but the calico shirt beneath was too threadbare for my liking. I had gathered the courage to ask Muir if he had a roll of cotton bandage for my chest; he had, and gave it to me, though he turned red as a berry.

I could smell the dirt on my face, feel the night air flowing unaccustomed across my neck. Not knowing where my hands should be, I plunged them into the pockets of the jacket, where I had hidden the rosary. Its smoothness against my fingers was a comfort.

Muir, after examining me, let out a great guffaw, and I could not help the frown that crept onto my face.

'I swear it, Sister, you look like any fool boy with more hat than sense. But *no talking*,' he repeated, as we guided Rattle through hacked stumps toward the road. 'If it comes to it, jus' play dumb and I'll tell them you're my brother's boy, an' slow, to boot.'

Muir mounted Rattle, still chuckling. He seemed to be gathering a great deal more enjoyment from the pretense than I, yet even his jesting could not put me at ease. I was nervy as a colt as we entered the town. The sounds that greeted us were deafening after our lonesome ride through the foothills.

Every building was a saloon, crowded with men. The gambling tables were full, windows fogged, people spilling out onto the street. Nowhere could I see a full set of teeth, or an outfit that might pass muster in civilized company. It seemed to me that all the men of the mountains were there, spitting and drinking, watching our passing with suspicious eyes and roaring curses across the unmade road.

Huge stacks of timber lined the streets, wood shavings everywhere, mingling with the alkaline dust and the reek of dung and spilled liquor. In the darkness of one street corner, something was hanging, twisting gently, a long, heavy shape against the blazing lights. I hurried to match Muir's steps and was most relieved when he stopped by a stable. He hitched Rattle to the post outside.

'Going to see about a mount,' he hissed over his shoulder. 'Like as not someone'll sell for cheap in this hell-hole. Stay here.'

Then he was gone and I was alone. The shouts and laughter from the saloons grew louder, coarser in the darkness. A group of men passed close by, and it was all I could do not to bolt. I steadied my breathing, resting my face against Rattle's neck for comfort. He snuffed me a few times, then as if to state his opinion, lifted his tail and released his steaming contribution to the town's olfactory delights.

I laughed, but it was a thin sound, my nerves held together with little more than cobweb. Then, below the din, I heard it. Finding its way through pitch-pine smoke was a tune, familiar to my ear. A memory: a woman's voice, accent slipping on the words of a new country. Warm bodies, pressed against mine, small hands and heads as soft as down . . .

I followed it without realizing, until I was brought up short in the doorway of a saloon. It was filthy inside, the song competing with the sound of logs spitting in the fireplace. Men crowded ten to a bench, all of them ragged, a collection of skins and hides suggesting trappers, who had taken to the mountains at the first call of the army's bugle. Here and there was a flash of Union blue: standard issue jackets swallowed into common dress. Muir was evidently not the only man in town evading the law.

The landlady had the sad, rimmed eyes of a gull and carried out meals on tin plates, the smell of which turned my stomach. I peered through the smoke for the source of the music.

A piano, battered and leaning, stood against one wall. A man was sagged on the bench before it, dark head lowered, picking the tune out slowly upon the loose keys. It seemed that no one could hear his melody above the din but I, yet the voice of those wavering notes drew me closer until I could hear them echoing within the frame, spilling unevenly from his hands.

There was something strange about his playing, like someone accustomed to sprinting who now stumbled. I was nearly at his shoulder when I saw: one hand was maimed, a bandage covering the space where two fingers ought to be, an exact copy of the injury I had inflicted upon another . . .

The sight made me stumble backward. I tripped and my elbow connected with something hard. Liquid seeped insidiously through my sleeve. Muir had told me not to look at anyone, so

I shuffled away, muttering an apology, but a thick hand shot out and seized my collar. I looked unwillingly upward.

The man's face was round as the dinner plates and covered in a mass of red hair, beard stiff with a paste of road dust and meat fat.

'Sonuvawhore!' he bellowed. 'Tha'were my drink!'

He was armed, like the rest of his table, each more wild than the last, vest pockets bulging with revolvers, knives, carbines resting against boots. I gave one great twist, and was momentarily free, but the ruffian was fast, striking out with the butt of his revolver.

I lunged to the side, a cry escaping me. The man's gaze grew wide at the sound of my voice as he stared down at my chest.

'You . . . you're a . . .'

My hand shot out for the nearest object; glass met my fingers. I smashed the whiskey bottle down upon his matted head. In a single, wordless movement, the room was on its feet, surging to take part in the latest brawl. The piano notes died away as the pianist turned, his song clinking into the floor as I stood exposed, the neck of the broken bottle blood-stained and guilty in my hand.

4

Vain is the horse for safety

'*Stay put*, is what I said,' growled Muir, breaking the silence.

We had fled the town at an awkward scramble. Muir had hauled me out of the saloon just as the first punches were being thrown, pushed me onto a horse I had never seen before and slapped it off into the night before I could argue. He was angry with me. I tried to explain that I had no intention of starting a brawl, but he only glowered and kicked Rattle into a gallop.

Finally, it grew so dark that I almost rode clear past where he had stopped upon the road. The moon had hidden itself behind the clouds, and the path we followed was little more than a bruised shadow in the night.

'Warm bed,' Muir was muttering as I drew close. ''S all I wanted. A warm bed, under a roof, and a drink, jus' for one night.'

There seemed little use in arguing with him, so I leaned forward to examine my new mount. I had only caught the barest glimpse of the animal before Muir had shoved me into the saddle.

He was a short, squat thing, a hard mouth and wide shoulders, wholly contrasting to Rattle's bony height. There was something of the wild horse in his thick, crumpled face and I noticed, now we were idling, how he shifted beneath me, as if itching to run.

'What is his name?'

The patch of shadow that was Abe stopped muttering.

'The horse,' I repeated, 'I assume it has a name?'

'He does. Damned stupid one at that.'

My expectant silence eventually got the better of him.

'Pokeberry,' he mumbled.

I reached forward to pat the animal's neck. 'Pokeberry,' I said firmly, 'we shall be friends. How much did you secure him for?'

'Cheap. Owner were desirous of shifting the beast on account o' the fact he's stolen.'

The bridle prickled in my hand. Riding a stolen horse was a hanging offense in most parts, as Abe well knew. I could sense that he was waiting for me to object. Yet what were the alternatives? We were fugitives in any event. After a moment's thought, I composed myself.

'Well, Mr Muir, I am no expert in these matters, but I notice that it is dark. Ought we not find shelter for the night?'

With as much confidence as I could muster, I dug my heels into Pokeberry's sides. He lurched forward awkwardly. Behind me, I heard Abe follow, grumbling all the while.

'I think Pokeberry is a fine name,' I said, sometime later. 'I have heard that such berries are used as medicine by some Indian tribes.'

'There's not one won't laugh at a name like that on a beast.'

We approached a fork in the road. Woodsmoke drifted through the chill air toward us, and after a few minutes I saw lights shining through a stand of trees. Not the flickering of a campfire, but the steady, yellow glow of oil lamps. Muir signaled that we should stay quiet. We rode gingerly up a path that widened into a yard of sorts, where several cabins stood. A dog barked in the darkness.

'Now remember,' Abe hissed.

The look I gave cut him off, even in the dim light.

No sooner had we dismounted than a door opened. Standing on the threshold of one of the cabins was a young woman, thick brown hair illuminated from behind.

'Pa,' she called, 'we got some drifters.'

The cabin, as it turned out, belonged to an Englishman by the name of Jameson. He came to greet us in a threadbare waistcoat and shirtsleeves. He had the look of one who had lost a good deal of weight and even more cheer in a short span of time.

'There's a whole pack of teamsters, bedded down in the barn

yonder,' he told us brusquely. 'You can join them. There's hay if you can find it. Supper's long done, but Jessie can fetch you a morsel if you've the money.'

'We have,' grunted Muir, pushing me forward. 'Don't mind the lad here, an' if he don't remove that hat. He's a mite touched.'

Before I could glare, Muir was gone. I took a seat near the fire, which burned high, settling myself into the shadows away from scrutiny. I prayed Abe would not be long with the horses. Apart from Jessie and her father, there were three other children, two of them infants and the third an older boy who lay on a cot with his back to the room. None save the girl paid much attention: evidently they were used to strangers at their hearth.

It was a rough place, but clean enough, the wind blowing through chinks in the log wall. The girl drew near me, setting a kettle on the fire and bending low to stoke it. She glanced up at my face from beneath dark eyelashes.

'You're a quiet one,' she smiled, peering coyly. 'Don't see many as young as you in these parts. Most've gone away to serve.'

I shrugged, hoping that might satisfy her curiosity, and tugged the brim of Muir's hat a little lower. Her father seemed to make no note of her behavior, cleaning a rifle on the other side of the fire. Unconsciously, my hand moved to take hold of the rosary in my jacket pocket, and as I stared into the flames, my evening prayers came to mind. It had been many days since I had been able to perform my dedications, and I ached to see them through, if only in my own mind.

The warmth of the fire, the clatter of plates served to drive away some of my anxiety, and the words came, rolling silent and languorous to my lips. I must have been whispering aloud, for with a jolt I looked up to find Jessie's face before me.

'What's that you got there?' she demanded, eyes on my hand. I tried to hide the beads, but she was quicker than I, plucking at my sleeve and dragging it forward, the rosary tangled about my fingers, tell-tale cross at its end.

Her eyes grew wide as she stared, first at my hand, then up at my face. I tried to pull away, but she lashed out and knocked the hat from my head. I stood undisguised before her.

'Pa!' she shrieked, her hands flying to her mouth. 'Pa, it's them!'

my face. I tried to pull away but she lashed out and knocked the hat from my head. I stood unrecognised before her.

'Pa!' she shrieked, her hands flying to her mouth. 'Pa, it them!'

5

Their feet are swift
to shed blood

Jameson stood slowly, the rifle in his hands. Jessie was still shrieking, setting the infants off crying and the dog barking. Instinctively, I reached for the pistols at my hips, but Jameson brought his weapon up, and leveled it at my throat.

'Stop that noise,' he told his daughter firmly. 'Go fetch that paper those folk brought from the city, quick now.'

'Sir,' I began softly.

'Just you hold still,' he interrupted. 'Jessie, let me see that likeness.'

The girl had rushed off when he spoke; in a moment she returned with a large bill clutched in her hand. She cast me a look, half fearful and half victorious, as she thrust it at her father.

'It's her, Pa. I knew there was something strange, moment I saw—'

'Hold your tongue.'

The man was looking slowly from me to the paper and back. I could not make out the particulars written, although I could see a drawing of two faces.

'Well I'll be . . .' Jameson breathed.

The next instant the door was kicked open. Jameson and his daughter whirled around. Muir stood upon the step, shotgun pointed dead at the girl's stomach.

'Lower that stick of yours,' he growled at Jameson, 'or so help me I'll blow a hole through your girl's pretty blue dress. Sister, with me.'

Silence dropped upon the cabin. Behind us, a child was wailing. In the firelight I could clearly see the faces in that room: Jessie's, white and trembling; her father's, closed and wary with fear; Muir, with death in his hands and the ugliness of the world in his eyes. I could bear it no longer, so folded my hands before me, and sat slowly down upon the bench.

Abe gaped, opened his mouth as if to argue, but I raised my chin.

'*Memorare*, O most gracious Virgin Mary, never was it known that anyone who fled to your protection, implored your help, or sought your intercession, was left unaided . . .'

'It's a trick, Pa,' Jessie shrilled, but Jameson held up one hand, allowing me to continue.

As I spoke my prayer, he lowered the rifle, until it rested on the floor near his boot.

'. . . O Mother of the Word Incarnate, despise not my petitions, but in your mercy, hear and answer me.'

I heard Jameson's voice, joining me. He hesitated over the words, but we recited them together. When I reached the end, I looked up.

'Amen,' he said, eyes closed. I heard his daughter hesitate, then follow suit.

Silence stretched through the room.

'Ah, hell,' Muir swore, glaring at me as he dropped the gun. 'Amen.'

6

He that sweareth to his neighbour, and deceiveth not

'So is it true, the stories they are telling?' asked Jameson later, over his dish of tea.

Since we had discovered reconciliation through prayer, we had been invited to sit with the family, although some tension remained. Muir glowered as though he was being stuck through with pins, and Jessie sat close to her father, her tears having subsided into the occasional hiccup.

I sipped the tea, enjoying its warmth.

'I am afraid you shall have to be more specific, Mr Jameson,' I said. 'We have been rather outside of society of late.'

Jameson returned my smile, and reached across to hand me the paper. Although he could not have been more than forty, his hands were thickened and knotted by labor.

'We keep all the announcements and papers that come through these parts,' he told me as I started to read. 'Worth our while to keep an eye out, after all.'

WANTED tall letters bragged, stamped carnival-high on the page.

The fugitives Sister Thomas Josephine, formerly of St. Louis, Missouri, and the deserter Abraham C. Muir, for Sundry Crimes against the State, including the Violent & Bloody Murders of the Brothers Paxton of Stillwater, the New State of Nevada.

I could not proclaim my innocence of either crime, not without implicating those who had aided me, so I merely handed the paper wordlessly to Abe. He scanned it, scowl deepening.

'The bounty is one hundred dollars apiece,' I breathed to him, over the hissing of the green logs. 'What does this mean?'

'Means we're in more trouble than we reckoned,' he murmured slowly, eyes fixed on Jameson.

The man was staring steadily into the flames. Beside me, I could sense Abe shifting his weight, freeing up his gun hand.

'A tempting sum,' Jameson's voice had grown soft, 'and for little work. Yet what sort of man would hand over a woman of God for money?'

His gaze found me then, brown eyes heavy.

'Sister, you are welcome here. We shall not betray you.'

'Bullshit,' Muir's voice was hard as splitting wood. 'He'll turn coat and run for town the minute we shut an eye.'

Jameson's look was sharp, and I saw something of the man he must once have been, before frontier life wore him down: intelligent and fierce.

'I should not expect you to understand, Mr Muir. I admit, I would not scruple in turning you over to the authorities, were it not for the fact that the lady has clearly placed her trust in you. That, and I know what hunts you.'

The breath caught in his throat and he was obliged to spend some time suppressing a cough that raked his chest.

'Heard talk, a few days ago,' he continued. 'There's a man, been making enquiries. Many were too scared to say more, and that takes some doing in these parts. They said he was like a devil, taller than any and dressed in the pelts of a dozen animals. He was looking for you, and I'll wager his fee is twice what's advertised here.'

A shudder rose under my skin. Muir found his voice first.

'What is he? Bounty hunter?'

Jameson twirled the dish in his hand.

'Aye, seems so. Working for someone with ready funds, as well. Like I said, many were too afeared to say more.'

He lapsed into silence then, contemplating the fire.

'I was a good man, once,' he finally said, in a softer tone, 'a better man than now. I know as well as any the damage that can be wrought by a false word upon a page.'

We drank more tea then, ate a cake made from coarse ground

flour and sour cherries, and did not speak further of hunter or hunted. Somewhat grudgingly, Abe produced a twist of raisins, perhaps as a sign of truce. We finished them in silence, as the pine blazed and the wind shivered through the cabin walls.

Jameson told us his story. How the war had ruined him, how his wife had succumbed to typhoid fever in their first hard months as settlers.

'Yet we learn,' he told me, with a smile worn almost to nothing, 'and we strive. It is too easy to forget that we are all Christian souls.'

Jessie had not spoken once through the evening, and looked at me in undisguised dread when her father instructed her to share her blankets with me, in a tiny closet room with the other children. I would have readily stretched out on the floor beside the hearth, yet could not protest and accepted graciously.

I must have fallen asleep as soon as I closed my eyes, fully clothed save for my boots. When I awoke, all was silent. In that cramped space, I felt one of the infants shifting beside me. All at once the memory returned, as it had done in the town, when I had heard the piano's tune.

Small hands, warm bodies. My brothers and sisters, all of us wrapped together in a bed. A woman singing away the fears of the night. It was a faded recollection, as meager as the light from the lamps we had once made with wisps of cloth and an inch of fat in a dish; not enough to sustain and too soon extinguished. Dead now, that woman, the children too, eternal infants under the care of the Lord. All gone.

All save me.

That memory was a door rarely opened, and in the closeted darkness of the rude cabin, with the wind whistling outside, my whole self seemed turned inside out. I felt a tear spill unbidden from my eye. I wiped it away carefully, so as not to disturb the girl who slept beside me.

It was then I realized that the blanket felt slack: she was not there. I stared blindly, ears straining for any sound. Perhaps she had just stepped out . . . Yet the longer I waited the more I doubted, and my doubts spoke with Abe's voice, remarking how the girl had looked at the price on the poster. How her father had promised we would be safe. But never a word from her.

As silently as I could, I crawled from the bed and pulled on my boots. The gun belt was by the door, and I held it close to prevent any noise as I crept into the main room. Muir was stretched out beside the fire, the boy and Jameson slept soundly upon the cot by the wall. The door stood slightly ajar, a wan strip of moonlight painting its edge.

Heart pounding in my ears, I stole into the yard, round to the corner of the cabin. Jameson's words were in my head, his stories of the demon-man who hunted us, and every sound took on the shape of footsteps, approaching over my shoulder. The yard was so black that – were it not for the pale edging of her dress – I would have missed Jessie as she hurried back from the barn, the paper clutched in her hand.

She did not see me, though she came close enough that her skirt brushed my legs. I armed the gun. In that vast, sleeping night the sound of the levers falling into place was as terrifying as a snarl.

'How much?' I whispered, an inch from her back. 'How much will you sell us for?'

She drew a breath to scream, but I rested the muzzle of the gun against her ribs.

'What did you agree?'

The fight went out of her. 'I was to take you to the stable,' she whimpered, 'at dawn. Take Pa's rifle and tie you there 'til they can fetch the bounty man from town.'

I gauged the hours of darkness left to us.

'In that case, Jessie,' I told her slowly, 'we had better be ready to meet them.'

127

7

He bowed the heavens
and came down . . .

The morning came, sun rolling red over the mountains. In its wake trailed a colorless sky. The riders split the mist that rose from the damp earth, tangling about feet and stirrups.

They dismounted a distance from the cabin, leading their horses silently over the cold ground. A wail pierced the still morning.

'They have found her,' I murmured. 'Come, we must hurry.'

I kicked Pokeberry into a trot. We had ascended a hill that rose above the cabins, where we could watch, hidden from sight. Beyond us I was pleased to see a small creek: the water would serve to cover our trail.

'What did you do?' called Muir as I urged Pokeberry down the bank.

'Nothing the Lord will not forgive,' I said over my shoulder. 'She will not have been harmed.'

'That weren't how it sounded.'

'The only thing they'll hurt, no doubt, is her pride. I do not believe she took kindly to having her hair shorn.'

After a few moments the silence was punctuated by a great laugh, clear and sudden, and I looked back to see that crooked grin I knew so well but too seldom saw. I could not help but laugh in return, my heart lifting for the first time in many days. We splashed across the creek, Rattle balking at the icy water, and I related how Jessie had planned to betray us.

'As soon as we were asleep, she must have run to the teamsters in the barn and asked them to fetch the bounty hunter. I caught her red-handed. I am afraid your hat was a casualty of battle,' I explained, for my head was now bare. 'It was necessary that she look enough like me in the darkness to fool them for a few moments.'

'So you lopped off those pretty brown curls of hers?' Muir laughed.

'I hope it will teach her some humility,' I justified calmly. 'The Lord knows, her father deserves some peace.'

'Little cat,' he cursed, 'going against her pa's word an' all . . .'

'You should not blame her for what she did,' I pulled Pokeberry up, in order to see his face. 'Their need was great.'

'I've seen worse suffering, Sister, and by those who'd pull their own teeth rather than break a vow.'

There seemed little use in pressing the matter, and I will admit, I did not want to dwell upon it. The new day's air was fresh, a welcome relief after the poverty of town and cabin. The mountain pines rose steep and green, and the sky wheeled out, a high, unbroken blue. A kind of elation took me, the like I had rarely felt, a simmering in my chest. With a deep breath, I dug my heels into Pokeberry's flanks and he took off, pounding the pine needles into the earth, their resinous scent trailing behind us through the deep forest.

'Did she send for the man that Jameson warned of?' questioned Abe, when we had once more slowed to a walk. 'The "devil" in furs?'

'I am not certain. Jessie said that the teamsters mentioned a name. It was strange, I recall, a flower perhaps—'

I had to haul on Pokeberry's reins to prevent him colliding with Rattle. Abe had stopped dead on the path.

'Lillie?' he asked quietly. 'Was the name Lillie?'

I told him I believed it was. A change came across his face, darkening with a memory.

'That man *is* a devil,' Muir told me. 'He tracked the Wylers for six months, clear 'cross the Rockies, before they finally gave up an' stopped running. I shall not tell you what he did to them.'

He fumbled for his flask and took a gulp of water.

'Jameson was right, work such as his don't come cheap. Broke place like Carson City couldn't afford him. Someone else is after us.'

A creeping certainty came upon me, sending trails of nausea into my stomach, making my whole skin flush as in a fever.

'Abe,' I began slowly, 'who was it paid your bail back in Carson?'

His look was sharp.

'Never knew,' he revealed, rubbing unconsciously at his wrists. 'That lad, the nervy one, jus' told me a man had come, paid the bail, and more beside. He denied it, but I reckon someone got to him first, put the idea of tricking Paxton into his head.'

I drew the poster of us from inside my jacket, pointed to the list of crimes for which he was wanted.

'How could they have known about all of these?'

Muir stared at the words blankly.

'I did not read it.'

I pushed the paper forward again, only for his jaw to tighten further. Then I knew.

'You mean you could not.'

He opened his mouth to reply, but a shot rang out across the slope. In the distance came the unmistakable cracking of feet over fallen twigs, the grunt of voices.

'Hunters, most like,' he turned in the saddle. 'Come, shouldn't linger.'

'Abe?' I tried, but he kicked Rattle into a trot, avoiding my gaze.

'Whatever you say, Sister, it don't change the truth. Someone didn't want you to hang; and I'll wager it's 'cos they got their own private revenge planned. You know as well as I the name of the man who's set the devil on our trail.'

I did know. It was Carthy.

8

. . . and darkness was
under his feet

'What is it?'

Muir cursed and dropped back down beside me.

We had made good time the previous day. Muir gauged that we might be able to make it into the mountains and across the state line to California before dark, if we hurried. The season was turning against us, each morning colder than the last; we had to cross the passes before the first snows, or be stranded until spring.

Scrambling to my feet, I peered over the rock to see what had caused Abe's alarm. We were perched on a ledge, overlooking a wooded valley. One end was dominated by the solid rock wall of the Sierras, jutting toward the sky in ever-higher peaks, our gateway to the west. At the other end, sheltered behind a mound of scree, was a camp. There was great activity across the valley floor. The earth had been torn up into a wide ditch twenty paces wide, men swarming in lines along its length. Now they were cutting into the mountainside with hand and haft, iron and fist. From above, it appeared as though some colossal worm was eating a course of destruction through the rock.

'What are they doing?' I whispered, eyeing the barrels and slag piles, sawn timbers stacked six feet high.

'Railway builders, or a blasting crew, looks like. Heard the Central Pacific was out this way. It's a damned nuisance. We got to get clear through them to make the pass. They're—'

Then all at once the mountainside exploded, dust and fragments hurtling out into the air. A deep booming struck me in the chest. The next thing I knew I was blinking my eyes to clear them, and Muir was shaking me, his voice muffled by a ringing in my ears.

'Sister? Don't fret, 'S only the black powder—'

'Nitroglycerin, matter of fact,' came a slow voice from behind us.

As one we turned. A man stood there, chewing steadily. His threadbare vest had a cloth patch with some kind of insignia on it. He signaled with his rifle that we should stand. I kept my head as low as possible, for I no longer had Muir's hat as disguise.

'"Dead-in-a-hurry",' the man drawled, 'that's what they're calling it in the towns. Sure cuts through rock good, though. That what you goin' to report to your employer?'

He spat, keeping his eyes fixed on us from beneath a shapeless hat.

'What the hell you talkin' about?' Abe demanded. 'We ain't got no employer.'

'Sure you don't.' The stranger jerked the rifle again. 'Move it. Boss'll have to figure what to do with the pair of you. These your mules? Bring 'em down. Got need for horses. They keep dyin' on us, see.'

We had little choice but to obey, although I saw Abe's eyes flicking back and forth to his shotgun, resting across the saddle. The man must have noticed too, for he delivered a sharp rap across Muir's knuckles when he reached for the gun.

'None o' that. Make like the boy there and get a move on, quiet like.'

Just behind our rock, a path led down toward the other end of the valley and into the makeshift camp. No wonder we had been visible in our position. When we entered the place, the man with the rifle gave out orders here and there, as if he was an overseer of some sort. He did not seem inclined to violence; perhaps we might talk our way out of the situation yet.

Foreign eyes met ours as we were forced through the camp, staring out from beneath tents and temporary shelters, blackened with scorch marks and rock dust.

'Chinese,' our guide drawled as we walked. 'Couldn't get no other workers, account of the war, but they do the job like they was born to it. Don't need to understand no language neither, jus' "make hole, boom".'

He prodded us into a shack. Maps and papers littered the walls. A weary-looking man was seated at a desk, eyeglasses pushed up his forehead. In front of him stood what looked like a huge mass of fur, and I had to look twice, thinking for an instant that he was in conference with a grizzly.

But it was not a bear. It was another man, taller than any I'd ever seen, and broader, swathed in furs of every kind, from shoulder to shin.

'What is it, Ed?' the bespectacled man sighed. 'Can't you see I'm talking? My apologies, Mr Lillie . . .'

9

And coals were kindled by it

The breath caught in my throat. I felt Muir take an involuntary step back, only to be prodded forward again by the rifle.

Lillie, my mind raced, *Carthy's hunting dog.* The huge man was turning to look at us. His eyes were set so deep in his heavy brow that they did not appear to be eyes at all, just a dark swipe of shadow across his skin. I kept my chin lowered as far as I could, but the heat rose to my cheeks under his scrutiny. I clamped my arms tighter about my chest. His gaze was flat as a predator's.

'Found these two snoopin' up yonder, talkin' of black powder,' the overseer sneered. 'Road agents, spying for Union Pacific, most like.'

'Now look here, we ain't nothing but—'

The overseer drove the butt of his rifle into Muir's stomach. 'Keep quiet,' he growled. 'You ain't talking 'til we finished.'

The man at the desk rubbed his face with both hands. An abandoned pen and ink pot stood by his elbow.

'State your names and business,' he snapped at me, 'I have no time for games. We got important guests arriving.'

'Sister,' the overseer supplied, staring down at Muir who was still doubled over. 'This 'un called the boy "Sister".'

Lillie had not moved, yet the air around him seemed somehow charged. He was raising an arm, so slowly that it was almost unnoticeable, like a snake shifting. I tried to think, asked the Lord to come to my aid, for I knew our time was short.

'Joseph Sister,' I heard myself stuttering, voice low. 'That's Mr, uh, Rattle. We are just travelers.'

Through the buzzing of fear in my head, I prayed for the Lord to forgive the falsehood, even as I cast about desperately for a means of escape.

'I find that unlikely in the extreme, lad,' the man in the glasses retorted. 'We have been plagued by you Union spies since the day we started work here and—' He broke off. 'Mr Lillie?'

Lillie had turned himself right around to face me. In his hand was a paper, dwarfed by his grip. I recognized it well enough. It was identical to the one stowed in my own jacket.

'Sister,' he rumbled.

For one, endless moment all was still: Abe doubled over, the overseer's finger on the trigger, Lillie before me with his air of unstoppable force. Then the Lord was in my body, guiding my movements. My hand shot toward the desk, seizing the pot of ink and flinging it into Lillie's face.

Fast as I was, Lillie was faster. He swung, twisting like a cat, a blade flashing in the light. It caught me across the collarbone as I dived past, pain searing the skin an inch from my throat. I went tumbling into the overseer, but Abe was ready for him, his face grim as he spun the man's weapon upside down and discharged it at point-blank range into his stomach.

Then we were running, stumbling out toward the horses. Pokeberry was rearing at the gunfire. Shots peppered the air around us, and I heard Muir cry out, but he motioned me to hurry. Glancing back as I leaped onto Pokeberry, I saw the bespectacled man at the doorway, fumbling with a revolver. Hands shaking, I dragged out one of the pistols at my hip and fired clumsily toward him.

The shot was far from accurate, but it made him duck. Then a huge, dark shape flung him aside. Lillie hurtled toward us on his own mount, monstrously huge, a blot of shadow and death upon the landscape, the ink winging across his face in dark feathers.

The passage came to my head unbidden: *the sun became black as sackcloth of hair, and the moon became as blood.* I was so afraid I could not tear my eyes away, even as Muir bellowed my name.

An explosion tore the air to my right, sending rock flying. I shrieked as my skin and hands were battered, and Pokeberry stumbled, whinnying in protest. For a dreadful moment I thought we would fall, be left helpless and crippled before an oncoming demon, but the Lord caught me once more, sending my heels kicking back, my voice screaming the horse on.

Faster than ever before we galloped, breaking free of the small camp. Abe was ahead, face white with strain. A trail of blood from ear to neck spoke of a brush with a bullet, but he seemed in one piece. We rode the valley floor, climbing up the blasted gully toward the mountain face. Building materials, piles of rock and timber littered the ground, and we wove through them, cantering to a discord of fire and thunder.

Muir was pointing Rattle toward a steep path that disappeared sharply into a gulch, but it was no use. Our horses were not fast enough, not strong enough to outrun Lillie for long; without stopping him somehow, we would be taken before we had even covered a mile.

Possessed by these thoughts, I almost rode Pokeberry clear into a crate that blocked the track. It stood alone, as if someone had been afraid to shift it further. There was a stamp upon it, and the words had me pulling the horse to a standstill. Black liquid oozed from one corner. I scrambled down from the saddle and sent the horse lurching after Abe with a hurried slap.

Guide my hand, I prayed, as I armed the pistol, *be my sight and savior in this hour of need.*

'What are you doing?' cried Abe, higher on the ridge. I set my feet firmly.

'Take the horses and ride!' I yelled back, 'in the Lord's name, ride!'

I did not look again to see if he had obeyed, for Lillie was closing in. The knife was in his hand, held low to cut a person down. Beyond him the smoke had cleared and the camp was in uproar. From my high vantage I could see a coach grinding to a halt, men pouring from its interior. For one moment, the distance seemed to contract as a pair of pale gloves appeared at the window frame, followed by a face, heavenly in its beauty, framed by golden hair and with eyes of impossible blue . . . .

'Dead-in-a-hurry,' I whispered grimly, and fired into the crate.

10

Dark waters in the
clouds of the air

The climb was relentless. Steeper and steeper the gulches rose, the cliff face falling away like a yawn of fear on one side of the narrow trail. The path turned to fine dust and loose stones, making the horses' hooves jerk and slip.

Pokeberry fell twice, each time more heart-stopping. I could not endure the thought of him breaking a limb, so I dismounted and led him by his bridle. Abe shouted back at me not to be a fool, but Rattle was faring little better and soon he too was on foot, struggling toward the distant summit.

Fear was coursing through my body. My head pounded, and my ribs were one spasm of hurt from where the blast had thrown me. I prayed none were broken, yet there was no time to stop and make certain. The cut across my collarbone bled sluggishly, but mercifully did not seem deep.

A chill grew in the air, hard in my gasping lungs. All at once the great, eyeless crags were looming above us. Sentinels of the Lord sent to crush me and to reveal the sins upon my soul. They called to me hungrily. My knees buckled in awe and dread and the knowledge that I was to die, that they would take me to meet my maker.

The cold brought me to. I spluttered as Abe threw away the handful of snow.

'Air,' he wheezed, white with his own difficulty. 'S'rare up here; look straight ahead, try and stay calm.'

We were at the snowline now and I thought we might finally be safe. But Muir's eyes squinted to the peaks, up into the sky where, magnesium-white, the sun was swallowed by cloud. In the harsh light, every line on his face seemed magnified. So too his years, his sins and sorrows, until he stood thrice-aged before me.

'Fast,' he whispered. 'We got to move fast.'

It was not only men we were fleeing – flesh and blood and armed with fire – but a storm.

The fog rolled in as the temperature plummeted. The cold was thick and insidious, creeping through seams and buttonholes to chill the skin beneath. Oftentimes, I could only make out the slipping shape of Rattle's back hooves, and nothing of his master, but I pressed on, following their trails in the growing frost.

Ice, a hard crust over snow that never melted, began to send me to my knees. I had no gloves, unprepared as we were for the cold, and soon my palms were scraped raw. Abe's wheeze drifted back to me. I murmured a prayer of resolution, of strength, and began it again each time I fell.

'Dear Lord, give me courage, for I lack it more than anything else. Give me strength, against men and their threats . . .'

A faint cry was all the warning I had before it struck. I had seen blizzards in St. Louis, yet only ever from the safety of the convent. This was fierce: a blast with crystals in its depths, not fine and sparkling but smashed into shards. After one minute my skin was screaming, after another, my hand came away flecked with blood. I dragged the kerchief from my neck, wrapped my face as best I could. Poor Pokeberry's mane was heavy with icicles, frost creeping into his nostrils. I tried to brush them free but found the bridle frozen in my hand.

I had begun the prayer again when I fell hard, my boots skidding out, sending me crashing twenty hard-won paces back down the mountainside. Pokeberry slipped with me, his hooves clattering dangerously near my head, the whole weight of him ready to crush me in one breathless second.

I thrashed my way to a stop. The reins had come loose from my hand and I prayed the horse had found his feet. My muscles screamed in protest as I tried to rise, eyes flooding in pain. I blinked them clear, but a moment later my eyelids were freezing closed.

The mountains, which had seemed so glorious only a short time ago, were cold with condemnation. I cried out, and the peaks took even that, swallowing my voice without even the hint of an echo. There was no sight, no sound, no air left for me. Just pain and cold and the weight of the sky upon my limbs.

Different pain, sharp, hard upon my cheek! I clawed at my eyes, but still they were sealed closed. There was a brushing against my wind-stung face and I felt warmth, faint and whipped away, but settling again and again, until the crystals began to give.

One eye came free, then the other beneath my scraping fingers.

Muir cradled me, breathing the warmth of his living body upon my face, melting the ice from my eyes. His hands held my head and for one, illimitable moment I felt as safe as a child.

Yet the storm raged and there was pain and he pulled me roughly to my feet, the frost cracking in the creases of my clothes.

Stay with me, his look said, black in the face of the tempest. *Stay with me, or we perish.*

As silver, tried by the fire

I remember little else from that ride. I recall a feeling of being pulled from the saddle, limbs unbending, of being laid on a floor unable to do anything else save shudder, my thoughts too slow even to pray. All that came to mind was a relentless image, blue eyes through a dust cloud, and words I could not shake: *his head and his hairs were white like snow, and his eyes were as a flame of fire* . . .

I must have been muttering them, for Abe was at my side. I could not see him, but I knew his presence. His hands were chafing mine, pushing warmth back into the fingers, but still the words circled in my mind.

White like snow . . .

I felt myself drifting into sleep, only for something to strike me hard across the cheek. My eyes flew open then, struggling to focus in the gloom.

'You sleep, you die,' Abe croaked. 'Start moving, or you'll freeze.'

But it was as if my body had turned to stone, the blood sluggish in my veins until there was no flesh to bend or give. Movement seemed impossible. Yet I felt Muir's eyes fixed upon me and gritted my teeth, shifted my legs a little.

'So,' he encouraged, 'now the arms. Come on, fingers too. How will you pray if you got no digits?'

I dragged myself into a sitting position, rubbing my arms and legs in the way that he instructed. Inch by inch, feeling returned, and with it pain. The nurse in me took over then, creating a catalogue of hurts: an ache in the ribs, the cut across my neck, which still bled. My pounding head, skinned hands, knees in no better state, face and lips ripped raw by the wind. And something else . . . I raised tingling fingers to explore my cheek.

'You hit me!' I gasped. 'Mr Muir, I . . .'

Abe gave what might have been a chuckle in any other circumstance. He too looked dreadful, but had recovered his wits quicker than I.

'Only way, Sister. Couldn't get my fingers free or I would've settled for a good pinch.'

Undoubtedly he had saved my life, and I held back any further rebuke. Before, I had been too mind-numbed to wonder that we were out of the storm. Now I saw we were in some form of cabin, crudely built from logs. Snow blew in through gaps in every wall, but it was shelter. I blessed whoever might have built it, be he vagabond or saint.

'Looks like a trapper's place,' Muir told me, opening a saddle pack with agonizing slowness. 'Abandoned for winter, no doubt. Most folk don't wait for the first snow.'

Every inch of me throbbing, I staggered to my feet. Between us we managed to start a fire in the makeshift hearth, for there were some logs remaining in an old lean-to, open on one side, that now housed Rattle and Pokeberry in reluctantly close quarters. Muir had begun to unroll the sodden blankets from their packs when an image came to me, enough to make me want to flee into the blizzard outside.

'That man, Lillie . . .?'

'We've no choice, Sister,' he told me, spreading the cloth out as best he could. 'Can't venture further 'til the storm lets up. Lillie too. He's a man; he'll have to wait it out, just like us.'

'Carthy was there.' I stumbled on the thought, even as I spoke it. 'I saw him, in the camp. He must be following Lillie.'

Muir was still for a moment, staring into the flames that struggled against the draft. Then the drifter in him seemed to take over, stating that there'd be time for talk and plenty, but that what we needed was food and warmth unless we planned on dying. Our provisions were frozen; the tin of pork fat had to be set in the heart of the flames before it softened. We ate like savages, scraping it up with pieces of hardtack before it could turn solid.

At another time in my life, such fare would have been

repugnant to me. But necessity pushes every boundary, and in that frozen climate, food was life. I found a handful of raisins that had spilt into the pack, gritty and hard as gravel. I made Abe pause before we wolfed them down, and say grace with me, or at least listen as I gave thanks for the food and shelter.

Although we banked the fire up as much as was safe, rolled ourselves close to it in the damp blankets, I still shuddered with cold. Muir said that we should lie alongside each other, for warmth. Propriety warred with my icy skin, and finally I agreed that we should roll ourselves top to tail, like children in a bed. Snow blew over the floor in fine sheets, so that I was obliged to cover my face, lest my eyes freeze again.

'Mr Muir,' I murmured after a time, for I was sure he was not asleep, 'you did not read our warrant?'

'You know I couldn't,' he grunted, and even then the note of pride in his voice made me smile.

'I know. Only—' The words tangled themselves in my throat. In truth, I did not want to say them. Was I being selfish, to withhold such information?

'Only?' came his distant reply.

'It is nothing. I shall teach you some letters, if you have a mind.'

There came no reply, and I sensed that he had at last given in to exhaustion. My own eyes were weighted with fatigue, yet I could not help but see the words he could not read; the phrase 'Wanted: Alive' set in huge letters below my likeness, but missing from his own.

12

Day to day uttereth speech,
and night to night sheweth knowledge

'You know, you wouldn't be bad with them things if you knew how to aim.'

We were huddled by the hearth, as close to the flames as would allow without scorching ourselves. Abe had been seeing to his weapons, cleaning the rifle and shotgun, and I took it upon myself to do the same with his pistols. I had seen him eyeing them at my waist on a number of occasions, and wondered that he did not ask for them back.

'The wielding of a firearm is not something we traditionally learn at the convent, Mr Muir,' I responded, perhaps more tartly than I intended.

Hands, frostbitten and scarred, came into view, steadying the chamber as I cleaned it. The cold dulled many things, yet abruptly I was aware of the smell of his skin, always like embers, as if some part of him had been irretrievably burned away, leaving only ash. If I'd had blood to spare it would have risen to my cheeks, but as it was I relinquished the pistol, started on the other one.

'Should you care to learn?'

His eyes were on my face. The cabin walls seemed too small, and I wished the storm raging outside would abate, so that I could feel the wide air on my skin, the breath of God in the wind. Here, I felt hidden. Trapped.

'I shall have little need once we reach Sacramento. I intend to reclaim the life of a nun once there. Visitandine Sisters have no use for firearms.'

For a moment Muir's mouth tightened, but then he merely shrugged, twisting the chamber.

'Plenty of dangers 'tween here and California, Sister. No one saying you got to use them, but say trouble did come; would you not rather know where you're aiming, who you might be striking down?'

The pistol fell still in my grip and I hated him then, for it was as if he had reached into my mind. Indian tricks, Carthy had called them, this way Muir had of laying bare my thoughts, and for a moment I could not look upon the face of the man who knelt there, whose eyes had seen so much death yet looked upon me with compassion.

It was too cold to move away from the fire, yet all the same I felt stifled, legs cramped beneath me. I fumbled in my pocket for the rosary, for I could feel emotion threatening my chest, like rain a beat before it falls.

'It ain't easy,' Abe's voice stopped me, as effortlessly as if he had taken hold of my arms. 'Never knowing if you've taken a life, or if your soul's still clean of blood. Once you know, there's no way back. Men like Carthy, like Lillie, they got something amiss in their heads that lets 'em lock away such thoughts, but believe me, they ain't free of them. Death by your own hand, once you seen it close, watched it spill, knowing that there's one less life on this earth, a life grown from babe, to child, to man, and it's you that dealt the end – there's . . .'

Something closed his throat, and he stopped. Slowly, I removed my hand from my pocket and placed it upon his arm. The sight of my fingers, scraped and filthy, but still those of a woman against the dull hide of his coat, sent a strange chill through me.

'Very well, Mr Muir,' I told him then. 'You may teach me to shoot.'

We could not fire in the close quarters of the cabin, but Muir showed me how to load and re-load the pistols effectively, how to draw them with speed from the belt. This in particular he made me practice over and again, huddled in his blanket while I paced the room. There was something of a holiday air to the activity, Muir imitating a schoolmistress now and then. It reminded me of a previous revelation.

'Did you never attend school yourself?' I questioned, during a rest.

Muir's face looked as if it would close again, and I could see he struggled to sound easy when he answered.

'Some,' he shrugged, 'when I were right small. There were a lady taught us young 'uns the bible and our letters, but we never got far. Sioux raided when I weren't more than eight. Not much cause for reading after that.' He shot me his grin, hard-edged this time. 'But, I can track better than most folk and skin a buck faster than you can say grace if I'd a mind.'

Abruptly, I reached into the jacket, pulled free the crumpled paper that showed our faces, smoothed it on the rough floor.

'You know your alphabet?' I questioned firmly.

For a moment he scowled, then looked abashed.

'Aye,' he mumbled, 'most I reckon.'

'This here's your name, how it's spelled,' I pointed to the black letters. 'Can you make them out?'

We spent some time picking letters out from the warrant's text and reading them aloud, even while the storm blew and stray scatterings of snow had to be brushed from the paper. I took a piece of charred wood from the hearth, and with it, Abe drew his name upon the ground, in shaky lines at first, but growing strong.

Some time during that night, the wind abated and the gusts blew less fiercely into our shelter. By the time dawn came, all was still. Muir slept, but I shuffled to the door, in order to take stock of the conditions.

Wonder met me. All around towered the mountains, rising proud and splendid into the air, a crown for a king vaster than imagining. There was no gold more fine than the light that struck the highest peaks, spilling liquid radiance, no color more joyful than the shades of amber-pink and lilac. The Lord smiled down His fairest face upon that morning, and I wept to see it.

It was a long while before I could tear myself away from such sublime beauty. When I did look back into the cabin, tears lingered chill upon my face and I laughed. Abe was packing near the fire, and his expression then was so strange it almost shook me out of my trance. A deep pain, a longing, a hope . . .

'Better get moving,' he sniffed, and the spell was broken. 'Like as not the dogs will be back on the trail before long, and we got some ground to cover if we're to see you safe to Sacramento.'

13

Who hath made my feet
like the feet of harts

The skies remained high and blue for us, the way clear, as if we had come through the darkness of our trials and the path lay open ahead. The going was slow, the horses wallowing shoulder-high through great drifts left behind by the blizzard. Yet by nightfall we reached the cove of a great lake, pines rising black against the gray dusk.

The moon provided light for our solitary trek through the rocks and trees to the settlement below. It was a quiet place, and isolated. There had been no news of us there, and we passed the night unobtrusively at the hearth of a family.

Our previous dangers seemed to fade the further we rode, until memories of the blasting camp, of Carthy and Lillie and the explosions seemed little more than a tale. My hurts were healing fast, lungs growing accustomed to the thin freshness of the altitude. Oftentimes, it brought upon me a sensation I had rarely felt, until nothing would do but to nudge Pokeberry into a gallop beneath the thick branches.

I continued my prayers, morning and evening, and whenever I found time in between, yet could feel my body changing, muscle where there was none before, flesh lean instead of thin, face whipped brown by the high, irritated blue of the mountain sky.

The solitude and the growing ease of our travels made me bold with the pistols. Muir still oversaw my practice, but now I could strike near a target, and after a week I hit a rabbit who been startled from his hole. Muir taught me how to skin it in one piece, how to remove the paws for trade.

I grew accustomed to my blanket bed, rolled out before a

147

stranger's stove, or cushioned by pine needles upon the ground, a fire our protection from the cold and the cries of beasts in the forest. Muir chose tracks seldom used and was adept at concealing signs of our presence. Sometimes he would talk as we rode or rested, telling me of the war, or his childhood with the tribe, but more often than not he would ask me to tell a story from memory, a lesson from the bible or one of our Lord's acts.

More than two weeks after we had left the cabin, I was halfway through such a tale, relating the trials of Abe's namesake, when he stopped dead before me. Through a gap in the ridges, the trees thinned to reveal a vista of the country below.

'There, Sister,' he murmured. 'There she is. California.'

Startled, I gazed upon my new home. That 'land of plenty' was indeed glowing, as if a brush full of yellow gold dust had been swiped across my vision. Grasslands rippled away into the distance, threaded through by the deep, dark green of trees, pine becoming oak, lining the creeks that ran in all directions like veins, feeding the land with water and life.

Nearer to us, deep tracks scored the mountainside, growing shallower into the foothills where rivulets of water flowed slow and brown to the plain below.

'Run-off from the prospectors,' Abe observed, 'tell them all you like the gold's gone, but still they come, buryin' themselves into those hills like ticks.'

He pointed far and away, into the distance. 'It's down there, Sacramento. When folks say there's no God west of the Missouri, sure as hell that's the place they're thinkin' of.'

148

14

My lots are in thy hands

The remainder of our journey passed in near silence. Muir seemed displeased with everything, and when he spoke, it was only to talk about how he would run his land, and what crops and cattle he should raise, once he had his payment.

He will not to settle, a treacherous part of my brain hissed, *after so much wandering.* As we drew nearer to our destination, I could not help but feel relief. The longer I was away from God's house, the more my faith suffered and the wilder grew my soul. I had seen a great deal more than I could ever have dreamed, and done things upon which I would dwell until the end of my days. My feelings too were such that no Bride of Christ ought to know. I was afraid that they would not be easily forgotten.

We made good time, for neither of us seemed much inclined to delay, especially once we left the slopes for the long, dappled grasslands. There had been no sign of our pursuers since we had crossed the state line in the mountains, but still we approached the city with caution, for word would surely have been sent to the law there.

It was near dark when we finally approached, and in the shadows, that flood-plain settlement reeked of rotting vegetation. We picked our way through the ragged town of tents and hovels that straggled from the city limits. Everywhere raw materials were scattered, roads half paved and dug out, timber and piles of stones making the streets seem like a building project that had been abandoned.

The endless houses, the litter, the stench of mud and sewers near overwhelmed my senses after the purity of the Sierras, but

I called upon the Lord to give me strength, for I was here to do His bidding, to bring His light into this place.

The streets were not named, and we were forced to ask several strangers as to the whereabouts of the Catholic mission run by Father Laverman. Most did not know, but finally one pointed us to a makeshift wooden structure.

If it was a church, it was more than humble, and I swallowed the dismay that threatened to show on my face. The walls seemed to have been rebuilt time and again, and now stood, leaning precariously against each other on the edge of a partly vacant lot. Some attempt had been made to neaten the ground around it, but weeds grew, thrusting through brick and mortar.

As I dismounted, my heart tried to beat itself from my chest. How was I to be received? I, who had strayed so far from the ways and words of the Church. My clothes I could not help, but I tied the kerchief around my head, hung the rosary about my neck and prayed that the Lord would grant mercy and understanding to Father Laverman.

I knocked, and the silence echoed around us. Finally, I heard bars being lifted and a face peered out at us, expression taut. Barely had I opened my mouth to speak when the man's eyes dropped into wonder.

'Praise the Lord,' the priest breathed, opening the door to us. 'Sister Josephine, you are alive.'

15

Burn my reins

'I received the news by telegram,' Father Laverman told us. His hands shook as he poured the water to make coffee. 'It said that you had left St. Louis, but were nowhere to be found. We prayed you would make safe passage here, eventually.'

We were settled in a small kitchen. It was plain, but seemed luxurious after weeks of eating strips of meat with our fingers, fish caught from freezing creeks, acrid from woodsmoke. Abe had stabled the horses at a neighboring saloon, and hunkered uneasily upon a chair, his expression as unknowable as that first day I met him upon the plain.

'There are questions, of course, as to your conduct and your ... methods of ministering during the journey.' The priest shot Muir a glance, which was returned, twice as hard. 'Yet I believe the Church feels there were extenuating circumstances. Of course, confession will secure the necessary absolution.' His smile wavered as he struggled with the large kettle. 'In any case, you are most welcome here. As you can see, I am not in the finest state of health.'

'Father Laverman,' I began when silence had fallen once more, 'Mr Muir has been my guide these past months, and indeed, I am indebted to him for my life, for he came to my aid on more than one occasion.'

Despite the pistols at my waist, my wind-toughened skin, I felt like a child, fumbling my words.

'I promised him remuneration for his actions. Might we ...?'

'Say no more, Sister. I will write to the bishop as a matter of urgency tomorrow. In the meantime, I hope you will abide here awhile, Mr Muir? We have little in the way of comfort, but no doubt you are accustomed to rougher.'

For a moment, Muir looked ready to refuse, but at a glance from me, he merely grunted.

'Sister Josephine, please excuse me a moment. I will see to your cell. Then perhaps we might say compline together?'

I inclined my head in agreement as he shuffled away.

'Sister,' Abe began in earnest, the moment Father Laverman was out of earshot.

'Mr Muir,' I interrupted, 'would you be so ungracious as to refuse shelter from Father Laverman? He is risking much to aid us.'

'Something ain't right,' he hissed, 'we should—'

'There is no "we", Mr Muir,' I broke out, struggling to keep my voice calm. 'You have performed your service admirably, and now I am where I belong.'

My hands trembled as I struggled to release the belt with the pistols, which had weighed upon my hips since our arrival. I pushed them toward him and turned away.

'I am not an outlaw, nor a deserter. I am a Visitandine and have no further cause to behave in any other fashion.'

16

To shoot in the dark
the upright of heart

I sank onto the narrow bed. The familiar words of compline, the relief that came from hearing another's voice praying in unison with my own, coursed through me. Yet it could not rid me of the heaviness in my chest.

I had washed in cold water, tried to cleanse myself of the past. I had stripped away the clothes of my adventure and replaced them with an old habit of Father Laverman's that hung awkwardly upon my frame. This was now my life: a poor room in a busy city on the western edge of the world. I lay in the sacred silence and clutched at the missal Father Laverman had lent me as if it were the hand of an old friend.

I must have slept then, though it cannot have been for long. There came a noise in the darkness, and voices. To break the Great Silence meant grave trouble, and immediately one hand flew to my hips where the pistols had rested.

My fingers met nothing but rough cloth, and I felt sick, that my first impulse should be toward violence even in a holy place. I did not have time to rebuke myself further, for my door crashed open, bringing with it cries of pain. Father Laverman was flung down upon the boards.

'Sister!' he cried, blood on his teeth, but a boot swung, driving into his stomach with a force that made me gasp, silencing him. The attacker was in the doorway, a silhouette that towered over the cowering holy man, and I had nothing to defend myself save the words of God.

'Dear Lord, have mercy upon us . . .' I began breathlessly, as a rough hand seized my face.

'Quiet, God damn you!'

I knew that touch, the roughness of those fingers upon my skin, all too well.

'Abe!' I lashed out, pushing him away. 'What are you doing?'

Father Laverman groaned, and Muir was on him again, although I shouted for him to stop. He dragged the priest's head backward by the hair, and pressed a pistol into his throat.

'Tell her,' he demanded, voice thick with a fury, more animal than man. 'Tell her what you've done!'

'Sister, call him off,' Laverman begged, but Muir struck him across the face. Bone cracked and the priest crumpled to the floor, blood streaming from his nose.

I had seen enough. It was the work of a moment to leap from the bed, to grasp the remaining pistol from Muir's holster and pull it free, the way he had taught me. It was loaded.

'Get out.' My voice shook, dark with anger. 'Get out, or God help me I shall shoot.'

Abe's sneer was terrifying in the darkness. He straightened, lowering the pistol to his side. His lips were flecked with spittle.

'Hear that?' he hissed to the man on the floor, eyes fixed on mine. 'Hear that? She's protecting you.'

'Father Laverman, come to me.' I returned Muir's gaze from beyond the pistol. 'He shall not harm you further.'

The priest made a strange gulping sound, coughed up bloody mucus. I realized then that he was weeping.

'Forgive me,' he choked, 'forgive me, I had no choice . . .'

'Found him, sending a signal from the window,' Muir told me with disgust. 'Sold us like lambs to the slaughter. Would've opened the door to them that hunt us, while we slept under his roof.'

'Please!' Laverman was crawling toward me, reaching a hand for my feet, bare upon the boards. 'You do not know what he is like, the things he has done . . .'

I lowered my weapon. Still watching Abe, I knelt, raising the wounded man's head so that he was forced to face me.

'Who made you do this?' I asked, as softly as I could.

'Please,' the priest was whimpering, 'you must leave, now;

they'll be here at any moment . . .' His bloodied hand reached up, trembling, to trace a cross upon my forehead. 'God forgive me.'

There was a deafening crash in the corridor, a great splintering as bolts gave way, as the front door was torn from its hinges. Through that violence, through the thundering of my heart in head, I heard one voice, magnified above all the others.

'She is here,' called Carthy.

Nunslinger: Book 4

The Habits of Strangers

The True Tale of how the Wanted Fugitives Sister Thomas Josephine of St. Louis, Missouri and Abraham C. Muir escaped San Francisco in Disguise and fled for the Mexican Border

I

Three things are hard to me, and the fourth . . .

'Father——!'

A hand closed around my face, sealing the cry within my mouth.

'You want them to hear?' hissed Abe.

There was a tremor of fear in his voice; the skin pressed against mine was icy with sweat. I tried to hear beyond my own rapid breathing, into the silence of the recently faded gunshot.

'We got to run,' he said, shoving one of the pistols into my arms. 'We got to find another door.'

I tried to think, but my emotions were in disarray, bare feet barely able to stagger mechanically after Muir.

'What about Laverman?' I asked.

'Dead,' spat Abe. 'Carthy wouldn't trouble long over that.'

Another shot exploded through the building; I could hear boots pounding on the floor above. They belonged to men who would seize my arms, who would drag Abe away into the darkness and press the cold cylinder of a gun against the back of his skull. Fear cleared my thoughts and showed me a way to run.

'Through the sacristy!' I cried.

I found Muir's sleeve and dragged him with me. Near, too near, was the man who hunted us. I had begged the Lord to hide me from his sight, yet still he pursued. I quickened my pace, praying beyond hope that we might once again escape our enemies.

The glow of a lantern snaked into the corridor behind us, reaching almost to our heels as I pulled a door open and shoved Abe inside. The chapel was in darkness, the smell of wax lingering from where we had prayed so peacefully not an hour before. We tripped through the benches. On the far side of the room was an alcove, and beyond, a door. Too panicked for stealth, I flung the bolt aside and threw it open.

The yard outside was a mass of swirling gray, fog – thick and impenetrable – rising from cobble to rooftop and into the blind sky. I reached out a hand and could barely see the end of my arm.

We stumbled away from the building, the cold ground bruising my feet as we ran. The stables where Pokeberry and Rattle were being kept were barely twenty paces away, yet before we had even reached the alleyway, a shape was looming before us.

Moisture clung and glistened to a mass of fur, rippling like raised hackles. A man on a horse, both of them silent: not even their breath disturbing the lifeless mist. It was Lillie, the bounty hunter.

We froze. Lillie began to turn his head almost as if perplexed, first one way then another. He could not see us, I realized. We were hidden by fog and the shadow of the building.

Our breathing seemed loud as church bells to me. My hands began to shake, both from fear and the cold that seeped into my skin. The rosary slid from my palm before I even remembered it was there. Beads hit stone, hard and dry as seeds.

Lillie's head swung around. I lunged for the rosary. The moment it was in my hand, silver sliced through the air where my head had been only a moment before. Abe hauled on my arm and we ran like a pair of wild things, barely telling up from down in the fog.

A wall loomed up and we banked hard. Lillie was running us down, sparks spitting from the horse's hooves. Along the wall I searched desperately for an opening, a doorway, anything.

My feet found the way when our eyes could not. My heel skidded on the wet ground and I reached out a hand only to connect with air. I cried a warning to Abe, too late. He crashed into me and together we fell, down through the fog, tumbling and spinning over wood and brick into the darkness.

160

2

... the depths have broken out, and the clouds grow thick with dew

I must have been knocked senseless for a moment. Then I smelled mud, filling my nose and mouth. I coughed it free. There was a shifting nearby, animal or human I could not tell, and I searched the ground for the pistol that had fallen from my grip.

My hand found a plank, rough-hewn and damp, then another. Stairs. I heard boots hit stone above, a horse snort in protest.

'Sister. . .'

Lillie's voice drifted down the stairwell to us, as harsh and low as I remembered.

'Abe?' I whispered urgently.

A groan from the darkness. I crawled blindly toward the sound, wet earth sinking under my knees.

Muir lay upon his side, grasping at one leg.

'Lillie?' he said.

'Above. Quickly, we must move. I think we have fallen down a set of stairs.'

'Here,' he shoved the pistol back into my hand, rosary tangled about it. 'Damn thing tripped me up.'

Tucking both under my arm, I dragged him upright. Barely had we taken a step when he bit back a yell. His weight pushed down on my shoulder.

'Leg's bust,' he said through gritted teeth. 'You get on ahead, I'll follow.'

He was wet through from the fog, but I could see beads of sweat adding their salt to his brow. I knew I was trembling, that the cold might be chilling my body beyond repair, but I pushed such thoughts aside.

'Abraham Muir,' I said, throwing his arm around my shoulder. 'Sometimes I believe you have cotton for brains.'

Behind us, I could hear Lillie feeling his way down the stairs, but slowly, for even he could not see clearly. We seemed to be in some kind of courtyard. I prayed that there would be a door, or a passageway somewhere in the darkness, and that the Lord would guide my steps toward it.

A handful of torturous paces forward, and my hand hit brick. A wall, closing us in. My muscles strained under Muir's weight. I turned, took another five steps. My bare foot splashed into a puddle, and I stifled a yelp. There was a change in the air, a scent drifting toward us. Through a gap in the fog I saw a narrow alleyway leading to a street, smelling of old mud and water.

'This way!' I gasped, too loudly, for I heard Lillie's steps quicken.

We staggered into the open. All the while I expected to feel a blade at my back, a savage hand close over my face. The stones changed beneath our feet, sloping downward. The smell of water grew stronger in the air, pungent with effluence. A desperate plan was forming in my mind, half madness, but perhaps our only chance.

There was no time to reconsider. Out of nowhere, a hand snatched the back of my habit and pulled. Fabric jerked tight across my throat, near throttling me as I was thrown to the floor. I saw one huge hand seize Abe, the other unsheathe a knife.

For a breathless moment I stared up through the fog at Lillie's face, mouth gaping for breath, hand ready to slice into Abe's gut.

My feet were under me, pistol gripped firm. I threw myself into Muir, the force of my body ripping him from Lillie's grasp and sending us both crashing into the icy river below.

3

But a net is spread in vain before them that have wings

The cold drove the air from my lungs. All thought left me except the urgency to breathe, and I fought my way to the surface, thrashing at the water with the pistol, still clenched in my hand.

The river was terrifying, black and empty around me, shrouded by fog. I could no longer see the bank, or the street, or whether Lillie still waited there. Worse still, I was alone.

I tried to call for Abe, struck out blindly, not knowing which direction to turn. I had only managed a few strokes when the surface exploded before me, water roiling as a hand clawed for air, then sank.

Some long-forgotten instinct sent me diving under. The cold closed over my scalp, numbing everything, but at last my searching fingers found fabric and I pulled with all my strength, kicking for air once more.

Abe broke the surface with me. He retched and spat, half vomiting up a lungful of water. I tried to hold on to him as best I could.

'—mn fool,' he rasped, 'damn crazy fool . . .'

I ignored him, staring about me. Nothing: water like ink and mortal fog, except for a light, pale and blinking ahead.

'Abe, I think there is a boat, we must swim.'

'Leg's bust,' he choked. 'Can't hardly bend it.'

'Swim or drown,' I heard myself gasp.

One hand caught up in his shirt, I began kicking. He wallowed along with me, now going under, now spluttering curses, but I persisted toward what I hoped was a lantern, a sickly yellow halo through the fog.

I had not swum for many years, yet by sheer necessity the

ability returned quickly, warming my blood, quickening the breath in my lungs. I felt my muscles bunch and release and realized that I too had grown strong. One last surge and wood grain appeared, the side of a small boat.

'Help!' I cried through numb lips. 'Help us!'

4

Flee from it, pass not by it:
go aside, forsake it

'How did you know?'

I pulled the blanket tighter around my shoulders. Although we now sat before a stove, I could still feel the cold biting into my bones, chilling me as though I would never be rid of it. We had been rescued, somewhat reluctantly, by a pair of boatmen who had been out searching for a skiff that had drifted away in the fog.

Once they saw that I was a woman, they spoke more kindly and brought us into their shack to dry out. We had not been disturbed in the hours since; with luck we had evaded Lillie again.

Slowly, the night wore away into dawn. One boatman snored, the other – not altogether trusting – chewed steadily at tobacco. I could hear his sputum hitting a bucket now and again.

The shack was made of planks, scavenged from boats. Outside the river birds were hacking and cawing their bankside chorus. The sound was familiar, frighteningly so, a noise from my past.

'How did you know?' Muir repeated, and I forced my attention back to him. 'How'd you know Lillie wouldn't follow us?' His eyes were squinted against the dim light.

The question was not an easy one for me. The answer belonged to another life, to a little girl who had woken every morning to damp river mud and the voice of the docks.

'Skins,' I croaked, and cleared my throat. 'All those skins he wears, they are too heavy to swim in. I knew he wouldn't jump in after us.'

Rather than answering, Abe swayed in his seat. I caught him, steadied him against me. Even from the distance of a hand's width I could feel his skin burning hot, although he shivered.

'You are not well,' I murmured, peering into his eyes. 'Abe, tell me what is wrong?'

He only mumbled, frowning as if in pain, arms locked tight about his chest. If I had ever been in the habit of swearing, I should have done so then. The river water was filthy. I had spat as much of it out as possible, but Abe had gone under again and again; no doubt it had found its way into his belly, his nose and lungs.

'Excuse me,' I called out over my shoulder, 'do you have any liquor?'

'Sure do,' drifted back the boatman's reply. 'It ain't for free drinkin' though.'

'A half-measure only. Please, my friend is sick.'

Footsteps approached, and with them the man's scent, of long ingrained sweat from winter-worn clothes, estuary slime and tar. I glanced up. His face looked as though it had sunk in upon itself, a trapper's hat lodged so far upon his head it seemed an extension of his hair.

'Don't look good,' he mused, then cast a look over me that made me squirm. 'Liquor, were it? He'd do better spewin' up if he drank a belly full o' the Sacramento.'

He shuffled away and returned with a bottle, the glass clouded by fingermarks.

'You a whore?' he said, staring at my bare head and shorn locks as I pulled the cork. 'Must'a been hard up to go sellin' your hair.'

'Watch your tongue,' I rebuked. He shrugged and moved away, but my nerves still hummed. I pushed Abe upright, and held the bottle to his lips.

'Abe, you must wake up,' I said, urging him to drink. 'We must find a way out of here, it is not safe.'

He swallowed weakly and choked, whiskey spilling from the corner of his mouth into his beard.

'. . . keep you safe,' he slurred, slumping against me once more.

I screwed my eyes shut. Once, a different voice had

murmured those words to me: a boy, his hand in mine, calling me a name that was mine no longer.

'Christopher,' I whispered.

But it was no use. There was no one to take my hand now, to lead me from danger and to promise that all would be well in the end. The second boatman was still lingering. I could smell him, idling closer.

Propping Abe up with one arm, I felt into his pocket, impatient of the flush that rose upon my face at such an intimate act. Mercifully I felt coins, and I pulled the handful free.

'You there,' I directed to the man coldly. 'What size are your boots?'

5

As a pilot fast asleep
when the stern is lost

Ripples were lapping somewhere near my head. There was movement – not the bone-shaking rattle of a stagecoach, but a slow rolling. I smelled the river again, a different scent now, dank vegetation rather than the reek of city run-off. I opened my eyes.

In the heavy afternoon light, I saw that we were underway. We were surrounded by cargo: crates and sacks piled high, a wicker coop that rustled with wings, barrels and strongboxes. The boat, low and flat, pushed lazily upstream, powered by a paddle at the rear. The bank that drifted past through the fog was a tangled network of winter-black trees.

Nearby, Abe slept on a pile of seed sacks. I was thankful for it. There was no saying how he would react when he woke, especially when he found out that I had spent the last of his money.

Most of it gone to the boatmen, to buy a pair of boots twice the size of my feet and an ancient coat that smelled like it had been salvaged from a corpse. I had been forced to use the rest, and – to my despair – barter one of the pistols, to secure passage out of the city.

'Afternoon there, ma'am,' a voice hailed as I stepped out onto the main deck. 'Trust you slept well.'

I shrugged further into the threadbare coat and returned the man's gaze.

'As well as could be expected. Where are we?'

'Jus' coming up on Freeport,' the man puffed, teeth clenched around a stained pipe. 'Well, seeing as you're rested, you remember our deal?'

'I remember it.' Instinctively, one hand went to my neck,

seeking the rosary. I pulled the coat a little tighter. 'Show me where to go.'

The work we had agreed upon continued until evening fell.

'Mrs Rattle?' the man in charge of the boat was peering down at me through the gloom, the end of his pipe glowing orange. 'Your fella's awake.'

I staggered out onto the deck, legs all needles and pins. The boat had been anchored for the night. The fog persisted in the air, yet the atmosphere was different. I could smell grasses, the distinctive must of sand. In a makeshift den of sacks and canvas, Abe was sitting upright. His eyes were bloodshot and bleary, but his look was sharp.

'Where in God's name are we?'

'Hush now, dear, you are not well,' I said loudly, kneeling at his side and making a show of fussing with the tarpaulin that covered him. 'We are safe, do not worry. You've been ill with a fever,' I whispered.

Abe was gaping at me. 'Why'd you call me "dear"?'

'I had to tell them that you were my husband.' He made a choked noise, and I pressed him back down onto the sacks. 'They wouldn't agree to take us without a few questions.'

'Who are they?'

'Traders. This is a delivery barge,' I said. 'They were coming downstream and it was needful we left that city as soon as we were able. So I made a deal.'

'What kind of a deal?' Muir's eyes were fixed on mine as he struggled upright again, and gripped my arm. 'What kind? I swear, Sister . . .'

'Ledgers, Abe,' I interrupted, before he could agitate himself further. 'Their man who can read and write has fallen sick, so I am seeing to their accounts.'

To my surprise, I felt a smile growing upon my face at his confusion. Before he could say more, I left him, and stepped back onto the deck. While we had been talking, I had caught the scent of woodsmoke, fish being charred over a fire. I was ravenous, and wondered if I might beg some from the men.

So absorbed was I in thoughts of food, that I paid little heed to my surroundings, until a shadow fell across my face. I looked up and the breath caught in my lungs. In the thin, gray moonlight, a shape loomed beyond the starboard side: huge and imposing, with masts like the slash of an ink pen. I leaned forward, craning to see the rest of the structure.

'Quite a sight, ain't it?'

The captain was lounging upon a crate, the pipe cupped in his hand. The glint of an eye showed that he was watching me, though he had been nothing but shadow a moment before. I wondered, not for the first time, how much he might have guessed about Abe and myself.

'It's a ship,' he said, voice low, as if afraid to disturb the mist. 'Done grounded itself there a year ago. When them that owned it came to shift it away, they found it had filled with sand. No movin' it now.'

I could not say why, but against the night, the ruined craft seemed almost sentient.

'Perhaps it was no accident that led it here,' I murmured. 'Perhaps it was intended to be a guardian of this river.'

The man stretched out his leg with a grimace and rose to his feet. I could not tell in the darkness, but I had the feeling he studied me as he passed.

'Go on down to the fire,' he said, almost kindly. 'They've saved you a bite.'

Although Abe protested, I insisted that he sit wrapped in a blanket while we ate. The men had handed over a whole trout on an old tin plate. It was the length of my forearm and had been cooked in the embers of the fire. I felt as though an age had passed since I had been able to eat, and I attacked my half of the fish like a savage, skin and all, its oily flesh filling my mouth like a blessing. Only after I nearly swallowed a bone did I remember to mumble a prayer of thanks.

Eventually, we were able to talk, although the fish still claimed most of my attention.

'I did not have a choice,' I told Muir. 'The horses were being

170

watched and the fog meant that few boats were leaving the city. I found these men making their deliveries downriver. It cost everything you had in your pocket to pay for passage, after the clothes. And I was forced to give the captain one of your pistols in payment.' I patted my pocket. 'I still have the other.'

I had been dreading telling Abe of the exchange, knowing what the weapons meant to him. But he said nothing, an unfathomable expression flashing across his face.

'Passage?' he questioned after a beat, pulling the last scraps of fish with his teeth. 'Where is this?'

'A few hours from a place called Suisun Bay. From there they say it is half a day to San Francisco.'

'Why?'

In truth, I did not know. My only goal, through months of hardship and misfortune, had been to reach Sacramento. I had told myself so many times that there I would finally be safe, and yet now, that surety had been ripped from me. As to the future: was this to be my life, fleeing always from danger, wanted by the men who sought to govern the land? It was too frightening to consider, that I should never again be able to serve the Lord as I had been ordained. Yet all I knew for certain was that we had to run.

Abe's face was white and drawn in the darkness.

'You tried to tell me, before,' I sighed finally, gathering up the remains of our meal. 'You warned me that the justice I placed my trust in had no power in the west. I did not listen, and now a man is dead.'

'Sister, it were Carthy who killed the priest.'

His sincerity brought a smile to my lips and tears to my eyes all at once. My flight from danger had only begun; his, I knew, had lasted years, yet he had still risked everything to help me. I pulled the remaining pistol from my pocket and laid it in his lap.

'The powder got wet,' I sniffed briskly, wiping my nose. 'They are fair useless without new bullets.'

Muir stared at the weapon, then at the deck around him. No packs, no saddlebags, not even a jacket.

'Sister . . . What will we do?'

'I do not know, Abe,' I whispered.

There was silence for a long time between us, as the river lapped gently and the fog made its eerie passage across our skin.

'I do not know.'

6

Who leave the right way, walk by dark ways

By the next morning, the food and the sleep had worked their good, for Abe's fever had abated. He was weak, and complained about the stiffness in his leg, yet was able to bend it, take a few tentative steps. He brushed me away when I tried to make him rest.

Before too long, the waterway began to broaden, and we found ourselves in the mouth of a wide bay. I was completing my work on the deliveries ledgers in the wheelhouse when the captain entered.

'Just comin' in to Suisun,' he mumbled, 'be in Frisco 'fore sundown. You had coffee?'

A dented pot had been set upon the stove that kept away some of the damp. He found a mug and poured for me. The liquid was so strong it resembled tar, but I thanked him nevertheless and drank it gratefully.

For a time, we stood in silence watching the weather, while he made adjustments to the boat's course now and then. A breeze had picked up, strong enough to whip tears into the eyes. It shredded the fog that had surrounded us since Sacramento until the way ahead was clear, clouds retreating into the low winter sky.

'It's comin' off the sea,' the captain told me with a sidelong glance, 'but shouldn't clear upriver until tomorrow.'

For a brief moment, I had forgotten our pursuers. Whatever the captain suspected, there was nothing to be done while we were passengers, although I kept a close eye on the crew whenever we docked to load and unload cargo.

Instead, I stared avidly upon this new part of the world, eager to examine the towns drifting by and the traffic upon the water. Vessels such as ours were joined by huge boats that belched white clouds over our heads, churning the water with their paddles, skiffs zigzagging between them.

The bay widened further and further until I could barely comprehend that such a stretch of water should exist. I had seen lakes and swollen rivers, but they had always been encompassed by banks. This water yawned outward, the boats that sprouted white on the surface little more than paper toys. At first, the city was nothing more than a smudge in the distance, but as we inched painstakingly across the expanse, it began to resolve itself, and for the first time I felt a tremor of anxiety.

In the afternoon light it rose, brown and black into the hills. Smoke and steam competed in trails. Wharves hunkered low to the ground, stretching out into the bay like fingers, sheds and cargo houses balanced along their edges, until I could not tell land from water.

It seemed a city peopled by the hungry. It seethed and grasped, sucked up and spat out life. I quietly wrapped the beads of my rosary around my wrist: as a comfort, and as a ward from harm.

Soon, the men were hitching the craft to the dock. Abe and I stood among the last of the cargo.

'Where are you goin' to now?' the captain asked, staring down the gangway.

'We don't rightly know,' Abe replied awkwardly. 'Things didn't turn out upriver.'

'That so.'

'The Lord will guide us, I am certain,' I interrupted, extending my hand. 'You have my thanks, sir.'

Instead of offering his own, he stared at me closely for a moment, then slowly produced the pistol I had traded him from his pocket, and pressed it into my hand.

'Have this back,' he said. 'Don't know who you are or what you done, but you kept your word with me. Reckon you'll need it more than I.'

My heart went out to the man. I wished I could have done more

174

to thank him, and told him so, as we shook hands. I gave the two
pistols to Abe, who took them wordlessly. A pistol restored to each
of his pockets, he handed me up to the dock. Then we were alone,
surrounded by a maelstrom of handcarts and barrows, sailors and
horses, all jostling for space on the narrow piers.

'Where shall we go?' I had to shout to be heard above the
activity. 'To the stage office?'

'Not a chance,' Muir's head was lowered like a dog on the
watch for threats. 'Road ain't safe. We got to get south, across
the border.'

'You mean we should try for Mexico?' I asked, elbowing my
way through the confusion. 'How?'

'I reckon the steamer's fastest,' he said 'straight down the
coast. It's the best chance we got.'

'Abe, we have no money.'

'I got ways of solving that.'

Casting a furtive look around him, he pulled me into the
shade of one of the buildings, beyond the stream of activity. He
faced me directly, brown eyes serious.

'Sister, we are in a mighty fix here. Way I see it, we got two
problems: one, if we want to live, we need funds. Two, every
person in the goddam Unified States is on look out for a nun
with a pair of pistols.'

'I cannot help that.'

'No,' he agreed. 'But it'd be a damn sight harder for them if
you changed your appearance somewhat.' He plucked at the coat
collar. 'This thing looks like you hauled it off a dead prospector,
anyhow.'

'It was the best I could do!'

'Well we need better. I got a notion of how to fix this mess
we're in but it may involve a few things that your Lord won't be
so approvin' of. Nor the law, for that matter.'

I hesitated for a moment, grappling with my conscience. Abe
was right; we needed money and clothes if we were stand any
chance at all. He had put his trust in me, and I resolved then and
there to return that trust.

I stuck out my hand.

'A bargain, Abraham Muir,' I said firmly. 'You protected me from danger when you could have turned your back. The Lord grant that I may do the same for you. Now, won't you tell me your plan?'

The corners of his mouth hooked upward into a smile that revealed sharp incisors.

'Well, seein' as we are somewhat short on both time and assets, I figure we only got one option.'

He shuffled closer, as the rain began to sluice down from the dockside roofs.

'And what is that?' I asked.

He barked a noise then, half laugh, half snort of disbelief.

'I never countenanced on asking this to a nun, but . . . where does the Lord stand on breaking and entering?'

7

Stolen waters are sweeter

Night had fallen. The smell of food began to drift through the air: meat grease and toasting corn. In the silence of the alleyway my stomach protested loudly. Abe shot me a look from six feet above, where he was balanced upon a precarious construction of lumber and refuse.

'Food comes later,' he hissed, clinging to the ledge of a window. 'First we got to—'

A piece of wood jerked from under him, sending him tumbling to the ground.

'Damn it,' he swore through gritted teeth, rubbing at his bad leg. 'This ain't working.'

Despite his certainty, Muir made for a clumsy thief. We had prowled the streets around the dock for long enough to find a store that sold what we needed; one that had been closed for the night and backed onto a conveniently dark alleyway.

As Abe growled and hopped upright, I shut my eyes for a moment, questioning once again the course upon which I had set my feet.

'Perhaps we are acting rashly,' I attempted, one last time. 'Surely, there must be some in this town who would show us charity? The church must be powerful here. They would not allow themselves to be corrupted.'

'You were as certain of Laverman,' Abe said, re-stacking his timbers. 'S'pose the preachers here are different. But s'pose they can't or won't help, just the same.' He turned to me, travel-stained and resolute. 'Ain't only your life being staked here. You—'

'I promised, I recall,' I said brusquely.

For a long moment I allowed the rain to fall upon my upturned face, asking for the Lord to make His will clear. If He had answers for me, He did not see fit to share them.

'Stand aside,' I sighed, clambering up. Under my lesser weight, the stack did not creak or shift so much. A grimy window was now level with my chest. On the other side was what looked like a workroom, a table scattered with shreds of cloth. All was dark within. I studied the window. The catch was on the other side. A memory returned to me in a flash, of watching someone punch through glass, of pieces falling to shatter on the ground. I wrapped the habit about my right elbow and drew my arm back, bracing myself for the impact to come.

'That wise?' Abe said, reaching out to stop my arm. 'Don't want you getting hurt.'

I thought for a moment.

'Is there paper in the mess down there?' I asked.

As Muir hunted around, I murmured a prayer to the Lord, to forgive the sin I was about to commit. Abe's hand came into view holding an old bill, its ink blurred by the rain. Carefully, I folded it to size.

'Pass me the pistol.'

With quick fingers I fitted the paper to the pane of glass and snapped the butt of the weapon forward. Glass cracked; it was the work of moments to knock free the shards and reach in to release the latch.

'You didn't learn that in no convent,' Muir muttered.

Ignoring him I clambered through the window, and he followed. Once inside, we crept silently from the workshop and into the store beyond. The front windows had been shuttered, and the barest light found its way from the outside.

Gradually, I made out a large space, divided into sections by shelves and cabinets. Abe strode forward, and I followed. Buckles and pins were piled into baskets, yarn was stacked in balls next to folded leather. He had chosen the time well; all the town was at supper, and the city was quiet. After a long moment of listening, Muir began to root through hanging bundles of cloth.

'Best be quick, we don't want a surprise now,' he whispered.

He dragged out several lengths of pale-colored fabric, discarding them after a brief inspection, before shaking out something dark that had the texture of calico.

'Here,' he said, tossing it toward me.

I allowed it to unravel in my hands. Only when I realized what the garment was, did I drop it to the floor, as if it had burned.

'What is it?' Muir was staring over his shoulder. 'What's wrong?'

I shook my head, eyes still fixed on the floor.

'Sister,' he sounded exasperated. 'We don't have time for dawdling. If you're scared of bein' caught—'

'It's not that,' I managed impatiently. 'I have never . . .' The words stuck in my throat. I swallowed hard, and tried again. 'I have never worn . . .'

Abe was standing at my side, a look on his face that I had not seen before. For a moment, I thought he might laugh, but then I realized, it was pity.

'You have never worn a dress,' he said incredulously.

'Not since I was a child. And my clothes then were little better than rags.'

'The law's looking all over for a *nun*; they ain't going to stop a lady.'

When I did not move, he sighed. I felt a breath of air, as he rubbed at his face.

'You dressed in men's gear,' he reasoned, 'fired at an armed killer, near got us drowned, bartered passage with traders, an' you're scared of a dress?'

'I would not expect you to understand.'

'Damn right I don't.' He seized the garment from the floor, pushing it back into my hands. 'You better get accustomed to the idea, an' fast, for if you leave it to me, I'll be choosing another for you that even Rattle wouldn't care to be seen in.'

With that he stumped off, leaving me alone.

179

8

As vinegar to the teeth,
and smoke to the eyes

My exit from the store was far less dignified than my entrance, for I was hampered by the strangeness of my new clothes. The bodice wrapped tightly about my chest and waist. Perhaps the woman for whom it was intended would have thought it a good fit, but after a shapeless habit, the close-fitting fabric made me feel naked.

Once outside, I did my best to straighten the garment. Abe had insisted that I also take new boots, a bonnet and shawl. I had chosen the most humble ones I could find. Now, I placed the hat firmly upon my head, wrapped myself in the shawl, for comfort more than warmth.

Abe, on the other hand, had looted the entire store. There was no denying the guilt I felt when I considered my hand in the theft, yet most of all I disliked the stolen dress, that told a lie to the world.

It was a necessity, I repeated to myself. After a struggle, I placed the old habit from Sacramento onto a pile of refuse. My fingers sought the rosary hidden in my pocket as I waited for Abe. He scrambled down into the alleyway a moment later, wearing a new coat and hat and carrying a bulging bag.

'Heard voices out front,' he whispered rapidly, checking over his shoulder. 'We better move.'

We hurried into a dark street, then another, Abe limping as he went, until music and brightness began to leak from saloons onto the stalls that lined the muddy road.

'Damn misers didn't leave any cash there,' Muir said, hefting at the sack. 'Reckon I've enough here to pawn, though . . .' His voice trailed off as he looked me over.

I followed his silent gaze down to the dress I wore.

The gown was dark and plain, but well made. In the light I could see that it was the color of mahogany, a hint of red in its depths. Thankfully, the shawl I had chosen appeared to be black; I glanced up at the bonnet, also black. His silence lengthened.

'Have you nothing to say?' I demanded, self-consciously.

Pink crept up his neck and he looked away.

'Jus' stranger than I thought, to see you like that,' he mumbled, before shaking the sack once again. 'Hope this'll do fix our fare. Got some fine gloves, buckles, even a fur or two in here.'

'Perhaps what we have done is necessary, Abraham Muir, but it does not mean I shall take any joy from it,' I said, my voice crisp as I tried to beat back my embarrassment. 'What of those we have stolen from? What of their misfortune?'

'No doubt they already know that a man's got to take what he can in a world like this,' Muir retorted. 'You seemed to understand that an hour ago.'

In sullen silence we made our way through the thoroughfare. I tried to pray as we trod the streets – for our sin, and for those who had driven us to commit it, and for those whom we had wronged. By and by, Abe found a trader and began haggling for the belt buckles. Unhappily, I turned away. The next stall over was stacked with trinkets and curios. In a basket that hung from a nail, something caught my gaze.

Paper flowers. Their brightness seemed at odds with the gloomy street. Once, I had carried such a bundle in my arms, clean and perfect against my grimy skin. I remembered how it felt trying to protect them from the elements. Twisted paper and thread – that was all they were, yet they seemed to hold a magic of their own. I pushed a few aside, reaching, despite myself, for petals of an impossible blue.

'Sister.' Abe was at my arm. I snatched my hand away, in time for him to shake a handful of coins into my palm. 'That'll do for some supper. There's an eatin' house over yonder. Looks good enough. I'll meet you there; got to finish some business.'

I felt his arm at my sleeve once again. One of the pistols slid into my grip. I looked at him inquiringly.

'You can't be too careful, Sister. This is a dangerous town,' he murmured.

Resolutely, I pocketed the gun, turned my back on him and strode toward the establishment. It felt wholly unnatural to be greeted 'Ma'am' and offered a table by the window. When the waiter arrived at my elbow, I nearly leaped from my skin. I ordered what they had – a cutlet and radishes, bread, and coffee – and paid my ten cents uncomplainingly.

I had traveled the plains alone, with no one but a horse for company; I had half starved in jail and eaten fish caught cold from mountain streams. Yet I had never ordered a meal at a table and been served with polite disinterest.

I was so hungry that most of the food found its way into my stomach before I had a chance to consider how or what I ate. The meat was tough, the bread gritty, but to me it was a feast. By the time I had cleaned my plate, I felt almost at ease.

Across the street, beneath the sickly gaslight I could see Muir, haggling over the contents of his sack with the traders. I realized then that he was trying to spare me pain, in his own way. He was taking responsibility for our theft. I had promised to aid him, and he had sent me away to profit from our sins, idle.

Calling the waiter over once more I ordered a pair of buckwheat cakes, hot with syrup, and asked him to wrap them. When he returned with them, I left the restaurant to surprise Abe with the food.

The patch of light where he had stood was empty. Carefully, I crossed to peer into one black store window, then another for a sign of that familiar profile, the angle of his shoulders. The syrup began to seep through the paper onto my fingers as I stood in the open.

He cannot have strayed far, instinct told me. *Perhaps he has stepped into the next street for a moment. But if I leave, he will not know where to find me.* Torn with indecision, I heard a noise echoing from a narrow passage that ran between the stores. The light from the lamps did not reach far enough to see clearly. The sound was a strange gulping cough, like that of some creature in pain. I took a few steps forward, reluctant to leave the circle of light.

A tiny figure was huddled, just out of view. I made out bare arms in the night, and eyes, large in a thin face, staring toward me. The noise came from the child's chest – whooping cough, it sounded like, wracking the small frame with its violence.

Forgetting all else, I hurried into the alleyway and knelt beside the child. It was a boy, not more than six. He flinched when he saw me, but I offered him the cakes.

'Please,' I coaxed, as gently as I could. 'Please take them.'

For a moment he stared. Then the cakes were gone from my hand, one of them already disappearing into his mouth. He did not waste another glance at me, before cramming the second down too.

'Slow down, child; it will not run away,' I heard myself saying.

But the boy did not wait, scrambling to his feet to bolt into the darkness, faster than a jackrabbit. I sighed, considering the coins that remained from supper. I slipped a hand into my pocket and jingled them, lamenting the lost opportunity to help, when the hand clamped over my face.

'Easy now, little miss,' a man's voice breathed onto my neck, 'jus' stay quiet now. What other goods might you be carryin' in that skirt?'

My eyes searched frantically through the gloom as I cursed myself. I had fallen for one of the oldest street tricks. The man's hand dug into my flesh, pulling my neck back painfully.

Another thief was grappling with my skirts, searching for purse or pockets. They both stank of raw liquor, of urine and old tobacco. I kicked out instinctively at the second man and felt my foot land somewhere soft, heard a grunt of surprise. The hand tightened across my neck, and my eyes narrowed, not with fear this time but with anger.

In one swift movement I wrenched my arm free and smashed my elbow across his face. Cartilage and bone cracked; I felt his grip loosen, and lunged away. But I had forgotten the other man. A blow caught me across the head and I stumbled, the bonnet falling back. My hand flew for my pocket, fingers closing around the pistol's grip. A moment later it was pointed at my assailants.

They fell instantly still. I could feel blood, warm and wet upon my scalp, but did not flinch as it ran a trail down my face. I held the pistol steady. A grim smile found its way onto my face as I cocked the weapon.

9

He that trusteth to lies, feeds the winds,
and runs after birds that fly

Abe found me beneath the gas lamp, nursing my pounding head. The edge of the shawl had served to blot away most of the blood but I felt battered and bruised.

'It is just as well that this wool is dark,' I said, as he approached, 'for I have already managed to soil it.'

He frowned at me, uncomprehending, and I was glad that the darkness hid my state. The blow must have knocked the sense from my head, for I found myself grinning at his expression, even though it caused the injured flesh of my scalp to pull painfully.

'Where have you been?' he demanded, sifting through his coat. 'Never mind. Here, we get twenty dollars apiece. Fifteen for the steamer an' five to eat. There's a boat that leaves at dawn, an' I intend we should be on it.'

'We need ammunition,' I told him sternly, handing the weapon over. He looked at me strangely again as he pocketed it.

'Got some. C'mon now, I want to make the ticket office 'fore it closes. Can't waste money on lodgings though, so it might be a rough night.'

'Can't get rougher,' I said cheerfully.

I allowed myself to be towed by Abe toward the waterfront. Whether he put my strange behavior down to fatigue or excitement I do not know. The ticket office was housed in a wooden shed. A few pale-faced men were stretched awkwardly on the benches there to wait out the night, hats and newspapers over their faces. I recall a seat sliding under me, near a brazier that drove away some of the damp chill that rose from the dock, but little after that.

I must have slept like the dead, for when I awoke, the first thing I felt was a violent thumping. It near blinded me, sparks bursting behind my eyes. I struggled to open them, and caught one glimpse of gray light through the smeared window before nausea swept me and I vomited.

The pain was unbearable, each convulsion sending a hot pulse through my head. Finally, it ceased, and I propped myself onto my elbows, shivering.

'Ma'am, are you alright?'

'Abe?' I croaked. A hand was at my shoulder, steadying me back onto the bench. I opened my eyes to see a handkerchief being held before me. I took it weakly and wiped my mouth.

'The man who was with you – your husband? – stepped out a moment ago to watch the steamer dock. Shall I fetch him?'

'Not my husband,' I managed to murmur. A stranger was perched beside me. His face was weathered and beaten by the elements, but he had kind eyes beneath graying brows. Seeing the mess I had made, I turned away, embarrassed.

'Let me fetch you some water,' he told me tactfully and disappeared from view.

Once he was gone, I felt up under the bonnet, exploring the scalp wound with my fingers. It was hot and swelling. I had been a fool not to mention it to Abe.

The man returned and presented me with a tin cup. I took a few sips, which helped to rinse my mouth and clear my head somewhat.

'Thank you,' I told him, breathing deeply. 'I struck my head a few hours ago, and I fear it has affected me worse than I thought.'

'That's as likely, ma'am. Blows to the head can cause something of a confusion to the brain.'

'A concussion, yes,' I sighed, wincing. 'I should have applied a compress, but I fear the sense was knocked right out of me.'

There was a surprised silence before the man spoke.

'You know your medicine.'

'Yes, I . . .' Something on his clothing caught my eye. In the glow from the almost exhausted brazier, a button glinted, as in sunlight across a plain. It brought to mind a column of men, marching, in what seemed like another life. Beneath his heavy coat, the man's clothes were faded blue. A uniform.

I struggled to my feet, though my head spun. Through the street side windows I saw more men, the gleam of bayonets over shoulders, leaning on either side of the door, examining anyone who came near.

'Do not be alarmed, ma'am,' the soldier told me, rising to steady my arm. 'There is nothing amiss; we are only guarding this place on orders. There's a couple of fugitives might try and get past us, see. Word is that they're fleeing for the border.'

I mumbled something in response, anxious to find Muir. If he saw ten Union men he would panic.

'What have they done, these criminals?' I asked vaguely, in an attempt to cover my alarm. 'Are they dangerous?'

'Afraid they might well be. They're wanted for all manner of crimes clean 'cross three states. Man and a woman it is, lady dressed as a nun, if you can imagine that. They murdered a priest, up in Sacramento.'

I did not hear the rest of what he told me, only remembered Laverman's terrified eyes, his bloodied hand reaching up toward my forehead in the shape of a cross, blessing me even as I called destruction down upon him. Tears blurred my eyes and I blotted them away with the shawl. Violence and pain seemed to follow upon my heels like a hound.

Looking up, I saw Abe through the dockside door, and hurried out of the building to take his arm.

'We must leave, now,' I hissed in his ear, and forced a smile onto my face for the soldier, who had followed.

'Sister, what—' Muir began.

'Sir, this is my brother,' I announced, for the man had overheard Abe's remark. 'He will care for me now. I thank you for your concern.'

Muir's face had gone white at the sight of the soldier.

'Brother,' I said, 'I had quite a turn back there, and this gentleman was kind enough to aid me in my hour of distress.'

Stiffly, Abe extended a hand, mumbling something about thanks. I could see his teeth clenching, sweat springing along his hairline. Other passengers began to crowd around us, impatient to board the departing steamer. Soldiers were pushing through the mass of people, turning back hats, checking faces and luggage.

'If you'll excuse us,' I demurred.

My hand was like iron on Abe's sleeve as we turned away in as calm a fashion as we could manage. Then, as one, we ducked into the crowd and fled for the gangplank. As we were ushered aboard and along the narrow deck, I risked one brief glance back toward the passenger shed.

The soldier stood where we had left him, a piece of paper in his hand. After a few seconds he looked up and opened his mouth to shout, but his voice was taken by a blast of steam. The boat began to drift away from the dock, gathering speed until he resembled nothing more than a child's matchstick doll across the water.

10

As a moth doth a garment,
and a worm the wood . . .

I must have fallen insensible once more then, for I recall little of
what passed next, save for Abe's arm around my waist, and a
narrow wooden corridor. The cool fabric of a pillow met my cheek
and I sank gratefully onto the bunk, only to rise again in panic.

'No,' I protested, struggling upward, screwing my eyes against
the light that spilled through the brass porthole. 'No, I cannot.'

'Sister, you're done in, look at you.'

I pulled at the ribbons holding the bonnet, until they came
loose. Abe hissed when he saw my scalp. My eyelids were heavy,
but I fought to keep them open.

'Concussion,' I told him, swallowing back nausea. 'You should
not let me sleep.'

'What in God's name? Did he do this, that man?'

'The soldier? No, he was kindness itself.'

I managed to tell Muir of what had passed in the alleyway,
one or two words at a time. The pain made me retch, until I could
not continue.

'Stupid woman,' Muir growled, though his hands were gentle
as he pushed me back. He woke me again minutes later, dabbing
at the wound with a damp cloth. I felt the blood that was crusted
around it give way beneath his ministrations.

'Here.' A glass was at my lip. 'Brandy and opium, best I could
do from the ship's medicine chest. They've no doctor aboard.'

I had never had cause to use opium myself, though I had
administered it on many occasions, but the pain was so great I
swallowed the liquor down in a gulp.

'A cold compress will help,' I told him, and he began to
dampen the napkin again.

'Those bastards,' he murmured, as he pressed it carefully onto my scalp. 'Hurtin' a lady like that.'

Perhaps it was his tone, the lightness of his hands as he smoothed the cloth, but at once I felt as though everything was crumbling away, sand in a flood. Sorrow broke upon me, and I had nothing with which to hold it back.

'What's this?' Muir questioned, and I knew then that I was sobbing, chest shuddering and tears flowing as if they would never stop. The world was tearing at me on all sides, clawing at my faith, my strength, at my very being, until there would be nothing left save the raw meat of my soul.

'You've weathered worse than this, Sister. A bang to the head won't kill you.' His voice was gentle.

'It is no use,' I choked out, 'no use in going on. They will destroy me.'

'You know that ain't true.' Abe's face floated above me. His brown eyes, for once, were entirely unguarded. They claimed my attention, until I was able to gasp in one long breath, then another.

'You have work to do,' he continued, 'an' the strength to withstand this.'

He pushed my rosary into my fingers, and closed my hand around it with both of his own.

The opium and brandy were working, for the edges of my vision had softened into shadows. Dimmer and warmer the room grew, until the tears from my eyes slowed, only now and then tracing my cheek.

'Tell me a story,' I whispered, as the world opened around me. 'Please, tell me of something good.'

'Ain't much good ever happened in my life, Sister,' Muir sighed, and his words seemed one with the motion of the sea that swayed the bunk. 'There were the Injuns, then the ranches, the war . . .'

'One good time?' I murmured.

'Sure, there's one,' he said after an age, so long that I was unsure whether I dreamed. 'Bright as a new penny it is, when I call it to mind, even after all these years.' His voice grew younger as I listened, losing its sullen edge, its reluctant rhythm.

'There were a dance, one town over. Grand affair – can't recall the cause, but it were a great excuse for merriment. Whole town an' more beside were out in the streets. The start of summer it was, air fresh as new grass. Warm too, enough to roll up your shirtsleeves an' feel the night on your skin.

'Group of us lads from the ranch went into town, lookin' for trouble and to drink ourselves silly, truth be told. But instead I found her. Jus' as soon as we rolled into town I saw her, leaping about in a dance beneath them little flags and burnin' lights in the dark. Her hair were the color of aspens in fall: a great stream of it, all over her shoulder. And her dress, like yellow mustard seed.

'I must'a looked like a shadow beside her. I always been dark, and were darker then from the sun, but she smiled at me, an' I knew I was done in.

'Ruth was her name. Said she were a trader's girl from the next valley over, an' her friends laughed at me.

'But we danced, and that whole night was in our mouths, in our very eyes, the dust of the ground kicked up beneath and the band swelling like a cloudburst as we hurtled past. She smelled like clean linen, an' sweat an' lemons.

'I can't 'a been more than sixteen, but it were like I could see life before me, I held it in my arms, and it would be all I ever wanted, long as I lived.'

His voice faded, and I found myself drifting back, away from the dusty town of the past, until the lights were a mere pinprick behind my eyelids.

'Where is she?' I breathed, as the opium washed over me.

'Never knew.' His voice was soft. 'Lost her in the crowd. But always seemed to me she were the only true thing, in all that darkness.'

I squeezed his hand as I fell asleep, and thought I heard his voice, though it could as easily have been my own, whispering.

'Not the only one.'

11

Take away the rust from silver

Two days later found me near the prow, watching the coastline stretch by. I licked the spray from my lips, only for the wind to renew it again. A slight chill was all that remained of the December cold that had plagued us in Sacramento.

It was the first time I had seen the ocean. The glimpse I had caught through the cabin porthole had been enough to send me scrambling outside like a child. A bright winter sun flashed upon the waves, and gulls called, bearing my spirit aloft. I felt the Lord's presence all around, and for a while, it was enough to make me forget all else.

Fresh air and sleep were fast restoring my strength. I spent a good deal of time alone on the deck, meditating about the path I was carving through the world. I was growing accustomed to the gown, and sometimes barely noticed that I wore it, but then a man would tip his hat, or a sailor's eyes would linger for a fraction too long and the old anxiety would return, like a worm in my stomach. I feared that I was beginning to forfeit the life I had pledged to follow until the end of my days.

I prayed all the harder at night, head resting upon the hard edge of the bunk. If Abe noticed, he never said. His leg too was healing well, and though he often limped, he would not let me examine the injury. Instead, he had cared for me, as gentle as a nursemaid that first day aboard. He had cooled my head, brought me tea, talked of everything and nothing to keep me calm, though in truth I remember little of what he said.

Now that I was well, he seemed almost shy, especially sharing the close confines of a cabin as we were. He rose early from his own bunk, so that I might have privacy.

That morning, with careful fingers, I had been able to wash my hair. My whole head felt lighter as I dabbed away the water with a cloth. In the tiny cabin mirror I examined the pale curls – shorn in Carson City – which had begun to creep down toward my ears once again. Rather than pushing them back until I could find a pair of scissors, I ran them through my fingers, loosened a few and allowed them to fall around my face.

A strange tremor ran through me; the unnerving sense that I had been dropped into another woman's life. The life that might have been, had I never been brought to the convent. A few months before, I would have thrown the bonnet aside, hacked the hair back to within an inch of my scalp and prayed for my vanity to be forgiven. Yet now, all was different.

My legs felt strong beneath me as I stepped out into the air. The ship we had taken was not the grandest, but it was smart enough, wooden decks scrubbed clean, paint shining white in the Californian sun. I strode around a corner, only to collide with a body.

Embarrassed, I murmured an apology and was about to turn away when I caught a glimpse of the man's face. His eyes were fixed on me, wide as my own.

It was Abe, but not as I had seen him before. His hair had been combed, back and away from his temples. Stranger still was his face: the thick, untidy beard that shadowed his features was gone, replaced by oddly pale skin, clean and smooth.

'You . . .' we began in unison, and snapped our mouths shut.

'Were a chap below offerin' barber work,' Muir flushed, running a hand over his cheeks. 'Thought might be wise, seeing as we're to travel unnoticed.'

'Wise indeed,' I added hurriedly, clasping my hands so that I did not push nervously at the bonnet. 'We should appear respectable.'

'"Appear" because we ain't?' Muir asked with a quirk of a grin.

I noticed for the first time the shape of his jaw, its angle. The years seemed to have fallen away from him. A smile had appeared on my own face, and I fought to control it as a couple passed us, arm in arm, nodding our way.

'Respectable or not, we should act as they do,' I murmured when they were from earshot. 'Mr Muir, your arm?'

Abe looked bewildered for a moment, then offered his elbow. I settled one hand upon it and together we began a slow promenade along the deck, in the manner of other passengers.

'This weather is very fine,' he observed, casting me such a lofty look that it was all I could do to keep myself from laughing.

'We can at least converse to appear less awkward,' I told him, amused. 'Do we know yet where we shall disembark, near to Mexico?'

'Later,' he said, dismissing my question. 'There's somethin' I been meaning to ask.'

'What is it?' I tried to keep my voice light, though my heart kicked its heels against my chest.

'You were talkin' in your sleep, when you were out. Kept sayin' a name. Christopher.'

His words stopped my feet upon the deck as if I had reached the end of a rope. For a long moment, the name echoed in the air between us, before I was able to shake free of my trance. The memory returned, stronger than it had in years; a face, lean and solid, with gray eyes like mine.

'Christopher was my brother.'

12

As a tempest that passeth

'Do you remember what I told you about my childhood, Abe?'

We were seated on the quiet, seaward side of the ship, sheltered from the wind. Behind us was the great constant washing of the paddle, the bursts of steam that pushed us boisterously south. The distant coastline was a dark shadow, where all of our dangers waited.

'You said y'all were orphaned, stuck in a poorhouse?'

'Abandoned, not orphaned. As far as I know, I have a father still living. My mother is the one who died.'

I fiddled with my rosary. The beads seemed to hold my voice back, until I was forced to put it away in my pocket. Abe watched my action, a frown upon his face.

'These things are difficult to speak of,' I explained with a half-smile. 'We are not supposed to dwell upon our past once we take holy vows. To serve the Lord, we leave behind all that we were: names, sins, even memories.'

'Then "Thomas Josephine" . . .?'

'Is the name I chose when I gave myself to God. I had a different one, once.'

His expression then, bursting with a question, made me laugh.

'No, Abraham Muir, I cannot tell you what it was. That girl is gone.' I took a long sip of the glass of lemon water that stood by my elbow.

'But Christopher?'

'Christopher, yes.' I sighed. Ordinarily, I had no trouble in finding the words I needed, but now they slipped through my fingers. 'There was more to our life then than I told you,' I began clumsily. 'Before the orphanage, I mean.

'Our parents had come on a boat from Germany. They got by at first, working at whatever they could find, and we were poor, but we grew. Then came news of the mineral rushes: of men pulling gold and silver from the rivers. Mother tried to detain our father, but in the end he set off alone for California with all the money we had, eaten away by greed. We never heard from him again. Mother grew weaker every day after that, and could not work. She sometimes went to scavenge coal from the dockside. One day she never returned.

'We ran wild. There were mouths to feed, and we found ways to do it. Children can know a city better than any law enforcer, if they've a need. We could get everywhere, into warehouses and pocketbooks alike. We lived near the docks, and often escaped by diving into the river like rats, as we did with Lillie. But in the end we were caught. I was nine, I believe, and Christopher was twelve. He got free, but they took me to the jail, and then to the orphanage. I never saw him again.'

'You were a thief?'

Muir's words shattered my recollections. Of all things, amusement was growing in the corners of his eyes. I stared incredulously at him for a moment.

'I was abandoned . . .'

'You were a thief, admit it.' He settled back onto the bench, a look of utter satisfaction upon his face. 'Knew it soon as I saw you. First day out on the plain, I said to myself, "Abe, this one'll be trouble. She'll have the very boots off your feet 'afore you can blink."'

Muir ducked as I snatched the slice of lemon from my glass and flung it at his face, where it struck him square in the eye. I could not repress my laughter then, and for long moments, was doubled over at the sight of him, grimacing at the piece of fruit in his hand. He flung it over the railing with great ceremony and a salute.

'There now. It's behind us. Like all things,' he said.

His eyes were on me again. His grin had softened.

'We cannot hold ourselves in debt to the people we were, Sister,' he told me. His hand hovered for a moment above my own. 'You're the one taught me that.'

13

There is a lion in the way,
and a lioness in the roads

That night we went ashore for the first time since we had set sail. It was customary for the steamer to make for land in the evening, to exchange passengers and mail. Muir and I usually hid in the cabin during these stops, for fear of being seen, yet we had grown braver. The weather had warmed. We had passed Los Angeles and were speeding further and further south.

From the deck, I could see orange trees clustered on the hillsides, ripening globes and dense leaves. I leaned far over the ship's rail, excitement coursing through me. I was two thousand miles and a lifetime away from St. Louis.

Still, I could not help but feel some unease as we walked down the gangplank into the little Californian town with the other passengers. Muir's pistols hung heavy in each of my pockets. We surely had the advantage over our pursuers, Muir reasoned, as we left the ship, traveling at such speed along the coast, but we should be on guard, and no one would suspect a quiet and respectable lady of being armed.

There was an eating house near the dock, a makeshift affair of tables set outside upon the dirt street. Yet it was merry enough, with the passengers all descending for entertainment, and a group of old men playing a jumble of instruments.

Muir and I sat slightly apart from the rest. As the light faded, we ate cornbread and beef, seared over flames, and gorged ourselves on tart oranges, the juice sticking our fingers together until we were forced to lick them clean.

Before long, the steamer sounded a blast on its horn, a sign that it would soon be ready to depart once more.

'Will you be safe here a few moments?' Abe questioned, his

eye on some activity further away in the town. 'I've a mind to see if there are any traveling back Sacramento way, who could carry word 'bout the horses.'

I patted my pocket and assured him I would be perfectly safe. Alone, I allowed the sounds and scents of the night to flow around me: the heady sweetness of orange peel crushed into dirt by passing feet, the tang of salt and seaweed from the beach, the sun-baked dust. The group at the table nearest to me exploded with laughter, and I leaned closer to hear the cause.

'I swear, it is true,' a man was holding forth to the rest, a pipe dangling between his fingers. 'May the Lord strike me down if I lie, an' the ground open to purgatory, that is the news from upriver.'

His voice was undeniably southern, a good-natured drawl whatever the situation, be it grave or joyous. He sported a moustache that curled thickly at the corners, one side a little higher, adding to the look of mirth about him. His waistcoat was worn plum-colored velvet, and spoke of better times.

He was likely a new passenger, come to join us on our journey south. I had not seen him before, but I recognized his companions from the ship. I smiled, and closed my eyes, listening.

'I cannot believe you are in earnest,' one was saying. 'The whole thing seems like the work of the scandal sheets.'

'Why, ma'am, the journal I represent carries only *bona fide* news,' the mustached man protested. 'The *Californian* has the third largest weekly circulation in all the western coast states and territories now, and we pride ourselves on our fine reporting of God's honest truth.'

He rewarded the company with another smile.

'I myself was in the city when it occurred,' he continued, conspiratorially. 'Just picture it: half the Federal Guard hot-footin' about the wharves under command of a cavalry lieutenant – a handsome specimen, ladies – one Theodore F. Carthy, who has chased the fugitives clear from the Nebraska Territory. They had another unit down from Sacramento and all of 'em were rubbing their beards and cursing each other that they'd been hoodwinked. Ain't every day a five hundred dollar bounty pair goes strolling on out of Frisco. Now, ain't that a peach?' He leaned back, settling a hand upon his ample stomach.

The hairs on my neck began to rise, and I shielded my face, grateful of the twilight. The old familiar anxiety began to uncoil in my stomach, so that I was almost prepared for the next words when they came.

'The soldiers were there when we boarded,' exclaimed one woman excitedly. 'They must have been searching the dock. I cannot believe anyone could have slipped past dressed as a *nun*. The whole thing is absurd!'

'Why, the very thing, ma'am!' The man gestured with his pipe to the enraptured audience. 'There's talk from here to Denver that she ain't a woman at all, let alone a holy one, but a man in disguise. I figure as much.' His eyebrows had shot up toward his hairline as he spread his hands. 'How could a woman, fine and fresh as your own dear selves, commit such shameful crimes? For, ladies and sir, we are looking at murder, theft, kidnapping, reckless destruction and mutilation, to name but a few of "her" wrongdoings.'

'And they could be traveling with us now?' The woman's voice was no longer quite so gleeful. 'Even on our very ship?'

'Indeed, ma'am, so I hear tell. But y'all have no fear. I, Franklin Templeton, intend to conduct a survey of passengers just as soon as we are underway. The cavalry unit I have been traveling with are but half a day's journey behind. They quite depend on my information, so I took the liberty of sending a telegram to the nearest station to let know of my intentions.'

I heard no more, for my heart was pounding in my ears. Even if we could evade this man on board, the damage was wrought; Carthy knew we were traveling by ship. They would have the law searching for us in every port between here and Mexico. If we stayed ashore, we would surely be overtaken. If we boarded the ship once again, we would be placing ourselves in the path of most danger.

The man with the moustache was rising from his seat, shaking hands with the assembled company, and moving toward the ship – no doubt to begin his survey.

Muir was nowhere to be seen, and there was no time to delay. I gripped the pistols through the fabric of my dress and stood. As the man passed, I muttered one brief prayer and stepped into his path.

14

He is drawn like a fool to bonds

'Cabin 12, did you say, ma'am?'

'Yes, to the left here.'

Up close, the smell of Templeton's tobacco was almost over-powering. It was a cheap blend, no doubt cut with all manner of unsavory things. I tried not to grimace as I felt his arm supporting my waist.

'I must thank you again,' I fluttered. 'I felt quite faint for a moment.'

'T''was the heat, dear lady, take my word for it. This Californian climate sure can get to a soul.'

He was puffing and sweating from my weight, the skin of his neck red and blotchy beneath a layer of dust. He propped me against the doorway in order to open the door of the cabin.

'If you'd be so kind as to light the lamp up for me, sir,' I whimpered, wafting a hand before my face.

As soon as he was inside, I cast one brief look around, then slipped in after him. It was the work of a moment to lock the door.

'There. I'm sure you shall be fit as a new fiddle . . .' He trailed off as he turned to find himself nose to nose with the muzzle of a pistol.

'Do not move,' I said quietly, staring into his eyes. 'I would hate to kill you.'

His smiled dropped into surprise, his face turning red, then white.

'What's the meanin' of this?' he blustered. 'Let me pass.'

He raised a hand to push away the gun and I brought out the other pistol, jamming it against his fingers.

'The last man who attempted that did not fare well,' I told him coldly. 'In fact, I believe you are acquainted with him. Now, sit down.'

He stood his ground and looked as if he would say more until I placed one of the pistols against his forehead. Two months ago I would have trembled to perform such an act. Yet now, a great calm filled me, as after long hours of prayer, when I felt certain that God was at my side.

'My dear sweet Lord in heaven,' he whispered, face falling slack. 'You're she.'

By the time Abe arrived, the man was seated upon the side of the bunk, nursing the imprint of the pistol on his forehead.

'Sister,' Muir stormed, as I pulled open the door one-handed. 'Where did you—' He stopped dead at the sight before him.

'Sister! I darn well knew it!' Templeton cried. His trembling had subsided, and now there was a sort of fevered glint in his eye. 'The traitor Muir and Thomas Josephine, here on this very boat.' He began searching his clothes in a kind of frenzy. 'My notebook – I *must* have a notebook.'

'Who in the hell is this?' Abe's eyes were fixed like a dog about to attack.

'Whoever he is, until recently he has been traveling in the company of a certain lieutenant,' I said calmly.

'I am Franklin Templeton,' the man hiccupped, a pencil clutched in his hand. 'Of the *Californian*. It has the third highest circulation in all—'

'You'll stay silent if you've a care to keep that tongue,' Muir growled. 'Why in God's name did you bring him here?' he directed at me.

'I had no choice. He knew we were traveling on this boat.'

'We could've damn well dealt with that,' Muir fumed. 'Now we got to try and get him off the ship—'

Beneath us, there was a judder; a horn blast sounded and the distant noise of great, washing blades began to echo through the walls, interrupting him. For one long moment, we all exchanged glances. I realized that the man was about to move an instant before he did.

But Muir was ready as Templeton lunged toward the door, catching him across the throat with a jab that was almost casual, and sending the newspaperman choking to his knees.

'This is a damn mess,' Muir snapped at me. 'Gimme that bonnet, quick now.'

I loosened the hat and tossed it to him. Unceremoniously, he ripped the ribbons from it, as well as a length of trimming. He bound Templeton hand and foot, sitting on him when he tried to struggle. Then for good measure, he pulled a blanket from the bed and rolled the man up tightly.

'There. Won't be tryin' that again.'

Templeton squirmed around so that he was facing us. Only his head protruded from the blanket, round cheeks pink. For someone who was trussed up like a sausage, he looked remarkably cheerful.

'Well, he was right about you and no doubt,' he wheezed up at me. 'Said you were prettier than a blue-nosed mule.'

Muir made to drive a boot into his stomach, but I stopped him, knelt instead by Templeton's side.

'It was Lieutenant Carthy, who said that?'

He nodded, and some of the jollity seemed to drain from him.

'In all truth,' he swallowed, 'I do not think the man is entirely sane. But he has money to burn and the ear of his higher-ups. He is *quite* bowed up over y'all, though. To hear him speak of the coward Muir, as he calls him, and of yourself . . .' Templeton lapsed into silence and slid a quick glance at Abe, poised above. 'Why, I should not care to repeat it.'

'What of Mr Lillie?' I asked. 'Was there a man, a big man in skins, traveling with Carthy?'

'You mean that great black bear creature? Yes indeed; he scouted ahead more often than not. I did not seek his company. Few would.'

Abe pulled me to my feet and into the far corner.

'We'll reach San Diego 'fore dawn,' he told me. 'It's the last town before the border. If what he says is true, like as not there'll be a whole fortful of men waiting on us.'

Templeton's eyes were on my face, and I found I could not concentrate on Muir's words.

'We have to get off this boat,' I whispered. 'If we can get to shore, maybe we have a chance.'

'There's a skiff tied up on the starboard side,' murmured Muir doubtfully, 'but there's no way we'd get it loose and away without bein' seen.'

My gaze returned to Templeton, trying to roll himself free.

'Unless no one was watching,' I said.

'Sister, I do not care for that thinkin' look of yours.'

'Abe Muir, you will have to trust me.'

'Aw, hell.'

'Mr Templeton,' I announced calmly, and he stopped his fidgeting. 'Can you swim?'

15

As the divisions of waters,
so the heart is in the hand of the Lord

'Man overboard!'

I cried it again with all the force I could muster as we sent the newspaperman splashing into the black Pacific. Templeton's head broke the surface of the water like a duck, kicking furiously to compensate for his bound hands. I ran for the other side of the boat just as my fellow passengers flocked to the railing to peer into the dark sea. Abe was waiting by the winch. I fumbled with the thick coils of rope, heart beating against my chest. But finally the knot was loosed, and Abe was shoving me aside to release the windlass.

The small boat hit the water with a splash. There was no time to check whether we had been heard. I clambered over the side and slid awkwardly down a rope, dropping the final six feet into a craft that bucked and swayed dangerously. Behind us roared the steamer paddles, thrashing the sea into foam and spray.

I steadied the sides with rope-burned hands, gasping as salt bit into my flesh. Abe landed clumsily beside me. Muscles protesting, I gritted my teeth and hauled upon the oar, the frenzy of flight coursing through me. Had not the Lord made me strong for this? Had he not given me courage to defy a world that sought to crush me at every turn?

We did not slacken pace until the lights of the boat had diminished, until Muir's ragged breathing finally reminded me of my own bursting lungs. There came no sound of pursuit, but it was only a matter of time. Even if the captain chose not to send men after us, the boat would soon dock in San Diego with news of our escape. Time was running short.

As if our minds traveled the same path, Abe and I pulled upon the oars once again, slower this time. All was darkness, and pounding waves. My hands seized up, stiffened by sea salt, but still I rowed.

'There,' after what seemed like an age, Abe was shaking me, pointing ahead in the distance. 'There, she's turnin'.'

The few spots of light that were the boat floated ahead. As we drifted further, I saw the land swoop away in a curve, forming the mouth of a bay.

'San Diego,' murmured Abe. 'If we can get past the city an' up onto land, we'll be in Mexico. With luck they'll have the tide against 'em.'

I flexed my fingers as he talked. My knuckles were swollen, blisters forming on each palm under the rope-burns. The thought of taking hold of the rough oar again nearly brought bile to my throat.

'Lord give me strength,' I murmured and leaned over the side to plunge both hands into the water.

The salt seared at first, bringing tears to my eyes but I blinked them away. Eventually, the cold became soothing. Abe said nothing in the face of my silence, only ripped his kerchief in two and offered the pieces to me.

'How long until dawn?' I questioned when I found my voice, tying the fabric into clumsy bandages.

'Three hours, maybe less,' Muir's voice was soft in the darkness. 'Sister, we . . .'

'I know, Abe.' I composed myself, and renewed my grip on the oars, pushing aside the pain. 'This is our final trial and we must rise to meet it.'

I turned toward him on the bench, and felt that he had done the same; smelled the familiar sweat from the edge of his collar, a wisp of his breath before it was whipped away to open sea. 'They will not take us.'

16

But in the end,
it will bite like a snake

It must have been the Lord who lent us strength in the hours that followed. We felt each other's pain, one pulling all the harder when the other faltered, until the world seemed reduced to the next stroke of the oar, and the next.

False gray had crept into the sky when the tide finally began to pull us toward the shore. We let it take us, beaching the craft, until we could stumble to dry land. I felt my knees buckle and lay down, right there on the seaweed. The surf tugged cold at my boots, and I let it.

'You alive?' a voice croaked beside me after a while. A smile stretched my salt-cracked lips, and I rolled onto my side to see Abe slumped in a similar position.

'We should get away from the shoreline,' he muttered, as I checked my pockets to see that the pistols were yet dry. 'Reckon we're safe, but I ain't sure 'til I can get a look from up there.' He squinted up at the cliff edge above us. 'What do you say, Sister? Shall we watch sunup from Mexico?'

Our bodies were battered and aching, yet we pressed on, forging a path up the sloping rock face. After a time it grew steeper, and it was all I could do not to look down, for a misplaced foot would mean a fatal plunge to the rocks below. Grasses aided us and I sometimes found myself scrambling on all fours, until at last I hauled myself onto the cliff top.

Abe stood some paces away, staring down coast. I followed his gaze. In the distance, I could make out the bay of San Diego: low houses along the coast and smudges of white that must be ships docked near the shore. The first ray of sun flashed upon a distant window.

He turned then, filthy and pale but with a look of such wonder on his face that for a strange, endless moment, I could not breathe. Then he was bounding toward me, letting out a whoop like a child from school.

His arms tightened hard around my shoulders, and my face was crushed against his as he leaped about, and laughter was breaking from both of our chests, tears too, all confused together.

The breath was gone from us after a few moments, and we clung to each other's arms, keeping ourselves upright. I could feel his face against mine, damp with sweat, the edge of his mouth lifted into a grin. He pulled away a few inches to reach inside his coat.

Cradled in his palm was a paper flower, a blue rose, its petals slightly crushed, but bright as a jewel in the new day.

'Saw you lookin' at them in San Francisco,' he muttered, eyes still creased with mirth. 'Just remembered. Thought it might make you smile.'

I had not moved away from him, and at that moment, I could not stop myself from taking his hand, the rose held within, and raising it to my lips.

But then there was thunder, and a cry and he was ripped from me. A shot blasted through the early morning stillness again and blood exploded from his chest, sending him stumbling back toward the cliff. I reached out desperate hands, caught one glimpse of his eyes staring over my shoulder, and then he was gone, empty air where Abraham Muir had stood only moments before.

Nunslinger: Book 5

Litany for the Brave

The True Tale of how Sister Thomas Josephine of St. Louis, Missouri, came to Seek Repentance but found Bloodshed in the town of Altar, Mexico

I

And when they brought the fifth, it tormented . . .

The sea frothed at the impact of the falling body. It was deepest blue, calm for a moment, before another wave rushed in to smash itself against the rocky coast.

The wind took my voice as I called out, but even then I knew it was hopeless. He was gone; taken by bullets and the might of the ocean.

I do not remember how the guns found their way into my hands. All I felt was their weight against each palm. Where my thoughts had once been of God and grace there was now only a roaring, like a thousand steam engines, stoked to breaking and hurtling toward oblivion.

Carthy had not moved, his arm was extended still, staring through the smoke. The weapons in my hands spoke for me. They howled for justice like a zealot at the altar.

For Abe, I thought and let the pistols loose, sending bullets to bite into flesh and release a spray of blood onto the salt air.

By the time the final echo faded, my will had been done. A bullet had found its home, in the stomach of the lieutenant. His eyes – cornflower blue – rolled back in his head.

In truth, I remember little after that point, for the world seemed to fold itself up like a fan, showing me only what must be done, one moment to the next. Walk. Kneel. Listen.

Then dusk was falling. I almost heard it, rushing outward, bringing a vast and empty sky. Dread prickled the back of my neck as I looked around.

I was in a desert, red dirt and boulders streaked with cinders spreading out in every direction. There was nothing, no landmark or mountain to suggest where I might be. I knew neither where I was, nor how I'd gotten there.

A breeze blew, loaded with dust, whisking my warmth away into the night. Beneath me, a strange horse shifted. Carthy's mount. I stared down in astonishment. It snuffed the grit from its nose softly, head swinging round to look backward.

Something was draped over the saddle behind me, bulky and awkward. Gingerly, I dismounted from the horse, boots crunching on the night-cold sand. With one hand, I pushed at the bundle.

A head lolled backward, vomit staining chin and chest. I bolted away, ready to leave the horse and lifeless rider alone in the wilderness where they belonged.

Yet another voice, one that was far more distant, would not allow it. She forced me to take a rope from the saddle, tighten the ties that held the man who had killed Abraham Muir, so we might drift together, through the emptiness.

2

She walks not by the path of life

My own gasping awoke me, hard and labored. I lurched upward in the dark, trying to hear beyond my hammering chest. All seemed quiet. My nightgown was soaked through with cold sweat and tangled about my legs as I crawled from the bed.

The desert wind washed over my skin as I threw open the door. As always, there was little light, save for the stars, wheeling above me, impossibly numerous. The moon was invisible. I had heard a story that it was too afraid to shine over such a barren place, in case the dark sands should drag it to earth and consume it.

Nearby ran the pretense of a road. It led out into a no-man's-land, but that was the way I preferred it.

A trader had spotted me, riding aimlessly, burned from the sun and the wind. There had been money in one of the saddle packs and I had thrown it at his feet without a care for how much or where he was going.

He hitched Carthy's horse to his train and offered space in his wagon, gave me water and food at dawn and sundown. For two days we traveled thus, and all I recalled was the glare of the light through my eyelashes, until we arrived here.

Altar, the town was called. When I first heard the name I laughed and laughed, and could not stop until tears ran down my face. That the Lord saw fit to send me to somewhere of that name – when all else had been stripped from me – seemed a grand mockery.

It was barely more than a village, beleaguered by arid winds and sucking at one lonely well. The people there did not know I was a Bride of Christ. They thought me only a woman in need.

When I fell from the wagon to my knees in the dirt, they took pity on me.

Now my face had nearly healed, skin deepening from red to brown, lips no longer peeling. I took another deep breath of the night, allowing the quiet to calm me. During my first days in the desert, I had thought it empty, but now I knew better.

Thousands of small lives lived and died in that solitary land, marvels of the Lord's creation even in the depths of utter loneliness. Birds made burrows, snakes traced their ancient tracks, coyotes howled and howled.

Inside, I lit a candle. The yellow flame sputtered, reaching out to encompass dirt walls, a straw mattress, a table made from two casks and a length of wood. The water in the jug was warm and gritty with dust, but I drank anyway, poured some into my hands to sluice the sweat away from my neck. There would be no more sleep for me. I reached for my clothes.

Bone rattled against the wall, stopping my breath. The rosary was hanging on a nail and swayed, pale and dry. I stared. It might have been a minute or an hour that I stood there, before I was able to dress.

I had traded the stolen outfit from San Francisco at the first chance I got, bartering instead a length of brown cloth and black-dyed cotton to sew myself a rough habit. It was coarse fabric, grazing my skin in the daily heat, but it was honest. My boots stood by the door. I shook them wearily, as I had been told to, in case spiders and scorpions had crawled inside while I slept. The shoes were mercifully free of life.

As I went about my first errand that morning, the familiar anxiety took me, and I only prevented myself from biting at my newly healed lips by muttering prayers for patience.

The folk of Altar were early risers, already stirring by the time dawn rose over the distant hills. Within minutes, the sun was heating the earth. In the kitchen outside my shack I scooped a handful of corn from a bag, mashing it with a stone, then dropped it into a pot. A little fat that I had been able to get the day before went in too.

Soon, it was time.

Another building stood near my own. It was larger and fitted with a stout, fastened door and I moved to unlock it. I had taken the barn intended for livestock, and people had laughed to see me make my bed in there, until they had heard the cries that echoed from within the other walls. Then they stayed away.

I tried to turn the key slowly, so as not to make any noise, but was forced to lean my weight down, freeing it with a squeal. This was the moment, every day, when I wished I could hold my rosary, feel its comforting presence upon my skin without being assaulted by memories. But I knew I could not; it was better left on its nail.

Resolutely, I pulled the door open. The stench of stale vomit and urine and old sweat rolled over me. I shoved the door wider to allow light into the room, upon the bed and its occupant. Irises bright as heaven stared out at me.

He was awake.

3

Her steps are wandering, and unaccountable

'Who's there? Elizabeth?'

The voice came quavering from the shadows, like a frightened child. Breathing courage into my body, I stepped into the room.

'You know very well who it is, Mr Carthy.'

Now that I was closer I could see his face, skin taut across cheekbone and jaw, where once had been proud muscle. Yet that gaze held me, something in its depths begging me closer. I realized then that a grin was stretching his mouth.

'I do know.'

'I see that you were unwell again in the night,' I observed in as bland a voice as I could manage, edging around the pool of vomit next to the bed. 'Did you manage to keep supper down, at least?'

'Muck not fit for crows,' he spat, grin gone. 'You are trying to starve me. Am I pitiful enough for you yet, Josephine?'

He lay slumped upon the sheets, wheezing against the fluid that plagued his chest.

'That is not my name, nor will you address me as such.' I turned away so that he would not see how my hands shook. 'It is time for your breakfast.'

He drank from the cup of water I offered without fuss. Only when I dipped into the bowl of cornmeal mush, loaded up the spoon and raised it to his mouth, did his eyes flare. He cradled his ruined hand to his chest, protectively.

'You will not feed me like some brainsick whelp,' he snarled. 'I can manage alone. You only do this to laugh at me. I hear you mocking me out there, you and your lover Muir.'

'Abraham Muir is dead,' I said, my voice cold.

Cornmeal dripped off the spoon back into the bowl as the silence lengthened. I remained still until Carthy's mania retreated and his jaw slackened once more.

'Will you eat?' I tried, more gently.

He nodded, avoiding my gaze, and swallowed the mouthfuls I proffered, flinching away from the cloth I held under his chin to catch what he could not manage.

'I will clean here later,' I told him when he had finished, desperate to be free of the heat and the smell and his presence. 'And change your bandages.'

His head only lolled in assent; breakfast had exhausted his strength.

'Sister?' His voice was weak.

The sigh halted me at the doorway. It sounded clear, almost regretful, the voice of the man I had once seen upon the plain, when he was fire and righteousness. He was whispering something, head pressed into the pillow in pain. 'I wish . . .'

'What did you say?'

I was forced to lean close, barely a hand's breadth from his mouth. As I did so, his eyelids sprang open, lips stretched again. 'I wish you would come down here with me.'

I stumbled to the door, slamming it behind me. This time the lock needed no coercion. I rammed the key home so hard that metal squealed. Part of me hoped it would never be opened again.

4

Leave it not, keep it,
because it is thy life

I threw open the lid of the crate impatiently, not caring that its sharp corners left deep gouges in the wall where it struck. Inside were the few worldly items I considered mine. Some scraps of cloth left over from sewing, an old bible, traded for the stolen shawl. The pistols.

My hands shook as I pulled them free by their newly made straps. There was a leatherworker in Altar. As soon as I realized what a desperate place it was, I had paid him a visit and over-ridden his reluctance by offering him the last of Carthy's dollars in exchange for his services.

He had flinched away from me while measuring my wrists and arms with a knotted string, but he had done as I asked. Now they were mine: sturdy, raw leather worked into bracers that ran from my elbow to my wrist. Some of the anger began to abate as I buckled the straps, clipped the pistols into their holsters. They weighed heavily at my arms, but with them in place, concealed beneath wide sleeves, I could ride without fear.

The horse's hooves beat rhythmically against the ground, muscles bunching and releasing as we cantered headlong into the desert. Pale dust rose and flew about us. The sun was already high and burned my eyes, yet I persevered; I kept my head low over the horse's mane, the scent of inhuman earth and living animal filling my senses.

The horse ran itself out and began to slow. I believe the beast felt the same release I did, fleeing into the landscape, away from walls and the noise of humans. Small puffs of dirt sprang under-foot as we shifted and stopped.

I turned back: a smudge on the horizon was all that suggested a village lay behind us. The desert was silent, blessedly silent. The horse went to nose hopefully at some withered scrub. I dismounted and sat down upon the baked earth and rock. Above me the sky spread out, blue in the heat. Tiny flecks of black wheeled: buzzards, on their daily scout for flesh.

In the saddlebag was an end of bread, wrapped in cloth, and the bible. I chewed dutifully on the food for as long as seemed necessary and took up the book. It had seen much use, its leather cover wrinkled and faded by the sun, the thin paper of its pages edged by the grease of many fingers. It was written in Spanish, and would have been of little use, had I not known Latin. As it was, I struggled by.

The wind picked up after a time, a long harrying sweep that tore at the pages and whipped dirt into my eyes. I dragged out a neck scarf and tied it around my nose and mouth. The book fell open at the center.

A paper flower quivered in the calming breeze, as if breathing. It was blue no longer, but stained with dried blood, as if blighted by disease. Nonetheless, I took the petals in my hand, raised them toward my lips.

The horse whinnied in recognition. I could see a dust cloud on the horizon. From the size of it, I guessed at ten riders, maybe more. I closed the book on the flower and crammed the missal into my pack, pulled myself into the saddle and waited. There seemed little use in running.

Twelve men drew up to me. They were all dressed in the sun-bleached hide of the desert, faces covered, wide brims casting the narrow strips of their eyes into shadow. Grime coated their mounts, their boots, clung to the sweat of their collars. They stopped just out of range of my pistols, and for a time we merely eyed each other.

After some commotion, a youth was shunted forward by an older man. His horse looked more like a mule, all jutting teeth and bones. As he muttered to one of the men, I examined what little of his face I could make out. He looked familiar.

'You from Altar?' someone called, with a heavy Mexican accent.

Calmly, I nodded, crossed my arms slowly into the sleeves of my habit. To raise a hand in haste was to welcome a bullet. As if accepting this as permission, the older man rode forward, dragging the youth along with him.

He pulled the kerchief from his mouth, and halted ten paces away. 'What do you do here?' he said.

'Who is it that wants to know?'

The silence that followed confirmed my suspicions right enough. No names, no uniforms. Bandits. My hands tensed within the sleeves.

'What do you want?' I called to them.

'You come 'cross the border, bring a man with you. A Yankee.' The leader smiled. 'You hide him in the town.' He was young, I realized, younger than his voice suggested.

'I hide no one,' I said.

The youth interrupted hotly in Spanish, gesturing at me, then back toward the village. I recognized his voice, had heard it shouting after his siblings when dusk fell and families gathered to eat.

'My friend say he has seen this man you hide,' the leader insisted, 'that he is a soldier in blue.'

'Ask him if he is certain of what he saw.' My voice was muffled by the cloth, but still it rang out, cold. 'His eyes might have deceived him.'

The leader repeated my words in Spanish. The lad looked as though he wanted to speak, but shut his mouth instead, sullen and silent.

'The tales of the young,' I told the older man. 'They seek adventure where there is none. Now, if you'll excuse me – good day.'

Before I could turn my horse, the man had a rifle aimed at me. The youth scrabbled to follow suit as the rest of the company bristled closer.

'*Sì, è vero,*' the leader said, riding forward. 'But my master, he too hear this tale. He tell me to go look, for the nun with blood on her hands, and her Union soldier.'

Despite the beating sun, his words chilled me. Easily, all too easily, I released the pistols with my fingers, pulled them free. The wood glowed in the morning light.

'Blood indeed,' I muttered, fixing him in my sights and cocking the pistols in one move. The first bullet passed cleanly through the crown of his hat.

For a long moment, only the wind voiced its outrage. Through the dust, I could see the men arming guns, surging forward. I held my ground. When they were within spitting distance, I shook free the scarf that covered my mouth and calmly placed the other pistol against my own temple. The men hauled upon their reins, dancing to a halt uncertainly.

'I know my sins,' I called. 'I will atone and I have made peace with my God. Have you?'

The leader raised a hand, and the men fell back. Carefully, he removed his hat, examining the ragged hole that now adorned its center. He tilted it toward me.

'*Hasta la próxima, Madre.*'

5

She hath no guide, nor master,
nor captain

The village was busy when I returned, as much as was possible in a town of fewer than four score inhabitants. The children had been released from their morning lessons to tumble through the streets like infant wolves, browned to a crisp, discarding their shoes to run through the dust on nimble bare feet.

They scattered out of my path. *Cuervo*, I had heard them call me, for my dark habit, a blot against the desert sands. *Crow*. They were not the only ones who stayed away. Few would look at me directly, since they had discovered my vocation, and even fewer would speak to me. Some made the sign of the cross when I walked about the town, through respect or fear I did not know. Neither did I much care.

Many of the larger houses stood near the town well. I stopped before one of them to hammer on the door. It was nearing time for the midday meal, and people were gathering around the well, vying for the next turn, kicking up wet dirt with their shoes and sharing gossip already repeated twenty times over. When they saw me, they fell quiet.

Scowling, I hammered again, feeling their eyes prickling the back of my neck.

'Doña Luisa?' I called.

A dog yelped nearby, the economical greeting of an animal always hungry, and a stringy yellow mutt skittered out from a passageway that ran beside the house to stare at me. I strode toward him and he led the way, through a broken back gate.

I stepped into what looked like a garden, baked stems and thin, drooping leaves where there should have been lush foliage. A woman was attacking the ground with a shovel. She was shorter than me by a head, robustly healthy, skin leathered by years under the Sonoran sun. A huge straw hat eclipsed her face. I lingered next to the furrows. If I expected a greeting, I would have a long wait.

'I saw your son, today,' I told her bluntly.

Doña Luisa made no comment, levering up the soil to reveal a shriveled potato. She threw it into a bucket and dug the shovel in again. Sweat soaked into the collar of her blouse.

'He was with some men, ten or so, without uniforms,' I said.

'*Bandidos,* they come east,' she interrupted, picking out another potato.

'They knew something of me,' I pressed, following her progress. 'What stories has your son been telling? I believed we had an arrangement.'

'*We* do.'

Doña Luisa was something of a matriarch to Altar. It was she who had taken pity on me when I staggered into the town with my just-living burden. She had given me use of the buildings we occupied, which had belonged to her late husband, and enough corn for a few meals. She was a pious, practical woman, and treated me with exactly the amount of respect she deemed me worthy of, not an ounce more.

Because she was the only one to speak to me, several times a week I found myself drawn to her threshold, especially when the town itself could not yield up what I needed. She tolerated my occasional company, and as the weeks wore on, I had come to take comfort from her terse manner.

Now she straightened with a grimace, cracking her back. She stumped toward the shade of the house, and I followed, knowing better than to wait for an invitation. There, she thumped a pitcher of water and a half-empty bottle of spirit onto the table with dirty fingers.

'My son has joined with Cortina's men,' she said, pouring the spirit into two small glasses, and poking one toward me. 'Cortina was a Señor once, with a hacienda the size of the desert, before the Anglos moved the border. Now he says he fights for freedom,

225

but,' she shrugged dismissively, dispatching half of her drink. 'Those men have no loyalty. People say he trades with the old president, Juárez, with the French, even with you *norteamericanos*.'

'They knew of me,' I repeated, impatient. 'Why would they have an interest? I am no one.'

She sipped again, slowly.

'I tell my son not to trust them,' she said. 'They are dangerous, but he does not listen. Like his father.'

She wiped her hands on her apron, nodded toward my own drink. Dutifully, I drank half of it down, struggling not to grimace at the taste of rough alcohol.

'Word travels far in the desert, *Madre*,' she told me briskly. 'These are Cortina's lands. He does not like surprises, or strangers. Now, what do you need?'

'Iodine?' I murmured hopefully, still pondering her words. She shook her head. Pursing her lips, she pushed a cork into the bottle of liquor and handed it over.

I studied the pale yellow liquid. Carthy's condition was serious, and the lack of supplies threatened his life still further. I wondered how long I could improvize in such conditions.

'Why do you heal him?' Luisa demanded, as I took my leave. I pretended not to hear her, as I hurried away through the buzzing furnace of the noon street.

6

Put a knife to thy throat,
if thy soul is in thy power

My fury earlier that day had been too much for the rusted door to the building where Carthy lay, and I had to spend several minutes working at the lock before I could push it open. I covered my face with my sleeve, assailed by the stench of the room.

Carthy tried to speak to me, but I resolutely ignored him, opening the shutters to allow any scrap of breeze to enter, washing down the floor with precious water to rid it of his earlier mess. Only when that was done did I have the courage to pick up my basket of supplies and approach the bed.

He stared up at me listlessly, mouth open in the heat, reminding me of the birds that sought the scant shade of fence posts on unbearable days, wings spread and trembling. Clenching my jaw, I began to fold back the sheet that covered him.

'Why do you bother?' The trace of bitterness in his voice was not enough to cover the despair I saw in his face. 'I am a dead man walking, Thomas Josephine. You killed me weeks ago. There will be no miracles here.'

The reminder of my sin was like a blow to the chest. Doggedly, I raised the hem of his shirt. Once, such an action would have been enough to send me running. Yet this was a body in need of healing, nothing more. I told myself this over and over until I was able to look upon his pale skin and wasting muscles without fear.

The bullet wound decorated his abdomen like a rosette, the flesh around it red and streaked. Although I had retrieved the bullet, and was satisfied no organs had been pierced, it refused to heal. I worked the soiled bandages free. Here was proof of my sin, driven into flesh. Proof that I had once lost all I thought inviolable about myself.

'This will hurt,' I told him as gently as I could, and pulled the cork from the bottle of spirits with my teeth.

His cries echoed back from the walls as I cleaned the lesion with spirits and cloths. He raged at me, cursed me in as many blasphemies as I had ever heard, but grimly I worked on. By the time I had finished tending to the wound, folding a new bandage over it, his fury and agony had subsided into whimpers.

'Please,' he said grappling with the sheet, feeling weakly for my hand. Tears of pain slid out from beneath closed lashes. 'Please, Thomas Josephine, let me die. I cannot live this way.'

He brushed up against my sleeve, tried to hold on with the three fingers that remained, but I jerked my arm free.

'You will live,' I pronounced, fighting back tears of my own. 'You will live and you will repent, Theodore Carthy. No man's soul is beyond salvation, and I intend to fight the devil for yours.'

228

7

For they sleep not,
except they have done evil

'"And when the wicked man turneth himself away from the wickedness he hath wrought,"' I read, '"and doeth judgment, and justice: he shall save his soul alive."'

The candle flickered in the rising draft from the doorway, and I hitched the blanket a little higher around my shoulder. I had not slept more than a few hours in many weeks, for fear of the nightmares that always returned. Now my eyes blurred with fatigue; I felt them droop closed.

'"Because he considereth and turneth away from all his iniquities which he hath wrought, he shall surely live, and not die,"' Carthy said, his voice snapping me from the doze. He was staring at me through the yellow light, eyes clear.

'Ezekiel,' he offered with a twist of the lips and flopped back onto the pillow. 'Eighteen, twenty.'

'Eighteen, twenty-seven,' I corrected, clearing my throat.

'Do you not wonder why I should know that, Sister?' he said.

I said nothing, unwilling to enter into conversation until I had gauged his mood. He had trapped me this way before.

'Do you think I am unaware of my iniquities?' he continued over my silence, staring up at the wooden ceiling. 'I feel the sins eating away at my flesh. I would be a strong man still, if not for that. Perhaps I would even be a husband by now, with a brood of boys at home to take my name. If I was strong, you would be the one, lying here at my mercy.'

I pushed the stool aside and made for the door, pulling the blanket tight over my chest.

'Wait,' he called, as I reached for the key, 'forgive me. Do not leave me alone.' He held my gaze. 'How will you make me repent if you leave me alone?'

Shakily, I returned.

'The first step,' I told him later, as I poured a cup of water, 'is to acknowledge and accept the wrong that you have done.'

I held the cup to his lips and he drank, meek as a lamb.

'Well now,' he said, 'that might take some time. Sister, should I keep a record? I believe I saw a pencil here someplace.'

He made some show of hunting about the bed, and I bit back the smile that twitched my lips.

'You know very well what I mean.'

'I know that I was wrong to make an enemy of you,' he rebutted, 'you have made me pay for that, with life and limb.'

His tone was light, free of the mania that seemed to flare without warning, but there was something else in his manner that put me on guard, yet prompted me to pull the stool a little closer to the bed. He seemed to be working some words around his mouth, as if trying to rearrange them there before they were spoken.

'The lives I took, they were all in the call of duty,' he said slowly. 'Even the ones which were not so heroic – those heathen women and children. Until I met you.'

His eyes were fixed on mine.

'Because of you,' he said, 'I killed, and *those* deaths were not necessary to my mission. Those were people who would still be living peaceably, had you not crossed their path. That priest.'

My heart thudded sickly. I felt the blood rise to my face yet could not seem to speak.

'I see him now,' Carthy continued relentlessly, rising on one elbow, 'begging me to spare you, even after Muir had near beaten the teeth from his head.'

'He did not have to die,' I whispered.

'Have *you* repented for trying to kill me, Sister? Or is it only Muir you regret? You mourn for him, yet you would not for me.

Was he such a better man? Tell me, what was he to you, Josephine?'

I stood and left the room though he shouted after me; bolted the door upon his cries, leaving him to bellow alone into the night.

8

He stealeth to fill his hungry soul

They came before dawn. Long after the last shutters had banged shut, after the woodsmoke had died in the chimneys. They came as shadows, black and gray and dun in the darkness, their footsteps muffled. At first I thought it was my nightmare come true, that the men and women and children who were rotting in the ground by Carthy's hand had returned to bear me to hell.

But the voices were real, feverish with restrained violence. I barely had time to rise from my bed before the door was kicked in. Instinctively I reached for the pistols, but a boot stamped down, just missing my hand, while another kicked the weapons away into the darkness. Hands were grappling my arms behind me, and I drove my head backward, connecting with a skull.

A man yelled in pain, yet my triumph was short, for the blow stunned me, enough that I felt rope binding my wrists before I could struggle. I was dragged backward, bare heels scraping through the dust. A dark figure followed behind, tucking my rosary into his pocket. I screamed my rage. A rag, sour with must and sweat, was stuffed into my mouth.

There were voices to my right, and I twisted painfully, in time to see the door to the other building flung open, to hear a familiar voice crying out in surprise, then in pain. Frantically, I spat the cloth free.

'No!' I shrieked toward the men, toward anyone who would hear, 'He is wounded! Leave him, please!'

But fabric was crammed between my teeth again, with enough force to make me retch. A sack was wrestled over my head, and I fought and thrashed, kicking out at whatever flesh I could find until my head grew light and I was forced to slow my breathing or suffocate.

I felt myself being lifted bodily, smelled horseflesh as I was hoisted over what felt like a saddle, which dug painfully into my ribs. I made one last attempt to escape, throwing my weight backward, only for a hand to grasp my neck.

'Quiet, *Madre*,' a man's voice hissed. Then we were moving, and I stopped struggling, for to fall would be death beneath a horse's hooves.

The minutes dragged interminably into hours; I was crushed and bruised all over, winded by the motion of the horse. I forced my body to be happy with the little air that found its way through my nostrils.

I only knew that time was passing from the light that needled its way through the hessian sack, from the heat of the coming day as we left the dawn hours behind us. From what little I could fathom, I judged we were riding east.

The nature of the land changed, sloping upward. Stones began to clatter past hooves and I smelled something that might have been vegetation, passing in a flash. Then voices crying in Spanish, metal clanging and dogs barking, movement all around.

These things I noted carefully, anxious to glean any clues about my surroundings. I was lifted free and set on my feet. Much to my consternation, my legs collapsed beneath me, numb from the long ride.

I sniffed beneath the hood before they hauled me upright. Somewhere, meat was cooking. It was strangely comforting when all else was fear and pain and unknown.

When the time came to move, I could not yet walk, and so was half carried, half dragged across the ground, down a step into a darker space, where the heat of the desert was kept at bay. Cool earth greeted my bare feet.

A man's voice, rough from tobacco and long days of silent rides, was issuing commands. He sounded indignant. The sack was yanked from my head and I blinked dust-stung eyes.

The outline of a man: broad shouldered and proud, a

233

bandolier slung over one shoulder, revolvers at his waist. All I could make out of his face was the glint of dark eyes beneath heavy brows, drawn into a frown.

'Sister Tomás,' he murmured in heavily accented English, 'I am Juan Cortina.'

9

A generation that for teeth hath swords

Gingerly, I lifted the nightgown over my head. It was ripped in places, filthy from ingrained dust. My muscles protested as I began to examine my limbs. Bruises were blooming dark where I had been manhandled, but I had dealt with worse in the past.

Thankfully, a pitcher of water had been placed in the locked room where they had pushed me. I washed with clumsy handfuls, gratefully rinsing the dirt from my face. Cortina's men had taken all of my possessions from Altar, perhaps to make it seem as though I had fled in the night of my own volition. My homemade habit and veil had been returned, along with my boots and even the missal, but not the pistols. I wondered what had become of them.

Something else was caught in the folds of cloth; I shook it free into my hand. It was the rosary, beads warm from the day's heat, as if living. I ran my thumb over the cross, grown smooth with use now. Instantly, I saw a flash of teeth, bared into a half-grin, the shape of a jaw, strong and wind burned next to my own.

As I feared, sorrow assailed me and I dropped the rosary onto the bench, clenched myself in tight, shoving away every memory of him one by one as they arose, until I was able to open my eyes, to dress myself with shaking hands and mutter through a prayer for strength.

There was nothing to do then but wait. Cortina knew my name, I recalled, staring down at the beads. What had he heard from across the border? I had hoped to be safe, so far away from civilization. What that knowledge meant for me, for Carthy, was still uncertain.

I was called for as the sun shimmered hot toward noon. I was escorted out, squinting in the light that bounced from sand and stone. The camp squatted on the floor of a narrow plateau. Steep hills jutted around us, as if they had been expelled from the earth by force, streaked ocher yellow and ash black. Tangles of weed sprouted here and there, baked to skeletons.

The buildings were a collection of tents and shacks, hastily assembled with cloth in their windows, and held together by wire. None of it would have been visible from the desert below. It seemed Cortina's men had found the perfect place to conceal themselves, hiding in the open, sheltered by a trick of the land.

One of the buildings looked sturdier than the others. Within sat Cortina, taking a meal. It took my eyes a moment to adjust after the glare of the day, but as they did I saw another man next to him, slim and golden. Carthy had been bathed and dressed in borrowed clothes; a dark shirt and neck scarf that made his golden hair seem even brighter. Weakly, he raised a cup to me and drank, his eyes triumphant over the rim. Beside him sat Muir's pistols.

I lunged, snatching for the weapons, even as my mind told me that it was useless. A moment later, I was wrestled back. Anger crackled through me, but also shame, that I could react so violently and without thought.

Behind the table, Cortina mopped at a puddle of spilled wine. 'Sister Tomás Josephine,' he greeted me in an almost friendly manner. 'I am sorry for your treatment, but I must take precautions. I have heard much of you already.'

He leaned back in his chair, rubbing at his beard thoughtfully. Satisfied that I was calm, my guards slackened their grip.

'Whatever you have heard,' I said, eyes flicking from Carthy, 'no doubt much of it comes to you stained by prejudice.'

'But who do you refer to, *Madre*? You have angered many people, it seems. The Union, the Church ... I was raised a Catholic, you know,' he smiled.

'And you treat a woman of God in this fashion?'

'Ah, I was *raised* this way, that is all. I might have honored the Lord still, were it not for the French; they invade my country and send a greedy emperor blessed by Rome to take what they can from the land.'

'Perhaps you should consult your own conscience where greed is concerned,' I snapped.

Cortina nodded once or twice, expression hidden by his beard.

'My new friend told me of your intelligence,' he continued, after a time. 'You have for certain left your mark upon him, Sister. I was not so quick to trust the stories, but now, I believe.'

He rose from his chair, weapons clinking as he came toward me. I saw him clearly then, a man of conflict, tempered by the sheer will of staying alive. He addressed me eye to eye.

'I kneel for no master and no Church. The imperialists in the capital would break us, yet still I might trade with them. One of their own, a renegade to be silenced, for a price.'

I held his gaze, refusing to look away until he wheeled around and returned to the table.

'But our guest,' he said, 'the lieutenant, he tells me of a bounty, five hundred American dollars for you, if we were to take a pleasure-ride across the border. I am friends with the Union, right now.' He indicated the camp outside. 'My men are riding with them. They are like brothers to me.'

'He is lying,' I told Carthy flatly, over Cortina's shoulder. 'Whatever he has promised, he will have no qualm in breaking his word.'

Next to the bull-like bandit leader, Carthy appeared little more than a ghoul. I could see that he was weakening rapidly from his exertions, sweat beginning to matt his fine hair.

'Be that as it may, Señor Cortina has given me something of great value,' he said, baring his teeth below trembling lips. 'You.'

He signaled to the guards, who took hold of my arms again. 'Let us see how you enjoy playing the prisoner.'

237

10

It is better to dwell in a wilderness, than with a passionate woman

With Carthy as my jailer, I prepared myself for the worst. At first I prayed, as well as I was able, asking the Lord to grant me wisdom, and forgiveness for my trespasses as well as those of others, for I had wandered far from the path of the righteous.

The afternoon wore on, and still I was left alone. Finally, I grew restless and began to pace the small room like a caged coyote, muttering prayers and thoughts beneath my breath until I wore myself ragged. I had held myself on guard for many hours, and now fatigue clawed at me. The bench was narrow and hard, yet I stretched my aching limbs upon it. As much as I feared the dreams and memories that came with sleep, it would be as a blessed relief.

Just as my thoughts had grown quiet, I was shocked awake by a harsh rattling. Through the narrow window cut into the door, one of my guards smirked, banging a tin cup back and forth against the wood. His nose was bruised and swollen, his eyes blackened. I remembered cartilage cracking beneath my skull during the assault, and wondered whether this was the man I had injured.

I glared at him until he stopped and left me alone. I waited. All was quiet, and soon I felt my eyelids slump closed once more.

The rattling started up again, just as I had dropped into sleep. Furious, I staggered over to the doorway.

'Did he tell you to do this? Lieutenant Carthy?'

Still smirking, the man only shrugged and returned to his seat.

It was mid-afternoon. Outside the building, the sun slammed down, driving away shade, sending men and animals alike into hiding until it slackened off into the west. I watched the heat ghost over the ground for a time, making even the flies listless.

A snorting wheeze came from outside my door. Silently, I padded across to stare out at the guard. He sagged, head lolling to his chest, contented snores riffling the air.

For a moment I considered creeping back to the bench, to snatch what little sleep I could. Yet the sight of that tin cup changed my mind. It was far from Christian of me, but as I knelt on the earth floor, I could not help but smile. Calmly, I took a deep breath, and began to sing, in as loud a voice as I could manage.

Though I tried to keep my expression calm and devoted, I had a good deal of trouble not to laugh when I heard the guard's cursing from outside the door. I had chosen one of the longer dedications. By the time I reached the final, long 'amen', a truce had been brokered. We both retired to sleep in mutual silence.

When my eyes opened next, it was twilight. There was a distant clatter of metal that might have been pots and pans. Through the narrow window, a blue haze was smudging the landscape into chalk. I had sat at liberty on such an evening, eating oranges on the Californian shore. The memory of a blue paper rose swelled, unbidden, to mind.

Thought it might make you smile.

The door creaked, and I swiped the moisture from my eyes, determined to remain steadfast. Yet rather than the guard, or Carthy, a woman was staring in at me.

Her eyes were heavy-lidded, black as a raven's; in the shadows there seemed no white to them at all. Irrational though it was, I felt myself take a step back. Then she was moving through the room, setting down a tray, refilling the pitcher of water as any woman might.

I thanked her hesitantly as she set a dish of food upon the bench. She remained bent over her task, long hair swinging forward to hide her face. It was as black as her eyes and plaited loosely into a braid that fell to her waist.

Other than this, there was nothing remarkable in her manner,

239

or the homespun fabric of her clothes. I tried to catch her eye, thank her again, but she turned and left, as if I was nothing but empty air. I sank to the bench next to the food, shaken. Although it now seemed absurd, for a fleeting moment, I had been convinced that what I had seen in the woman's eyes was not entirely human.

II

Bind it upon thy fingers,
hang it about thy neck

The guard reappeared to bolt the door when I started on the plate of food. It was meager, cornmeal mashed with bacon grease, beans in a sort of spice I had never encountered before, but I dug in with the spoon and ate ferociously. After a moment, fire burst upon my tongue, spreading through my mouth and I choked, terrified that I had been poisoned and cursing my foolishness.

The hated tin cup came into my vision, and I looked up through streaming eyes at the guard. He was smiling again, not the same ignorant smirk, but with an expression one might lavish upon an errant child. Past caring, I seized the mug from him and gulped down its contents.

Beer. The unexpected taste made me cough, yet it washed some of the fire from my tongue, leaving behind only a gentle heat, and my streaming nose and eyes.

'Thank you,' I rasped, wiping my face and poking at the food. 'What is this?'

He told me in Spanish, and though I did not understand, he took the spoon from me, demonstrated taking a little of the beans, along with the cornmeal. I was reluctant to try again, yet he seemed insistent. In this manner, I was able to finish the dish without further commotion. The guard went back to his seat, seeming to think it unnecessary to lock the door. Instead he continued with his task, rolling tobacco and humming tunelessly to himself.

'That woman,' I tried after a while, through the doorway, 'who was she?'

He looked at me blankly, so I indicated the plate, pointed. '*La señorita?*' I tried again.

Nodding, he shrugged dismissively and answered in words I could make little sense of, although from his actions I grasped that he thought it not a worthwhile exercise trying to talk to her.

As the evening wore on, the door remained open. Every minute, I expected Carthy to appear, filled with the hollow joy of his mania and the freedom to enact its commands, yet he did not come. Instead, the guard offered me a smoke, and though I declined, I could not help asking, with signs and halting Spanish words, why he was showing me kindness.

Jamming the tobacco between his teeth, he fished around beneath his shirt and pulled out a chain, upon which dangled a disc of beaten silver, stamped with an image of the Virgin. I smiled my understanding, and pointed next to his nose, placing my palms upon my heart in what I hoped he would understand as an apology.

He grinned beneath blackened eyes, and waved my hands away. Before I could return the smile, the outside door flew open and two men came sprawling in, sweat staining their shirts, blood on their hands. Their eyes were frenzied as they came forward to grasp at my habit.

I staggered with them out into the camp. Night had fallen and oil lamps flared, casting the place into strange shadow. There was no one to explain where I was being taken, but the guard had joined in with the others, pulling me toward a group of people and horses.

Even at ten paces I caught the smell: blood, too much, spilling bright and fatal from sundered arteries. I was pushed into a knot of carnage.

Cortina was already there.

'Indian attack,' he told me grimly. 'Twenty of my men I lend to the Union. Forty men in all and only these six return. The lieutenant tell me you know some medicine?'

I dragged my eyes away in order to nod at him.

'Very well,' he said. 'I offer you this: my men live, you walk free.'

'How can I trust your word?'

'You let them die then.'

I was trapped and Cortina knew it. I began to roll up my sleeves.

'I shall help them,' I told him coldly, 'for the Lord and for their souls. Never for you.'

I will utter my spirit to you;
I will show you my words

The night that followed was one of the longest I can recall – endless, lost minutes of panic and pain and momentary relief. To give Cortina's men credit, they followed my instructions without hesitation, translating for each other as I sent them for clean water, for bandages, or to hold down the wounded when the agony became too great.

Of the six men, four belonged to the Union, and I forced myself to swallow fear at the sight of the familiar blue uniforms. They had been chasing an Apache raiding party across the border from Texas, I was told, having paid Cortina's men to act as guides and extra hands. Despite this, they had been no match for the force they encountered. The slaughter of troops – both American and Mexican – had been wholesale.

The survivors had been moved to a large tent that housed supplies, laid out upon makeshift beds of crates and sacking. Their wounds were horrific. Not only from bullets, but great slashes that cut through muscle, blows that had split flesh. They were broken men, bone glistening in the light of the lamps, their bodies spilling the secret workings that should never be seen by human eyes.

I pitied them. They did not care now for what they had been fighting, only for the pain and the terror of death. Yet even as I condemned the hands that had wrought such violence, I remembered Abe's voice telling me of another slaughter, of women and children, cut down as they ran away.

Losing concentration, I staggered, nausea washing over me. A hand steadied my shoulder, and I looked around at the man who had been translating my commands all night.

'You must drink,' he murmured, waving to someone at the entrance of the tent. Hesitantly, the woman who had brought my meal earlier entered. Her eyes lingered over the men, the bowls of bloodstained water, the saturated bandages. She held a jug in her hand, and two cups.

'This is Maria,' the man told me, as she picked her way through the debris. 'She will help you now.'

'Who is she?' I rasped, my throat dry.

'She came looking for her man, a few days ago, is working for keep 'til he return. He is riding near the border, with Juárez's men. She said he is her husband, but . . .' the man shrugged, breaking off as the woman approached.

Wordlessly, she poured coffee from the tin pot and offered it to me. Her eyes strayed constantly to the wounded men. It must have been horrifying for someone unused to violence, I realized, the groans and cries and stench of fresh and drying blood.

I wiped my hands on a cloth and drank. The coffee was strong, laced with sugar and liquor, and I gulped it. There was much work to be done, and I needed my strength.

'You need not stay here,' I told her, handing the cup back. 'If it is too much, there are blankets to be washed, water to be boiled.'

'I have no fear.'

Her voice was quiet, lower than I expected. She looked up at me again, the rapid glance of a bird as she set the coffee down and began to tie a cloth around her head.

'What should I do?' she said.

Her accent was strange, like none I had heard before, but there was no time to wonder. One of the men had come to himself, thrashing in pain. He had been close to scalped, the skin at his hairline sliced deep from earlobe to crown. His face was a mask of blood, impossible to find detail in his features, except for his teeth, unnaturally white against the gore.

It took two men to hold him down as I worked. We had nothing to numb pain except liquor, which was of no use when a man was screaming so. Forcing my hands to be still, I threaded a needle and stabbed it into the heart of a flame.

'Maria,' I called, 'would you—?'

But she was already at my side, holding the flesh in place so that I could begin stitching. She did not flinch at the task, only stared down in stony silence at the man's writhing face.

It was terrible, dirty work. My fingers slipped time and again in the man's blood as I tried to close the wound. The feeling of thread pulling through skin set my teeth upon edge, yet I put all such thoughts aside, focused only as far as the next task.

Thankfully, he had fallen unconscious again by the time I finished. I surveyed my work. The stitches were hurried, yet it might heal, with time. I left one of the men sponging the gore from his friend's face, and moved on.

Maria worked beside me as the hours rolled past, holding limbs as I reset bones, wiping away blood, cleaning the mess that the men could not help but make. She spoke only to ask for instruction, and never trembled, never broke her expression of absolute stillness with smile or frown, even when one of the men we had tended succumbed in a final struggle. The holy words of the *viaticum* died in my mouth when I realized he would breathe no more.

Sensing that the man's passing was imminent, I had begun to mutter the prayer, even as I fought to stem the bleeding from the stab wound in his gut. I had faltered over the words, interrupting them to call for more cloths, for a hot iron to try and sear the wound closed.

Now, we both stood quietly, looking upon the ruined corpse of the man I had failed to save. He had been unconscious at the time of his death, a small mercy. My hand was slick with his blood, but I traced the sign of the cross upon his forehead, fingers trembling.

'*Requiem aeternam dona ei,*' I breathed, '*Domine, et lux perpetua luceat ei. Requiescat in pace.*'

Dawn was filtering through the door of the tent, stripping the lamps of their glow, illuminating the evidence of my fight against death, soiled and strewn across the floor. There was no glory in it then, no wonder at the divine mystery of life, only grief at the hopeless waste.

It was all I could do to stagger outside, suck the clean air into my lungs as if I had not breathed all night. Knees buckling, I lowered myself to the ground in case I should faint. My hands were tacky with drying blood as I rested my head against them, incapable of thought.

I felt eyes upon me before I knew who was watching. The camp was stirring, the sky sloughing off darkness. Movement from a doorway caught my attention. Carthy stood, one hand pressed against the frame, hair mussed as if from sleep.

My sadness was physical in that moment, and I had nothing to offer, no strength or defiance as I met his gaze. Cortina too appeared, crossing the distance to where I sat.

I told him that I had done what I could.

13

The heart of a man is like deep water

'Sister!'

The cry was weak, but audible. I looked up, trying to locate its source, but the crashing of waves, the harsh whipping of ocean wind eclipsed all else.

'—ter!' I heard again, the voice of a bird caught in a storm.

An anguished moan ripped from somewhere near my feet. Carthy lay there, pale and frantic, clutching at his torso. A hole oozed liquid, seeping dark into the blue jacket.

The pistol was in my hand, cocked and ready to fire. Distantly, I remembered reloading it with bullets from his belt, calmly pushing the charges in one by one. My finger had frozen upon the trigger. The barrel hovered, aimed dead between Carthy's eyes.

'Do it,' I heard him spit through the roaring in my head. 'Finish me, Josephine. Send me to hell. I shall be there waiting for you.' He dared a glance down at the wound and shuddered, sweat beginning to bead his upper lip. For the first time, my hand trembled.

'Merciless bitch,' he half-laughed, 'Muir would've killed me cleanly.'

Every inch of my being screamed for me to end it: the pressure of a finger, nothing more.

A flickering movement caught the corner of my eye. Something sapphire and rustling, easily crushed, was lodged in the tuft of seagrass where I had stood only minutes before. Abe's flower, a stain webbing across its petals. Twisted paper and thread, wet with precious blood. All that was left.

Something broke inside me the moment I let that pistol fall from my hand.

No man is beyond salvation.

'Sister!'

'Abe!'

My own voice jolted me into wakefulness. For a long moment I gasped, disorientated. No cliff top but rough walls, a blanket and the dying day outside the window.

'Not Abe,' said a familiar voice.

Carthy sat in the corner of the room, leaning against wall and crutch, one hand pressed protectively to his side. How long he had been there I did not know. Alarmed, I looked down, for I wore only my old nightgown.

His lip curled into a pained laugh as he watched me tug at the blanket.

'Do not concern yourself, Thomas Josephine. I lack the strength, if not the will.'

'What do you want?' I said impatiently. Now that I was awake, my head had begun to pound. I was exhausted from the long night. I rubbed at my temple, wishing he would leave.

'You trembled to look at me, once,' he said. 'Perhaps you do not fear me, any more?'

'Not today,' I sighed, closing my eyes. Memories of the cliff, of Abe's face, warred behind my lids. 'I am tired. Whatever taunts you have in mind, would you make them, please?'

Something landed upon the blanket with a rustle. I looked up to see what he had thrown, prepared for the worst. Instead, there was a tangle of flowers, tiny clusters of pink blooms above stringy gray leaves. A scent rose from them, impossibly sweet and fragrant for something created of that forbidding land.

Carthy kept his gaze fixed upon them.

'I watched you with those men, last night,' he began, almost grudgingly. 'You did not care that on any other day they would have hunted you down to be hanged without a thought. One or two would have had their fun with you before you reached the hands of justice. I have heard them laugh over just that in the past. You could have killed them, and no one would have known. You could have killed me.'

249

'The Lord—' I began.

'This was not the work of the Lord,' he dismissed, 'it was done by your hand and yours alone.'

We stared in silence at the flowers, lying bright against the coarse blanket.

'"No man is beyond salvation",' I heard him whisper. He would not meet my eyes, though I searched his for some explanation as he struggled to his feet. 'But I wish to God you'd killed me.'

14

Who hath wounds without cause?

Evidently, my work had not gone unappreciated by Cortina or his men. As darkness fell, Maria visited my room once more, bringing with her a tray of food, far finer than the previous day's offering. She also bore my habit and veil. They had been scrubbed clean of blood, and although they were spotted in places with dark stains, they smelled of rough soap and sun. I discarded the nightgown gratefully, and pulled the garments over my head. Finally, after a moment's pause, I added the rosary to my outfit.

I thanked the younger woman for her assistance as she poured coffee. 'I have seen such things in the past, but it must have been disturbing for you,' I said.

She only shrugged, continuing with her work. 'I did as asked.'

Her voice had the same careful tone I had noticed the night before, as though she were choosing each word before she spoke it.

'You did more than that,' I smiled, rising to help her. 'Those men might have died, if not for you.'

The jug slipped from her fingers and burst open upon the floor, hot liquid spilling out into a puddle. I stooped to retrieve the shards with her, asking what was wrong. My hand brushed across hers and she jerked backward, as if she had been stung.

'Nothing, *Madre,* forgive me.'

She stood to leave, but saw the flowers, lying untouched on the blanket.

'Lieutenant Carthy,' I began clumsily, sweeping them toward her. 'I do not want them.'

Slowly, she gathered up the jumble of trailing stems. I saw the

251

skin of her arms for the first time, scarred in rings from wrist to elbow, like recently healed burns. A tiny lift of a smile twitched upon her mouth.

'What are they?' I asked, curious at her response.

'*K'ineesh*,' she said quietly, turning them in her hands.

'What?'

She retreated into herself again, face closed.

'That is their old name,' she told me, throwing the flowers into a bucket by the door.

She lingered at the threshold, as if to ask me a question. The only thing that hinted at her state of mind were her heavy brows, lowered into a frown. Finally, she raised her eyes to mine – that same black, disquieting gaze.

'They will die soon,' she said.

If I wanted to follow her, I was not able to. Two men remained posted outside of the room. It seemed I was neither prisoner, nor free to leave, though Cortina had given his word. I stared at the discarded flowers and pondered my future.

I would leave that place alone, I decided. I had redeemed myself. Carthy would no longer be a yoke around my neck, a reminder of my transgressions. I had the lives of five men, Mexican and American, to act as credit on my account. It was time to remember what I had left St. Louis to do; find some place in that world where I could work good. I would discard the darkness in my soul, the violence that came too easily to my hands, and live a life of penitence with the memories of my sin.

When Cortina came to visit, as the night grew cooler, I was prepared to meet him.

'Sister.' He bowed slightly as he entered. Deep lines swept beneath his eyes. Much of his arrogant manner seemed subdued by the events of the previous night. 'I have come from the men.'

'How do they fare? I would like to see to them myself, if I am permitted.'

'Their wounds are bad still, yet I think they live.'

He fished a wad of tobacco from his pocket and pulled off a hunk, chewing thoughtfully upon it for a good while. I decided to allow him time to address our bargain, for my release would no doubt pain him.

'I am a difficult man,' he sighed, lowering himself to the bench. 'We know this. I have no desire to chase always right or wrong, the good or the bad. But my men, they trust me. They come to me from the madness of this country, looking for a father who will fight. And so, I hate to lose any of my sons. You understand?'

I nodded, though I did not – not fully.

'I made you a promise,' he said. 'Five of six, they live.'

'And I hope they shall spend their days in peace, as much as this world will allow,' I smiled, offering my hand. 'I will stay to see them healed before I go, then there will be no more debt.'

'*Claro*,' Cortina agreed, climbing to his feet. My hand hovered in the air between us. 'But you see, I look to my sons, as a good parent must. Their lives, and our fight, it needs money. American dollars go far, in the right places.'

My heart began to thud in my throat.

'You promised I would be free,' I managed, though my jaw was tight with anger. 'You gave me your word.'

'*Madre*!' said Cortina, banging at the edge of the door. 'You said yourself you acted for the Lord alone, never for me.'

A clank of metal came from the hallway, and I backed away, knowing what would come next. Sure enough, two men entered, bearing iron cuffs, a length of chain between them.

'No!' I cried.

'Five hundred dollars,' called Cortina over my struggles, the men pinning my arms between them, forcing the metal closed across my wrists. 'And the good will of the Union. Do not struggle. You will be in the New Mexico Territory before the month is out. But I will treat you well. I will not lock you here, like an animal. You will be allowed still to care for my men. I am not unreasonable, Tomás Josephine.'

I dragged at the chains. Coarse iron cuffs chafed my skin, links the length of my forearm hanging between them. I refused to satisfy Cortina with fear, but stood defiant, staring him in the eye.

He had paused in the doorway to examine the flowers in the bucket. 'The lieutenant will no doubt return with you. You do not like his gift?'

'*K'ineesh*?' I said, bitterly. 'Is that what you call them? I did not think anything worthwhile could grow, out here.'

'*Madre*, even here there is some beauty. But they are *alfombrilla*,' he corrected me over his shoulder, as the door was swung closed. '*K'ineesh* is their Indian name.'

Had he waited a moment longer he would have seen my expression freeze at his words. As it was, I remained motionless, despite the drag of the chains upon my wrists.

I saw again Maria dropping the coffee when I talked about the men, saw her stony face as one by one they writhed in pain beneath her gaze. I heard her, murmuring those parting words as she dropped the flowers, in an accent so different from any other Mexican woman I had encountered.

Her voice was a terrible promise: *they will die soon*.

15

As clouds and wind
when no rain followeth

It was an hour or more before I was permitted to leave my cell, to make a visit to the patients who remained in my care. I hurried across the camp, as fast as I was able without arousing suspicion. It was quiet; those who were on watch observed my progress across the open space, but did not stop me.

I was trapped, they knew. Even if I was not chained, the desert spread vast and deadly, all around. Bullets or horses would stop me before I made twenty paces out of the camp; and if by some miracle they didn't, the heat would serve as executioner in their place.

Perhaps I had been too long among the savagery of the west, but my nerves had been thrumming a warning ever since Cortina's words: *that is their Indian name*. For all my anxiety, I prayed that my suspicions were unfounded.

My feet moved with silent speed as I reached the tent and pushed through the canvas. An oil lamp had been left burning low, and now cast its shadows upon a scene of horror.

Blood dripped from every bed, soaking into pillows. The men's throats had been slit. Many of their eyes were open, as if in surprise at the blade that had cleaved through flesh and arteries. Movement caught my eye; a Union man's chest was jerking, the last life draining from his sundered neck.

Four of five were dead. In the darkest corner of the tent, the final survivor slept. Standing above him was Maria. Her face was composed despite the blood spattered across her cheeks, and for one, endless moment, she held my gaze, eyes hollow. Then she was moving; one hand pulling back the man's hair, dragging a curved blade through his skin.

I ran forward too late, my choked cry lost in his own, in the hiss of blood that burst from his flesh. I knelt upon the covers, trying desperately to hold the wound closed with my shackled hands, even as I felt his life stream through my fingers. He was an American whose leg I had re-set the day before, who had thanked me, as he had sweated in pain. Now his eyes begged wordlessly. They were the same color as Abe's and I felt my tears spilling as he convulsed twice, three times and died.

'I'm sorry,' I sobbed, again and again, 'I'm sorry.'

I heard a ripping sound and spun, terrified, expecting a knife to come slicing toward me.

The canvas at the back of the tent billowed open, split to make a doorway. Lurching to my feet, I stared wildly out into the night, but the woman was gone.

'Mother of God!' a man's voice croaked behind me. Carthy stood in the tent opening, frozen. Behind him I could see a group of men, hear their jovial chatter as they came toward the make-shift hospital wing, bearing bottles and plates.

'What have you done?'

16

The fire never saith:
'It is enough'

Six pairs of eyes traveled the room, to fix upon me, the only living creature at its center. Blood dripped from the iron at my wrists. The knife was at my feet, discarded in the dirt, red with guilt.

One man began to retch, and the stunned silence finally cracked open with cries and curses and weapons withdrawn from belts. None were quicker than Carthy. Wounded as he was, he limped into the room with such fury that the men fell back behind him. In his good hand a pistol shook, armed and ready to fire.

'I knew it,' he rasped, eyes bright. 'I knew that I was right to hunt you down, you cold-blooded bitch.'

My mind had ceased operation. I stared at the inlay of the familiar pistol, Muir's beloved possession so alien in Carthy's hand.

'This was not me,' I heard myself saying, as if correcting a simple misunderstanding. 'It was the woman.'

Several of the men surged forward, murder in their eyes, but Carthy barked at them to stay back, all at once inhabiting the body of the soldier he had once been. Reluctantly, they obeyed, flanking him on either side.

'Was this *revenge*?' he demanded of me, face twisted. 'To strike at Cortina for breaking his word? Some of these were your countrymen!'

'I saved them!' I protested. Alarm finally broke through my shock, as I realized the danger I was in. 'You watched me, all of you.'

'*Puta*,' the man who had translated for me spat.

'Saved them to preserve your own skin,' Carthy sneered, before I could speak.

'No, I—'

'Go and get Cortina,' he ordered, interrupting me. All but one of the men set off at a run. 'He must know of this. And fetch some rope. We shall have to restrain her.'

'You know this is not true,' I cried, taking a step toward him. He only brought the pistol up, to aim all the truer.

'Do not give me reason to fire, Josephine,' he whispered. 'It would be too brief an end for you. I want you to have time before you die, to think about the lives you have taken. How many is that now? How many times have you failed your God? You tried with me and now you have succeeded with these miserable souls.'

'You are the one who drove me here, across the country, across the desert,' I shouted. Rage finally broke through every restraint I had struggled to keep in place. 'Were it not for men like you—'

'Men like me?' Carthy crowed. 'What kind is that, Sister? Those who fight for their country, for honor?'

'There is no honor in your fight! You know nothing of justice, or mercy!' The chains rattled at my wrists, but I stared unflinchingly into his eyes. 'Abraham Muir understood. He was a good man. You might have been too.'

Carthy's jaw was trembling, whether from exertion or emotion, I could not tell. Eyes never leaving mine, he swung the pistol around and fired at point-blank range into the remaining guard's chest.

'I am a good man,' he moaned, even as the guard writhed upon the floor.

He returned the gun to my head, eyes wild. I knew then that his mania was no temporary affliction: that he was truly mad. I threw my hands protectively before my face as the gun exploded a second time.

The chains shattered at my wrists, hot metal flying. When I opened my eyes, he was already limping toward me, through the smoke and the powder in the air, shoving the pistol into my

hands. The barrel still smoked. His ruined fingers were scrabbling to release the second gun and the holster.

I tried to speak, in protest, in question, but he only grasped
one of my bloody hands and dragged it down his face. I felt his
skin, burning and damp with sweat, and for a moment, I held
on. Then he pushed me toward the back of the tent, pain twisting
his face.

'To hell with you,' he gasped, as shouts began to echo across
the camp. 'To hell with you. Go.'

Nunslinger: Book 6

The Judgment of Abraham

The True Tale of how Sister Thomas Josephine of St. Louis, Missouri, journeyed through the Desert to fight alongside Rebels at the Battle of El Paso del Norte

I

After him they brought the sixth . . .

My ears rang from the noise of gunshots, thundering against the canyon walls. Orange starbursts flared. Rock and dust exploded near my head.

I had run in blind panic, stumbling into the rocky hills and gullies that surrounded the camp rather than fleeing toward certain death in the desert. And now I crouched, surrounded by sharp rocks and black night.

The darkness was terrifying, near absolute, with barely a scrap of moonlight to see by. I did not know what I was doing, I only knew that I had to run, and it had to be far, had to be fast. The drying blood upon my palms became mingled with dirt as I fell, plunging blindly down slopes, taking the narrowest paths, where men and horses would not be able to follow.

There had been no time for thought. No time to get my bearings, to be logical. My hands still burned from the feel of Carthy's skin as he pushed the holster into my arms, from the wildness in his voice as he cursed me, even as he saved me.

My foot skidded on loose stones and I tumbled from a ledge, landing heavily. Somewhere above, I heard the holler of dogs, snatching up my scent. I was being hunted, not for bounty but for revenge.

In the weak moonlight I saw a hill, a slope so steep it was almost vertical. It would be a difficult climb, yet it might slow down my pursuers. I began to scramble upward. Steeper and steeper it became, the dirt sliding away beneath my boots, until I was forced to cling with my fingertips.

The ground was a long way below me now; if I fell it would

be into the hands of my enemies. I could hear them beneath, quarrelling in the darkness.

I clawed my way up another few feet, praying I would reach the top soon. A bullet skimmed past, inches from my head, but I refused to stop, refused to contemplate what would happen if I felt hot metal pierce the flesh of my back.

Finally, I dragged myself to the top of the ridge and stood. Triumphantly, I caught one fleeting glance of the barren landscape that surrounded me, shadows pooling in endless rocky valleys, before the earth shattered beneath me.

I lost my balance and fell into the unknown blackness below.

2

The way of a ship
in the midst of the sea

I do not know for how long I lay insensible. I felt grit beneath my body, but could not move or summon thought. Then the pain began, gradually at first; a deep pounding in my head that grew sharper with each heartbeat. I felt like I had been beaten as I rolled over onto my back.

My ears rang, but beyond that there was nothing. No shouting or gunfire, no sound save for a papery whisper, rising and falling like the wings of moths. I opened my eyes. Plants surrounded me, sprouting waist-high from the dust and sand. All were dead, bleached pale as parchment. A wiry moon had come out to illuminate them. There was no decay there, just an absence of life, scoured clean by the scavenging desert.

I rose to my knees. My arms and legs were a tapestry of scrapes and grazes. After a brief hunt I found the holster, thankfully with pistols intact. I thought I heard a snatch of human voices upon the breeze, but they were far away.

For the first time it struck me, as I watched a gust of wind rattle the skeleton stems, that I was alone. I had run yes, had evaded my would-be killers, but to what end? I was lost in a land where life and death were a matter of hours, rather than years. I had no food, no water.

I staggered to my feet, desperate for the Lord to send me a sign, give me guidance. I looked for Him in that cruel landscape, tried to see a trace of His hand, but all was darkness, and pain. I recalled Carthy's words, warning me that I would die slowly, alone with the memories of those I had wronged. By an act of mercy he had spared me, and by that same act I was condemned.

My foot caught on something and I fell sprawling among the wasted scrub. The dead leaves scraped at my face like fingers. I closed my eyes in despair.

I was woken by the sun, sliding inexorably across my face. The chill had already ebbed from the earth. All too soon the heat would become unbearable. I sat up. During that long night I had struggled, had prayed and found no answer. Yet there was no way back. I could only move forward, as I had done since St. Louis, and trust that my feet were firm upon His path.

In any case, walking seemed a better occupation than staring at the dust and waiting to die. Wearily I climbed to my feet. The rosary clattered around my neck, miraculously intact. A superstitious part of me wondered whether it was somehow alive, whether the beads would not allow the world to break them apart. I put aside such thoughts and began my morning devotion.

By the time I had finished, my brow was damp with sweat. My ankle throbbed when I placed weight upon it, but held. I had no excuse now, nothing to prevent me from pushing through the scrub and walking onward, into the wilderness.

3

The way of a serpent upon a rock

The desert spread before me, too much and nothing all at once, fading into the horizon. Craters sagged here and there, as though the ground had been pocked by some ages-old disease and never healed.

"'In a desert land, and where there is no way, and no water, so I have come before thee,'" I whispered, "'to see thy power and glory.'"

It was not long before my mouth became too dry to recite, before my head began to swim with the heat. I looked upon death, waiting for me on the plain, and walked out to meet it.

My mind began to play tricks on me; showing shimmering pools of water that were not real and could never be reached. Sometimes, the sand beneath my feet grew so deep that I found myself sinking, and had to fight my way upright.

The sun roared past its zenith as I set one foot before the other. My eyelids drooped closed for two paces, three. When I opened them again, I found myself staring at a tall, dark shape. It was black as ink on the clear blue horizon, and looked like a figure.

As I approached hesitantly, it resolved itself. A tree, gnarled branches thrown to the sky. It was old, bark scored by centuries of buzzard claws. I reached out to touch its surface: warm as flesh and flaking away. It was life, of a sort, a fitting place to end my travels. I sank down at its base, dropping the pistols beside me. I would not need them any more. They would be a gift, for whoever might find me here, one day.

My strength was exhausted, my skin burning and blistered. I felt the day pass, the sun sink toward the horizon, felt night seep in. I had begun to shiver when the noise started up, a sound like bones rattling against each other, the dead rising.

I grasped the beads at my neck as the sound continued, hard and sharp. Abruptly, I heard Abe's voice, a ghost from another lifetime, telling me the story of how Rattle got his name . . .

My eyelids flew open. The snake was coiled behind my pistols, raised up and ready to strike. Blind fear sent me lunging for the weapons. The creature struck faster than I could have imagined, fangs sinking into my outstretched arm like a dart. I cried in pain and fell back, dragging one of the guns free. My boots scored tracks in the sand as I scrabbled away, trying to arm the weapon. The serpent gathered itself to strike again, and I fired wildly. Its head blew apart in a mess of scales and flesh.

Two small puncture marks upon my arm pulsed and bled, the skin around them already beginning to swell. Dry sobs of terror rose in my chest as I tried to rip my sleeve to form a tourniquet but found my fingers too weak.

The bite sent spasms of pain toward my chest and I crumpled to my side. Through the gathering darkness I thought I heard a horse approaching. I struggled to turn my head, terrified of what horror the desert might subject me to next, and found myself staring into eyes, liquid dark as a raven's, above the glint of a knife.

4

The way of the eagle in the air

I smelled twigs burning, hot ash brushing across my skin. Above me, the stars were punctures in the night sky. A woman was there. She looked like Maria, but her every feature shifted through the smoke, distant one moment, close the next. She leaned in and I tried to cry out as she set her teeth against the mottled flesh of my wounded arm.

I felt her suck at the snakebite, spitting free mouthfuls of blood and saliva. I thought I saw something of myself spilling from the wound into the sand – part of my soul, draining irrevocably away. The pain came again, crawling across my shoulder to squat upon my chest.

I saw Maria put a handful of something in her mouth and chew upon it. Her lips and teeth were black with flecks. She opened her mouth to reveal a blackish mass, and I flinched away as she gathered the darkness from her tongue and pressed it to my wound.

Then the edge of a flask appeared, liquid trickling over my lips, and I was afraid, because to drink the water was to drink the night and the emptiness of a tomorrow I thought never to see.

But see it I did. I next opened my eyes to twilight and a sky like the skin of a peach. For a moment, I dreamed I lay upon soft grass, with early summer all around me. But soon I heard movement, smelled the scratch of flaming twigs. I struggled to raise myself on my good arm. Maria knelt before a fire pit, coaxing flames from a heap of the dried offerings of the desert.

I was too weak to try to flee as she looked up at me through the smoke, eyes opaque. Not until the fire was burning well did she approach.

'You have slept,' she told me bluntly. She began to untie a strip of cloth that wrapped my lower arm. The skin there was still inflamed, I noticed, but less so.

I had too many questions, abhorrence at the memory of her with the blood of men upon her hands; yet I could not find a way to bring my thoughts together.

'Am I going to die?' My voice was cracked from lack of use. 'The rattlesnake?'

The woman snorted dismissively.

'That was no rattlesnake,' she brushed away a layer of dried leaf matter from the wound. 'A crooked snake only, you saw its trail?'

When I looked blankly, she ran her fingers through the dust next to me, in 's' shapes.

'He hide his tail in the dead leaves,' she said, 'makes them rattle like the rattlesnake. You hear that.'

'But the poison.'

She shrugged. 'It is not so bad. You made it worse, getting scared, making your heart beat fast. Even a child knows; stay calm after snakebites.'

Despite my state, I took exception to her tone. 'How did you find me?' I demanded. 'There is nothing but desert for miles.'

'You made a lot of noise,' she said, sitting back on her heels, obviously relishing my outrage. 'Like a buffalo.'

I tried to sit upright, but she pushed me back with ease, retrieving a water flask.

'We all watched you,' she continued, 'the coyotes, the lizards and me. Drink.'

Had my thirst not been great I would have struggled to swallow the mouthfuls of stale water for anger. She had seen my suffering and let it go unaided, until it was almost too late. As it was, I let the liquid soothe my parched throat.

Maria returned to her seat by the fire, to a pile of fur on the ground. It was a jackrabbit, absurd ears hanging limp in death. She smoothed them for a moment, before skinning it with a few deft strokes, the knife an extension of her arm. As she gutted it

270

and skewered the carcass on a stick, I thought about her hands slicing through human throats, as if the men were nothing more than beasts.

'You are a murderer,' I whispered.

If she heard me, she made little sign of it. I shifted closer to the flames. My arm ached deeply and was still swollen to the shoulder, but I could move it. I tried to convince myself that it would be ungodly to share a meal with this woman, yet as the meat sizzled, I found that hunger overcame my resolve.

I had not eaten for a night and a day, and fell upon the food, tearing into the meat with my teeth. Only after a moment did I remember to give thanks to the Lord, and set my portion down to begin a hasty prayer.

I had lowered my eyes and begun to whisper when a noise broke through my concentration, grease being sucked from bones. I looked up. Maria was staring at me, chewing deliberately.

'Do you not pray?' I snapped.

She was piling the slippery bones in front of her, sorting through them as if they were puzzle pieces, and she a child at play.

'No.'

'You have death on your hands,' I could not help myself from saying, 'they were innocent men.'

She stood abruptly, taking up the knife and jamming it into her belt. Her hair was loose and draped her face like a shroud.

'Maria,' I began.

'That was never my name.'

She strode off into the night. When I called again, she stopped, just at the edge of the firelight. I could not see her mouth move when she spoke.

'Those men were not innocent.'

5

The length of days
is in her right hand

I was woken before dawn by the sounds of the woman who was not Maria moving about, kicking the smoldering embers into the ground and covering them with dust. A horse stood nearby. Whereas my own flight from Cortina's camp had been made empty-handed and in panic, she had been prepared to go. The realization that she had planned the attack made me furious.

'You intended to kill them,' I accused, swiping the sleep from my eyes. 'You murdered them in cold blood.'

She ignored me, striding forward to tug the blanket on which I slept from under me.

'Did you not hear me?' I demanded.

'It is time to leave,' she said, her voice calm. She moved to the horse and tightened the straps of its saddle. She looked dressed for traveling. Her long hair was braided tightly, a broad hat sheltering her brow. She had replaced her homespun skirt with a thick pair of men's trousers, the long knife she had used yesterday sheathed at her belt.

'Who are you?' I was anxious for any clue about her. 'Please, tell me. Cortina said that the name you gave those flowers was Indian.'

'Yes. He knew of my people,' she offered blandly. 'I would have killed him too, were he not so well guarded.'

'But do you not see?' I said, following her. 'It is not for us to mete out judgment. The Lord will condemn sinners when their time comes.'

'As you did, *Madre*?'

The words were bitter in her mouth. As I held her gaze, I saw again Carthy's anguished face, pushing me away, crippled by the wound in his stomach.

'I know my sins,' I whispered, 'as you know yours.'

'I know nothing of sin.' She swung herself up into the saddle. 'A man kills and is killed in return. That is not sin, only life.'

She clucked her horse forward. It was only then that I comprehended the reality of the situation. The ground around me was empty, save for the pistols in their holster.

'Wait,' I called, slinging the weapons awkwardly over my shoulder. 'Where are you going?'

'Toward sin,' she said, her voice mocking. 'You would not like it. Better to stay here and die well.'

'Why save me then?' I stumbled after the horse as fast as I could. 'Why did you save my life if you intended to leave me here?'

'My fight is not your fight.'

I stopped running then and laughed, a harsh sound. My response made her pull up short. By the time she looked back, I already had a pistol aimed at her head.

'I would gladly lay down my life in service of the Lord,' I told her grimly, 'even if it was to repair only one of the wrongs in this broken world. But I cannot do his work if I am dead. Take me with you, and I shall pray for your salvation.'

She tilted her hat back to see me clearly, one dark brow raised. After a moment, she indicated the space behind her saddle.

With difficulty, I clambered up, and took hold of the cantle with my good hand. I remembered riding thus with Abe, my arm secure around his waist, his skin warming the hide of his jacket. I clung on as the woman kicked the horse into a trot once more.

'You should load those pistols, *Madre*,' she said.

6

Come, let us lie in wait for blood

It had never been my intention to ride pillion with a murderer, and knowledge of that made my journey far from easy. I was silent, doubtful of the Lord's intention to throw me in with this woman. Yet I had no choice: it was ride or die.

Somewhere, men were hunting me. Cortina or the Union, or both. I had no doubt that news of my transgressions would spread; that my bounty would be increased. And what of Carthy? Was it his madness that had spared me, or his conscience? If he had truly begun to repent, he might yet convince the world of my innocence.

The woman before me shifted in the saddle, and I glared at the brim of her hat. *She* was the guilty party, yet was acting as though nothing had happened.

'Where are we going?' I snapped. The silence that had held for the past few hours was beginning to grate.

'Does it matter?'

I swallowed a sharp retort. The sky did not help. It was a flat, blinding sheet of cloud, turning the air thick in my lungs, making my head throb along with the ache in my arm. I could feel blisters forming from where I kept a tight hold of the saddle.

'I should like to know,' I tried, more patiently.

'East,' she said.

'And what is east?'

'My business.'

'Which is?'

She did not answer. After a brief prayer to the Lord for wisdom, I tried again.

'You know my name. What am I to call you, if not "Maria"?'

For a long while, I could hear only the beat of the horse's hooves against the hard earth. A breeze had picked up, so that when she finally spoke, the sound was almost lost.

'*Náscha*,' she murmured softly. 'In my language it means "owl". You may call me that.'

'That is your name?' I said.

'It is the one I have taken. I had another, once, but I cannot wear it any longer.'

I thought of a small girl running wild in the muddy St. Louis streets, blonde curls matted with dirt, stolen money clenched within her fingers. I too had a different name then, one that could not be worn by Sister Thomas Josephine.

'How did you come to choose it?' I asked less sharply.

It was a long time before she replied.

'My people believe that they carry evil on their wings, the owls,' she answered. 'They bring death wherever they go. It seemed to fit.'

'You mean you have killed before?'

She turned her head a fraction, and I caught the edge of her look. Beyond, cloud was gathering into a boiling mass, cutting the horizon in two.

'There is a storm coming,' she said.

We did not speak again as the sky grew sick and heavy, clouds rolling violently overhead, whipping the sand into our faces. The rain came before we could find shelter, pounding down in sheets. Finally, the side of a crater reared before us, and the horse was steered into a narrow cave. We shook and shivered from the damp after the heat of the day, until the woman who was called Owl hunted out a pile of soggy twigs and started a fire at the lip of the cave. It smoked more than burned, yet offered comfort. As my habit began to dry, I stared into the weak flames, lost in thought.

'They stole my life.'

Her voice broke over the crackling, startling me out of a doze. The rain continued to beat down, water on dust. She stared through the smoke, not at me but into me, as if she could do away with speech and place the words inside my skin.

275

'They stole my life, those men, others like them,' she continued. 'My people were the *Diné*. Our home was in the canyons north of your border with Mexico. They cut it smaller and smaller over the years, but still they came, the men in blue. They were not content with the land they stole. They wanted more. Our animals, our holy places, they wanted all that gave us hope.

'They had a great hollow inside them, and they ate and ate to try and fill it. We fought back in our ways, and they theirs. We took supplies: they burned our food. We stole guns and they poisoned the water. Through hunger and sickness and battle, they sorted living from dead.

'Those who survived, marched. Hundreds of miles, to unknown places, the men with blue jackets driving us on. Their faces were not of proud fighters but of wolves, starved from winter, ready to eat the flesh of their own kind.

'Others came to prey. The slavers waited in shadow for those who fell behind, sick. They killed us, or took us. They tied us hand and foot, drove us into Mexico to be sold. And the men in blue knew this. They did nothing.'

She pushed back the sleeves of her shirt, raising her forearms to the faint glow of the fire. The scars I had seen before circled the flesh, a dozen times, wrist to elbow.

'They forgot we could hear,' she said, watching my face, 'the men who bought us. And they talked and talked. I learned Spanish, that way. I learned English. And when I knew enough—'

'You escaped.' The sound of my voice took me by surprise.

Owl settled back against the cave wall.

'No,' she told me, closing her eyes with a sigh. 'I began to hunt.'

7

Then thou shalt mourn at the last

'How many men have you killed?'

Try as I might, I could not keep the edge of disgust from my voice. While the rain had fallen, we had reached a truce – albeit uneasy – yet I could not forget the woman's crimes, even dependent as I was upon her good will. I gripped the rosary, trying to find a way to see her in the light of God's mercy.

Owl did not answer me.

'Were they all Union men?' I tried again.

As usual, she ignored me, hunting through the saddlebags for the few tools she carried to set up camp. The rain had finally ceased, and outside the evening was calm.

'Feed the horse,' she ordered, wedging a smaller knife into the top of her boot. 'I will find food.'

After she had gone, I sat still and spent time flexing my aching arm. Finally, with nothing else to do, I went to find the corn and look to the mount we were sharing. It was a large beast, with a chestnut coat that would have shone had it not been for the dust. The saddle also bore the marks of wealth. Stolen like the horse, no doubt. It had patterns tooled into the leather, and silver details, some of which had been hacked free. Trying to ignore the guilt I felt at looking through another's possessions, I began to search the packs for my bullets.

They were not there. Nor did I find anything else of use. The woman lived as spartan an existence as was humanly possible. She owned nothing beyond one homespun skirt, a faded blue scarf, several bags of dried beans and corn, a pot and some matches.

'You want these?'

I had not heard her approach. I felt my face redden, caught prying. She was holding out a handful of the bullets.

'Yes,' I said, raising my chin. 'I should like them back.'

'What does your God say, a holy woman with a weapon?' She crammed them into her pocket, and dropped down before the fire. I saw wet dirt upon her fingers; the water flask dripped nearby. In the other hand, she carried a large lizard. Her fingers were dark with its blood. I tried not to retch as she worked the small knife through its beaded hide, revealing gleaming muscle.

'I thought you were looking for supper?' I swallowed, turning my face to the fresh breeze.

'This is supper,' she returned, absorbed in her task. 'You did not answer my question.'

I could not watch as she cleaned the animal, so I looked out to the desert.

'The Lord moves in mysterious ways,' I answered slowly, 'and so I must believe that this is the path He has chosen for me to walk. I have sinned, and no doubt I shall sin again before my time is through. I had hoped that I might work some good in the west, no matter how small.' I risked a glance over my shoulder to find her watching me, knife poised. 'I do what I must.'

She held my gaze for a long moment.

'I have killed nine,' she told me softly, 'not all Union. Not all men.' She held up a bullet. 'I also do what I must. You have these back, *if* you help me.'

'I will not kill.'

She waved my words aside before I could finish. 'There is a ranch, a day or two from this place. They took some of my people for slaves.'

'You want to free them?' I said.

She returned to work on the lizard. 'Alone, it is hard. With another to watch, to shoot,' she shrugged, 'perhaps no one will die.'

'Do I have a choice?'

'You could stay here.'

Grudgingly, I held out my hand, allowing her to pour the

ammunition into my palm. I tried to ignore the ease with which I slipped the bullets into the chambers, the feeling of comfort that came from holding a fully loaded gun.

Across the fire, Owl was grinning at something. When I grunted in question, she held up the freshly skinned, spitted lizard.

'Heads or tails?'

8

And poverty shall come as a runner, and beggary as an armed man

It took us three days to reach the ranch. By the time we saw the thin line of smoke fading into the sky, we had become accustomed to each other, and so I did not hesitate to follow when Owl slid from the horse in order to creep closer under the cover of greasewood bushes.

I had quickly learned that it was unwise to mention the crimes that stained both of our hands, unless I was prepared to withstand hours of strained silence and biting remarks about my own transgressions. Instead, we shared the sound of the desert, the flurries of life against the sandy ground, the high, mournful circles of buzzards. As my arm lost its stiffness, I taught her how to hunt jackrabbits with the pistols, the way Abe had taught me. She in turn showed me how to catch food with nothing but a blade, and smirked at my disgust the first time I tried to skin a snake.

I did speak of my adventures, sometimes, when the fire burned low at night. Owl listened, sitting so still that I almost forgot she was there. Once, I told of our escape from the steamer, described Abe rolling Templeton up as if he were a pudding. The laugh that burst from her was so unexpected that for a moment I only stared, before my own laughter joined hers. Too soon though, I remembered that my old friend was no longer with me. I lay and watched the heavens turn, drowning myself in their remoteness.

Now, the woman next to me snorted in annoyance, eyes narrowed to peer at the lonely ranch.

'I see no one,' she murmured, 'only a hound, but there is smoke.'

'We shall have to get closer,' I said.

'They will see us.'

'And what if they do? They will not shoot women, out of the blue,' I whispered. 'Take off your hat.'

She scowled but obeyed, cramming it under her arm as we strode out of the scrubland and toward the wooden structure. We had not taken more than twenty paces before the door flew open and an old man stumped out, an ancient rifle in his hands. I began to call a greeting only for a bullet to whistle past my head.

'"They will not shoot at women,"' Owl mimicked, ducking low. There was nowhere to run or hide, no cover from the onslaught.

'Perhaps he cannot see properly,' I shouted.

The dirt exploded several inches from my boot.

'We must run, come back when it is dark,' Owl was saying, but before she could finish I was pushing her aside, commending myself to the Lord as I hid a pistol in my sleeve and fumbled for the rosary at my neck. She yelled for me to come back, but I ran into the open, hands raised.

'Stop!' I cried, expecting every moment to feel a bullet smash into my ribs. 'We wish you no harm, in the name of the Lord!'

An empty shell clattered to the wooden porch as the echo of gunfire faded away. The man peered at me, mouth open, as though I were some strange creature that had wandered into his yard. His hair was more yellow than white, frayed by the sun and the wind. His eyes were clouded with rheum; otherwise his aim might have been true.

'What in the name of damnation,' he whistled around a brace of teeth. 'Is that a *nun*?'

I felt the heat rise to my face, tried to keep my voice steady as I approached, hands crossed into my sleeves in a show of peace.

'I am a Bride of Christ,' I said. 'We are just travelers, looking for—'

The man began to wheeze like a pair of old bellows. His gummy eyes watered as he doubled over with laughter.

'A goddam nun,' he hiccupped, over and again. 'A real goddam *nun*.'

I gently moved the barrel of the rifle aside, to stand on the porch beside him.

'Sir,' I began.

Still grinning, he began to inch his finger back toward the trigger.

'You come to the wrong place, Sister; ain't nothing but sinners here,' he said.

I groped for my pistol.

'I know, my son,' I told him, and struck him hard on the side of the head. He went down like a sack of potatoes before the smile had even faded from his face.

9

Be not with them that
fasten down their hands

As we had feared, the ranch was mostly deserted. Owl found a young Mexican boy hiding in the stable and dragged him into the house, where we had tied the old man to a chair. He had recovered his consciousness, if not his wits, but refused to answer any of my questions, alternating between groaning and cursing. When he saw the boy, he began roaring for his gun, until I was forced to arm the pistol in order to quiet him.

'We will not hurt you,' I told the child impatiently, with a stern look at Owl. She loosened her grip upon his shoulder, a little. 'We have some questions, is all. You speak English?'

'Damn bitch, goddam nun bitch,' the man snarled, and I waved the pistol at him again.

The boy interrupted in Spanish, and Owl listened closely for a moment.

'He says that the old man does not know what he says, that he is mad.' She muttered a question at the child. 'He says he does not like to be left alone here with him, but that the master has gone to town.'

'I know you!' the old man opened his cloudy eyes wide to stare at me. 'The crow from out east, they done told us about you!' He lapsed into laughter, spluttering to himself.

'What does he mean?' I demanded of the boy. The hairs on the back of my neck had risen, despite the sweltering cabin. 'What is he talking about?'

As Owl repeated my words in Spanish, the child's expression began to change. He backed up into her grip, which before he had been so eager to avoid. His face turned pale as he stared at the pistol in my hand, words tumbling out rapidly.

'He says that men rode through here,' Owl translated, 'a day ago. They had news of a slaughter in one of the camps, east of Altar.' She lapsed into silence, allowing the child to finish, and her mouth straightened into a hard line.

'What is it?' I demanded.

She shooed the boy into a corner, pulling me away from the old man. 'Cortina,' she whispered. 'He has sent out men, to all the towns. They are calling you *Cuervo*, the Crow. He is offering blood money for your head. Dollars and pesos.'

'And what do they say of you?' I said.

My chest was tightening in anger. I was being hunted once more, pursued by men like dogs, eager for my suffering. Owl shook her head slowly. Her face was closed, as ever, save for a shifting of her eyes.

'They do not know my name,' she confessed.

I lost control of my emotions, shoving her backward in rage and frustration, bringing my pistol level with her brow.

'Those deaths are on your head,' my voice shook, 'but now I will be the one to suffer for your crime.'

Her expression changed from shock to cold fury. I felt pressure against my side and glanced down to find one of her knives pressed into my ribs.

'You promised to help me,' she said, voice low. 'Keep your word, and I will help you in return.'

'How can I even trust you?'

'I am no liar.'

My anger subsided, leaving my head buzzing. I lowered my arm and Owl pulled away, sheathing her knife. The old man was leering up at us in toothless interest, but the boy had vanished. Owl swore and ducked out into the yard, where settling dust was all that remained as evidence of the child's escape.

'He will ride for town, for El Paso del Norte,' she announced, gathering up her hat. 'He said that is where they have taken my people to be sold again. There is another horse in the stable.'

I nodded curtly. What need was there to fret over a stolen horse when I was wanted for murder? I snatched up the old man's rifle and slung it over my shoulder, though he hollered blasphemies at me, and turned to follow the other woman. Owl stopped in the doorway. The flaring sun cast her face into shadow.

'*Madre*,' she said, 'if you aim at me again, I will kill you.'

They eat the bread of wickedness
and drink the wine of iniquity

El Paso del Norte was two days' ride to the east, Owl said. The boy had taken one of the horses from the ranch's stable, and must have known another path, for we did not see him again.

The rest of that day, Owl's silence had a sharp edge, and she often rode ahead. My new mount was most capricious, but I could not bring myself to be harsh with him, for his bony gait reminded me of Rattle.

The land around us began to change, exchanging burned scrub for spiked green plants. The ever-distant hills grew closer, until they shed some of their haze and began to catch the shadows, like the mottled skin of a reptile.

My anger had long abated, calmed by the quiet ride. The situation was bleak, yet the worse it became, the more determined I was to cleave to my oath. Once more, the world had spat in my face, but if I could not meet it with charity and compassion, then I was not fit to wear the habit of a servant of the Lord.

When we finally stopped for the evening, in the first slopes and crevices of the hills, I produced a bag from one of my packs.

'Salted beef,' I told Owl, taking out the items one by one, 'beans, flour, and this.' The last was a bottle of spirit, an old yellow color. Owl pulled the cork and sniffed at it, recoiling with a grimace.

'Tequila,' she pronounced, and placed it on the ground, turning her unfathomable eyes upon me.

'From the ranch,' I explained, arranging my trophies. 'I did not think that old demon would miss them.'

'Why share them with me?'

I shifted awkwardly. It was true, I had planned to save the

provisions for myself, in case the time should come that I had to ride alone. Yet now . . .

'I am sick of eating snakes,' I retorted, and was rewarded with the faint trace of a smile.

After days of stringy game, the food was a feast. Owl used the flour and a little of our water to make flat rounds of bread, which we cooked on the embers of the fire, wrapping them around the chunks of beef and cramming them into our mouths like children with sweets. We even drank some of the tequila, perhaps in celebration of our unspoken peace, perhaps in anticipation of events to come. The night felt restless and aware, as if a great being lingered out of sight, waiting to be entertained by our rush toward danger on the morrow.

'El Paso del Norte is half a day, maybe,' Owl said, taking another sip and wincing. I had shuddered at the drink's taste too, yet now my chest felt warm, my mind less troubled than it had been in many weeks. 'They took us there to be sold, the slavers,' she explained.

'We will never be able to walk in the gate,' I told her, wiping my mouth and handing back the liquor. 'You heard that old man, I'm the *Cuervo*. They shall be out looking for me.'

'The Owl and the Crow,' she snorted into the bottle, 'it is like a story.'

The sky was crowded with stars, single, multitudinous. For a moment, I wished I could lie down and never venture further.

'A story that will end in death,' she continued, slumping back. 'Do not allow yesterday to swallow all of today,' she murmured a few moments later. 'My grandmother told me that. But she did not live in such times. There was life ahead, for her.'

I did not answer, for her voice in that stillness reminded me of another's. Of a man – a stranger then – with shadows shifting across his face as he warned me:

Some are ventured too far to return.

287

I I

If thou shalt seek her as money . . .

'This will never work.'

'*Madre,* you have not lived in a camp with men such as these. They are stupid and greedy.'

'What if—' I tried.

'Enough, there is no time,' she interrupted. 'You are prepared?'

Frantically, I checked the pistols and rifle. All were loaded.

'Yes, but—'

Owl kicked her horse into a gallop before I could finish, spraying me with grit. I peered out from behind the rock. She had changed into her plain skirt once again, unbraided her hair so that it streamed behind her as she rode. I watched as she drew level with a heap of boulders, smoke drifting from behind them. She pulled her horse to a stop in seeming surprise. Distantly, I heard male voices.

We had seen the men that morning from a ridge. Three in all, and a cart, piled high with something under a stained canvas tarpaulin. The track they followed was rutted with wheels and hoofprints; we were drawing close to El Paso del Norte.

The strategy was simple enough. Owl would ride up and distract the men, offer them the bottle of tequila, which was still full enough to dull their wits and senses in the fierce noon heat. Then . . . I did not want to think about the remainder of the plan. She had dismounted now and was walking out of sight, behind the boulders.

I closed my eyes for a moment and laid a clammy hand against my brow. My heart was pounding, and my mouth felt like I had been swallowing paste. Silently, I cursed the old man at the ranch for his volatile liquor, and myself, for being fool enough to drink it.

The sun had slipped a few inches further across the sky when I heard her shriek. I sat up as another cry rang out, hastily muffled. It was the work of moments to haul myself onto the horse, kick it fiercely into life. For once, it obeyed, pounding up the dusty track toward the camp.

The rifle was already in my hand as they came into view. Three men who looked Mexican, road dirt baked into their skin. The color of their jackets was impossible to discern, not that it mattered. One of them was wrestling a knife from Owl's hand while another grappled with her legs. His trousers were already unbuttoned and hung loose about his thighs. I dragged the horse to a stop, sighted the rifle just as I had seen Abe do, and fired.

The moment he collapsed to the ground in pain, Owl rolled to her knees, pulling the smaller knife from her belt. Before I could shout she had plunged it into the throat of the second man, twisting viciously and ducking aside as the blood began to spurt freely. I did not see him die, for the third man came staggering out from behind a rock, where he had obviously been engaged in his own business.

'Leave him!' I called to Owl as she raced toward him. The third man's face was pale beneath the dirt as I nudged my horse forward. Owl came to lay a hand upon its mane.

'Are you hurt?' I asked her, eyes never leaving the man.

'We should kill them all,' she said through gritted teeth.

'I would rather not have another soul upon my conscience.' I turned my attention back to the one man still standing.

'Remove your boots and jacket,' I ordered. When he hesitated, I fired into the ground at his feet. He seemed to understand my meaning after that, and did as I demanded. 'Now walk.' I indicated with the gun, away from the path. 'That way. And keep walking.'

'You shot *that* one,' Owl commented as I dismounted, watching the man I'd taken down whimper on the ground. 'Is *he* not also a soul upon your conscience?'

I walked over to the figure. He clutched at his behind with both hands. The bullet had embedded itself firmly in the muscle.

'No, he is a buttock on my conscience, which is another thing entirely,' I murmured. 'Ask him what he knows, and *try* not to kill him. If he moves, tell him I will shoot the other cheek.'

I turned to check the progress of the walking man. My heart was thudding in my chest, enough to raise the blood. Not through fear, entirely. I could see the fleshy speck that was his face pointed toward me, and raised my rifle again. He whipped around and resumed his pace.

No, it was not fear I felt, but excitement.

A strange gurgling noise pulled me from my thoughts. Owl had one knee pressed to the man's chest, the long knife buried in his throat. I cried out in exasperation. Her eyes found mine, flat and uncompromising as she pushed back her hair with a bloodied hand.

'He moved,' she said.

Thankfully, he had also talked. They were survivors of a recent skirmish that had spilled over the border; a turf war to gain control of the weapons supply going north between the Confederacy and the Union. The men had sided with the Confederacy, who had triumphed. Their dubious reward had been responsibility for the transportation, back to the temporary headquarters in the city.

'Transportation of what?' I asked Owl, heading for the covered cart. The smell should have warned me. I threw back the canvas – stiff with stains – and the stench rolled over me. Death, sickly sweet, filled my nostrils and throat like tar. I covered my face with my sleeve, trying to cough it free, but it was too late, the rotting smell was inescapable.

'The dead,' Owl said briskly, peering over my shoulder at the bodies piled high in the cart. 'Our way in to El Paso del Norte.'

. . . then shalt thou understand
the fear of the Lord

'I cannot breathe.'

Owl shushed me. 'We are coming into the city. There are sol-diers nearby.'

She pushed me down, squashing my head beneath the canvas. Together, we had cleared a small space among the bodies for me to hide. I had been violently opposed to the idea, but I under-stood – as she did – that the likelihood of sneaking into the city any other way without being seen was slim. The cart lurched over a pothole and an arm landed near my face. I covered my mouth, shut my eyes tight, and prayed for the mess of lost lives around me.

Through a tear in the canvas I saw lamplight flicker, heard the horse's hooves change tone as we clattered through a gate into a half-paved square. Night had fallen.

I had insisted on offering some final words over the bodies of the two men Owl had killed. She did not like it, but left me to pray for their souls as best I could. She contented herself with rifling through their saddlebags and tying their horses to the back of the cart. In their possessions she found more bullets for my pistols and a large knife. This she took for herself, looking pleased, hiding it at her waist with the others.

I held my breath as the cart clattered to a stop, trying not to think about what would happen were I to be found; I, a wanted fugitive, hiding beneath corpses, armed to the teeth with the guns of dead men.

I heard her exchanging curt words with someone in Spanish. The conversation was short, to my utmost relief, and we had just started to move again when a different voice called out.

'Wait there! What is this?'

Had I been in the habit of swearing, I should have done so then. The voice was American, a thick, southern drawl. I could not help but sneak a look. A man was restraining the bridle of Owl's horse, peering up at her. His jacket was a threadbare, vegetable color, yet I saw gold thread, glinting upon the collar. *Confederates*.

'What do you do here?' he demanded.

'She come from near the battle,' a Mexican voice explained hesitantly. 'Some men pay her to bring the dead.'

'And you were going to let her through?' The soldier's eyes were bloodshot from too long in the sun and too little sleep. 'Those Lincolnites are trying everything to get at us here. We must be careful.'

The Mexican mumbled what might have been an apology, but I did not hear him. The Confederate captain was moving toward the cart.

God help me, I thought and tugged at the bodies. Their lifeless weight rolled on top of me, smothering me with the stench of death and decay. My eyes watered as I tried to keep nausea down. I saw a flicker of light, felt a gasp of fresh air as the tarpaulin was pulled back. For a moment, I was sure that the captain's weary eyes found mine through the tangled limbs, but then he too was covering his face with his sleeve, pale beneath his sunburn.

'Goddam waste,' he said, to himself. 'Tell her to take them to the garrison for identification,' he barked at the Mexican, wiping his hands upon his trousers as he left, although he had not touched anything except the canvas.

The next few minutes were some of the worst of my life. With every jolt, the weight of the bodies grew more suffocating, and panic began to fill my mind: the thought that I might be killed by dead men. By supreme effort I stayed calm, until finally I heard Owl's voice whispering above me.

'We are at the garrison; the man said this is where they hold prisoners. Are you ready?'

I tried to make a noise in response, but there was no air in my lungs. Owl pulled the tarpaulin off and pushed the bodies away, allowing me to fight my way out from under them. I leaned over the edge of the cart, gulping at the clean air and shuddering all over. She looked down in disgust.

'Why were you underneath them?' she said. 'You will smell terrible.'

My face must have warned her that to continue to speak would not be the wisest choice. She motioned for me to hide, and I reluctantly ducked back under the canvas as she called out in Spanish for someone to open the gate. As quietly as I could, I armed the guns. Through the hole in the tarpaulin I made out a brick building, hastily patched and extended with raw wood. We were in some form of courtyard, the ground churned and pitted by boots and debris. The gate clattered shut behind us.

'Aw, hell,' I heard an American voice swear nearby. 'Jack, come help here.'

'What you yellin' for?' came a second man's reply.

'Some woman's brought them boys from upriver. Heard they got shot up good,' the first man said, drawing closer. 'Heard they're a goddam lead mine, every one of 'em. Let's get 'em laid out, poor bastards.'

I waited until the last moment, nerves thrumming through my body. Finally, as the tarpaulin was pushed back I sprang upright and leveled both pistols at the man's face. The other soldier made to cry out, only for the sound to be cut off by the blade that appeared against his throat.

'*Ave,* gentlemen,' I said.

13

For she hath cast down
many wounded

The man cast rapid glances back toward us as we made our way down the corridor. He was slight, with drooping moustaches that gave him a hangdog look. One hand was pressed to a small cut on his neck. Owl had suggested that we only needed one man. I had restrained her from killing either, but compromised by knocking the larger of the two senseless with the butt of the rifle. It seemed less messy than the alternative.

'Prisoners are down there,' the soldier said, indicating a set of stairs into the older part of the building. It was dark and musty, made from heavy bricks that absorbed the light.

'How many guards?' I asked.

'Ten,' came the answer, too fast. I raised the pistol to his face. 'Two,' he amended, sheepishly.

'Why so few of them?'

'The Feds been gatherin' 'cross the river for days now,' he said, 'all the rest of us been mustered down there.'

'And the prisoners?'

'I dunno,' he shrugged. 'Couple of farmers caught runnin' arms, some Injuns what the general wanted took.'

'Shall we kill him now?' Owl whispered, digging the blade into his back.

'*I* should prefer that we do not,' I said to the man calmly, 'but I cannot vouch for my companion. Have you any intention of acting rashly?'

He shook his head, lips tight in the gloom.

'Very well,' I said. 'Walk ahead. If you cry foul, there shall be a hole in your skull before the word is finished.'

We descended, the stairs creaking beneath our weight. Owl

drifted silent as a ghost behind me. The quiet murmur of laughter reached us. At the bottom, lamplight spilled from an underground corridor. I saw heavy doors with bars set into the wood, four of them, another passageway at the end.

I nudged the soldier into the light.

'Jack!' came the greeting from an unseen guard as the man took a shaky step forward. 'Come see this mouse; he's runnin' like the devil his self!'

As I had predicted, the man opened his mouth to cry a warning. He did not get far before Owl rammed the knife into his shoulder, and his words turned into a shriek.

'Be quiet,' I snapped, as I pushed past him, guns raised. 'She will not kill you if you stay still.'

'Who the hell are you?' the guard blustered. I could see that he was far in his cups, his shirt sagging from his trousers, holster draped over the back of his chair. He had been playing a game with a starved-looking mouse, trapping it under a tin bowl. I knocked it over and the creature scurried away.

'An unarmed man should not ask questions.' I plucked his revolver from its case and threw it behind me. 'I want the keys,' I told him softly. Up close, I could smell the liquor on his breath. His lips and teeth were stained with tobacco. There was something familiar about his scent, but I shook it away.

I caught the glint of eyes at the doors, fingers wrapping around the bars as the prisoners rushed to see the commotion.

'*Shádí!*' called Owl, straining to see into the cells and retain her grip on the soldier. Voices answered her, hesitant at first but growing stronger.

'The keys, now,' I demanded.

'You're her, ain't you?' The guard was fumbling with his belt, and I heard metal jangle. 'You're that crazy blackcap what slaughtered them Union men.'

My muscles tensed with every breath as the guard struggled to extract the keys. The longer we waited, the more danger we were in. Finally, he extended them toward me. I reached out and saw his eyes flick to the soldier.

'Owl!' I cried, as the men lunged at us. The guard grabbed for my pistols, using brute force to try and wrench the weapons out of my grip. He almost had them when I heard two Mexican men yelling at me from a cell. Their hands were reaching through the bars. I threw myself into the man's stomach, knocking him backward. The two prisoners caught hold of anything they could grasp, his shirt, his hair, until I was able to get one of my legs free and drive my knee into his groin.

The guard let go and I pushed away, leaving the prisoners to smash his head against the door until he sagged into a heap. Owl had the keys in her hands. Her soldier lay on his front, twitching, a long, deep slash across his back.

Her fingers slipped as she searched for the right key.

'Quickly,' I told her, rubbing at my burning arms. 'There is not much time.'

Four Indian women came tumbling out of the first cell. Owl looked into each of their faces, questioned them brusquely and turned away. They in turn shrank back, afraid.

'What is it?' I asked, as she shook through the keys a second time. There was a kind of desperation in her eyes that I had not seen before.

She did not answer, flinging open the second door to grab at the people within. Three men and a young boy shakily answered her questions. Frantically, she unlocked the third, which contained the Mexicans who had near-killed the guard. She shoved them aside impatiently, running for the fourth cell. It was empty.

The keys fell from her hands as she stared into the small, damp space.

'What is wrong?' I repeated, risking a hand on her shoulder. She was limp, defeated.

'My sister,' she said, distantly. 'She should have been here.'

14

Death and life are in the power of the tongue

One of the Mexican men was tugging on my arm as he staggered past, pointing to the passageway. He and his cellmate were manacled together, but they did not waste another glance back before they raced for the stairs.

'What did he say? Owl?' I shook her and she knocked my hand away, stooping to retrieve her knife from the back of the soldier.

'He said there was another. I do not know who he meant.'

'Another guard,' I murmured, as the sound of hurried footsteps grew close. 'He means there is another guard.'

Our eyes met. Owl shoved the freed prisoners aside to position herself flat against the wall. I stepped over a pool of blood, aiming my pistols directly at the doorway.

A man came staggering round the corner, eyes down as he hauled awkwardly at a revolver holstered at his waist. One arm was fastened across his chest in a dirty sling. Owl was on him the minute he crossed the threshold. He raised his face and for a moment, my entire world froze. Only when the first blood had spilled from his neck could I scream for her to stop.

The guns shook in my hands. I tried to level them, but the shaking just increased.

'Sister?' The man wheezed against the knife that was balanced at his throat.

'No,' my voice cracked. He repeated the word, and I screwed my eyes shut.

'*Madre*, you know him?' said Owl.

'No.' Cold sweat sprang up along my hairline. It was not possible. It was not him, just another man. 'No, he is dead.'

'I ain't dead.' The man sounded chagrined. I heard him shifting away from the knife against his neck. 'Must you do that?' he asked Owl.

'Is it . . .?' she began.

'No!' I burst. 'I told you, Abraham Muir is—'

'Alive, no thanks to you,' the man interrupted. I heard uneven footsteps limp toward me. I wanted to turn and run, but stood my ground. The man came forward until the barrels of the guns pressed into his chest. I looked up into a dead man's face.

15

For the ways of a
man in his youth

'I called for you,' he said, old shadows flickering against his skin.
'I shouted your name 'til I had no voice left, and you did not
come.'

'But I saw . . .' My voice trailed off, helplessly.

'You did not care what you saw, once *he* appeared.' Abe's
jaw was tight, a muscle twitching from the strain. 'You did not
care to look, to see that I lay six feet below, bleeding out on a
ledge.'

I could not speak. I heard it again in my mind, that faint bird's
cry on the cliff, snatched away by the wind, my ears deafened
from the retort of the pistols.

'Abe, I . . .'

The weapons fell from my hands as I gripped Abe's good
arm, though he flinched away. The feeling of warm skin through
the shirt, of blood pumping strong through his veins, was a fresh
horror.

'I thought he killed you,' I whispered. 'It was retribution.'

'You should have saved your anger,' he jerked away to pick
up one of the pistols. 'You couldn't even finish the bastard, I
heard it all.'

Abruptly, I was furious with him, in a way that left no room
for calming thoughts or prayers. I had tormented myself with his
death, for failing to save him, had pictured his face again and
again in my mind, yet all he could think of was revenge.

'Do you not know me at all Abraham Muir?' I demanded,
following as he limped toward the table. 'Was I supposed to leave
him? Ride away while he bled to death?'

Muir flicked open the pistol's chamber one-handed, peered inside. 'Why not? You left me.'

For a long moment, silence stretched between us. Abe was breathing like he had been running, but he pushed the pistol back into my hand.

'We can't stay here,' he said finally, voice hoarse. He reached for his own revolver. 'There's trouble upstairs.' He looked around then, taking in the scene before him, and frowned. Owl gripped her knife, still hesitant. The Indian prisoners returned his gaze in confusion. 'What in God's name y'all doing here?' he finally asked.

'We can trust him, or not?' Owl eyed his gray Confederate uniform.

'I ain't one of them,' Abe explained, tugging at his sling. 'Though they saved my life, such as it is. One of their patrols found me, scraped me off the roadside near the border. They fixed me up best they could and drafted me in, even with a chest full of shot. They're that short on men.'

He looked about at the doubtful gazes.

'Hell, Sister,' he burst, exasperated. 'You know I never gave two cents for this war. But even scratchin' lice with the Graybacks is better than bein' a corpse.'

I nodded slowly, knowing that he spoke the truth. Owl relaxed her stance.

Abe nodded smartly in return and peered down at the guard, slumped and bloodied in the corner.

'He dead?'

'Not quite.' I guessed.

Abe grunted. 'He'd have corned himself into a stupor anyhow. Come on.'

Owl murmured something to the Indians, and they made for the stairs. Abe bent to gather up the other pistol before I could, cramming it into the back of his trousers before following on. I stayed silent; they were his guns, for all I thought of them as mine.

'New travelin' partner?' he muttered, as we crept upward,

slanting a glance at Owl. 'Wouldn't have had you down as bein' too friendly with a Navajo.'

'It is a long story. She calls herself Owl.'

'Mighty fitting,' he said, and in the darkness I saw the edge of his smile, crooked as an old fence. My heart raced with gladness, and despite the tension between us I thanked the Lord that he was alive, as rashly as a child.

'Why is it fitting?' I asked, trying to keep the emotion from my voice.

'As a partner for the *Cuervo*,' he smirked. 'Whole town's been gossipin' since the day before yesterday. I been half expecting you since then.'

'How did you—'

'Sister, how many nuns do *you* know with a brace of pistols and a bounty on their heads?'

At the top of the stairs, he stopped us, motioning that we gather close before we ventured further.

'Union made an attack few days ago, some ways west along the river. They're always scuffling, so chances are it won't have reached this far, but just in case . . .'

Owl hefted her knife, relaying his words to the Indians. Several of them, I noticed, had armed themselves with whatever they could find.

'What about once we are outside?' I whispered, handing my rifle over to one of the unarmed women. 'Can we escape? There are soldiers everywhere.'

'I imagine it will be as it always is with us,' Abe said, cocking his revolver. 'Gunfire, chaos and the devil's own luck.'

'Us?' I snuck a look sideways as I checked my own gun.

'Kinda miss having a bounty on my head,' he said, ''specially now I can read the damn warrants.'

The garrison was deserted, every soul rallied out for the fighting or hiding from it. As we crept through the building, we heard distant thuds and cries, growing ever louder, resolving themselves into the rattle of guns and the screams of men.

301

I threw open the door. The sky was orange with fire and smoke. From somewhere nearby came a sickening crash, and mortar shook itself free of the building above our heads.

'Hell,' Abe swore.

16

Thou art ensnared by the words
of thy mouth

Cannonballs shrieked through the air as we cowered, the world crashing down around us. The darkness spat hot dust. Venomous bullets flew past to shatter on walls.

'We got to get out,' Abe yelled over the noise. 'They're like to tear the whole city down 'fore they let it back into the hands of the secesh.'

'How?' I cried. Another deep thudding struck nearby. 'The horses are gone.'

'We run then,' he hollered.

'You're injured!' I plucked at his sling. 'What if we wait, hide here until the fighting is done?'

''til the Union find us you mean?' Abe raged, his breath hot on my face. 'Me a deserter and a turncoat and you a murderer and a thousand dollars for both our heads?'

'I did not know it was a thousand,' Owl grinned wildly, ducking toward us. 'I should have handed you in.'

My reply was cut off as a shell hurtled past us to slam into the courtyard wall not six feet away. The blast knocked us back, shards of brick and dirt flying into our faces. Ears ringing, I picked myself up, and looked around. One of the Indians was bleeding from a shallow gash beneath his eye, but otherwise all were unharmed.

'Abraham is right,' Owl's voice was muffled in the aftermath of the blast. 'We must run.'

'She got sense,' Abe coughed, elbowing my pistol straight with his bad arm. 'Get your people, Owl, tell them we're taking to our heels.'

For a breathless moment Abe and I exchanged glances,

standing shoulder to shoulder, gathering our strength. Then we were running, even as smoke darkened the air before us. Out on the street it was chaos. What little paving there was had been blown apart. Windows had shattered and from the gaps between buildings came rifle fire, bursts of red in the darkness.

We staggered as best we could through the ruined streets, away from the combat. The noise abated somewhat, as we left the worst of the fighting behind us. I could see Abe's chest heaving, sweat darkening the knot of the sling around his neck and I feared for him. My own eyes stung with smoke, skin speckled with blood from flying splinters, yet I ran as an animal might, eyes searching for movement anywhere in the darkness.

Owl was a shadow behind me, her hair gray with dust. The Indians raced alongside her, two of them half carrying the man who was wounded, the others with knuckles white around their weapons.

I saw the bell that sat atop the city gate upon the next street and pointed, yelling wordlessly to Abe. He bared his teeth in response, and I summoned one last burst of speed as we threw ourselves around the corner.

Had we been a smaller group, we might have been able to turn tail. As it was, one by one we collided in confusion at the sight before us.

A wall of blue, the color blinding after the smoke-filled streets. Fires burned in the corners of the square, streaking faces, flashing on belts and bayonets. A company of Union men stood between us and the gate.

For a gasping moment we stared, as though they were as shocked as we. Then a shot rang out in surprise and struck one of the Indian men. The woman beside him screamed in anger and let loose a bullet from her rifle. It flew wide, but acted as a signal to the others, who began shooting at the soldiers. I threw myself to the ground, dragging Abe with me, as shots flew, scrabbling to get my pistol clear. Someone on a tall horse was riding behind the Union line and I whispered a prayer as I took aim, knowing the chaos a wounded mount would cause.

But I stayed my hand. A voice was calling through the clamor, then another.

'Hold fire!'

The volley petered out. Beside me, Abe was ashen-faced from the pain of falling upon his chest, but all in one piece. One of the Indian women had been struck. Owl was propped on her hands, sheltering the young boy with her body, hatred twisting her face.

'Hold fire! I want them alive!' came the voice, again.

A man hobbled forward, leaning upon a crutch. I knew him then.

Hope and dismay warred in me as I watched Carthy step through the lines of men and limp boldly into the middle of the ground. His uniform was new, yet he looked thinner than ever, lines of pain etched deep into his face.

I climbed to my feet. Abe grasped my arm, pulling himself up with me. Carthy stopped at the sight of Muir, but his eyes were lit from within. My stomach clenched, for I knew the look of his lunacy.

'I thought I killed you,' he told Muir delightedly, 'but now, here you are, all dressed up as a Grayback. Sister,' he greeted me, eyebrows raised. 'What precious thing did you sell to return him to life? Or did you give something *freely*?'

'Bastard,' spat Muir, his hand inching toward his revolver.

'Weapons to the ground,' Carthy ordered. 'Or I shall tell them to shoot.'

Reluctantly, I let my pistol fall into the dust. From the corner of my eye I could see Owl tossing away one of her many knives.

'Lieutenant Carthy,' I began.

'*Captain* Carthy,' he interrupted, pointing to his collar. 'Reinstated with honor. For valiant service and for surviving you, Thomas Josephine. Are you proud?'

'I am innocent. You know that. Or you would not have saved my life, at the camp.'

A tremor ran across his face.

'Saved,' he muttered, 'as a good man might.'

305

I shifted forward a step. 'It is not too late for you.'

His eyes widened to me then, in such painful hope that I almost reached out. A hand jolted me backward.

'He's mad, Sister,' Abe sneered. 'That whore pox rotted his brain long ago.'

Carthy's mouth contorted. 'First squad, to me,' he called over his shoulder.

Bayonets flashed as thirty rifles were lowered onto us once more. A group of men pushed through the ranks.

'All here present are fugitives,' he told them. 'They are to be brought to justice. Except,' for a moment his face vacillated between triumph and uncertainty, 'except for the good Sister. She is innocent of the crimes of which she stands accused. Thomas Josephine, please come here.'

I could not read his eyes, inhumanly blue even in the firelight.

'Don't,' Muir hissed beside me, 'he'll kill you.'

'He saved me, Abe,' I said slowly. 'He will repent.'

'Sister!'

I released myself from his grip and walked forward.

'My men will ensure your safety, dear lady,' Carthy said, almost formally, as I reached him. 'Once they have done their duty by these criminals.'

He raised his hand, and I heard the sound of thirty rifles cocking.

'Wait!' I cried.

'Why?' he asked. His eyes were curiously blank. 'I see no reason to bring this matter to a court. All before us are traitors to the Union and a danger to the Nation.'

'You cannot do this!'

Owl stood perfectly still before the soldiers, gaze fixed upon me. Abe too, face contorted as if I were torturing him. One of the Indian women clutched the child to her.

'Prepare arms!' Carthy commanded.

'Please, in the Lord's name . . .' I begged.

'Do not force me to make you join them, Josephine,' he murmured, tenderly. 'Part of me would dearly like to. Aim!'

I reached out and covered his hand with mine. His skin was burning, slick with perspiration.

'Theodore Carthy, I forgive you your sins,' I said, with every ounce of conviction I could muster. 'Together we shall find salvation.'

His lips hung open, that final terrible instruction fading in a breath of air.

It was through my fingers, as I raised them to place a blessing upon Carthy's forehead that I saw Abe's arm fly to his back, for the pistol concealed there. Our eyes locked. He fired at the same instant I threw myself in front of Carthy.

Nunslinger: Book 7

Westward Orders

The True Tale of how Sister Thomas Josephine of St. Louis, Missouri, Escaped from Imprisonment, Evaded the Law and Rode the Mississippi River in pursuit of one Abraham C. Muir

I

For a just man shall fall seven times, and shall rise again

That day began the same as all others: I could not have known that it was to bring my future, carry it in the pair of cracked, mud-crusted boots that tramped the flagstones of the hall to linger outside my door.

They belonged to a man, that much I knew. Whoever he was, he had visited many times before. On each occasion, I listened to the silence of the corridor, and imagined that he was doing the same. Sometimes, I heard a whisper of cloth as he raised his arm, as if to knock upon the wood, but he never did.

If I wondered at all about who he was, I did not dwell on it for long. There were other thoughts that claimed me, thoughts that lengthened my days and stretched my nights into sleeplessness.

When I had first regained consciousness, I thought that I must have lost my mind. Above me rose familiar walls of white plaster and a scent that I knew: strong soap and linen. No dirt, no blood, nor fire. For one bewildering moment, it was as if I had never left the convent, as if I had dreamed the entirety of those cruel months in the west.

Soon I learned the truth. I had fallen in the chaos of the fight at El Paso del Norte, and the Union – not knowing what else to do – had sent word to my old convent in St. Louis. They had come, had taken me back into their charge with a head full of shot and a dead man as my legacy.

My sisters had pressed me with questions when first I woke, implored me to confess all to them and the Lord, but when I tried, I could not find the words. I allowed them to tend to the wound that had threatened my life, that would leave me scarred until the end of my days, but I did not open my mouth to speak.

There was little reason to. My wordlessness became a vow of silence, which in turn became my penance. When I was well enough to walk, they escorted me to chapel, and let me help with simple tasks. My sisters never let me from their sight. They nodded in their calm way and assured me that they understood my trials, but they did not. Not one of them had any notion of the doubt that daily raked its claws across my soul.

They had given me back my bone rosary. It was all that remained of my time in the west. I spent hours staring at it, picturing it covered with Wade Paxton's blood, or tangled around Muir's pistols. On the day the boots came it hung loosely in my fingers as I knelt in my cell, eyes fixed upon the sliver of daylight high above. I had begun to recite the *Miserere* in my mind, wishing I could release the holy words of contrition into the air, for they stuck in my throat.

Deliver me from blood-guilt, the verse begged. Muir's brown eyes had begged the same thing of me, even as he prepared to deal out death. I was so lost within the memory that I did not realize the stranger had come to stand outside my door again until a flicker in the light caught my eye: the shadow of feet, beneath the threshold. I waited for the mutual silence to begin, as it always did, but beyond all expectation, heard a voice.

'I trust you will be prompt in your enquiries, sir?' said Sister Beatrice Clement, the mother superior.

'I will not keep her long, Sister,' a man answered, his voice impatient. 'As we have discussed. Now, if you please?'

Keys jangled, scraped against the lock. The door swung open to reveal a man. He hesitated on the threshold, as if restrained. I blinked my eyes to clear them of the day's glare, and he came into focus. He wore a coat of thick, gray fabric that sagged at the pockets. He was huddled into its depths, but beneath the folds I caught the sheen of brass: buttons and a belt buckle, dulled through lack of polish.

I rose to meet him, slowly, in case I staggered. My legs were numb from the hours spent kneeling on the cold floor. His dark eyes surveyed me:

'Do I address Sister Thomas Josephine?' He spoke carefully, a Boston accent licking at his words.

Behind him, the Mother Superior's face was a pale oval, framed in perfect light and dark. Her cool eyes held mine in silent command. I nodded my head to the man's question.

'Sister Thomas Josephine,' he continued, 'I am US Marshal Benjamin Reasoner. I'm afraid I have some questions for you.'

2

With an iron pen and
in a plate of lead

Reasoner returned daily. He was apparently unperturbed by the fact I never made any sign of speaking, or acknowledging his questions. Instead he would enter and stand hunched in the doorway, flicking through his handful of worn papers, annotated edge to edge with pencil scrawl.

He began with the same question every time.

'Sister Thomas Josephine, you are currently held accountable for six charges of murder by the states of Nevada, California and the New Mexico Territory, for the deaths of the Brothers Paxton of Stillwater, Father Johannes Laverman of Sacramento and Privates Worth, Hemmel and Lee of the 1st Regiment New Mexico Volunteer Cavalry. Can you provide me with any information to the contrary?'

As always, I did not answer, but instead studied his face in detail. I had never heard of a black man being made marshal, and to try and figure his character became something of a hobby of mine. I had his face mapped by heart. I determined that his nose had been broken and re-set a number of times. His cheeks were roughened by the elements, and spoke of many months living in the saddle. His eyes were sharp, yet weary: weighed down by too many nights awake. They helped me place his age at around forty.

I believe my study disquieted him, for eventually he would snap from his expectant silence to stuff the papers back into one voluminous pocket and bid me good day.

On the fifth or sixth visit I rose to greet him. His eyes lingered over my feet. It was February, and bitterly cold. The glass in the high window of my room had frost on the inside, and the joints of my bare fingers and toes were angry with chillblains.

'Why do you do this?' Reasoner asked quietly, seeing me wince as I stood. I glanced over his shoulder to the sister who accompanied him.

'Thomas Josephine is a penitent,' she told him calmly. 'She is atoning for the sins she committed in the world by secluding herself here, and by the denial of material comforts.'

Reasoner scraped at his forehead and frowned. I thought he would speak his mind, but when he finally did open his mouth, it was to frame the usual words:

'Sister Thomas Josephine, you are held accountable for six charges of murder . . .'

The diocese had prevented him from arresting me, I discovered, saying that I was not in my right mind. The convent's walls protected me from justice. Reasoner knew this, but still he came and asked his questions, and every day I remained silent. I wondered why he should waste time in such a fruitless task.

On his seventh visit he completed his usual inquiries and stood, waiting for a response. I, in turn, was engaged in a study of his coat cuffs. They were frayed, evidently he had no time to darn them himself, and no one who cared to do it for him.

'Sister Josephine.' His words were hesitant through my contemplation. 'Do you know the whereabouts of Abraham Muir?'

It was the first time I had heard that name spoken aloud in many weeks, and the sound of it was a blow to the chest. For a long moment we merely stared at each other. I realized that I had opened my mouth, that the words I had not uttered were etched large upon the air between us.

Where is he? I ached to ask.

I clamped my mouth shut. The newly healed scar on my face prickled beneath Reasoner's gaze. I turned away.

The next day, of course, he was there again, in the doorway, shuffling to and fro in his worn leather boots. I had almost begun to look forward to his visits, yet now I resented his presence, for he brought the world with him, reminded me that somewhere, the relics of my sin were living and breathing.

'Abraham Muir,' Marshal Reasoner said abruptly, in place of his usual questions. 'You traveled with him, didn't you?'

I did not answer, but glared furiously at his hands, determined to withstand his probing.

'I have here,' he continued doggedly, taking another step into the room, 'a copy of a newspaper from a month or so ago, the *Californian*. It was sent to me by a lawman out San Francisco way. There's a rather astonishing article in here by a man name of Templeton.'

I glanced up at him sharply before I could stop myself.

'Shall I read it to you, Sister?'

Reasoner's hands were stained with printer's ink from the paper. Evidently he had read it many times. I turned away.

'Very well.' There was a rustle as he folded the article into his jacket. 'Another time, perhaps. Now, Sister Thomas Josephine, you are held accountable for six charges of murder . . .'

316

3

Thou hast indeed
numbered my steps

The scent of citrus, released in a spritz from tough skin, filled my gray cell like sunlight. Reasoner hummed tunelessly as he worked a segment free and put it into his mouth.

'These are very good,' he said, chewing. 'Are you sure you will not join me?'

Two more oranges rested beside him on the floor. He had taken to sitting down, propping himself in the doorframe as he asked his questions. With every visit he grew bolder, to my increasing dismay.

'Got these from a steamer, come up from Panama,' he continued, piling the skin neatly on the floor beside him. 'California oranges.' He sucked away contentedly for a while. 'You must've passed that way, on your journey to Mexico?'

I said nothing and concentrated on counting the beads of my rosary. I had passed that way, and the scent of those fruits was a potent jolt to my memory.

'That's right, I was going to read you that piece by Templeton,' the marshal continued good-naturedly. 'Here it is.'

He extracted the newspaper and smoothed it out against his knee. I looked to the doorway. The sister who was supposed to be standing guard was nowhere to be seen.

Reasoner cleared his throat.

'"On the twentieth day of the month now passed,"' he read, '"I, Franklin Templeton, correspondent for the *Californian* – which as you know has the third largest weekly circulation in all the western coast states and territories— "'

A breath of laughter escaped me at the thought of that

317

gentleman, rolled up like a cigar on the floor of the cabin, yet beaming all the while. Reasoner eyed me from under his lashes, before reading on:

"'—had the singular experience, both thrilling and terrifying, of being the prisoner of those notorious outlaws, the renegade Catholic Sister Thomas Josephine and the fearful traitor Abraham C. Muir.

"'It was aboard the steamer *Prairie Rose*, as she journeyed the Californian coast toward San Diego. Your humble narrator had been traveling in the company of the brave federal troops who had hunted the fugitives since their daring flight from San Francisco, right under the noses of the law.

"'I joined the steamer north of San Diego and just as we were set to embark, found myself going to the aid of a lady of astonishing pulchritude: a fair Madonna who was swooning in that county's climate. Being a gentleman of good breeding and humane consideration, I at once sprang to her assistance, and helped her to her cabin, only to find myself at the wrong end of a pistol! The lady in question had shed her disguise and her eyes blazed down upon me with all the burning righteousness of an avenging angel. It was the Sister herself!

"'"Be still and repent!' she cried to me, 'or I swear I shall strike thee down as David smote the Philistine!'

"'Before I could escape, in came rushing her fearsome companion. Abraham Muir, deserter and killer, who they say can speak ten Indian languages. Where she was lightness, he was dark, rangy as a wolf, the marks of a wild and lawless life upon him.

"'Needless to say, I put up a fair fight, which forced them to bind me hand and foot. Thus, I became instrumental to their escape plot, and was privy to a good deal of talk between the two.

"'The news from Mexico that they have escaped their final reckoning once again does not surprise me. Those who have encountered the pair say that the charges fired from the Sister's pistols are guided by the Lord himself, and are sent to find their

318

homes in the flesh of sinners. I am of such a belief, for where Muir must have the Devil's own luck, I am certain that Sister Thomas Josephine has the fire and fury of Our Savior himself by her side.'"

4

We are but of yesterday

Reasoner peered up at me over the paper.

'Is that last bit true, Sister?'

Although Templeton's narrative had almost caused me to break my silence with laughter several times, I only raised a calm eyebrow.

'Indeed,' the marshal agreed, 'I would not be surprised to find a penny dreadful in place of a bible in Templeton's pocket.' He re-folded the paper. 'However, his is not the only report of its kind. There are others which are not so poetic, or admiring of you. In fact there are many who wish to see you hanged.'

When I did not answer, he sighed, rubbed at his chin. 'Will you not tell me what you know?' he pressed. 'What happened back there in Mexico, when Muir killed Captain Carthy?'

I shut my eyes but it was no use, the image rose as it always did, clearer than the room around me: Abe, his expression begging me to move away, out of the path of the bullet he intended for Carthy, a moment before he squeezed the trigger.

Reasoner was still speaking.

'You are lucky to have survived, you know,' he said, picking at a thread on his cuff. 'I asked your mother superior. She said that without their treatment the fragments of shot in your scalp would have surely been fatal. Why do you insist on protecting the coward who shot you?'

I was shaking with anger. This man had arrived, unsolicited, to plague my days of contemplation; he had dragged the past with him like a dog with a long-buried bone. I stood and took a step toward him, to make him leave. He rose too, expression no longer casual.

'Muir was to be brought here, to St. Louis,' he told me bluntly, stopping me in my tracks. 'To be hanged publically at Gratiot Street Prison. General Sherman got wind of Captain Carthy's murder. He wants an example made of Muir.'

Where is he? I was desperate to ask, yet could not say a word. Reasoner spoke into my silence.

'Have you heard of a man named Colm Puttick?'

There was no need for me to shake my head.

'He's a demon,' the marshal said darkly, 'him and his crew have been terrorizing Missouri for years, especially out round the borders. They have allegiance to no one. Nothing but godless sons of—' Reasoner pulled himself up short. 'Sorry, ma'am. They are vicious men,' he continued, 'men who kill whole families in raids, for a handful of coins. I shall not tell you their methods.'

He took a step closer.

'Puttick and several of his men were finally apprehended not long after Muir. They were being transported together, in a chain gang,' he said. 'Report has it that Muir fell in with them. A week ago there was a skirmish: they killed four guards and broke free, somewhere north of Little Rock. Muir, Puttick, and three others. They fled into Indian Territory. Every lawman and bounty hunter in the Unified States is after them now. Their heads are worth more than gold.'

Reasoner's features had changed shape, tightening at the jaw and temple: what I had mistaken for fatigue was tenacity, I realized then; that of a single-minded man, sharp and inflexible as steel.

'We may not have the power to bring *you* to justice, Sister,' he said, voice hard, 'but by God we will see Muir answer.'

Marshal Reasoner stood less than an arm's length away from me, so close I could feel his breath stirring the air of my cell. I was at a crossroad, I realized. Two paths were open before me. I knew then that I had come too far; that all my efforts at penitence were for naught. There was only one road for me.

I shot out a hand, plunging it deep into Reasoner's coat. The service revolver that hung at his waist sprang to my fingers as if it were alive. I armed it in one movement before the marshal even had a chance to draw breath.

For the first time in many weeks, I felt a smile creep across my face.

'You should have listened to Templeton,' I said.

5

If I go to the east,
he appeareth not

I wrapped Reasoner's coat around me. He had not wanted to hand the garment over but had no choice, being at the mercy of his own revolver.

'Please,' he said, eyes blazing as the jacket settled onto my shoulders, still warm from his flesh, 'in the inside pocket there is a case. Take the coat if you must, but give me that.'

I reached in for the object. It was made from silver, thin leaves clipped together, the size of a playing card. There were traces of a design upon the metal but they were worn to nothing. It fell open in my hands, and Reasoner cried, as if I had wounded him.

Inside was a photograph of a young woman, her hair styled in the fashion of a decade before. She held a baby in christening clothes.

I shot Reasoner a glance, but he was staring fixedly at the photograph in my hand, would not look elsewhere until I tossed it toward him. He cradled it to his chest and met my eyes as I dragged the door closed upon him, bolting it from the outside. The look on his face told me plainly what I already knew: I had made an enemy.

Before I had left for California, a lifetime ago, the convent had been my home. Throughout my travels its memory had been a source of solace. It had remained pure in my thoughts, a reminder of a world in which goodness and faith were chief among forces, and whose walls were inviolable.

Those same walls had received me again, yet where once they had sheltered, they now confined. Now, I fled down the narrow passages that I had walked in pious contemplation. I was running from my own sisters, from my own Church, and the horror of that threatened to halt my flight faster than any lawman.

It would not be long before the sister who had escorted Marshal Reasoner returned to my cell. She would find it locked, but the man was already shouting the alarm. I took the back stairs, down toward the ground level of the building. The scents of fresh-baked bread and simmering soup drifted toward me: my sisters were at their midday meal. I crept toward the closet where donations were stored. I would not bolt out into the city unprepared.

Everything was as I remembered. It did not take me long to find the items that I needed, drop them into a sack I found there. I was slipping from the room again when I heard a sharp intake of breath.

A novice stood, a tray between her hands, staring at me as if I were the devil himself. Her name was Constance; she brought my meals. I raised my hand slowly, in a sign of peace.

'Please,' I asked her, 'do not say a word. A man's life is at stake. I must leave.'

Her eyes strayed from the sack I held to the revolver gripped in my hand.

'They were right,' she said, her voice trembling. 'The doctors, they warned Sister Beatrice that you had lost your mind, but she would not listen.'

'You don't understand,' I begged, even as she backed away. 'There is a soul I promised to save.'

'Sisters!' she was already crying, the tray of food clattering from her grip. 'Sisters, she is here!'

I had no choice but to run. Tears stung my eyes. I heard the women who I had counted among the dearest of friends crying in alarm at my escape. The light from the front hallway stretched toward me. I was almost free. Voices echoed down the stairs, and I threw myself into the shadow of the wainscot.

'Fetch the chloroform from the infirmary,' that was Sister Beatrice speaking. I caught a flash of her face through the banisters, strained in the afternoon light. 'We must treat her as gently as we are able, just as last time.'

They hurried away, and I allowed my head to fall back against the wall, clutching for the rosary at my neck. *Last time?* Had this happened before? Dimly, I recalled the hospital wing at night, recalled trying a door handle to find it locked, rushing to a window to smash a pane of glass before being discovered. Yet it was as if the memories belonged to someone else.

I glanced up at the statue of Christ in the entrance hall. Perhaps I truly had lost my mind. *Please,* I implored silently, *please tell me what to do.* His glass eyes looked down at me. He knew much, too much of my soul. Did He intend for me to always wander, unfit for the cloister, forever at odds with the world?

There was no answer. His carved face remained impassive in its holy suffering, even as Marshal Reasoner's voice bellowed from the floor above.

I waited no longer, but clutched my courage to me and plunged outside, into the winter streets of St. Louis.

6

But if to the west,
I shall not understand him

The docks smelled the same as they always had: damp wood and river mud, effluence both animal and human mingled with shaved wood and tar. Every steamer that berthed there was being loaded with coal before it departed for New Orleans. Whole streets were black with the dust. Fires were common in this neighbourhood – and feared – for half the city could be eaten up in a conflagration.

I pulled Reasoner's jacket tighter across my body. A wet mist was rising from the river. Soon it would encase the streets. Night was falling, opening the gateway to another world: a different city crept out of the seams, slick as a cockroach and twice as hardy, peddling hope and danger together. I checked the revolver in my pocket for the hundredth time.

The Lord had turned His face away from a place such as this, I knew, yet still I walked, stepping willingly into the under tide. The sack over my shoulder was light, containing only my habit. Once more I had shed my skin. Reasoner's coat was a blessing, thick and warm. Along with a battered hat, it helped to conceal my figure, to walk with greater ease in the men's clothes I had taken from the donations cupboard.

Ahead of me the sign for a bar swung out of the mist. It had been nearly fifteen years since I had seen it. I could hardly believe that the place still existed. The last time I had been inside, I was barely taller than the tables, and had spent my time creeping beneath them, stealing coins to feed my brothers and sisters.

I shrugged aside the old memories. Instead, I remembered Abe, laughing at my attempts at disguise, telling me that I looked too clean by half. I checked that the rosary was concealed around my neck and scraped up a handful of muck from the street.

Reluctantly, I rubbed a little over my chin and cheeks. There was no use in delaying further, and no use in asking the Lord to give me strength in such a place of sin. I pushed open the door.

The bar was quiet, something that I was grateful for. A few steersmen were slumped in a corner, no doubt drinking the last of their pennies before shipping out once again. Several better-dressed men were engaged in a game of cards. I did not remove my hat, but slumped over to the bar and ordered a drink in my gruffest voice.

Someone shoved a glass of beer toward me. I paid with a few of the coins I had found in Reasoner's coat. Taking a seat in a dark corner, I sipped it slowly.

Once I would have been terrified to sit among such company. Now, however . . . it was as if the bullet that had almost taken my life had stripped me of my fear. A cracked mirror hung upon the opposite wall, throwing back my reflection; a pale face scowling beneath a shapeless, brown hat. One hand crept self-consciously toward my head. Even in the gloom, the scar was livid. It started near my left eye, scored its way across my temple and back into my scalp. An inch further and the bullet would have killed me. Instead, it had only etched my skin before burying itself in Lieutenant Carthy's skull.

My arm jerked involuntarily and I slopped beer over my sleeve. I shoved down the panic that threatened to swallow me, and forced my attention back to the room. It had grown busier as I sat, lost in thought. The men at cards had welcomed a few others to their table. All of them were a shade cleaner and better presented than the general crowd.

I grabbed the arm of a passing boy, who bore a stack of greasy dishes, to ask who they were.

'That's the crew of the *Annabel Lee*,' he told me, sniffing. 'She's the fastest tub on the river. Made a fortune on a race last month, they did, so now they think of themselves as bein' heroes an' such.'

'Where do they run to?' I asked.

'Downriver to Arkansas, maybe Memphis. Far as the Feds got control, anyhow.'

I released him and gave him a penny, much to his delight, for he had told me what I wanted to know. The *Annabel Lee* was the boat I needed.

7

Shalt thou see as a man seeth?

As I watched the men, I thought on Reasoner's words. *Indian Territory.* That was where Abe had disappeared with this man Puttick and his gang. Had the marshal told the truth? Could Abe truly have entrusted his fate to a murderer?

Back in San Francisco I had made a promise to help him, to see him safe from danger. Twice now I had abandoned him in his hour of greatest need.

Yet he, in turn, had risked my life for the sake of revenge.

I took a larger gulp of beer and spluttered. My thoughts were tangled and left me reeling from confusion. I had no choice but to set my feet forth and pray that the Lord would guide me through the obscurity.

I counted the coins in Reasoner's coat. They were nowhere near enough to buy passage, even third class, on a steamer, and I knew I would not be able to follow Abe's example of looting a store and pawning the stolen goods.

Taking up my glass, I edged a little closer to the men the boy had pointed out. They had been growing ribald as the evening wore on, shouting and exclaiming over the pile of cards and money before them. I saw that the boy was right. Although many of them wore fine, new clothes, beneath they were tanned to leather, wind-whipped and rough-palmed: tell-tale signs of life on the river.

One man reached out to make a swipe for his winnings and swore in pain, clutching at his hand. A filthy bandage was wrapped around it, stiff with old blood, growing red at the edges where fresh stuff seeped through. He gritted his teeth and took a large swig of the whiskey before him.

329

This was my opportunity. I steeled myself and stepped into the light of their table.

'That needs stitching,' I called, trying my best to disguise my voice.

The table fell silent. Seven men blinked up at me, gaping. My cheeks flared and I hastily took a drink, to hide as much of my face as possible.

'What the hell you talking about?' one of them growled.

'His hand,' I jerked my head at the bandaged man, 'it needs stitching up, else it'll fester.'

'Go to hell,' the injured man spat, though he cradled his hand to his bulky chest. 'T'will heal soon enough.'

'As you like,' I shrugged and half turned away, feigning indifference, though my heart pounded, 'but if it isn't seen to it'll turn bad, then you'll lose the whole arm. Thought your ship's doctor would've told you that.'

'Ain't got one, lad,' another of the men slurred cheerfully. He had a shock of graying blond hair that had been tattered and bleached by the winds. He was also far in his cups. 'Cavalry borrowed the bastard couple o' months back, so we been fixin' ourselves. 'Cept Jim there got a mite too friendly with a windlass—'

'Shut your hole, Eli,' the bandaged man barked. 'You'll not go telling my business to all and sundry.'

'How d'you know, anyway?' another man asked me clearly. He sat straight and calm, nursing a drink, rather than gulping it. He was older than the others by a few years, his face covered in a peppered beard trimmed close to his chin. A pair of kid gloves sat on the table by his elbow. 'That his hand needs stitching, like?'

'I have been making a study of medicine,' I said quickly, praying that the Lord would forgive the lie. 'Now I am trained, I need employment. I was thinking of heading south, to see if the army want me.' I drained the last of the beer from the glass and tugged the brim of my hat at them. 'Well, if you'll excuse me.'

It will not work. My mind raced as I slouched toward the door. *They will not take the bait.*

'Hold up there!' I turned. The man with the gloves was drumming his fingers in thought. 'You reckon you could stitch his hand proper?' he asked.

'He ain't no more'n a boy!' the injured sailor protested. 'He ain't coming near me with no needle!'

'Dammit, Jim,' the blond man burst, 'you want a festerin' stump 'stead of five fingers?'

I shrugged casually, trying to keep the thrill of triumph from my face.

'Sure,' I told them, 'I could stitch it, if I had a medical chest and somewhere to work.'

331

8

Thou hast clothed
me with skin and flesh

The *Annabel Lee* was indeed a tub: it jostled between two grand steamships like a mongrel dog between greyhounds. From what I could make out in the darkness, she was a hodgepodge of dainty wood and coarse metal, painted from ten different cans. My stomach flipped as I set one foot upon the gangway, and I wondered what new trouble I was walking into.

'She don't look like much,' said Eli, the drunk, as he hauled himself up the rope alongside me, 'but Jim's the best goddam engineer on the Mississipp'. Ripped out her old boiler he did, made one new. Now she runs like the devil was chasin' her ass with a hot poker.'

I tried not to let the profanity unnerve me, yet my stomach did another small somersault.

'Weren't nothin' to it,' Jim replied gruffly, cradling his hand.

'Like hell there weren't,' Eli cried. 'If he loses his arm, lad, we'll be so far up shit creek—'

'Where shall I work?' I interrupted, grateful that the darkness hid my red face. 'I'll need some light.'

'Best come on up to the wheelhouse,' advised the older man with the beard. 'I'll get them to fetch the medical chest.'

'Who's he?' I murmured to Eli, as we climbed a set of rickety metal stairs toward the top of the boat. 'Is he the captain?'

'N'awww,' the man slurred, 'Hallow ain't no captain. He's the *pilot.*'

I had only the slightest clue what this meant, but from the tone of Eli's voice, it was clear that Mr Hallow was the most respected man on the ship.

The wheelhouse was a precarious glass and wood

construction; a crow's nest perched above the top deck with barely enough room for four people. There was an ancient stove, glowing with embers, and a cracked leather seat in the corner. It housed the ship's great steering wheel, surrounded by a strange network of pulleys and funnels.

Mr Hallow soon entered, bearing a lantern. Jim, with the injured hand, came after him. I shied away from the direct glare of the light, as we shuffled about to make room, and peered instead into the medical chest. It was poorly stocked. An almost empty bottle of morphine and a lack of bandages spoke of the crew's attempts to minister to themselves. I poked about. To my amazement I found a little tin containing two needles, thread, and an injecting syringe.

I held it up to the light: it looked clean, as if it had never been used.

'This is wonderful,' I murmured. 'I can get some morphine straight into you, to help with the pain.'

Jim was shuffling down the seat. I almost laughed to see such a huge man inching away from me.

'It is only an injection; it will not hurt overly much,' I told him, drawing a half-inch of morphine into the chamber and sterilizing the point in the lamp flame.

'Don't care for it,' he declared. Even in the darkness I could see he was turning pale. 'It ain't right. A good wash of river water'll sort this hand out.'

'Quiet, now, and let the lad work,' commanded Mr Hallow. 'You'll be no use in the boiler room if you can't hold a spanner.'

I unwrapped the rag from around Jim's hand. The wound ran raggedly across his palm, angry and oozing. I traced a vein in his wrist with my eyes.

'Now hold still,' I told him, before pushing the needle in and depressing the plunger. He gave one high-pitched cry, then his eyes rolled shut and he slumped down.

'He's swooned,' said Eli incredulously, tears of laughter springing to his eyes. 'Big Jim's done swooned like a girl.'

Despite their laughter, I was grateful for Jim's fainting spell, for it meant I could work quickly and firmly without him bucking about. I stitched the wound as well as I was able, trying to bring the skin together so that it would heal neatly. The morphine was doing its work, for when the large man came around he only blinked blearily down at his hand.

'Try not to use it for the next few days,' I told him sternly, 'else the thread will pull. And keep it clean.'

Jim was soon dispatched to his bunk on Eli's arm. I used a rag to clean away some of the blood on my hands and packed the medical chest once more. Mr Hallow was lounging beside the stove, staring out at the lights on the shore.

'Well now,' he said quietly. 'When are you going to ask about shipping out with us?'

I looked up at him, alarmed. We were alone in that small space. I realized how fragile my safety was.

'Weren't that the whole point of comin' over, in there,' he continued, jerking his head toward the bar, 'talkin' about Jim's hand like that? I'll wager you don't have more than a dollar in your pocket.'

I could feel myself flushing, and kept my head down.

'I was pleased to help,' I said, as low as I could. 'Now, I must be leaving.'

'You ain't going nowhere, miss.'

I froze, one hand in the medical chest. For a moment, all I could hear was the thundering of my heart in my ears. Hallow had shifted around behind me. Slowly, I closed my fingers around the cold glass of the syringe, while I inched my other hand for the revolver.

'What are you talking about?' I tried to sound dismissive as I stood, my back to him.

'That disguise wouldn't fool a child,' he laughed. I could hear the speculation in his voice as he took a step closer. 'No boy's got a face that pretty.'

I whirled around before he could move, the syringe raised. My trick worked, for he knocked the needle out of my hand, giving me time to pull the weapon free.

334

'Do not doubt that I will shoot,' I told him through gritted teeth, 'and be assured that I will choose somewhere lasting and painful.'

Hallow's face creased, his eyes filled and he began to laugh, slowly at first, but then in silent spasms, tears running down his face into his beard. It went on for so long that I was forced to ask him what he thought so amusing about being shot.

'Got to be,' he choked, 'got to be the worst interview I ever seen,' he wiped his eyes on his sleeves, and grinned at me. 'I was going to offer you the job.'

I gawped at him wordlessly, the revolver still between us.

'But, I'm—'

'A fine lad with a needle,' he filled in with a wink. 'Now, what d'you say? The pay's forty dollars per trip downriver. We leave in the morning.'

9

He striketh,
and his hands shall heal

And so I set out to ride the Mississippi River aboard the *Annabel Lee*. Evidently, Hallow had told the crew of my appointment during the night. They emerged bleary-eyed at sunrise, stumbling toward the galley for coffee, and none of them looked at me twice, save to tip me a wink and bid 'young Thomas' a good morning as they passed.

As yet, the pilot's motives for taking me aboard and keeping my identity secret remained a mystery. I prayed that the Lord had moved his soul to compassion and that he did not harbour any darker intentions. Meanwhile, the boat made ready to depart. Eli – who, it transpired, was the first mate – was as bright-eyed as a fox, despite his indulgences the night before.

'A pinch of cayenne and a raw egg,' he winked when he saw me looking, patting his stomach, 'sorts the men from the boys.'

Soon he was hollering the most colorful profanities I had ever heard as the deckhands hauled cargo into the boat, sweating beneath sacks and barrels on the gangway. I escaped onto a higher level – the hurricane deck, I heard the men calling it – and sat with my legs overhanging the action, bundled into Reasoner's coat, with the sun on my face for the first time in nearly two months.

Although there were a few passengers, most of those looking to buy passage down the river avoided the peeling, jumble of the *Lee,* whatever rumor said about her speed.

As the bells rang noon, it was time to depart. A whole wharf of steamers were straining at their lead-ropes, like horses wild to be given their heads. A crowd gathered on the rough planks of the boardwalk to watch, and see who would be first out into the middle of the channel.

The steamer chimneys had been belching out steam in preparation, and now the huge paddles began to beat the water into white-tipped froth. If there were any lawmen on the docks, they were lost in the excited halloos of the crowd. With a great shudder, the *Lee* was released from her moorings. There was scarcely a foot of room between the sides of the ships, but somehow we slid through a gap, jostling with the other bows to shoot ahead into open water. The sun flashed on a pane of glass above me, and I craned up to see Hallow, standing to attention at the wheel.

The last time I had ridden in a boat it had been with Abe, skirting California on the glorious fringe of the bright Pacific. The Mississippi was different: peat brown, lazy and wide. I had grown up on its banks, knew its twists and levees, its slime and its promise like the back of my own hand, yet I had never traveled its length.

For the most part the crew left me alone to watch the shore. Only when night fell and they gathered around the wheelhouse to smoke and drink did I find myself drawn into conversation with the men I journeyed so cautiously among.

'Ain't the worst I had by far,' Jim snorted, spitting out over the rail as I unwrapped the bandage on his hand. Of all the men, he seemed most ill at ease around me, and I wondered if he objected to my presence. 'Once took a fishhook, a great barbed one, straight through my foot.'

'Bullshit,' Eli cried, topping up a tin mug from a smeared bottle. 'Show us the scar then, you finagling bastard.'

'I ain't taking my boots off for no one,' Jim swore, settling back as I examined his hand. 'Y'all have to take my word for it.' He hissed in pain as I flexed the skin around the stitches.

'Looks to be healing well,' I told him, unrolling a clean length of bandage. 'As soon as it's firm those stitches can come out.'

'Now me,' interrupted Eli, staggering to his feet. 'I gots a doozy of a mark, an' it'll beat all y'all sons o' bitches.' He began struggling to free himself of his waistcoat and hitched up his shirt. To the left of his spine was a puckered circle of white scar tissue.

'What happened?' I could not help but ask as I packed up the chest. The men around me groaned.

'Well, I'm glad you should ask,' said Eli over their protests. 'Now, I was a farmhand when I was a lad, over in Illinois. My granddaddy had this mule, name of Hamish, most miserable cussed creature I ever did encounter. Took a mislikin' to me, on account of the fact I once hit him on the nose with an apple. Anyway, one day I'm standing in the yard, watching the clouds and generally minding my business, when Hamish turns around, calm as you please and kicks me square in the stomach.'

He took a swig of liquor.

'Would have hurt nothin' but my pride, were it not for the loose stake in the fence I fell clean onto. But, being a healthy buck I survived, an' Hamish went for glue. I made sure to buy a can in order to fix that fence and serve him right.'

I realized that I was laughing along with several other of the men. It only lasted a moment, before I remembered where I was.

'What 'bout you then, lad?' Eli grinned, swiping liquor from his beard. 'Where'd you get that slice 'cross your face?'

I ignored him, and finished my packing, wanting to be away from there.

'Let me guess,' the mate continued to probe, 'crime o' passion? Injun arrow? Tell us, young Thomas.'

I stood abruptly, the case banging against my side.

'A friend almost killed me,' I told him bluntly, before pushing up the stairs.

The wheelhouse was dark. The red-toothed grin of the stove was reflected in the windows. I shoved the case under the chair and leaned against the glass. It was loose in its frame, and a breeze pushed through the splintering wood to freshen the musty warmth within.

Eli's words had brought it all back; the moment that Muir's bullet had screamed its way past me. I remembered lying on the ground. There had been no pain then, only surprise that the blood running into my vision was my own. Carthy had fallen alongside me, laying a few inches away upon his side, like a lover.

One eye was a black hole, oozing with lifeblood. The other, heaven blue, remained open and fixed upon my face in death.

I pressed my forehead to the cold glass. Distantly, I was aware that the ribaldry of the men outside had subsided into murmurs.

'They don't mean no harm,' said Hallow, quietly. I had forgotten he stood there. His back was to me, eyes questing out over the river, though I could not fathom how he saw anything through the darkness. 'They're curious about you, is all.'

'And what about you?' I did not have it in me to be subtle. 'What do you gain from having me aboard?'

He must have heard the bitterness in my voice, throat tight from unshed tears, for he half turned in my direction.

'Well now, that depends,' he began. 'You're in some kinda trouble, that much is obvious. It's a marshal's revolver you got there in your pocket, and last I heard, they weren't letting no women go enforcing the law.'

I tensed, uncertain.

'You don't seem like a whore,' he mused, 'nor do I think you're out to disadvantage me or the crew in any way, so.' He threw a smile over his shoulder, teeth gleaming. 'Ain't it only proper to go helping a woman in need?'

'Not this much,' I insisted. 'If you're hoping that there is money in it for you, a ransom or some such, you are mistaken.'

Mr Hallow was silent for a long time as the boat cut through the black river, ripples hissing against the sides.

'I was in the army for a time, you know,' he said eventually. 'Early on, as a volunteer. Caught a fever, infection in the chest what couldn't be shifted, so they sent me home. Saw one battle though, if you could call it that. There were more dead boys laid to ground that day than cattle in a slaughterhouse. We came out on top, and grabbed us some secesh prisoners. Highest ranking of them was a doctor. Bein' hot-headed and drenched in our friends' blood, we was all for lynching him and sending his regiment back his scalp in revenge. But one of the captains stopped us, took the man and freed him. You know what he said?'

I could only stare through the darkness, until his face seemed to melt into shadow.

"'Don't kill the doctors,'" Hallow's voice was rapt. "'How many lives d'you think he might save, if he lives? You kill him, you kill a hundred men, and all that could come to pass with their futures.'"

He sighed, a long weary sound.

'I got some lives on my hands, miss,' he finally said. 'I figure if I help you, and you help others, that might go some way to payin' off my debt to the devil.'

10

The paths of their steps
are entangled

By the time we arrived at the port of Cairo, Illinois, a few days later, I had begun to learn the way of life on a steamer ship. There was indeed a captain on board, an idle fellow called Johnson, whom we rarely saw. Overall the running of the ship was left to Eli and Hallow: between the pair of them, they knew their vessel as if it were alive, right down to each gauge on the boiler, each rivet in the hull.

My days were easy. I sat in the sun on the hurricane deck and watched the river, or sheltered in the wheelhouse when the weather was bad. Now that I had put some distance between myself and the convent, I began to consider the severity of my deed. Not only had I burned the bridge to the only home I had ever known, I had made an enemy of Marshal Reasoner.

And what of myself and the Lord? Sometimes, I thought I felt Him with me, saw His plan in my good fortune at finding the *Annabel Lee*. At others times I felt utterly desolate. I had seen too much to live calm and cloistered. How, then, was I to stay faithful and serve Him?

Whenever panic threatened, I would stride to the bow, no matter what the weather, and turn my face to the south. *There* was work to be done, and a promise to be kept. Abe was hunted through the wilds, thrown into the company of desperate men. I had failed to save Carthy's soul, but I would not give up on his.

The levee at Cairo was bursting at the seams with other ships, sailing for New Orleans or back up north. Hallow had handed out a week's pay to the men, myself included, and though I was reluctant to leave the safety of the ship, there were purchases to be made in the stores that lined the river.

I was no stranger now to traveling in the wild, and bought those things I thought necessary: ammunition for the revolver, matches, a small knife. I was making my way back to the ship when I noticed a cartographer's shop. If I was to venture into the unknown, then what I needed was a map.

It was busy within, full of pilots exchanging news of the river and its fluctuations, seeking out maps of this stretch or the other, and Union clerks, frantically gathering information for their regiments. The sight of the blue uniforms set me on edge. The army had sent Sister Thomas Josephine back to St. Louis and would be held accountable for her disappearance; here, I tried to remember, I was just 'young Thomas'.

I asked the beleaguered sales boy for any maps relating to Arkansas, and the Indian Territory beyond.

'They ain't well drawn, for the most part,' he said brusquely. 'There's none too many care to risk their heads on account of mapmaking. But we've a few. They're laid out yonder. That negro's looking on them, currently.'

A man was stooped over a pile of papers, further along the counter, leaning so far in that his nose almost touched the wood. I approached, meaning to stand alongside him when he turned: crooked nose, unshaven cheeks, eyes the color of a winter pond.

My heart stopped. It was Reasoner.

I I

The flood divideth the people

'Have you nothing with more detail?' Marshal Reasoner snapped at the clerk, 'These maps have nothing but "Comanche" scrawled on them.'

My lungs were barely drawing air. Reasoner wore a different coat, one that fitted him badly across the shoulders. I began to edge sideways out of view, but he straightened and turned my way. There was nothing I could do except lunge for the counter, and bury my head in a pile of papers displayed there.

'You wait a moment,' the clerk sneered at the marshal. 'There are other customers—'

Reasoner pulled back his coat to reveal a badge with a star.

'I do not have a moment,' he growled. A vein beat in his neck. 'I have flogged four horses near to death to get here from St. Louis; if you do not supply me with what I need, you will be standing in the way of half the law in Missouri.'

'Then we are fortunate that this side of the river is Illinois,' the clerk shot back with a haughty sniff. 'You will have to wait your turn.' To my horror, he turned to me. 'These are the maps you asked for, young man. Do you see any to interest you?'

I could feel my skin turning red from collar to scalp beneath Reasoner's scowl. Surely, he would recognise the scar on my face, his coat, but he only muttered in frustration and turned away. I grabbed the first map I saw and thrust a handful of coins at the clerk.

'A good choice for the Indian Territories,' the clerk said loudly, counting my money. 'One of our more *detailed* maps.'

Reasoner swore in frustration. I spun away from the counter only to collide with his shoulder. For a moment, he glowered

343

down into my face before his eyes settled on the jacket. His frown faltered.

'That's—' he began.

I ducked away from him with all the speed I could muster, pushing through the crowded room in an attempt to make the door. Reasoner was bellowing behind me, but I was smaller, and faster, and burst onto the street.

Dodging through the crowd I raced back toward the ship, the map crushed in my fist, fear making my breathing short. I glanced behind me, and saw him staggering from the shop, fumbling for his weapon. A horse-drawn carriage was rumbling past, and I threw myself behind it with inches to spare.

At the dock, the *Annabel Lee* stood newly loaded and primed for departure. Eli was lounging in the weak spring sunlight, smoking and sharing a bottle with some cargo men. I scrambled up the gangplank as if it were on fire, and yanked on his sleeve.

'Is everyone aboard? We have to leave, now,' I gasped, searching the levee desperately for any sign of Reasoner.

'Now then, young sir,' the mate smirked, 'we're all here and ship-shape, so what's got you all riled—'

There was a commotion in the crowd, some way along the bank. Without another word, I sprang past him and kicked the gangplank onto the dock. The men below cried out in protest as I frantically began to ring the bell that signaled departure.

'What in all hell are you doing?' the mate fumed, dragging my hand away and shaking me like a puppy.

'Thomas!' Mr Hallow's head was sticking out the wheelhouse window. 'What cause for alarm?'

'Life or death, Mr Hallow!' I yelled, twisting free of Eli's arms. 'We must leave now!'

With a single nod, the pilot disappeared. A moment later, I heard a different bell clanging in the depths of the ship and felt a great juddering as the paddles began to turn.

Five boats away, four, men in uniform were swarming up the gangplanks. Reasoner was on the dock, shouting for them to search every craft. For one heart-stopping moment we hung in balance between land and water. The marshal turned his face toward our stern, and our eyes met. Then a great convulsion shook the ship, throwing every one of us off balance: something was straining, metal squealing in protest, and I lost sight of him.

'The rope!' cried Eli, leaping for the railing.

The boat remained anchored to the dock by a thick rope, stretched to breaking. Eli was fumbling with the complicated knot that fixed it in place, calling for Hallow to stop. A few more inches and the whole of the rickety stern would rip free. The mate's hands were slipping; there was no time.

I pulled the revolver from my pocket and armed it. I had never fired such a weapon before, but I imagined that I held one of Muir's pistols, and sighted it the same way, praying that my bullet would find its mark.

'Stand back!' I yelled to Eli, and fired.

The rope exploded in a shower of fibers. The *Annabel Lee* lurched her way free of the other ships at her famous speed. As I looked back at the dock, the wind caught the map that I had dropped, sending it flapping and curling across the distance like a broken wing, to scud to a halt at Reasoner's feet.

12

Now I am turned into their song

The men stood around, looking at me expectantly. They were gathered on the wheelhouse steps, as was their way, yet rather than the usual jibes and noisy chatter, silence reigned, save for the odd snort or cough.

'Well then,' Eli said, arms crossed. 'You promised an explanation.'

I looked pleadingly toward Mr Hallow, but he remained impassive. After our flight from Cairo, Eli had dragged me up to the pilot and demanded to know who I was. The men were scared, he said; they had seen the lawmen on the dock. There was no denying who they were after. The mate had wanted to turn back and hand me in, but Hallow had overruled him. I should have the chance to explain, he said, before they decided what to do with me.

The truth was a specter, touching all of us with its presence: unseen but felt and feared. My mouth was dry with the need to confess. I did not know where to start, how to correct the falsehoods I had willingly spun. *Deceit is in the heart of them that think evil things: but joy followeth them that take counsels of peace.*

I crossed myself, and set my chin firm.

'I am a woman,' I told them, fixing my eyes on the wheelhouse door, 'and a fugitive. I am sought by the law for the murder of six men. Until a few weeks ago there was a bounty of five hundred dollars upon my head.'

There was a long silence. Eli cleared his throat.

'Well I knew the woman part,' he said hoarsely. I looked up at him incredulously and he shrugged. 'Worst disguise I ever seen.'

'I knew it and all,' interjected Jim, 'never seen fingers like that on a man.'

346

The rest of the crew looked somewhat guilty. I could tell they were trying not to glance at Hallow.

'Figured it were none of our business,' offered Eli as an explanation. ''Til now, that is. You bring the law down on us, you *make* it our business.' He looked around. 'Anyone got questions? Because I sure as hell do.'

'Who were the men on the dock?' the night watchman demanded.

'Where'd you learn to shoot like that?' a young engineer butted in at the same time.

Before I could answer, Jim stood up angrily.

'She ain't telling the truth, you idiots,' he snarled. 'Who the hell ever heard of a woman with that size bounty on her head? The only one who's come near was that crazy blackcap, what's her name, one killed those brothers and that priest and them men, down in Mexico.'

The young engineer started forward at his words. He looked as though he was figuring a sum in his head.

'That's six,' he said slowly, turning a little pale. 'What you just said, Jim, those killings, it makes six. And she said . . .'

I felt the weight of their eyes upon me. With a heavy sigh, I reached beneath my shirt and pulled out the rosary that hung there. The cross swung between my fingers.

'Holy mother of God,' swore Eli.

347

13

I was the brother of dragons

'Is it true you once blew a fella's head clean off?'

I looked at the rapt faces around me. The senior men among the crew had retired below deck with the captain in order to decide my fate. The lower-ranking members remained, crammed into the wheelhouse, where the assistant pilot had taken over steering. I had changed into my habit; once my identity had been revealed, it seemed a falsehood to remain in trousers. If anything, this new costume increased the crew's curiosity ten-fold.

'*I* heard that y'all escaped a mining camp in California by callin' down the wrath of God upon the mountain,' said the engineer importantly.

'That is nonsense,' I told him, though I could not help but smile. 'A crate of nitro-glycerine is hardly a substitute for the mighty fury of the Lord.'

'So you were there?' the cabin boy pressed. 'Me an' Bill, we was trying to figure where you went, after we read 'bout you skipping the gallows in Carson City. We heard 'bout that, 'bout you an' the traitor.'

'Abraham Muir is—' The sentence stuck in my throat. I could not help but see Carthy, eyes desperate in the flames that consumed El Paso del Norte, silently begging me to call him those three words before he died: *a good man.* 'I would rather you did not speak of Muir,' I said quietly, 'but yes, we traveled through the Sierra Nevadas. We survived an ice storm.'

There was a murmur among the men.

'You still ain't said where you learned to shoot like that,' the engineer continued. 'Nuns ain't supposed to shoot like that. Hell,

I couldn't shoot like that.' He gaped as he realized his blasphemy. 'Sorry, miss. I mean, ma'am.'

I nodded in thanks.

'I was no good at all in the beginning,' I assured him, and the others crowded in to listen. 'I learned in the mountains, on jackrabbits first, then in the desert, in Mexico. I had time to practice.'

One of the older men whistled.

'Thought I'd seen a deal of this country,' he said around the stem of his pipe, 'traveling this river the way I done. I been to Ohio, all the way down to New Orleans. But California, Mexico,' he shook his head, 'those are wild lands. Wouldn't catch me out there.'

'Have any of you ever been into Indian Territory?' I ventured.

The men laughed incredulously.

'You ain't serious?' the engineer said. 'No one goes into Indian Territory, save for the rustlers an' scalp hunters, and even they end up dead more often than not.'

'I do not have a choice,' I said resolutely, swallowing the distress that had risen at his words. 'I took a vow. There is a soul there that I've promised to save, and I would walk through a thousand such places before I let him go to the devil.'

The silence that followed my assertion was broken only by the shifting of coals in the stove, the gentle slop of water in the darkness below. The oldest of the men poured a measure of whiskey into a tin mug, and came forward to press it into my hand.

'I swear it, Sister,' he told me, a little misty in the eyes, 'whoever that man is, he's the luckiest son of a . . . he's dern lucky in having you on his side. Makes me wish I never lost my faith.'

'Faith can never be lost,' I replied, staring down at the mug, 'even if we turn our faces from it.'

He toasted me in agreement, and I raised my drink in turn, but no sooner had the metal touched my lips than the assistant pilot let out a curse.

'What in hell's name—?'

A second later he was hauling on ropes and levers, yelling into the speaking tube that fed down to the boiler room.

'Run her back, run her back, goddamit! There's something in the current!'

The boat shuddered as gauges were shut off, as pistons began to squeal and reverse their oiled imperative. The paddles, in turn, streamed with water and groaned as they began, ever so slowly, to turn in the opposite direction.

We crowded to the windows. A hundred yards away, something huge floated upon the rolling surface of the Mississippi, drawing ever closer. It was burning. Great plumes of orange fire made it seem as if the river itself was aflame. The moon illuminated smoke and steam, as if a great maw had opened to disgorge its hot breath into the night.

A piece of wreckage came drifting toward us. There was no denying its shape: part of a deck, railings torn and twisted at either end. Alongside floated what looked like a body.

'It's the *Admiral Milton*, from Cape Girardeau,' breathed the engineer. 'She's destroyed.'

14

The giants groan under the waters

The carnage was absolute. That thick, alluvial darkness was a circus, the wreckage smouldering red and white, throwing the faces of survivors into grotesque detail.

I stood at the railing of the *Lee,* unable to speak. Below, the crew were busy anchoring us upriver from the ruined boat, gathering ropes to drop one of the cargo rafts into the river. The middle section of the *Admiral Milton* was utterly gone; toward the far shore I could make out one of the chimneys, floating like a great log. The bow was already under water. I could see pale wood beneath the surface, sinking deeper with every passing minute. By some miracle, part of the stern remained afloat. It was this that survivors were clinging to, although those who could swim had struck out toward us as soon as we had come into view.

However difficult my path, here were people who suffered and lives to be saved. I raced up the stairs to the wheelhouse to gather the medical chest. I slung Reasoner's coat over my habit, for the night was cold.

I arrived on the boiler deck just as Eli was about to put to river upon the cargo raft.

'Ain't no way you're lettin' the nun go,' Jim protested, as I made to clamber over the railings. 'She'll bolt first chance there is.'

'Don't be a fool,' I snapped at him, as I tossed the medical chest down to Eli. 'I fixed your hand up, didn't I? There are people over there twice as deserving of my help.'

I did not wait for him to reply, but slithered down the side of the ship onto the raft.

'Let's go,' I told Mr Hallow.

He gave a short laugh as we pushed away, leaving Jim to splutter above us.

Soon, any laughter was erased by the horror we encountered. We pulled aboard two young crewmen, one of them unconscious from a blow to the head and another badly burned and half drowned. Hallow questioned him as Eli pushed us carefully closer to the wreckage.

'We was running well,' the injured man sobbed, as I gently cut away the remains of his jacket, scorched into his flesh. 'Captain was pushing us hard, with the boat crowded as it was. Had near two hundred passengers aboard and not space for fifty. He wanted to make Memphis afore they ruined the cabins . . .' He choked in pain as I worked free a wad of fibers. 'We pushed too hard. Ran too hot and the next thing we know, four of the engines just burst. The whole of midships was thrown in the air, and with it, bodies, falling back into the water . . .'

He subsided into chokes then. Hallow and I exchanged a glance as I filled my needle with morphine and sent some into the man's skin.

When I was done, Eli handed me his neckerchief.

'Tie it round your face,' he instructed grimly. 'The steam's what kills. Scalds folk to death – it can burn you from the inside out if you breathe it.'

We pulled five more from the water. All were wounded, some horrifically so, their skin seared raw. As we approached the slowly sinking stern, we saw another craft, drifting close through the fog.

'Hello the boat!' Eli called out. 'Who goes?'

A large skiff emerged from the flickering darkness, rowed by two men. One of them was broad-shouldered, wearing the rough calico of a farm laborer. The other was dressed all in black, save for a gleam of white at his collar.

A preacher.

15

Wise men confess
and hide not their fathers

My stomach gave a strange tremor as I studied the man. He was solidly built, with closely cropped hair and a pair of tiny spectacles wedged onto his face.

'Rescue party,' came the reply as they drew up alongside us, 'from Lodestone, 'bout a quarter mile downriver. We heard the explosion.'

The preacher wiped his hand on his jacket and extended it first to Hallow, then to the mate. 'Josiah Falk,' he said, blinking through the smoke and steam toward me. I stared back, and watched his eyes widen as he took in my habit, my rosary. His hand hung empty for a moment, before he quickly retracted it, and touched his head.

'Sister,' he murmured in greeting. 'I am sorry, you surprised me.'

'Have you discovered any alive?' I asked briskly, ignoring his abrupt change in manner.

'One or two,' he coughed, reluctant to meet my gaze. 'We set them on the bank, yonder. They said there were some crew trapped in the wreckage still, so we came back.'

'Like as not they're already drowned,' said Eli, 'if the steam hasn't got to them.'

'We must try, nevertheless,' I said quietly.

Hallow shook his head. 'That wreck's going to sink any moment. We have only minutes, if that.'

'I shall go aboard, even if you will not, Mr Hallow,' I told him, meeting his eyes. 'There may be lives to be saved.'

'I shall go too,' Preacher Falk spoke up, tying a cloth around his face. 'It is what I returned to do, after all.'

In the end it was decided that Hallow, the preacher and I would row across in the skiff, which was secured to the raft by a rope in case of danger. As we drew close, I felt my courage waver. The wreckage was buckled and twisted. Water bubbled up to the surface, speaking of the network of destruction sinking to the bottom of the river. The air was thick with the stench of oil, scorched metal, the distant sweetness of charred flesh. I was grateful for the cloth around my face.

Falk went first, hauling himself aboard. The deck was almost at a right angle to the water and his boots scrabbled for purchase on the wood. The wreckage creaked beneath him but held.

'You do not have to go,' Hallow was saying, but I was already on my feet, hanging the medical chest over my shoulder on a makeshift sling.

'I have debts to repay too, Mr Hallow,' I told him, and allowed Falk to pull me aboard.

'Five minutes,' the pilot called up from the skiff, 'then we must row clear.'

Gingerly, our feet slipping in spilled oil and water, we traversed the wreck. Falk would stop to call, listening in the darkness for any sign of a human voice amid the ominous creaks and groans. We were standing silent on one such occasion, when I felt icy water lap at me. I glanced down: my habit was sodden to the ankle.

'We are sinking,' I told the preacher, as calmly as I could. 'The boat is sinking.'

'Then it is too late for these poor souls,' the preacher replied. 'We shall pray for them,' he shot me a glance, 'each in our own fashion.'

We had come a fair distance from the skiff, and I could hear Hallow calling for us to return. Foot over careful foot we made our way back. I cast my eyes desperately into each window and opening we passed, trying to see a hand, a scrap of clothing, anything. We were almost returned, when I heard a faint cry, a whimper only, choked and rasping like a dying bird. I halted in my tracks, and screwed my eyes closed, trying to hear.

Whatever it was, it called again. Immediately, I whirled around, scrambled toward the other side of the sloping deck. The water was deeper here, and soon I was wallowing, knee-deep, clambering over obstacles as the cry grew louder.

Halfway down the wreckage was a metal door. It had been staved in by a piece of debris. I thought about the *Lee,* her layout, and realized that it would lead to the boiler room. Through a crack, an eye gleamed out at me, contorted with pain.

'Man alive!' I screamed.

Against a leaf,
that is carried away on the wind . . .

I tried to comfort the trapped man, waiting for the preacher to fight his way through the water behind me. It was creeping up my legs now: in a few minutes the entire wreck would be beneath the river. The man was wild-eyed in fear and pain. I reached my fingers through the gap in the door and he grasped at them.

'I can't die here,' he gabbled over and again, 'not here, please, get me out.'

'Are there any others down there with you?' I asked, trying to peer into the darkness behind him.

'All dead,' the man choked, 'blown to pieces. Please, be quick; one of the boilers – it's still going.'

Falk waded up behind me.

'Sister,' he told me breathlessly, 'Mr Hallow said we have barely a minute before this whole heap is gone.' His face paled at the sight of the man behind the door.

'Help me,' I commanded, taking hold of the twisted metal. 'We have to free him.'

Falk stood alongside me and together we pulled upon the ruined door with all our might, even as the water inched up our bodies.

'It is no good,' the preacher panted, sweat streaming down his neck to stain the white collar, 'the blast has bent the metal, it is stuck fast.'

'We must try something else,' I insisted, only to be interrupted by a cry of warning from Mr Hallow.

We did not have to wait to discover his meaning. The next moment there was an almighty boom from the depths of the ship, sending us both staggering back. Behind us part of the deck exploded, steam blasting from the hole like a geyser. I could feel the dreadful, searing heat of it.

'It's the boiler!' the trapped man was shrieking over noise. 'It's gone, please!'

He began to throw himself bodily against the door, thrashing like a caged creature, clawing uselessly at the gap.

'We must go,' the preacher told me, eyes fixed on the trapped man, 'we cannot help him now.'

He reached out toward the door.

'My son,' he called, and caught the bloodied fingers. 'Go with grace to the Lord. He will end all of your suffering in a land of eternal peace.'

Falk made to turn away and take my arm, but the man dug his fingers into the preacher's sleeve.

'You don't understand,' he begged, 'the water down here – it'll boil me alive!' He found my gaze too, held it. 'Please, not like this!'

'I am sorry,' the preacher's eyes flicked toward the boat, where Hallow was screaming for us to return. 'If only I had a way . . .'

The man began to cry then, in terror of the agony to come. Trembling, I reached inside my jacket. There was Reasoner's revolver, still dry in its holster, loaded and ready.

'There is a way.' My voice came from very far off, as I stared down at the instrument of destruction in my hand.

The trapped man had seen it too.

'Yes,' he whispered, eyes fixed upon the weapon, 'do it, please.'

Wordlessly, Falk took the revolver. He stared at it for a long moment, lip twitching.

'Get back to the boat,' he muttered at me, and armed the gun. I was surprised at the ease with which he managed it.

I did not move, rooted to the spot, even as the steam howled toward us. Falk took aim through the gap. The man lowered his head and locked his hands together in readiness.

'Forgive me,' whispered Falk.

No shot came.

I looked up into the preacher's face to find it white as lime, mouth slack and drooping. The gun shook in his hand, so violently that I thought he might drop it.

'Forgive me,' he murmured again, 'I cannot.'

Below us, the boat gave a tremor and sank a few inches lower. Fire flashed from the darkness behind the trapped man. He shrieked and clawed desperately for the gun.

Falk was backing away, but I stepped into his path, wrenched the revolver from his fingers. The trapped man looked into my eyes.

'*Benedictio Dei omnipotentis*,' I called, 'admit this soul into the glory of the Lord, who lives and reigns, world without end.'

'Thank you,' the man whimpered, 'thank—'

The weapon exploded in my hand.

Nunslinger: Book 8

The Brother of Bone Orchard

The True Tale of how Sister Thomas Josephine of St. Louis, Missouri, fell into the Company of Outlaws in pursuit of one Abraham C. Muir.

I

And the eighth
was the preacher of justice

The bandage slipped from my hand. Dawn was breaking and my eyes could no longer focus on their work. I rubbed at them and caught the smell of blood too late: metallic and animate. I was too weary to wipe it away.

The groans had ceased. All around me lay the wounded and dying. Fire and water had pulled at the seams of their bodies. I had patched what I could, given relief in shots of silver metal to veins, but I was no miracle-worker.

Blearily, I looked up. The survivors from the *Admiral Milton* had been carried to a barn near the riverside. The hours had passed in frenzy. The crew of the *Lee* had steered us to the bank, had shaken the townspeople from their beds to provide aid. Now all was quiet. Something at the back of my mind rattled a warning, but I was too exhausted to heed it. I stood and left the barn.

Outside the wooden door I came face to face with a crowd. They stood silent, stony-faced to a man. When I looked into their eyes, many glanced away. Preacher Falk was at their head.

'Are you done?' he muttered, voice hoarse.

I nodded.

Through the crowd, I looked for familiar faces, for the crew of the *Lee*. They stood a little way back from the rest. Eli was swaying, drunk and pale, staring at the ground. Jim glared at nothing, just rubbed his hand as though he would wear a hole through the bandage that I had wrapped around it. I looked to Hallow.

His eyes were hidden in the shadow of his hat. His mouth opened to form words, but none came as he shook his head.

I took a step forward in dismay, but my legs buckled under me and I dropped to my knees in the dirt. From the crowd, I heard a woman cry out in alarm. For a long while, nobody moved to my aid. Then footsteps were coming toward me. A hand pulled at my arm. It was Mr Hallow. I caught his scent as he knelt: river water and smoke and the sweat of a long night.

'We can't take you, Sister,' he whispered to me in the wan light. 'The crew are scared by what you did.'

I inclined my head to show that I understood, but at that moment I wanted nothing more than to slide into the mud of the riverbank, into cool, dark oblivion.

'She will be safe here?' Hallow's voice was hard as he spoke to Falk over his shoulder. 'I am holding you to oath, Preacher.'

'I cannot protect her from the law,' came Falk's reluctant answer, 'and if they come calling, I will not lie to save her. But none here shall harm her.'

I tried to speak out, to tell them that I had to journey further, that I could not remain in some backwater town and wait for the law to find me. Panic swept over me and I opened my mouth to plead with Hallow, only for my vision to sway and shift, my head spinning until I lost all sense of who I was.

I must have fallen, for I felt someone lift me in their arms. I wanted to protest, to struggle, but my body would obey me no more.

'She must rest,' Hallow said to Falk.

'This way,' sighed the preacher.

I was vaguely aware of the crowd following as Hallow carried me away from the river. Their muttering buzzed in my ears like the noise of a swarm of insects.

My head lolled uselessly against the coarse cloth of Hallow's jacket. As we passed a window, I caught a glimpse of my reflection. The face that looked back was slack and pale as death, but the scar from Muir's bullet was visible, a livid-purple line disappearing beneath my veil. In the reflection, my eyes were boreholes in a swipe of blood.

Demon, I heard someone mutter from the crowd, and at that moment, I almost believed them.

2

My strength is not the strength
of stones

By the time I regained my senses it was night. The sun had already departed from the world, leaving behind a winter haze, ribbons of cloud etched red against the sky, reflected bloody on the water.

I hauled myself upright. My head pounded for lack of food. The room I was in was sparse: a wooden lean-to, dirt and straw on the floor. I lay upon a bed, covered with a quilt. There was little else, save for a desk and a shelf containing black-bound volumes of sermons. Preacher Falk's room.

The front door stood half open to the dying day. I let the chill breeze carry the sleep from my eyes. Outside stood a row of plain and honest houses. Yet over everything was another image, imprinted onto my gaze as if I had stared at a flame for too long: the man from the boat, a bullet hole black in his brow, his eyes shifting until they became those of another, with irises of perfect blue. I shuffled back onto the narrow bed, until I could press my face into the wall.

'I have acknowledged my sin to thee,' I murmured, beads of perspiration springing on my forehead despite the cold, 'my injustice I have not concealed. I will confess against myself to the Lord: thou hast forgiven the wickedness of my sin.'

I repeated the words over and over, the wall digging deep into the flesh of my brow and my hands, until all the moisture was gone from my throat and I began to cough. The sound of liquid being poured broke my concentration.

Falk stood in the doorway, a jug in his hand. I had not even heard him enter. Slowly, he extended a cup to me.

I drank greedily. My hands shook so hard that half of the

water spilled down my chin and into the fabric of my habit. It moistened the dried blood upon my fingers, and when the cup was empty I stared wordlessly at the dark matter caked beneath my nails.

Falk was moving again, pouring more water, but this time a different scent came with it: soap, made from lard and lye. He knelt beside the bed, setting a bowl upon the floor. He stared at my stained fingers for a moment, then, steeling himself, he reached out and pulled my hands toward him.

'What are you doing?' I demanded, for his grip was tight around my wrists.

'And Jesus said,' he muttered tensely, chafing at my skin with the soap, '"If I, your Lord and Master, have washed your feet; ye also ought to wash one another's feet. For I have given you an example, that ye should do as I have done to you."'

I pulled my hands from him, splashing water on the blanket.

The preacher was breathing hard. I could plainly see the anguish and the effort it cost him to touch me, yet still his fingers twitched, desperate to complete their task.

'"I came not to call the righteous, but sinners to repentance,"' he told me breathlessly, reaching forward again.

I pushed away, dragging myself to the edge of the bed.

'You cannot judge me,' I whispered.

He drew closer once again.

'What you did was a mortal sin, Sister.'

I was shuddering, whether from anger or fear I did not know. Everything within me was confused and shaken up together.

'It was mercy.' The words pulled themselves from my lips.

The preacher shook his head, relentless. 'It was murder. Only God has the right to take a life.'

'The gun was in your hand. You promised to aid that man, but you could not.'

The blood drained from Falk's face.

'I offered him comfort,' he blustered, 'a reminder of God's grace . . .'

'As did I.'

His mouth worked for a time. 'What you did was sin,' he said finally. 'I shall pray that the Lord will forgive you.'

He shoved the bowl and soap aside.

'Preacher,' my voice stopped him in his tracks, 'you cannot judge me for having the strength to do what you could not.'

His hands gripped the edge of the table, knuckles white with the effort to control himself.

'You are lost, Thomas Josephine.' He turned to the door. 'I will send word to the marshals upriver.'

He did not look at me as he spoke but addressed the evening. 'I promised Mr Hallow that you would not be harmed by my flock, but I will not stand in the way of justice.'

'Then I shall leave,' I said.

'And go where, Sister? The roads are impassable. There will be no stagecoach until spring, and the wreck has halted travel by river.' He unhooked his glasses to polish them, muttering as if to himself. 'No, it is best that you remain here, and await judgement. Surely you can see that is what is right?'

His face was set, stolid above homespun black and badly starched white. I envied him his conviction.

'"But we are all become as one unclean,"' I told him softly, '"and we have *all* fallen as a leaf, and our iniquities, like the wind, will take us away."'

3

Nor is my flesh of brass

So began my time in the town of Lodestone. It was a strange place, squatting on the edge of the Mississippi like a toad, low and brown and half submerged in the waters. In the summer it must have teemed with disease, the heat breeding mosquitoes and biting flies in the still pools along the banks. At the drag end of winter, however, it was cold and dark.

The town was also something of a pariah. During a flood the previous winter, the river had shifted its course downstream, and now no one could decide whether Lodestone belonged to Missouri or Arkansas.

'It don't matter anyhow,' one of the women told me, gathering up linens in her strong arms, 'as there ain't been no law here since war began. First they tell us we're controlled by the Feds, then the southern army. No one got any slaves here, anyhow.' She dumped her burden into a basket and left.

I gathered from her tone that it was not through any love for the Union that there were no slave-owning families among them: the town seemed to be suffering from the worst of deprivations heaped upon it by four years of anarchy and warfare.

I had no option but to remain until I could fathom an escape route. As for politics . . . at the convent my sisters and I had taken no side in the war that pitted God's children against each other. Rather, we strove to make ourselves useful, and help those in need. I would do so again in Lodestone.

There were few men left among the community; those who had remained were either too young or too old to fight. As such, Preacher Falk was their *de facto* mayor. It was clear that he had warned his flock against me, for most would hurry away whenever I came near, making the sign of the cross over their chests.

Not so with the laundry woman. Her name was Ellen, and thankfully for me her family was one of the most generous in the town. Ellen's husband had been killed early on in the fighting, leaving her at the helm.

I asked her why she ignored Falk's warnings about me.

'Pa were a minister,' she said, as we collected bandages, 'and there weren't nothin' holy about him. He'd snore an' drink an' belt us when we done bad, like any man. Falk might be in the grace of God, but he's still a man, an' no higher or mightier than you or me.'

Her face reddened as she finished speaking.

'Sorry, Sister,' she mumbled. 'Didn't mean to speak bad of a servant of God.'

I busied myself with rearranging a patient's blanket, thankful to hide my face. She could not have known my doubts. I visited the church as often as I could, kneeling on the cold floor beneath their crude cross. I did not attend the services, but rather heard them, Falk's voice roaring out across the village, expostulating on the sin and guile of Papists, on the wilful destruction of life.

At first I had slept in the same house that my patients had been moved to, until Ellen had thrown up her hands and insisted that I take residence with her. My bed was a blanket, rolled out on the flagstones before her hearth and I was grateful for it. I had slept thus many times during my travels with Abe, before.

Ellen had three daughters, all just grown, tall and awkward as herons in their faded print dresses. In the beginning they hung back as if I might spring at them, staring at the discolored scar beside my eye, but as I helped them in their daily chores, they began to lose their shyness.

It was immeasurably comforting to be among their company as we pounded linen clean or kneaded bread or rinsed the pans. Sometimes I would laugh among their chatter and for a few minutes forget why the other townspeople avoided me. But then

I would catch an uncertain glance, and remember. Such thoughts brought pain and the memory of a bullet hole to the forehead.

As the days passed, the river remained empty. We had heard blasts and distant shouts as men worked to clear the wreckage of the *Admiral Milton,* but in almost a week, no traffic had passed. I would be safe so long as the river remained blocked, assured Ellen. The roads were too bad for travel, and Marshal Reasoner would be a fool to ride alone through these parts.

'It's the bushwhackers,' she told me briskly, as we squelched our way through a patch of reeds just outside the town. 'They'd take your marshal for a slave, right off. They come through here often enough.'

'Are they part of the southern army?' I asked.

'No,' Ellen hopped to avoid a clod of mud, 'and yes. They're outlaws, but the army pays 'em, from time to time. Mostly, they just take what they want on their way back to Indian Territory and damn the rest.'

'Indian Territory?' I said, taking my eyes off the treacherous ground. My foot slipped into a puddle, sinking up to the ankle.

Ellen gave a hard laugh at my interest. 'Don't fret; it's near two weeks' ride from here, clear 'cross the state. All the better for us, seein' as every man on the wrong side of the law from here to the New Mexico Territory camps out there,' she said, pulling me free of the sucking mud.

We arrived at a clearing in the reeds where the earth was firmer. A makeshift coop had been cobbled together and six ragged chickens pecked at the ground within.

'Why do you keep them out here?' I asked, as Ellen stooped to root among the damp straw for eggs.

'Bushwhackers take what they *see*,' she said, examining two small ovals and handing them to me to place in a basket. 'The goat and the pigs were in the village,' she straightened with a sigh and cracked her back. 'They took them, even tried to take the cow, and kill't it when it wouldn't go with them. They don't understand, see. They're just foolish boys who ain't out for glory, only spoils.'

'Is there nothing that can be done?'

'You see any militia here?' Ellen's face was resigned. 'No, there ain't. They'll not lay a hand on us women, but there ain't nothing to stop them taking everything we have.'

Ahead of us, her daughters streamed toward the house, laughing and chattering.

'But we make do,' she said softly, watching them, 'and we pray for the time when things are better.'

4

Does thou desire to keep
the path of ages?

'Should you like to learn how to shoot?'

Ellen and I were peeling potatoes at her large kitchen table. Her daughters worked around us, sweeping the floor or tending to the fire. At my words, one of them dropped the poker she was holding into the soot.

'I beg your pardon?' Ellen's face was a picture of amazement, a long ribbon of potato skin hanging forgotten from her knife.

'I have been thinking,' I told her, as casually as I could manage, though my heart increased its pace, 'that if you could shoot, then maybe you would be able to defend yourself from those men.'

'Bushwhackers don't hurt women,' interrupted Lacey, Ellen's youngest. 'Everyone knows that.'

'She's just soft on their pretty hair,' accused Mary, the second oldest. 'They wear it long,' she told me, 'and they got these shirts an' ties, all bright red and yeller and green, like a circus. They say it's 'cos the Feds are such poor marksmen, they need all the help they can get in findin' a target.'

'They do look fine,' grinned Lacey.

'Sure do, if you like flea-ridden sons of farmers with a feather or two—'

'Enough, Mary,' Ellen snapped. She returned her gaze to me, drumming the knife handle upon the table. 'What if we did learn – think that'd make them leave off? They're wintering down south now, but come spring they'll be back, could bring half of Quantrill's raiders back with 'em.'

'You said yourself they were only boys, out for what they could plunder,' I said. 'What if you could dissuade them? You do not deserve to be afraid.'

Ellen stared at me for a moment.

'It ain't a woman's place,' she sniffed, and resumed hacking at the vegetables. 'A woman's got no business with firearms.'

'A woman's got no business having to hide her livestock way out in the reeds for fear of thieves, either,' I retorted.

'She's right, Ma,' Mary said. 'I *hate* tramping through those reeds. They ruined my skirt.'

'Quiet,' her mother barked. 'Ain't you got chores to do?'

A silence fell upon the kitchen, but it was thick with unspoken thoughts. *Please Lord*, I prayed, *allow me to aid these people*. I would help them in any way that I was able; surely that was with a strong arm and clear sight as well as prayers?

'How d'you know to shoot, anyway?' Ellen said after an age.

I remembered the rapt faces of the crewmen aboard the *Annabel Lee* as I told my tale. Here was a way I could win them.

'I have traveled a long, hard road to get here, Mrs Anderson. Out west there is sometimes naught but you and the rocks and the sky. You do what you must to survive.'

I tipped another few potatoes into the pot and leaned forward. Ellen's daughters, I noticed, had slowed in their work to listen.

'I learned how to shoot with pistols and a rifle,' I told her, 'and I practiced so that I could knock a man's hat clean off and not damage one hair on his head. I can hunt too, with a knife. An Indian taught me that, in the desert.'

'You traveled with an *Injun*?' exploded Lacey. 'Din't he try to scalp you?'

'*She*,' I corrected with a laugh, 'and no, she saved my life, after a snakebite. I traveled with her for a time, and we hunted lizards for our supper.'

'Lizards!' two of the girls exclaimed in unison, their faces twisted with disgust. 'How could you eat that?'

'When you have been riding all day on an empty stomach,' I smiled, 'those scaly legs start to look very tasty.'

They squealed and I found myself grinning, for the first time in weeks.

'Well there ain't no lizards here,' said Ellen crossly, 'only men.'

'Please, Ma,' Ginny, the eldest girl said, draping her arm around her mother's shoulders, 'I'd like to learn how to shoot. Remember when Pa used to bring home a duck? We could shoot ducks an' have good meat again.'

The older woman's face twitched between anger and amusement.

'Fine,' she relented, stabbing the knife into a potato. 'I suppose you realize we ain't got no weapon? What'll you teach us on? A shoe?'

'I had a revolver,' I reminded her, 'in my coat, when I left the *Lee*.'

'Falk's got it,' said Lacey, scrambling over to the table, 'I saw it the other day, when I took him his bread. It were on his shelf.'

'Then we shall have to get it back,' I smiled.

372

5

He shall give flint for earth

'Ain't sure I like deceiving the preacher like this,' complained Ginny, rubbing her hands nervously on her skirts.

'We ain't deceiving no one,' Lacey nudged her. 'Anyway, don't you *want* to learn to shoot?'

'It's her gun,' Mary reasoned, 'so it ain't stealing.'

I remained quiet. It would not do at this point to admit that I in turn had taken the weapon from someone else.

'Hush, all of you,' Ellen hissed. 'Here he comes.'

Further up the street, Preacher Falk stepped from the church and began to amble toward his house. Ellen shook out her skirts, and clutched a bundle firmly to her stomach.

'Stay quiet, the lot of you,' she ordered, and stepped out onto the road.

'Preacher!' she called in greeting, as he opened his door.

'Mrs Anderson.' He tipped his hat. 'I thought we were not on friendly terms of late.'

'I am sorry. I did not mean to allow that woman to come between us.' Ellen's voice was over-earnest. Beside me, Lacey winced.

'Ma's a terrible liar,' she whispered to me, before being shushed by Mary.

'I have baked some bread,' Ellen continued, holding out the bundle, 'and it would please me to see you enjoy it, by way of my apology. Them bushwhackers took most of our preserves, though, and I'm afraid it is rather plain without jam.'

'They know not what they do,' said Falk distractedly, peering into the bundle. 'I am comforted to hear you have not been deceived by the Sister. The sooner she is taken on her way, the better for us all.'

'Amen. Now let me set this down for you.'

She disappeared into Falk's house. As one, the girls and I held our breath; after a few moments, Ellen reappeared, shoving something beneath her shawl.

'I must be getting along now, Preacher,' she was saying, her cheeks very red. 'Good day.'

She increased her pace toward us, motioning us to move. The girls tumbled out from around the corner, hurrying me away, breathless with giggles. There was a cry from behind us and I looked back to see Falk throw himself around the doorway.

'Mrs Anderson, bring that back!'

'I do not know what you mean, Josiah!' Ellen called over her shoulder, gasping with laughter herself.

'Mrs Anderson!'

We bundled inside her house and Ellen collapsed against the closed door, fanning herself. Beside me, the girls were helpless with laughter.

'My, but he will be in a rage,' said Ellen, wiping her eyes. 'Here.'

She thrust the weapon toward me. My hand closed around the smooth wood of the grip. Almost immediately, I was back on that sinking ship, in a hellfire of darkness and danger, the jolt of a bullet through my muscles as a man sank lifeless into the black waters before me.

'You take it,' I swallowed, trying to summon a smile. 'It will be yours to practice on, after all.'

6

Can the rush be green
without water?

The Anderson girls knew of a little grove, far away from the town, where we might practice. As we tramped into the clearing for the first lesson, the girls were twitching with nervous excitement. Ellen was pale, but she too seemed eager.

'The first thing you must learn,' I told them, 'is how to load the weapon. It will be of no use to anyone sitting empty.'

I made each of them take turns packing charges into the chambers. Lacey managed to drop most of the bullets onto the damp ground.

'Never get them wet, if you can help it,' I said firmly. 'Keep the weapon where you know it shall be dry.'

'Where did you keep it?' Lacey retorted, cheeks dimpling. 'Do habits have pockets?'

Ellen swiped at her. 'Don't be disrespectful of the Sister,' she rebuked.

'When I was in Mexico,' I told the girl, 'I had special bracers that were hidden beneath my sleeves. That way, I was able to ride safe and keep my guns handy.'

The girl's eyes had grown round. 'Is that when you got *shot*?' she breathed.

I turned away with a smile.

'First,' I told Ellen, 'you hold the gun like so.'

Shooting lessons continued every day after that. I tied a rag to one of the tall reeds for target practice, and was gratified when, not long after, it was riddled with holes.

In return, Preacher Falk roared about the danger of weapons in his sermons, of a woman's place and her seemly duty, but the rumors of our shooting lessons proved too enticing. We were joined by others. We quickly ran out of ammunition, but Ellen bartered replacements from the wounded sailors and the old men in town.

'They know better than to cross me,' she said with a wink.

Winter was gradually releasing its hold on the land. The sun grew stronger, coaxing buds from skeletal brown trees. In another life I would have celebrated the spring as the birth of a new year, the glory of the Lord and his sacrifice. Now, however, it was impossible for me to know whether the season brought hope or fear.

One morning, while at my chores with Ellen, we were halted by the unexpected sight of a plume of steam from the riverbank, and the distant sound of washing paddles. In the middle of the vast river, a quarter of a mile away, a steamboat was thrashing its way past.

'River's open,' the other woman murmured.

We watched a while longer. The light caught upon the windows of the wheelhouse, and for a brief flash I ached to be aboard that boat, sailing once more, anonymous.

'I saw Falk leave this morning,' Ellen said, squinting out over the gray water. 'He must have figured the roads are clear. No doubt he'll ride for Osceola, see if he can get word to the law from there.'

'I must go west,' I told her, as a fresh breeze blew the scent of coal and oil toward us, 'to Indian Territory.'

She nodded. 'I guessed you might say that. It's suicide, but somethin' tells me that won't stop you none.'

'I shall put my faith in the Lord.'

'You truly believe that this is the path he chose for you?' she asked, as we walked back up the street. 'That he would send you into danger and suffering? I'll wager this was not the life you imagined when you joined your convent.'

'No,' I agreed, feeling a twist of a smile, 'but there is work to be done, out here, there are souls to be saved. I do not believe I would be of use in the convent.'

'I understand,' she said slowly, turning her eyes upon me. 'Better to be where you're most needed, even if that is the darkest of places.'

7

He gave a way for the
sounding storms

Time was on my side, for by dusk Falk had not returned. Ellen
had been making inquiries through the town, to see if anyone
would sell me a horse. I had money from my work aboard the
steamer, but few were willing to deal in Union greenbacks.

I slumped into a chair by Ellen's hearth in frustration. Every
hour I remained was an hour in favor of Reasoner and the law.

'How far is the nearest landing?' I asked Ellen. The door flew
open before she could answer and the girls tumbled in, skirts
mussed, faces flushed.

'What on earth is the matter?' their mother said, rushing
forward.

'The bushwhackers are back!' gabbled Lacey. 'We was feeding
the chickens and two of 'em came busting outta the reeds, but
Ginny scared 'em off!'

'Talk sense, Lacey,' Ellen ordered.

'She is, Ma,' interrupted Mary. 'Ginny were a wonder. These
two men, all mud and patches, came riding on out, and they
bid us good evening and the blond one says to the other, "these
look like federal chickens to me". And I try to tell them that
they's just chickens and they don't got no politics, but they pull
out their knives and start cutting the wire. Then,' Mary took a
deep breath and stared at her sister, 'Ginny says, "you ain't
gonna take those chickens". An' the men jus' laugh an' carry
on, so Gin gets the gun out and tells them to lay off or she'll
shoot.'

Ellen's face went dead white, but Mary gushed on.

'Well, they weren't laughin' so much then, and one of 'em
looks right mad, coming forward with his knife out, so Ginny

takes aim and bang! Straight through the hat! Jus' like you said, Sister, a big old hole.'

'Then they starts yellin' and we starts yellin',' chipped in Lacey, 'and Ginny tells them that unless they clear out the next one'll be through their bellies.' She gave a satisfied sigh. 'Wish you could'a seen it.'

Ginny had not spoken. Only now did she take the revolver out of her pocket. Her hands were shaking so much that the metal rattled against the table as she set it down.

'Weren't nothing,' she whispered. 'Sister Josephine's right, I were tired of being scared.'

Ellen pushed past me and tugged her daughter into a tight embrace.

'You foolish girl,' she said fiercely into her hair, 'that were brave but it were mighty stupid.'

'They won't come back, Ma,' said Lacey cheerfully, kicking off her shoes in front of the hearth, 'Ginny seen 'em off for good.'

Ellen met my eyes over the head of her daughter, who clung to her now, courage fading.

'We must pray that's so.' The woman's voice was harsh. 'For the Lord only knows what hell we may have brought down otherwise.'

8

My arrow is fierce
without any sin

That night I dreamed of Abe. I dreamed that we were traveling together once more – riding Pokeberry and Rattle through a forest. There was a fall chill in the air and we were moving quietly, so as not to disturb some unseen presence, something dormant, like a beast in hibernation.

From the corner of my eye I caught a flicker of movement. I steered my mount off the path and rode closer. It was a bird, with gentle gray feathers, trapped in a briar bush. I slipped off Pokeberry and reached in to pluck it out, only to recoil in horror: the bird had impaled itself on a thorn, the woody point driven deep into its eye. Black blood oozed, but still it fought.

I staggered away, grasping at my side for a knife, but slipped and fell into a pool. It was not deep, but the edges were slick with mud. I wiped the muck from my face, yet more ran into my eyes. I scrubbed at them, but it only grew thicker. I called for Abe and the mud filled my mouth, seeping over my lips and tongue. I spat it free but still it came, running down my throat until I began to suffocate in darkness.

I thrashed awake, only to find a hand clamped over my mouth. Ellen's face hovered in shadow as she knelt over me. Her hair hung loose over the shoulders of her nightgown. Beyond her I saw the girls cowering together, and beyond that a glow of orange in the night.

The first shot broke the stillness before I could speak, and was followed by a second volley. I could hear hooves thundering along the muddy street outside.

'Out of the house,' Ellen commanded shakily, pushing shawls

into her daughters' arms. 'Stay quiet and let them take what they want.'

'Mamma, no,' cried Ginny, white as thin milk, 'they've taken everything already!'

'She is right,' I said, hauling myself to my feet, nerves jolting with every gunshot from outside. 'They are thieves and criminals, if we fought them—'

'They might kill us,' Ellen snapped. She looked at Ginny. 'Let's pray to God they have poor memories for faces.'

Ginny reached resolutely for the gun, but her mother snatched it away, shoving it deep into her own shawl.

'Cover your head with a blanket, at least,' she snapped at me, 'or do you *want* to be discovered?'

Outside, the street was in chaos: cries and gunshots rang out from every direction, mingled with coarse laughter and bellowing. A pair of horses galloped past us, the riders, with long greasy hair and patched shirts, crowing and discharging their pistols into the air. Across the street an old man stumbled from his house with an agonized cry, his nightshirt soaked in blood.

The girls were sobbing and Lacey let out a scream, but Ellen pushed her away.

'To the church,' she called frantically. 'We must get to the church.'

I tried to turn toward the wounded man, but Mary's hand was like a vise around mine, dragging me away.

Ellen looked over her shoulder and cried in dismay. Behind us, her house was on fire, flames licking from a smashed window up into the roof.

'This is your doing!' She turned to me, wild-eyed. 'You taught them to fight and this is what come of it! Falk's right, you're a demon, nothin' but death and misery—'

'Mamma!' screamed Mary beside me. 'They got the preacher!'

At the top of the street, a man on a horse was pulling to a stop. Behind him, dragged along by a rope, was a figure in black, filthy and grazed. Blood matted the preacher's hair; the glass in his spectacles was missing, though the mangled wire frames still clung to his face.

'Found me an abolitionist!' roared the man on the horse.

Falk slumped to the ground, only to be yanked up again.

'This fella's riding north for his friends at the border,' the raider continued, drawing his gun. 'Jayhawkers been thin on the ground, and I ain't collected me a scalp for months. Guess this one'll have t'do.'

'Here, Morgan, don't that white collar mean he's a preacher?' another man interrupted. He sauntered out of one of the nearby houses, carrying a cooked chicken carcass. 'I got a notion that it's wrong to go scalpin' preachers.'

'That's him,' Ginny's voice shivered near me. 'That one with the chicken. That's the one I shot at earlier.'

'I'll not let him harm you,' Ellen swore.

The sound of their voices, though quiet, caught the chicken man's attention. He swung around to face us. 'Well now,' he cried, peering through the smoke, 'if it ain't the little lady who done took a chunk outta my hat.' He strutted closer, tossing away the bones and wiping his hands down his front. 'Y'see,' he said, grinning, 'got my chicken in the end. Told my friends too. Y'all could've saved yourselves a deal of trouble.'

'I'm sorry . . .' Ginny's voice was soft. 'I'm sorry.'

'Miss, there ain't nothin' to be sorry about,' the young man told her, leaning in. 'We got ourselves a coupl'a fine meals, and now we'll be on our way. Your preacher, though, he might be sorry.'

'You touch him, y'all will go to hell,' Ellen spat. 'That's for damn sure.'

'He chose his side and we chose ours, ma'am,' said the chicken man. 'Now if y'all excuse me.'

Beyond him, the men had set Preacher Falk atop a horse, and were busy throwing the end of a rope over the church gable. A noose was already around his neck. My muscles tensed. Mary tried to hold me back, but it was too late, I was ripping free of her grip, lunging for Ellen and the revolver concealed in her shawl.

381

I ran forward, throwing off the blanket that covered me as the men secured the final knot. Another booted the horse in the rear: it shot forward with a whinny and the preacher was jerked backward into space.

The gun was in my hand. For a moment, the memory of my past sins made my fingers shake, but the girls were screaming behind me, and a servant of the Lord was dying. Strength filled me as I armed the weapon, set my sights, and fired.

9

Let mercy forget him

Falk lay insensible, the charred rope around his neck smoking softly at the edges. A profound silence had fallen, separated from the general chaos: the sounds of looting continued – cries and shattering glass – but they were distant, muted.

Through the smoke I stared into the eyes of Falk's would-be murderers. They were gaping at me, too stunned to draw their weapons.

'Is that' – the man who had eaten the chicken squinted – 'is that a *nun*?'

His words broke the silence. There was a clamor as pistols, shotguns, knives were drawn and thrust in my direction.

'What the hell's a *nun* doin' in a place like this?' the man continued incredulously, and I swiveled to aim at him.

'You will let the preacher go,' I said evenly, 'for he is a servant of God, and I will not see harm come to him.'

'That were a lucky shot.' The man called Morgan spoke slowly, and began walking toward me. He looked to be the leader for the other men fell into step with him. 'But I'll warrant you could not make it a second time.'

'There was no luck to it,' I told him icily. 'Let that man go, or else I shall start taking limbs.'

'Morgan,' the chicken man started, 'ain't that—'

'I'm having a mite of trouble believin' you,' Morgan interrupted his man with a grin. 'See, if you really are a blackcap, there ain't no way you got it squared with the Lord to go about takin' lives willy-nilly.'

'Morgan,' said Chicken with greater alarm.

'So I'm thinking,' the leader smiled relentlessly, halting barely two paces away from me, 'that you are bluffing, ma'am, an' if you were to shoot right now, you wouldn't even clip a button on this here coat of mine.'

He was young, I realized. They all were. I could see that their faces were slender and unlined. Not one of them looked over nineteen. Whatever crimes this boy had committed to gather the loyalty of those who followed him, a hint of it came from his heedless grin, from his clear eyes that had never considered the debt of taking a life.

There was a groan from behind him and we both looked away. Falk was hauling himself to his knees, pawing weakly at the rope about his neck. He was rasping out words, his throat too raw to speak clearly.

'What's that, Preacher?' Morgan said, signalling one of the men to drag him forward. 'Speak up so as your congregation can hear you.'

Falk was dumped at the leader's feet. I heard Ellen stifle a sob of horror at the state of him.

'Preach,' Morgan said, squatting down companionably beside him, 'your neighbor here's been tellin' lies 'bout herself. Now, I don't remember me much of Sunday school, but—'

'No lies,' Falk wheezed, swaying. 'She's a killer.'

'I knew it!' burst Chicken. 'Din't I try to tell you, Morg? She's that one they're after! I saw the poster when we was down south. They want her for *six* murders! Sister Theobald or something.'

'Sister Thomas Josephine,' I corrected him coldly, 'and I believe it's seven, now. Is that not so, Preacher?'

'The law's coming,' he whispered, as he slipped to the ground again. 'You'll all see justice . . .'

Morgan's face hardened. He checked the sky, growing pale in the east, and swore.

'Kill him,' he barked at the chicken man, and turned away. 'We ride, boys!' he bellowed. 'Git on yer horses and ride!'

'I told you not to touch him!' I warned, even as Chicken armed his pistol.

'Shut her up,' growled Morgan.

384

I lunged forward and knocked Chicken's gun into the mud.

'Five hundred dollars,' I shouted after Morgan. He stopped mid-stride. 'That is the bounty on my head,' I continued clearly. 'You hand me in, you short the Union five hundred dollars.'

'No, Sister,' I heard Ginny whisper.

'Spare the man of God,' I said resolutely, 'and I shall go with you, willingly.'

'Fine,' shrugged Morgan, 'take her.'

Men were coming forward with rope. I let them pull the revolver from my fingers, bind my hands behind my back.

'Ellen,' I called behind me, 'quickly, help him.'

She and Ginny darted forward to drag the preacher out of the street, until he lay moaning in Ellen's arms. She looked up at me, swollen eyes full of questions.

'Indian Territory,' I mouthed to her, with a ghost of a smile. Then, someone was pushing me toward a horse, boosting me into the saddle. One of the men swung up behind me and I shuddered at his nearness, for he smelled of smoke and blood and battle.

'Fall out!' Morgan cried, trotting up alongside us. His pistol was drawn and the same, thoughtless grin stretched his lips. Without pause, he turned in the saddle and loosed a bullet behind him. Ellen screamed. I twisted around.

Blood was steaming from Preacher Falk's forehead.

'You ain't the only crack shot, Sister,' Morgan bragged, and I could only choke in horror as the men bore me away into the bone-gray dawn.

Silver hath beginnings
in its veins

From the moment Morgan loosed his gun upon Falk, I knew I had underestimated the men to whom I had ransomed myself. I had thought them to be foolish farm boys, out for adventure and to take what excitement they could in the wake of the war. So they were, yet they had long lost sight of any cause or call to valor. They had spilled the blood of their neighbors – of those who had seen them grow – and in doing so had scarred their souls beyond imagining.

Falk's death left me stunned. Over and again I saw that shock of blood, spilling from his skull, heard Ellen's screams fading into the distance. I had another life to add to my account.

I should have died, many times over, yet I had not. The gallows had called, the desert had clawed at me, and Muir's bullet had left its mark upon my skin, yet still I lived. I, who had promised my life and soul to the Lord eternal.

Had He saved me to do His work? Or had I wilfully misjudged His intentions, blundered wildly and selfishly after my own desires? I had sought to save Abe's soul, to guide him away from destruction and back toward salvation, yet if I was damned, then so was he.

We rode for several hours, the scenery passing without note before my blind eyes. When we finally jolted to a halt, the sun was far overhead and the landscape was entirely different. We were in a wood, the midday sun filtering weak and yellow through wet branches. There were more men now, standing about in a temporary camp. I was prodded toward a fire and sank down into the damp leaves without protest, for in that moment, I did not care what became of me. I sat, barely comprehending, as I was tied to a sapling and left alone.

Some time passed before I felt fingers loosening the bonds at my wrists. My hands fell to my sides, white and nerveless. Whoever had freed me hesitated and then began to chafe the skin. I numbly watched the dirty fingers at work, bringing pain and warmth to the surface. When I could move again, I pulled away and began flexing each joint the way Muir had shown me, when we had taken refuge in a snow-bound cabin, so many months before.

A dish of food and a steaming mug were set before me. I ignored them. Someone nudged the food closer.

'Got to eat, now.' That voice belonged to the chicken man. I saw his boots shuffling back and forth in front of me. 'There're others who'll take it if you don't.'

I allowed my head to drop back against the young tree they had tied me to, and closed my eyes. He was right. The food was eaten by another soon enough. Just as soon, we were riding again – but to where and for what purpose I did not know. As the day wore on, I grew faint from fatigue and hunger. Many times the man riding behind caught me as my eyes grew heavy and my body began to slide from the saddle. Eventually, muttering gentle curses, he bound my hands to the pommel. I did not fall after that.

When I thought that nothing would wake me from the abyss into which I had sunk, the scent of coffee reached my nose, hot and burned-brown, more welcome than wine. I raised my head, although my neck creaked in protest. It was dark. Ahead of me I could make out many campfires scattered through the darkness, the silhouettes of four or five bodies around each. I could even hear bacon sizzling. I was sick with hunger, and no amount of self-recrimination could stop my mouth from watering.

By the time footsteps approached, my eyes were clear.

'Food,' I croaked through a dust-dry throat. 'Water, please.'

'Thought you might be feelin' that way,' came the amused reply.

Chicken knelt, unstopping a flask. He held it to my lips and I gulped greedily, relishing even the drops that escaped from the corners of my mouth. When I had drunk my fill, he untied my hands once again, and I flexed them impatiently.

'Coffee?' I asked, eyes watering.

'No, ma'am, 'fraid it's mostly chicory,' he said, handing over a tin mug. 'We ain't had real coffee down here since snowfall year before last.'

The stuff was watery and bitter, but it was hot. I swallowed it down, warmth flooding my body. He handed me a plate with a hunk of bread, stale at the edges, and a pile of fried bacon. I crammed it into my mouth with clumsy fingers.

'Easy now, it won't scarper on you,' guffawed Chicken. He was squatting before me, the way Morgan had next to Falk, and the memory made my hands slow.

'Thank you,' I mumbled grudgingly through a mouthful.

'You got to eat,' he shrugged. He turned red when I met his gaze and swayed awkwardly. In the firelight, I surveyed his features. He did not look a day over fifteen, though the dirt entrenched in his skin made him look older. He was fair and freckled, with greasy red-blond hair and a beard like ground-weed on his youthful cheeks.

'We don't mistreat women, no ma'am,' he muttered, more for his own benefit than my own.

'You took their food,' I replied, working at a piece of bacon fat. 'You burned their homes, you killed their husbands and fathers and friends, but you think you have not hurt them?'

'The Union done far worse,' the young man said hotly. 'They killed our women, children an' all. Hell, we're showin' *mercy*.'

'Mercy,' I laughed bitterly, dropping the greasy rind back into the dish. 'You are the worst kind of fool. You have told yourself that for so long you truly believe it.'

He flushed angrily.

'You don't know nothing,' he spat. 'Don't know nothing of it.'

'I know what it is to destroy a soul.' I stared him down, the words burning my lips. 'I know what it is to look into a man's eyes, to see everything that made him, from babe to man, and to end it all. How many lives have you taken?'

'Twelve,' declared Chicken, though uncertainty edged his words like a tremor in the ground. 'Done killed twelve traitors.'

He finally looked into my eyes. I watched him blanch at what he saw there.

'Then you should pray,' I told him. 'Pray to remain ignorant with all your might, for, if you ever understand what you have done, it will kill you.'

When evil shall be sweet in his mouth

'Where are we going?' I demanded to the youth behind me, as he kicked his horse into a walk. It was dawn, and we had been traveling for nearly two days, yet no one had seen fit to share with me our destination.

'South,' came the taciturn answer.

We jolted along in silence for a while. I gathered my patience.

'How far south?' I pressed.

'Not much past Little Rock.' He sighed at my expectant silence and looked around. 'There's a detachment, somewhere near there,' he whispered, as if in a classroom. 'Morgan needs to talk with some of them that's higher up 'bout you, to negotiate proper. Then it'll be on to the city. Damned Feds've had control there for more'n a year now.' He paused uncomfortably. 'The *darned* Feds,' he corrected. 'Sorry, ma'am.'

I took a deep breath. The answer was not the one I wanted. I had hoped that we would ride west, into Indian country. Though I did not yet know how, it had been my plan to escape or barter my freedom once we had crossed the border, and then venture on alone in search of Abe.

'Morgan is brave, to go riding into enemy territory,' I tried. Again, there came the awkward silence of a boy uncertain of his own tongue. 'I had thought he would prefer to return to his camp in Indian country.'

'How'd you know where we camp?' the young man asked, alarmed.

'I read your thoughts,' I goaded.

He pulled the horse up short, much to its displeasure, and set me down immediately before backing the animal away, saying that I was witching him. Word went around after that, until none would carry me save for Chicken, who seemed to bear responsibility for all unpleasant tasks.

'What you gotta go saying things like that for?' he grumbled, as we swayed along. 'Ain't things hard enough for you?'

'It was a joke,' I sighed, trying to shift position. 'I cannot help it if the boy is slow-witted.'

Chicken's horse was a bow-backed creature, fat in the stomach and stout in the legs. It lurched rather than galloped, and I found myself remembering Pokeberry's smooth stride with longing.

'How'd you know about Indian country anyhow?' Chicken demanded. It seemed our conversation of the previous night had left him sour. 'Don't tell me you been there an' all.'

'Of course I haven't,' I replied wearily, 'but I've been told it's home to all manner of outlaws. I know of someone who is hiding there. A friend. He's traveling with a man called Puttick.'

To my surprise, Chicken let out a laugh. I felt my brow creasing. His tone was not pleasant.

'Do you know him?' I asked, anxious to keep him talking.

'I've *heard* of him,' Chicken said. 'Everyone *heard* of Colm Puttick. But no one we know of ever met the man. Or they ain't lived long enough to tell tale of him. He's a specter. Changes his face like a skin-walker, is what people say.'

'That's nonsense,' I dismissed. 'He is a man like any other, and wanted by the law, just as I am.'

Chicken made a noise of disagreement.

'He ain't human,' he protested. 'Some of the things he's done make Morgan look like a March lamb. Why, he won't take no men into the gang unless they swear themselves to him, then he brands them, like they was slaves, with an "X" on their chests.'

I felt him move and turned to see him tracing two lines beneath his collarbones.

'They do it willing too,' he sniffed. 'Then they're in with him 'til death, like. Anyone else sees that mark on a man that's not with Puttick, it means he split with the gang. That mark, it's a target. You see it and Puttick ain't there, you shoot at it, and send

391

the head to the Creeks for reward. They're Injuns,' he explained importantly, sensing my confusion. 'We got dealings with them along the border for safe passage, but they's loyal to Puttick most of all.'

'Is that where he is?' I asked, though my anxiety grew with every sentence Chicken uttered. 'With the Creeks?'

'Like enough,' Chicken said, obviously relishing his role as storyteller. 'He got camps in the forest. Law won't follow him in there no more. Tale goes they tried it once. Tracked him 'cross the plains all the way to the treeline. He lit some fires, lured 'em in.

'Now you ain't never been there, but it's a fright of a place; long, thin pines, deep as an eye can see, 'til you think you'll go mad with it, and round the edges these great black oaks, dark as night underneath.

'Anyhow, a posse followed Puttick in – thirty men and horses, they was – an' they never came out. Week later, they say, Puttick rode into the Creek camp, bold as you like, an' made the chief a present of thirty scalps, all sewn together. Injuns been scared loyal to him, ever since.'

Some of the boys who rode nearby had overheard Chicken's remark, and soon began their own tales of Puttick's brutality: they described burning farms and bodies strung from beams, whole families murdered and scalped. I saw their youth in the way they delighted in the grisly stories, yet even then, I believe they were sparing me details.

I listened in silence, made nauseous by every word. Were these the men to whom Abe had joined himself? Was he even now riding with them, looting and killing? I did not want to believe it, and yet, I had seen the way humanity could fall from a man the further he traveled from himself.

Whichever path I took, it would be one of grave danger. I had no allies, not any longer. The Union had no doubt renewed their reward for my capture, aided by Reasoner and his force; the Confederate Army were scattered, and those who remained were little more than outlaws and bandits, swarming the county in search of gain.

Then there were men like Puttick.

One wrong step, and my life would be cut short. Let the future bring what it may, I thought bitterly. If I was to do God's work then let it be among the fallen and the wretched, where conscience and kindness had long been forgotten.

"'And we are all become as one unclean,'" I murmured. The words came to me again, stronger and clearer than ever before. "'And we have all fallen as a leaf.'"

'What's that s'posed to mean?' Chicken demanded. I realized that I had spoken out loud.

'It means that we are all sinners,' I told him quietly, 'and it means that none of us are beyond salvation.'

12

He stretched out the north over the empty space

The next day dawned chill and bleak with rain. So followed our situation. Every road was a quagmire. Mud sucked at the horses' hooves, and more than once a rider was sent tumbling from his mount into the muck. The trees grew lower and darker, and beyond their trunks I saw water gleaming sickly, black with weed and decay.

When the rain set in, the temper of the young men suffered beyond all repair. Gone were the wild grins and stories told with jovial disregard for propriety. Instead, gazes were fixed ahead; talk was curt and brief. Behind me I felt Chicken shudder from the cold. The bushwhackers' clothes were little better than threads: they may have been colorful and draped with bright ladies' scarves, but they were worn to rags.

Sometimes we would come across a cabin or a farm, and the boys would kick their horses forward, eyes lit with anticipation. But all were empty, abandoned and looted many times over, bones sucked dry of their marrow.

We stopped in one such place for a few hours, and I was left standing in a long-forsaken yard, while the men kicked dejectedly at the walls. Beneath the mud at my feet I saw something pale. I stooped and pulled it free with clumsy tied hands. A book of common prayer, leaves torn away like a vegetable, rotted into a useless mass.

'This was not us, y'know,' came a voice from behind me. Morgan stood, leaning against his horse and watching me. His eyes were fixed, lips curved in terrifying vacancy. 'This were the Feds, when they charged through here a year back. Left the houses burning bright as torches and the pastures cut and bleeding out, all red.'

I turned away and stared at the book in my hands until the call came to ride out. The gang were looking for another town to raid: another place like Lodestone, unfortunate merely because it existed, eking out a living on the scraps and peelings of war.

After nightfall, one of the scouts returned and Morgan called a halt. There was nothing I could do but watch, tied up when even the dogs roamed free, as the young men armed themselves and fired each other up on swallows of stolen whiskey and stories of federal betrayal.

I closed my eyes then, for I could not escape it: the memory of Ellen's scream and her daughters', Falk's blood spattered across them. Falk had been wise to fear me, after all. Had he seen his own destruction in my arrival? Like the crow after which the Mexicans had named me, I had brought death, not glorious and brave but decaying and empty, in my wake.

Had I saved that man on the boat, or did he suffer somewhere eternal because of my deed? I felt a hot tear form in my eye and clenched my teeth at its uselessness. That single drop of water could not erase or atone, could not call a shot back into a gun or stop a foolish woman from imagining goodness into a pair of blue eyes.

I felt something brush my arm. Chicken stood over me, armed and ready to ride. Beneath one arm he held the rug that usually covered his horse.

'Hands too tight?' he asked, coughing awkwardly to cover his concern.

I shook my head. The tears had fallen despite my efforts, had slicked my face, but I could not even begin to speak to this boy, so oblivious to my turmoil. He knelt and arranged the rug over me.

'Might be gone 'til sun-up,' he said. His voice sounded bright, yet I saw the tension in his jaw as he shot quick glances toward my face. I did not fear the cold, but I did not wish to weather such a night alone.

'My rosary,' my voice was cracked. 'Please.'

With nervous hands he reached forward and plucked the

beads from under my collar, pulling them gently over my head, veil and all, until they pooled into my bound hands. I gripped them, beads made from bones that had once driven muscles to run and leap; that had once lain against Abe's skin and mine.

Chicken left me then, and soon the sound of hooves and clattering metal faded away. I did not hear another soul. Night fell black and starless. Through the trees I sometimes saw a brief flare of fire, smelled smoke upon the wind, but no one came. At first, I was afraid, but I found that if I tilted my head back, I could watch the boughs stroke the sky, tracing their patterns in artless grace.

God's touch was in their movement, in the chill breeze that cooled my swollen eyes. The night grew deeper, and for the first time in many weeks, even captive in the wild, I felt my thoughts calm.

13

The bird knows not the path

Near dawn, I was woken by the shifting of movement, by the brush of fur against my hands. My heart hurtled into fear. I opened my eyes and struggled to turn my neck, barely daring to breathe.

A large gray dog appeared in my vision, peering around the edge of the trunk to which I was tied. Blood stained its jaws, matted into the coarse hair around its muzzle, and for a moment it stared at me with eyes obsidian and endlessly deep. I felt hot breath misting from beyond its teeth. Then it made a noise in its throat and strolled forward to settle itself beside me, two front paws crossed as if to say, *well, is not this dull?*

By the time the riders returned in the ashen dawn, we had grown to some acquaintance. I had questioned the dog as to its name, place of abode and vocation, but he had simply answered by blinking up at me.

As soon as a figure began to walk toward us from across the clearing, the hound whuffed and stretched languorously before getting to his feet and loping off into the trees.

Chicken gaped after it as he covered the last few paces.

'Damned cur,' he said with wonder, watching the dog disappear into the forest.

'Where did it come from?' My lips were stiff with cold, tongue dry in my mouth.

Chicken set about untying my hands. While I went through the routine of chafing life back into them, he stacked a few dry branches together.

'That beast were in the town,' he said, setting the wood to smoking. 'Came charging on out when Morgan had its master by the hair – latched onto his leg like a bear-trap, right above the boot.' Chicken looked almost amused.

'What was it doing here?' I shivered.

'Here's as good as any place, I guess,' the young man told me without meeting my eyes. 'It don't have a home no more.'

A weak flame flickered into being in the pile of twigs, and Chicken spent the next few minutes feeding it. Around us the camp filled up, boys carrying sacks and trophies from their raid, some with lace curtains thrown over their heads, crowing over the night's crimes. I wondered how long those curtains had been in the making, how some woman had painstakingly tatted the delicate patterns that were now clenched in thoughtless fists.

The scent of woodsmoke rose around me, and food cooking, as if such homely things could disguise the destruction the gang had left behind them. From a pouch Chicken pulled out a hard round of yellow bread, and, nestled in a cloth, three eggs. I remained quiet as he poured water into a pot from his canteen and set them to boil.

Together we watched the water bubble.

'Din't kill no one,' Chicken told me, fiddling absently with a twig, 'not this time. Morgan did but he—' He broke off and threw the twig into the fire. 'Morgan don't think about it over much.'

'And you?'

My hands had fallen into their old pattern of feeding the rosary through my fingers.

Chicken met my eyes, but glanced quickly away, down to the beads.

'What they for?' he asked distractedly. 'Don't look holy to me. Look like something an Injun would wear.'

I smiled at the accuracy of his guess.

'They belonged to a man who lived with an Indian tribe,' I told him. 'He made me this,' I showed him the little wooden cross, dark with its stains, 'and joined them together, and that made them holy.'

'You got words to go with 'em?'

I nodded. 'Many. They give thanks to the Lord, and praise and remind us of the holy mysteries of our salvation.'

'Salvation,' he repeated, eyes on the steam that rose from the pan. 'That's what you said yesterday. You truly believe that, Sis? What if there's them that can't be saved? Them that's gone too far?'

I stared at him in surprise, for those same words had once fallen from Abe's lips. He had asked me that question on the night we shared our first fire, before I knew anything of the world and its pain.

'I do believe it,' I told him and reached for his arm. 'Every man, no matter how evil, was a child once. Men are driven to sin. They do not carry it in their bones.'

He left his sleeve in my grip for a long moment.

'These eggs is done,' he said, face coloring. 'What'd you say to some breakfast?'

14

Neither has the eye
of the vulture beheld it

The gang slept through most of the day, taking their rest while
the sky remained dry and the sun tentatively warmed the earth.
I followed their example, for there was little else to do. After we
had eaten together, Chicken had coughed and shuffled and fumbled with something in the bottom of his sack. It was a leather
book, a bible, pages well-worn from a generation of fingers and
thumbs and candlelight vigils.

He placed it in my lap. 'Got you this. Thought you might say
a prayer with it, for me, an' some of the others.'

His face was taut with shame as I stared at the object, stolen
from poor folk who must have cherished it and the hope it gave.

'Thank you, Chicken.'

He rewarded me with a smile. 'If you please, Sis, Chicken ain't
my real name. Jus' what they call me on account of my likin' for
it. My given name's Christopher. Might you call me that? No
one here does, see.'

'Christopher.' That name fell too easily from my lips. 'I will.'

When we next rode, the ropes that bound my hands were
looser. Christopher gave me a sack to keep the bible in, along
with a little food, just for me.

Evidently, this exchange had not gone unnoticed, for several
other boys rode alongside us over the course of the day. They
cleared their throats and looked nervous. Some blurted out
names; their own and others, sisters and mothers left behind.
They asked me to think of them in prayers, even once in a while.
A few brought trinkets to accompany their request: glass beads
or a pencil or a flowering twig.

The collection rolled and jumbled together in my lap. Boys,

400

born on the wrong side of a line that should not exist, who had followed brothers and friends to war, filled with courage but not with thought.

Morgan sneered when he rode past and saw these offerings, but he could not supress the superstitions of his gang any more than his own scorn. He was in a foul mood, Chicken whispered. The hound's bite was a nasty one and gave him a good deal of trouble. I would have offered to clean and bind it, but the memory of Falk made me unchristian, made me smile grimly at the thought of his discomfort.

We had traveled a good fifteen miles from our previous camp when I saw a flash of gray through the leaves. The hound was running alongside us, long legs stretching and bunching with the effort of keeping pace.

Chicken followed my gaze.

'Well I'll be,' he breathed and I felt his eyes settle upon me in awe. 'What did you do to that thing?'

'Nothing,' I whispered, watching the dog's joyous movement.

'Morgan'll shoot it,' Chicken warned.

'I've a feeling that he will not see it.' As if he heard me, the hound dropped away into the shadows.

The further south we traveled that gray day, the cheer brought about by full bellies and stolen coats subsided into anxiety. I asked Christopher why the others were so somber.

'No predictin' who's got control of this land, day to day,' he murmured. 'Last fall there was more of us, an' we was more than a match for Fed patrols and other gangs. But now . . .'

I had to get away, I realized, and soon. If we were discovered by the Union, or other raiders in a skirmish, I could be captured in the struggle, if not handed over outright.

If I did not escape, there was every chance I would never reach Indian Territory, let alone live long enough to rescue Abraham Muir.

15

The depth saith:
'It is not in me'

Before nightfall we made camp, and made it quietly, without fire. Few spoke, but as I ate, a circle of pale faces and wary eyes gathered around me. Christopher left my hands untied so that I might open the bible and read a lesson to those gathered there.

"'And the city was broken up,'" my voice traveled evenly through the dusk, "'and the men of war fled, out of the city into the night, they went by the way that leadeth to the wilderness.'"

Some sat with clenched eyes and clasped hands as if in Sunday school, while others nodded absently, playing with the leaves between their fingers.

'You all know the Lord's prayer?' I asked, when I had finished my reading. There was a chorus of murmurs, with only some affirmative. I asked if anyone could begin it for us, inspiring much debate over the first line, and I smiled. 'Join in as you can,' I told them, 'but remember to say "amen".'

"'Our father,'" started Chicken, "'who art in heaven . . .'"

By and by the prayers were done and the night grew darker. Chicken produced his rug and made to secure my hands to a tree once more.

'They could hang me, you know,' I told him softly as he knelt at my side. 'The Union or the law. But I did not flee St. Louis because of them.'

I caught his hands as he reached for me. Firelight and shadow traveled across his face like oil across water.

'I ran because I had to save a soul,' I whispered. 'There is a man who is lost out there. I promised him salvation, and I will not fail him. Please, let me go to him.'

The young man looked more of a child than ever as he hesitated in my grip.

'This man of yours – he's in Indian Territory?' he said, eyes bright. 'With Puttick?'

I nodded. 'His name is Abraham.'

He sat back. 'You'll never make it. It's near a hundred miles from here to the border.'

'I've ridden that far and further,' I said.

He faltered. A shout sounded from the main part of the camp, then another.

'Even if I did let you go,' he breathed, shooting glances behind him, 'even if I did ...'

'Please, Christopher,' I begged.

He looked wretched as he shook his head.

'Chicken by name,' he tried to laugh as he began to wrap the ropes around my wrists. 'Sorry, Sister.'

16

God forbid that I should judge
you to be just

Dawn broke, still and misty and cold. I stirred before the others; even the man on watch dozed quietly nearby. I heard the soft crack of a wet twig breaking, and twisted my neck around fearfully, only to find the hound padding toward me, its breath coming quick. I smiled my greeting and it drew closer. The scent of gunpowder clung to its fur. I frowned, when a noise split the stillness.

We both whipped around. Through the trees I could see movement, slight at first but coming closer – figures running, stooped low. The noise came again, and again, dead branches cracking beneath heavy boots. I opened my mouth to shout just as the savage bellow of a shotgun shattered the stillness of the camp.

Men in blue came swarming forward, roaring their challenge. The gang were pale and bewildered with sleep, scrambling to their feet, grabbing blearily for weapons. Pistols began to retort through the mist, and I saw one lad fall to the ground, his proud yellow shirt blooming with blood.

I strained at the bonds that held me, the rope cutting into my skin, already sore and red from days spent tied to tree or saddle. The cords twisted cruelly against my raw flesh but did not budge. As I screamed my frustration, the hound growled low in its throat, gaze fixed ahead. A shadow materialized from the smouldering ground that was already a battlefield, running head-first as if hell was storming up behind it.

I braced my legs and hauled myself upright, determined to meet death standing. The dog let out a savage bark and launched itself forward. Only when he was about to leap did I see clearly enough to cry out a warning.

The dog dropped back to all fours as if I had called its name. The figure careening toward us was Chicken, his pale eyes wild. He was bone white beneath a mask of powder blast, twin trails of blood streaming from his nose.

He found his footing and ran forward again. I could hear his harsh panting. His hands were shaking in terror, but held a blade.

'What is happening?' I cried, as he started to hack madly at my ropes.

'Federals,' he sobbed as he worked. 'Came so quiet we never heard them. Morgan's dead; one of 'em shot him in the face – I were right there, next to him. Would've killed me too, but his gun blew up,' Chicken laughed frantically, his voice saliva-thick, 'so I ran and I ran here.'

I felt the ropes around my hands give. The young man sank against the tree in my place, sweat matting his fair hair and running into the tears and dirt that streaked his face.

'Blue,' he gabbled. 'Blue coats and blood.' His fingers slid from the bark leaving a dark streak. I looked closer; his sleeve was soaked with red.

I caught him as he fell and pulled back his shirt: there was a ragged hole under his collarbone and another through his thin back, beneath the shoulder blade. Both pulsed blood.

'You've been shot, but the bullet has passed clean through,' I told him quickly, unravelling his neckerchief. 'You must stay still.'

He cried out as I pushed the cloth under his arm and cinched it tight across the wound.

'You got to run,' his lips were weak, 'they'll take you—'

'Do not concern yourself over me,' I said. 'Be still.'

'I'm goin' to hell,' he whimpered, eyes rolling shut. 'I can see it, Sis, I know it, they goin' to take me down there.'

'What did I tell you,' I said forcefully, pressing down on the wound. 'Do you remember?'

He did not reply, only wept in fear.

I sat back, eyes wide. The sounds of fighting were everywhere. I could hear voices within the cries, screams. Federals were murdering the boys who had taken me captive – who had brought me flowers, and sat around me like children in order to hear my prayers. Once I might have welcomed the men in blue as saviors, yet by their deeds they made themselves my enemies.

Chicken moaned weakly from the ground, reaching out a hand to me. I ignored it and began to unbuckle his gunbelt. One pistol was missing, but the other remained. It was shabby and ill kept, but it would serve. Grimly, I secured the belt around my own waist then retrieved his knife from the ground.

'Don't, don't go—' Chicken gasped. He snatched weakly at my habit as I rose. I stared down at him, armed once more. The dog padded over to stand at my side. It was as tall as my thigh. Absently, I rested a palm upon its head. My hands were coated with the boy's blood.

Beneath his gaze I reached down and dragged two fingers across the smooth skin of his brow: a red crucifix upon the pale flesh.

'No one,' I told him, 'is beyond salvation.'

Nunslinger: Book 9

Homily for the Damned

The True Tale of how Sister Thomas Josephine of St. Louis, Missouri, became a Vigilante and Braved the Wilds of Indian Territory in order to Rescue one Abraham C. Muir

I

And the ninth
was of darkness

Fear fell from my shoulders like a cloak as I strode out of those dark woods. With a loaded pistol in my grip I felt stronger than I had in many weeks. A man's blood coated my hands and arms. It was benediction: it set my feet and kept my chin high as I entered the chaos and slaughter.

The dog loped alongside me as I walked into the clearing where the fighting was thickest. Death filled the air. Amid the screams of animals and boys. Their bodies lay where they had fallen, their long hair trampled and bright shirts bloodied and torn.

The gunshots became dull bellows as I continued, thunder in my chest, smoke in my lungs. I made out blue-jacketed figures on horses. Fire flashed upon the end of a plunging bayonet and for a moment I thought I saw someone with fair hair, the color of wheat – someone from another life – turn toward me.

I stumbled, tripped over something soft and bulky, and hit the ground. Cold mud dug itself under my nails as I scrabbled to regain my footing. My boots caught upon the object again and I rolled to my knees in order to see.

A scream caught itself in my throat as I stared, horrified at Morgan's ruined skull. One side of his head had been utterly destroyed by the bullet that had taken his life. His lips were stretched in a grin, stiff with the blood that coated what remained of his face. I pulled myself to my feet and staggered away. I realized that the sound of fighting was abating. Many of the boys I had traveled with were dead or dying. My palms were slick with sweat as I shifted my grip around the weapon.

Ahead of me, a man in blue sat upon a horse. In the sickly

light of dawn I saw that his cuffs were dark with stains. In his belt was a pistol, the twin of the one I held in my hand, and I knew instinctively it had belonged to Chicken.

The Union man held a bushwhacker by his long hair. The strands clenched in his fist were the only things keeping the boy upright. He had been beaten, so badly that his face was a mess of flesh, but I recognized him as one of the lads who had knelt beside me in makeshift prayer only the night before.

His lips were split and he choked out a froth of bloody saliva as the federal soldier drew a knife and angled it toward the boy's scalp. I raised the pistol and pulled the trigger.

My shot rang out and the Union man screamed, dropping his knife to clutch at his hand. The bullet had shattered a path through his palm. I rushed forward, yelling for the outlaw to move. He only stared, battered and stunned, as I grasped hold of the soldier's clothing and pulled with all my strength.

Wounded as he was, the federal man held on to his mount with his good hand, bellowing and kicking blindly. The tip of his boot caught me on the chin and sent me staggering back; I raised the pistol again, only for a gray streak to rush past.

The hound launched itself at the man, locking its jaws around his arm and dragging him from the horse. The beast was rearing in fright, but I darted forward to seize the bridle. Within a moment I was in the saddle, the reins firmly in my grip. A bullet whizzed over my head, then another, as the Union soldiers ran to their comrade's aid.

With a scream I kicked the horse in the flanks. It reared and took off, the dog following. Tan and gray, horse and hound, we streaked through the confusion, through the smoke and gunfire, our stained heads low like wolves fleeing into the darkness.

2

The innocent shall divide
the silver

Reasoner slept like a man in debt to his dreams, head slumped and legs crumpled against the chair. The shutters were tightly closed against the coming day. A lamp flickered with a last few greasy sputters of oil. The light crawled over the lines that etched his face.

It had not been difficult to find him. The federals had given up their pursuit of me after barely a mile, eager to return to warm hearths and contemplation of their spoils. I had listened for them in the shadowy dawn, followed their noise and the trail they left behind. If ever I placed a foot wrong, the hound would pad ahead, nose to the ground and set me right.

They rode for Little Rock. There were few lights: it was still early when I arrived and most citizens were yet rolled up in their blankets. I followed the federals into the city, watched them tie up their horses and enter a hotel. Not long after they went inside, the lamps in the hotel windows died down, and the place subsided into quiet once more.

The dog panted softly as I ventured through the front door. The place was empty of customers, the owners not yet awake, save for a boy, dozing on the counter. He yelped in horror when I woke him, blood-stained and filthy as I was, but he directed me to Reasoner's room without making trouble.

The marshal had fallen asleep without locking his door. His hand hung loosely: the silver frame I recalled from our time in the convent had fallen from his fingers onto the boards. I shifted in the doorway, loud enough to wake him. His hand flexed convulsively for the fallen object before he even opened his eyes.

Within a heartbeat he regained his senses and lunged for the revolver that lay upon the table.

'Who's there?'

I stepped forward and his eyes widened with fear.

'God preserve us,' he whispered, beginning to make the sign of the cross upon his chest.

'From what, Marshal?' I asked, moving more fully into the room. His hand froze mid-gesture, expression thickening from fear to disbelief.

'Please, do not get up,' I said softly. 'I will not be staying for long.'

He ignored me and staggered to his feet, his hands moving to arm the gun.

I produced the pistol from behind my back and leveled it at his chest.

'Sit down.'

Reluctantly he dropped the weapon on a nearby table and obeyed.

'How did you get here?' he challenged, 'The patrol—'

'The patrol did not waste time in looking for me,' I dismissed, 'only in taking revenge.'

'You speak as if that were wrong,' snapped Reasoner. 'Your traveling companions were killers, Sister, every one. Have you already forgotten that preacher from upriver?'

The faces of the dead and dying rose before me: Falk, Chicken, Morgan. Abruptly, I was tired, too tired to fight this man.

'I tried to save him,' I said wearily, 'but the bushwhackers . . . they were boys, Marshal, just frightened boys, far from home.'

My head was spinning and I blinked, hard, trying to clear my mind. Reasoner's hand was creeping toward his revolver.

'Please do not try that,' I warned. 'I do not wish to shoot anyone else today.'

'I saw your work,' the marshal said slowly, sinking back into his chair. 'That man will lose his hand, you know.'

'Better that than to take another man's life,' I retorted. But my conscience prickled. 'Did the men bring any prisoners back?

One of the wounded boys had a bullet beneath the collarbone. Did he live?'

Reasoner shook his head.

'They left none alive.'

Nausea and sorrow swept me.

'May the Lord have mercy upon him,' I murmured.

'May he go to hell,' Reasoner said coldly. 'May he suffer for what he has done.'

I clenched my teeth. I could not summon the faces of killers or thieves to mind, only a young man, begging me not to leave him as he died.

'They have suffered enough already.'

Reasoner was silent, his face hard. I saw then that he did not comprehend me, that he sought to stand among humanity and cleave it in two, like rot from sound flesh.

'Saint or sinner, Sister,' he asked slowly, 'which are you?'

I sighed and transferred the pistol's aim to the silver frame that lay on the floor. 'Where is Puttick?'

Reasoner ceased all movement, staring down at the object.

'Well?' I demanded, steadying the gun with my other hand.

The air whistled out of his nostrils, as if he wanted nothing more than to rise up and smash the weapon out of my hand. That precious silver gleam held him in place, more effectively than if I had tied him down.

'Lower your weapon,' he growled.

'Not until you tell me.'

'West,' he barked finally, 'last I heard, in the Sans Bois Mountains.'

The lamp spat feverishly, sucking upon its final drops.

'Thank you, Marshal Reasoner,' I told him.

'We will find you,' he promised, as shadows beat about the walls. 'You *and* Puttick, if he's alive, and when we do there will be no mercy.'

'There never was,' I said, as the lamp died and the room was plunged into darkness.

3

I carry my soul in my hands

The city came to life before me. The streets filled as the sky shrugged off its dawn haze in favor of a steely gray morning. Boats puffed and scuttled along the riverbanks like steam-driven beetles. The city did not seem to be suffering under federal control. To the contrary, even from a distance I could see that the marketplaces and corners were bustling, crammed with opportunists and the politically casual, driven by a springtime hunger for commerce.

I had secluded myself in a clump of trees beside the riverbank. I looked down at the bundle in my lap. It was time. I had put off this moment for as long as possible, yet the future was barreling onward and would not hold itself for me. The blue garments were stiff and musty from poor laundering. Resigned, I pulled off my habit.

The hound watched me dress, chin on his paws, as I dragged the stolen trousers over my legs. I could not help but feel that there was something judgmental in his gaze.

'There was no help for it,' I told him, picking up the shirt and jacket. 'I do not like it any more than you.'

The clothes were ragged, and much too large, yet I had seen Union uniforms in far worse condition. The boy at Reasoner's hotel had acquired them, had brought them to where I waited, hidden at the edge of town after the patrols had streamed out in pursuit of me. He had handed them over with something like reverence, and I saw that he had done his best, had chosen the army issue garments as carefully as he could from what he could steal.

To top it off, he had thrust a large paper bill at me, newly printed. My own face stared up at me, this time adorned with the new scar. Falk's name had been added to my tally of murders. I had almost ripped the poster into shreds, yet the boy had presented me with a pencil and asked so timidly if I might sign it that I could not refuse.

His sisters played at 'the Six-Gun Sister', he told me excitedly; they fought for whose turn it was to wear one of his mother's linens around their heads. They'd be green with envy, he beamed. I tried to smile in return, yet my heart contracted as I watched his small figure run off, pretending that rolled-up bill was a rifle.

Whatever I had become, I thought grimly as I pulled off my veil, there was no way back to the woman I had once been. Freed from the cloth, my curls fell to almost beneath my ears. I passed the fair strands between my fingers for a moment before taking up Chicken's knife. I hacked the hair away, cutting it so short that only prickly clumps remained. Finally, I pulled the cap over my head.

'What do you think?' I asked the dog. 'Shall I pass for a federal lad?'

The animal remained impassive.

'You do not have to stay with me, you know,' I grumbled, as I rolled up the habit and veil. 'I never asked you to join me.'

I set about checking my stolen horse's saddlebags, in the hope of finding food. The beast was a mare, smaller and sleeker than the mounts that I had ridden in the past. She was a dappled tan, with a mane and tail so dark to be almost black. She snuffed at me, and I found myself looking into her liquid eyes.

'We shall have to disguise you too,' I told her, smoothing her nose. 'Rub some dirt into that fine coat of yours. Horse theft's a hanging offense, you know, and you're too pretty to go unmissed.'

Later, after the horse was disguised, hunger began gnawing at me. I discovered a twist of jerky shoved into one of the pockets of my stolen clothes. I tore off a hunk with my teeth and chewed ferociously. The hound was at my side in an instant.

'If we are to share a meal together, I should know your name.'

I offered him a chunk of the dried meat. He took it between his teeth with surprising delicacy, despite strings of drool.

'I imagine you had one, once,' I said.

The hound did not reply.

'You are gray,' I told him, 'so perhaps it was Smoky? Or Ash?'

He made a noise into the air, and continued his meal.

'Dusty?' I tried, brushing off my hands. 'Or Rabbit? Rabbits are gray, sometimes.'

I made several more suggestions to the beast, all to no avail, until I grew impatient.

'The only other creature that is gray is a dove,' I said impatiently, shoving my balled up habit behind the saddle, 'and you are not in the least like one of those.'

The dog glanced up at me, as if I had spoken his language. 'Dove?' I tried incredulously. He wagged his tail.

Abruptly, I remembered Abe's voice, somewhere in the mountain darkness of the Sierras, chiding me for Pokeberry's unbecoming name: *There's not one who won't laugh at a name like that on a beast.*

I hauled myself into the saddle and felt a smile twitch my lips. 'Dove it is.'

4

The young men saw me,
and hid themselves

I rode into town with the noonday sun simpering through the clouds. There were federal soldiers everywhere. I kept my cap low and tried to blend in as well as I was able.

Little Rock seemed to be peopled by two types: first were those who had weathered out the war under a Confederate flag and now paid the price, who walked the streets with their backs bent and their eyes to the ground; second were those who had seen the advantage of being a known Unionist in a recently captured city, who strode through the mud with their pocketbooks full and their heads held high.

Almost every storefront I passed flew the stars and stripes, and proclaimed themselves to be 'Lincolnite & Loyal!'. Everywhere were peddlers selling 'Yankee Notions' – buttons and knick-knacks – out of handcarts, dogcarts and from the back of mules. One man bawled '*Yaaaaankee corn*', as if the Lord himself blessed the ears that came from the north.

Posters and bills were pasted ten feet high on the walls of the courthouse. I drew to a stop and glanced up, only to pull my hat down even lower: my own face towered above me on two of the huge bills. I scowled from beneath the brim. It must have been Reasoner who had them printed fresh.

'She is surely a whore,' I heard a voice say nearby. 'Ain't no way those bushwhackers woulda let her be, out there on the road.'

'Can't speak about a lady that way, cuz,' another voice admonished. 'Let 'lone a nun.'

Behind me, two young Union soldiers stood gawping up at my picture. My heart thudded in my chest as I began to edge away.

'She *cain't* be a nun,' the first boy insisted. 'Nuns ain't so handy with pistols. You hear 'bout that cavalryman, 'cross the river? Shot a hole the size of a dollar coin clean through his hand, she did.'

'She got grit, alright,' said the second boy, admiringly. 'I've heard that her pistols is blessed by the Lord hisself. *That's* why she's so handy. Can't be killed by normal means, neither. God won't allow it. Anyone who tries gets sucked down straight to hell.'

'Balderdash,' scoffed the first, but he shifted slightly in his boots, before turning to me. 'Here, you don't think they'll send *us* after her, do you?'

5

Who are ready to raise up a leviathan

I managed to escape the conversation with gruff words and ill-tempered growls, yet their talk weighed heavily upon my mind. I had become a true fugitive, gossiped about in the saloons and bars, notorious across the United and Confederate States, yet I was more alone then I had ever been before. Even in Mexico I had traveled with Carthy, Owl or Muir: strange allies indeed, but allies all the same.

Here, enemies surrounded me. Since my flight from St. Louis I had been chased and hunted, judged and held captive in the wilds. I had initially intended to travel alone, after I had fled the convent, yet now I understood that if I was to succeed, I needed partners.

Where to find them? The main streets of the city were too full with genuine Union soldiers to be safe. I worried that at any moment some commanding officer would spot me and order me to fall in with a regiment. Instead, I hitched the horse outside a respectable-looking hotel and took to the back streets.

Dove trotted alongside me, his nose twitching. Although I grimaced at the stench as the streets grew narrower, to him the miasma of human and animal waste, mud, ash and rot was a rich bouquet waiting to be explored.

On a corner I asked a beggar where I might go if I was looking for men, those who knew the land and would be interested in the prospect of bounty. He held out his hand, whistling toothlessly. When no coin was forthcoming, he leered.

'Try the bars down by the wharf, my boy,' he gurgled. 'On Cart Street, ask for Macclehorse. He's after some huntin' I hear.'

I followed his directions. The alleyways grew steeper toward

419

the river, the buildings grimy and damp. Hogs rooted freely among the filth. Dove joined them in their explorations, soon trotting up to me with a curled-up boot held proudly in his mouth.

When I reached Cart Street, I stopped a woman, ragged and gum-eyed, and uttered the name I had been given. She shuddered and swore and pointed out the grimiest building. It was a saloon. Taking a breath, I walked toward it, Dove hard on my heels, still carrying his boot.

The smell of spilled liquor assaulted me feet from the entrance. If the saloon had a sign, it had long rotted away. Instead, a door made from an ancient tabletop stood propped against the wall, admitting a single bold beam of light into the dark interior.

I stepped cautiously over the threshold and muttered a brief prayer to the Lord that I might be able to conclude my business there before a knife found its way between my ribs.

The place sprawled out before me, long and low. The windows were smeared, there was barely light to see by. I walked across a floor covered with sawdust so clogged with chaw that it felt like a bowl of hominy underfoot.

Near the bar, a group of men, heavy-eyed and sodden, were sagged upon the benches. The man behind the counter looked like a weed beneath a rock. He swiped a rag at a few glasses.

When I approached, he mechanically upended one and glugged a measure of something cloudy and brown into it. He paid no mind to my appearance, and I sensed that a bear could have ambled into that place and been served in the same careless fashion.

'Hellfire an' fury!' a voice swore behind me. I turned. A big man at a nearby table was staring at me, his lips wet with liquor and spittle. 'Looky at the bluebelly!'

He staggered to his feet, upturning the table as he did so. His drinking companions casually lifted their glasses and bottles out of the way as he crashed forward.

'Blowhard mudsill,' he cussed, and tried to spit at me. The

projectile stuck to his beard as he tripped and careened into the bar. Groaning, he clung to it as he fought to regain his feet. He wore no coat or hat, merely ragged trousers and an old shirt , which stretched across his belly. Grimy skin showed through the patches. What remained of a waistcoat was stained and greasy below the lank brown curls of his too-long hair.

'Muckety-muck,' he burbled, as his elbow slipped and sent him tumbling to the floor.

I winced down at him.

'What did he call me?' I asked his companions. They stared back, glassy-eyed, their shoulders stooped with the kind of melancholy that no liquor could shift. Another man, alone in a corner looked up from his newspaper with interest. His eyes were as yellow as a hawk's in the gloom.

'Y'know perfectly well, y' damn Yankee,' the drunk announced from the sawdust, lurching his way upright a fingertip at a time. 'Yer a coward and y'know it. Acknowledge the corn!'

As he pulled himself up, the bartender poured him another drink. He knocked it aside with one flailing fist. The other swung toward my head with surprising speed, but I ducked and slipped to his side. The drunk's companions reeled to their feet as I seized a handful of his shirt and pinned him to the bar, kicking his feet from under him.

'Watch your tongue, sir,' I told him.

The man snorted in rage against the wood, straining to rise. He was strong, but so drunk he could not find his feet.

'I am looking for a Mr Macclehorse,' I announced to the room, 'and not for trouble. I have business with him.'

Five pairs of eyes flicked to my back as I spoke, and I felt the sharp point of a knife prick through my clothes, against my spine. I looked around, carefully. A boy stood there, staring up. His hair was long and matted and might have been red, if not for the dirt. His lip trembled constantly as if with palsy, yet his eyes were fierce as he pressed the tip of the blade harder against my skin.

'I should let that bear you've trapped go,' the sharp-eyed man

421

advised from the corner, glancing up from his reading. 'If you don't the boy'll leave you flopping helpless as a fish.'

Dove emerged from under one of the tables, boot in mouth. Rather than attack, the way I had seen him do in the past, he only gazed up at us in confusion. What might have been a smile flickered across the boy's face.

Reluctantly, I released my hold on the drunk. With astonishing speed, he spun and landed a blow squarely on my jaw. The force of it stunned me, but I had wits enough to stagger away, behind the hound. He was growling now, his prize boot forgotten, and the drunk faltered.

''M Macclehorse,' he slurred, focusing with effort. 'Who the hell are you?'

My chin was throbbing hard. The blow had driven my teeth into the side of my cheek, and I could taste blood. I spat out a mouthful before pulling the rosary from concealment. From my other pocket I extracted one of the bills with a picture of my face.

'Forgive them, Father,' I said, pushing past him to slap the warrant for my arrest down onto the counter. 'They know not what they do.'

6

Ask now the beasts,
and they shall teach thee

A gray slab of raw meat was dropped into my palm. It was far from its best, and the thought of placing it upon my face made me shudder, but Macclehorse was insistent.

'Thank you,' I told the redhead boy who offered it to me. He nodded and returned to his seat on the floor, where he had been wrestling Dove for the boot.

'If I'd'a known you was a woman,' Macclehorse began for the sixth time, eyes misting over, 'and a lady of God an' all . . .'

'There is no harm done,' I told him, wincing at the clammy feel of the meat upon my face. 'I would have spoken out sooner, had I been certain of you.'

'Still cain't countenance it,' one of the men leered. The stench of whiskey was sour upon his breath. 'The Six-Gun Sister herself. Them posters been going up round the city like wildfire. Is it all true? You kill seven men?'

Lurching forward, Macclehorse shoved the man, sending him tumbling backward off the bench.

'Shut yer hole an' show some respect,' the big man commanded.

'He has a point,' the hawk-eyed man said coolly, leaning against the bar. Apart from the boy, his was the only gaze unclouded by liquor.

Macclehorse bristled.

'Keep yer britches on,' the man on the floor snorted. 'I was just wonderin' at her being here, same as you.'

'I *had* intended to make Mr Macclehorse a business proposition,' I told them, 'for I'm in need of a bounty hunter.'

Most of the men collapsed into laughter, whooping and gasping until they saw my expression.

"'Pologies, Sister,' offered one of Macclehorse's friends, wiping his eyes, 'but whoever told you to seek out George here was runnin' you a merry dance.'

Even the man himself was laughing.

'It's true,' he said, red with shame. 'I ain't good for the hunt no more. Twenty year ago, maybe.'

I looked around at the assembled faces. The Lord had led me to this place for a reason. Drunk and dangerous though these men were, I determined that they would be the ones to help me.

'That is a shame, Mr Macclehorse,' I said, folding up the poster. 'There was to be a thousand dollars in it for you.'

My words silenced any remaining laughter. I took my time in gathering up my hat.

'Wait now,' Macclehorse wheezed and cleared his throat. 'That's a lot of dollars. Who you huntin' with a bounty that size? The King of France?'

His cronies smirked again.

'Colm Puttick,' I said, voice calm.

The silence fell abruptly.

'Sister,' Macclehorse finally managed, 'maybe you ain't heard. No one in their right mind'd go after Puttick, not any more. He's a highbinder—'

'I am not interested in lectures or stories,' I told the big man. 'I know who he is, and what is more, I know *where* he is. And I intend to find him.'

'Why?' said the sharp-eyed man by the bar. This time, no one threatened him. Their gazes were fixed upon my face.

'He has stolen something from me,' I told him slowly, 'and I must reclaim it.'

'Don't take this as dissuasion, Sister,' Macclehorse slurred, 'but I cain't figure what Puttick might've taken from you that'd be worth so much.'

I smiled, only to wince at the pain in my swollen jaw. Macclehorse noticed, and looked ready to cry with mortification.

'A soul,' I murmured, 'is worth infinitely more than gold.'

'Amen,' the sharp-eyed man drawled. 'Now, while I do not mean to interrupt, I can't help but notice we're one bartend short.'

He was right; the bar was empty.

'That there's a bill promising five hundred dollars for your head, ma'am,' he continued calmly. 'Somehow I do not think the landlord shares in our scruples with regard to your identity, nor as to keeping quiet.'

'Levi?' Macclehorse called. The alcohol was dropping its hold upon him even as I watched.

The redhead boy had been sitting on the floor, playing tug-of-war with Dove. He released the boot and stood up, exchanged one look and a nod with the big man, and set off at a run through the saloon. Before he disappeared, I saw the gleam of the long knife already in his hand.

'Never cared for the b—. . . the beggar anyhow,' Macclehorse said cheerfully. He suppressed a belch and cast me a look, with eyes that almost focused. 'Looks like I'm yer man, Sister.'

7

And the birds,
they shall tell thee

We decided that we should stay in the saloon while we fixed our plans. The others had sloped away, but Macclehorse had grabbed each man by the collar before he left.

'Keep it dry,' he snarled at them, 'or you'll be wearin' a marble hat.'

Most had glanced down at Levi, cleaning the blood off his knife, as they pledged their silence. Even the hawk-eyed man had obeyed upon leaving, though he did so with clear amusement.

As it transpired, Macclehorse was of no fixed abode. I suspected that he slept in the saloon more often than not.

'Had a place in the county up north a ways,' he said vaguely when I asked. 'Likely ain't nothin' but dust there now, since the fightin'. Came here t'join up last winter, but t'army din't want me.'

He looked around, on the hunt for more liquor. Wordlessly, Levi placed a short bottle down before him. He took a greedy swig and grimaced.

'Sarsaparilla,' he told me with disgust. Levi handed me my own bottle, and I drank gratefully.

'Is he your son?' I asked, as the boy returned to the doorway to where Dove lay basking in the pale sun.

'Not by a jugful,' Macclehorse coughed. He was looking sorrier for himself with every passing minute and took another disconsolate swig before he spoke. 'Found him few year back, down in N'Orleans, 'fore the war broke out. I were at a dogfight in some deadfall. I opine I had bin drinkin' some,' he acknowledged. 'Anywho, these varmints was on the swindle, so I had a mind t'check the hounds. Went back to the kennels, an' these beasts is hollerin' and howlin' like demons, ready to tear a body's skin off soon as look at him.'

Macclehorse leaned closer, and lowered his voice, eyes on the doorway.

''Cept there's this little fryin' size fella, not more than five or six so I can tell, an' he's in there, roped up like the hounds an' sleeping 'longside them like it ain't no bother. Turns out he was kept to patch up the dogs what got torn up in the fightin'. With anyone else they'd go haywire, but not him.

'Won my fight, but I couldn't allow leavin' him. He din't have no ma, or bub, or sis. Took him 'stead of my winnings. Been with me since, nigh on four years now.'

I watched as my vicious hound companion huffed contentedly and lifted his paw so the boy could scratch his stomach.

'And the barkeep?' I asked, though in truth I did not care to hear the answer. Macclehorse shot me a knowing look.

'Levi keeps my back,' he said slowly, 'an' I keep his. 'Tis our way.'

Abruptly, there was a scuffling at the doorway. Boy and hound were on their feet as one, fangs and knife at the ready. We squinted as the sharp-eyed man stepped into the gloom. He carried a large sack.

'Provisions,' he announced, hands raised. 'Mind calling your beasts off?'

I looked to Macclehorse in question.

'I know him,' he acknowledged in my ear. 'A deal, nohow. He's a tracker, I reckon. Passes through here couple times a season. Alright,' he called out to Levi, who lowered the knife. 'I ain't thought to see you back here,' he told the man, 'an' I'm damned if I can recall your name.'

'We've drunk together that many times, George,' the hawk-eyed man smiled. 'It's Bird. Bill Bird. Greetings again, Sister,' he said, in an accent I couldn't place. 'I have decided that I am for an adventure after all.'

Macclehorse and I exchanged glances.

'As I hear it, them dollars is going one way, which is inta my pocket,' the big man said bullishly.

Mr Bird shrugged. 'Could be. But I'll warrant you haven't traveled through Indian country in recent times.'

Macclehorse flushed. 'We'll do jus' fine,' he snapped. 'I dealt with featherheaders afore.'

'Territory's different,' said Bird reasonably, helping himself to a seat. 'You've got the Choctaws and the Cherokee in the east, the Comanche in the south. You had better ask the Lord and ask him again to keep you from their sights, Sister. Then the Creeks, up on toward Fort Smith—'

'The Creeks,' I burst out, remembering the name from Chicken's stories. 'They're allied to Puttick.'

'Right you are, ma'am,' agreed Bird. 'Now, I am of acquaint with most of these tribes, passing through often as I do, and I could guide you so y'all barely saw a breath of smoke from their campfires. Your Mr Macclehorse might've been a fine hunter once, but he's been out of the game a bit now.'

I turned to Macclehorse to find that he was studying me. Drunk though he was, I saw the glint of intelligence in his eyes, and knew he was no fool. He toyed with his sarsaparilla bottle.

'Ain't gonna whitewash over my faults,' he told me. 'I useta coulda whipped a dozen Injuns. But Bird's right. I ain't done no huntin' for years. Went prospectin', over in Nevada; got all chawed up from there from the mines. Bin beatin' the road since. Like as not John Law's on my tail, to boot.' He swilled some sarsaparilla around his tongue. 'I ain't gonna cheat you, Sister. If Bird's bettermost, then I'd welcome him.'

'My price is sixty-forty,' the other man responded. 'You will not make it ten mile without a good tracker.'

I could see Macclehorse figuring the sums in his head.

'Six hundred, four hundred,' he agreed and spat upon his hand. The pair shook, then each insisted upon clasping my own palm in turn.

'Amen,' Bird grinned at me.

428

8

Times are not hid from the Almighty

We set out that night, after Little Rock's backstreets had quieted down. Bird rode in front alongside me, and Macclehorse and Levi brought up the rear. They shared a cantankerous old cart-horse. It was so large and thick that it looked as though it had been hewn out of a lump of granite.

I kept my Union hat pulled low and nodded to the sleepy sentry at the gate, who did not bother to raise a second eyelid. Just as soon as we were clear, we rode. We rode like the devil himself was upon our heels, kicking up the loose mud of the roads and making for the forest.

West, Reasoner had said. The direction of the setting sun, where the world threw itself in a savage rush toward its ending. I asked Bird if he knew the Sans Bois Mountains. He said he did, and reasoned that we should head northwest. I left it in his hands.

We covered a great deal of distance that day. By noon Macclehorse complained that he was played out and that we needed to rest and eat. We halted in a stand of slim-trunked pines that carpeted the ground with brown needles.

Mr Bird rooted through his pack, produced a pan and a pot, and soon the scent of bacon and coffee filled the clearing. I began to whisper grace to myself, but Mr Macclehorse inter-rupted to ask that I pray aloud, saying that they should all abide by God's wishes.

I did so, and the act of seeing those hardened men, hands clasped tightly before their chests, filled me with hope, even if their eyes did stray to the sizzling meat now and again.

We rested after we ate. I shifted, uncomfortable still in the rough uniform. I ached to shed the jacket and trousers, to return to my habit and the security of my veil, but we had decided that it would be unwise. Bird pointed out wryly that while Union boys were ten a penny, he had rarely come across a fugitive nun in Indian lands.

After that, he read the newspapers as he was wont to do, licking his finger to turn the pages.

'What you want with all them newsheets anyhow?' snorted Macclehorse from beneath his hat. 'Cain't be nothin' you ain't heard before in there, Mister Cat shot Mister Dog at sucha place; south losin' the war, etcetera.'

'No harm in keeping an eye on proceedings,' Bird said rather sanctimoniously, before his hand hovered to a stop above a page. After a moment, a chuckle broke from him.

'Bless my eyes,' he grinned. 'Why I think you should see this, ma'am.'

9

Thou hast clothed
me with skin and flesh

NUN ON THE RUN! the headline bellowed. *SIX-GUN SISTER ESCAPES FEDERAL PATROL!*

I caught a glimpse of the article's author and groaned. 'Do not read it,' I advised, turning away. 'That man would sell his own mother for a story.'

'Well, I want t' hear!' cried Macclehorse, 'an' so does Levi, I'll warrant. Yer famous, Sister. With your permission?' he added hurriedly.

I nodded wearily and Bird cleared his throat.

'"In a stunning twist to this ongoing tale of murder and mayhem,"' he read mockingly, '"I, Franklin Templeton, leading correspondent and most daring reporter of the *Californian* – which as everyone knows has the largest weekly circulation in all the western coast states and territories – traveled at great personal risk and peril into Arkansas, where the Six-Gun Sister, Thomas Josephine, is said to have escaped like the divine spirit from the grasp of a federal patrol. Being of a bold and enquiring nature, I ventured into the Union camp where one soldier currently lies upon his death-bed, having encountered the Holy Sister.

'"With tears in his eyes and a bible upon his chest, he told me of how he had been preparing to revenge himself upon a captured border ruffian when a light shone, blinding as the dawn, and the Sister appeared from nowhere, a gun in her hand and a beast from the Book of Revelations at her side.

'"There was naught but a bloodied stump where his hand used to be. 'I raised it against God,' he wept piteously, 'and she took it in retribution.'

431

'"On the Sister's trail is US Marshal Benjamin Reasoner, a freeman previously of Massachusetts. While the marshal denies that he is pitted against the wrath of the Lord himself, he is attempting – and yet, it appears, failing – to apprehend the Sister with any expediency. With unprecedented access to the marshal's most private thoughts, I, Franklin Templeton, can reveal that Thomas Josephine is believed to be headed for Indian Territory, in order to reunite with the traitor and murderer ABRAHAM C. MUIR.

'"Muir – who as all good Christians know escaped the chain gang to which he had been confined – is reported to have joined the company of the notorious outlaw COLM PUTTICK: the most wanted man west of the Mississippi. When this boiling cauldron of devilry and divinity overflows its pot, why I shouldn't care to speculate . . ."'

'That is enough,' I said, my face burning. 'The man writes nothing but foolishness.'

I got to my feet and began to pack up my saddlebags.

'Foolishness or not, Sister,' said Macclehorse lurching upright, 'you never said nothing about no marshal—'

'I wonder that you should be surprised,' I snapped. 'You knew of the bounty upon my head. Who do you think set it?'

'But *Reasoner*—'

'Will not be a problem.'

The big man was shaking his head. 'He ain't no Johnny-come-lately. Got more arrests t'his name than any other marshal in the Unified States. Hell, he once disappeared into the Territory for two straight months, came out with a beard like a buffalo an' six outlaws all roped up together on mules.'

'Our big friend is right,' Bird spoke up from across the camp. 'He's got good horse-sense, that man, and book learnin' to boot. I hear he studied law, up in Boston. Came down country with a family, bought up a parcel of land 'fore the war, but lost it all. That place wasn't called Bleeding Kansas for nothing, ma'am.'

I thought of the photograph Reasoner so treasured, its frame worn away to almost nothing, the pretty young woman and the baby of a decade before never grown older. The men were still staring at me, so I busied myself with cinching the straps on my saddle. Eventually they moved away to do the same.

'Abraham C. Muir,' murmured Bird quietly as he passed. 'So that's what Puttick took from you.'

I met his hawk eyes with my own.

'Let's ride,' I said.

10

For the arrows of the Lord
are in me

We traveled hard those first few days. The horse's hooves ate up the scrubland and prairie, kicking brown dust into the chill air. Every day we stopped at noon when the sun grew warm in the washed-out sky. Eagles drifted lazily on air currents high above and what little indications there were of other travelers vanished entirely, erased by the winds that spilled over the ever-nearing mountain ridges.

Twice we looked behind us upon reaching higher ground to see smoke drifting rope-thin into the sky, some miles off. Once, I thought I saw a spark in the sunlight, and a smudge that could have been a line of riders. No one ventured a guess aloud, but Reasoner's name was on all of our minds. We pushed the horses all the harder.

Talk was scarce. Concern made our tempers short, and my mind was occupied with other matters. It was as if hearing Abraham's name spoken aloud had opened a floodgate: now, everything reminded me of him. Even the streaked brown earth made me think of the whipping scars I had once seen etched upon his back.

Bird said that we must skirt the forest before we reached the Territory. Soon enough we saw dark trees rise up to the west. They gathered up the sunset like a miser raking coins.

The prairie broke up into ridges, the foothills of the mountains, all loose earth and hardy trees. Oaks began to tower high among the pines. We made camp beneath the canopy. Perhaps it was the silence of the place, eerie after the winds of the open spaces, but Mr Macclehorse was making faster work of his whiskey than usual. Ordinarily he entrusted his liquor to Levi, to ensure that he did not over-indulge, but not tonight.

After a long swig, his eyes grew wide and I tried not to meet his gaze, having become familiar with his penchant for drama when inebriated.

'Sister,' he said, setting the bottle down to draw his pistol, 'stay perfect still . . .'

Without shifting a muscle I followed his gaze. A large rattlesnake had emerged from the rock upon which I leaned, drawn by the heat of the fire. Its tongue flickered in and out, tasting the sole of my boot.

Macclehorse was arming his gun with shaking fingers, blinking hard under the influence of the alcohol. Before he could take aim, I jerked to my feet and slammed my boot down onto the snake's neck, pinning it to the ground. The muscular body writhed and thrashed, beating at my legs, but I drew my knife, drove it into the skull and twisted the way Owl had taught me. After a moment, the beast quivered and grew still.

I returned to my seat, wiping the knife on the edge of my trousers. The big man looked pale.

We ate the snake that night. Macclehorse declared it the worst supper he'd ever eaten. 'I know,' he announced, 'that I am a no 'count, ornery old corncracker, but I *never* tasted nothin' bad as this.' He passed me his bottle. 'Better drink an' wash away the flavor of Mr No Legs, ma'am, or you'll be darn sorry.'

Grinning, I accepted a swig from the bottle. The whiskey was harsh as turpentine, and I choked. Macclehorse guffawed and clapped me on the back.

'Sorry, Sister,' he exclaimed, 'couldn't afford nothin' but pop-skull.'

'I have drunk worse,' I told him through streaming eyes. I helped myself to another chunk of snake, much to his amazement. 'I've eaten worse too.' I handed the bottle on to Bird.

'I can't countenance *that*,' sniffed Bird, passing on the bottle to Levi, untasted, who set it down. 'Even if this isn't exactly buttermilk cake.'

'It is a sight better than dried-out rock lizard, I can assure you,' I laughed.

The liquor did its work, warming our bellies. When we were sated and the pine knots in the fire popped brightly, Bird asked me what had truly come to pass, the winter before. In that still night it did not seem amiss to tell them my story as well as I was able. Levi lay alongside Dove as the hound worked over what remained of the snake, gazing into the fire with the rest of us.

More than anything, I found myself speaking of Abe: of our meetings and separations, wounds and lucky escapes. The night grew deeper, and moths began to appear, flashing in and out of life at the edge of our camp.

'I made a promise eternal to the Lord,' I finished, quietly, 'and when I die, I hope I shall live forever in his grace. But I made promises here on earth too.' I smoothed the beads of the rosary against my fingers. 'I pledged salvation to a man once and failed. I will not let that happen again.'

A guttural snore answered my words. Macclehorse was slumped against his saddle, chest rising and falling. Levi too had fallen asleep, curled next to Dove. I smiled at my foolishness, and reached for my own blanket.

Eyes, back-tooth yellow, caught mine and I started. Bird was a shadow, so still that I had forgotten he even sat there. I tried to smile, but felt a tremor of unease beneath that piercing stare.

He cast a glance over at our sleeping companions and leaned closer.

'What happens, Sister,' he asked, beneath the crackling of the embers, 'if a man does not want to be saved?'

I swallowed and told him that I did not know; that it was late to be discussing questions of theology. His needle-sharp gaze faded into his customary grin and he adjusted his blanket around himself, bidding me goodnight.

I lay awake a long time, watching the clouds and the stars through the branches, Bird's question echoing through my head.

What happens if a man does not want to be saved?

And the rage thereof
drinketh up my spirit

The next day dawned sulky, with a heaviness that clapped itself around my skull. The atmosphere crackled. Dove snapped and rumbled at nothing, and even Levi's small hand could not calm him. Macclehorse was bleary and sour from the night's drink, and Bird was oddly still, his eyes fixed ahead.

He peered through the trees, swaying his finger like a compass needle until it picked out a ridge, rising unevenly above us like a set of worn teeth.

'That's the border,' he told me. 'If we cross there we'll be in Injun lands. The Sans Bois start just beyond. If Reasoner's following, then like as not he'll take the easier pass, up north a ways.' He squinted over his shoulder and cursed. 'Looks like we got to move fast. That there's a storm on our tail.'

The hairs upon the back of my neck rose as we rode up out of the trees, which thinned away into a rocky plateau before sprouting once more into a second ridge: the one that marked the border. The thinning air throbbed like a pent-up scream. Darker and darker grew the day. As I stared at the looming mountains, a strange energy crackled in my chest, a desperate urgency to get beyond them. I found myself pushing the mare into a run, faster and faster until her tail streamed out behind us. Bird's voice called me to stop.

Then the rain came, fast and dark as demons. The clouds roiled and thunder crashed. Dove was howling, and the wind whipped Macclehorse's cries for shelter away. I rode like a woman possessed, icy water streaming down my face. Finally, the mare slowed, sides heaving, snorting the rain from her nose. Breathless, I looked up. I had come to the end of the plateau.

From here a steep trail led upward, disappearing over the stony ridge. The weather was abating now, drawing away its fury until all that was left was a feeling both full and empty, as after long, hard tears.

Shaking, I slid from the horse and rested my head against the saddle, wondering at myself. I was still there when my companions caught up. Dove padded up to me, whining and pushing his nose into my hand until I assured him all was well.

Bird was furious.

'What in the name of Sam Hill were you doing?' he raged. 'This is *not* where we should cross! You've taken us a damned fair piece out of our way!'

I had never before seen him angry. His rage was alarming, eyes snapping against the dullness of the day. I stood calmly before him.

'What does it matter?' I asked evenly. 'We can regain the path on the other side, can we not?'

Bird swore and stomped away. Macclehorse looked after him. He turned to me with an uneasy face.

'Bird's fit to be tied,' he said, his voice uncharacteristically serious. He rubbed at his neck. 'Cain't blame him none, Sister. You gave us a fright, tearin' off the way you did . . .' He trailed off and swallowed. 'Still,' he said loudly, squinting up at the brightening sky. 'We're outta the worst. Look, the devil's beatin' his wife.'

I followed his gaze up into the sky, bewildered.

'Mr Macclehorse means that the sun is shining, along with the rain,' a voice interrupted behind us. Bird stood there, hat in his hand, eyes lowered. 'I got to apologize for raising my voice against you, Sister, but you got to understand, these are dangerous lands.'

I accepted his apology, for there was no other choice. Within half an hour the sun shone full, lending the air a certain freshness and grace, as though the Lord wished to show that the hand which crushed in fury might also fall in gentleness. Raindrops sparked upon brown grasses and waxy new leaves as the clouds were brushed away into scraps.

The land felt different as we ascended the ridge, richer and wilder. Rain-shy birds found their voices. Finally, our horses scrambled up the summit. The trees dropped away and a sweeping vista opened out before us: huge swathes of jagged, pale rock plunging into valleys of dark forest, sheltered on one side by the mountain ridges, world-battered sentinels.

I gazed in amazement. I had thought that Indian country would reflect its inhabitants, wild and lawless, yet this was a glory; an ancient land that might have been the same since the Lord himself walked the earth. Macclehorse had to tug on my bridle in order to break my reverie.

We followed a trail that dropped down below the treeline once again. Beneath the trunks, a spring bubbled up from the ground to trickle downward. We paused to refill our flasks and Dove rushed in, to bark and frolic at the water. Levi and I laughed at him. I picked up a stick to throw, but my arm froze as I smelled the smoke. I grasped Macclehorse as he passed and he pulled the big carthorse to a stop, following my gaze.

Bird dismounted behind us.

'Is there a camp?' I asked warily. Bird shook his head.

'A trading post only. We can bypass it easy enough.'

'Now see here,' Macclehorse protested. 'I am clean outta whiskey after sharin' with you two fine folk, an' Bird, you was all outta tobacco last I asked for a chaw. Let's see what they're offerin'.'

'Are they Indian?' I asked.

'No,' said Bird, 'just a couple of old buzzards, and teetotal to boot.'

'All the same, Mr Macclehorse is right,' I reasoned. 'We could use some supplies. And surely it could do no harm to inquire if they have had news of Puttick's men?'

Bird's eyes were a flat gold as he shrugged and swung himself into the saddle. We did not have to ride far before we realized that smoke was wrong. There was too much of it, thick and black, rather than a neat plume from a chimney. The wonder of the previous hour was all forgotten as we made our way toward it, not knowing what we might find, save for misfortune.

12

And sets the terrors
of the Lord of War against me

The rain had extinguished most of the fire, but even so, the
carnage that greeted us was absolute. A cabin stood at the edge
of the clearing. Smoke seeped lazily through the broken windows. The door had been kicked to splinters. I stepped over a
chunk of wood as I approached the house. Behind me,
Macclehorse swore repeatedly. Two pigs had been skewered to
the walls on either side of the threshold, iron poles driven through
their bodies so deep that they were held there, like insects pinned
in a glass case. I touched the gentle pink ear of one as I passed.
It was still warm.

Nothing remained whole inside. It was as if a hurricane had
swept through, reducing everything in its path to fragments. The
daguerreotype of a young man lay shattered on the smoking
hearth, the glass ground to dust beneath a boot.

A tablecloth had fallen to the floor, caught under the ruined
furniture. I looked closer. Fingers protruded from beneath its
embroidered edge.

I pulled the fabric aside to reveal an old woman, clothed in
good, hard-working cotton. Her white hair was matted with
blood and her clear blue eyes sagged at the corners. They were
still, empty. Rage filled me, but I reached down and slid her
eyelids closed.

When I emerged from the cabin, Macclehorse came to grasp
my shoulders. There were tears of strain upon his face and he
tried to pull me away, back toward my horse, but I shook him
off and strode to where Bird stood, blank-faced, at the edge of
the clearing.

An old man was sprawled in what had once been a vegetable

garden, the green shoots of a new crop trampled into the bloodied earth. He lay facing the house, one arm flung out. There was mud beneath his nails, as if he had pulled himself forward one last inch toward his wife before he died. There was no need to ask who had committed the crime. The man's shirt had been scored in two lines, leaving a bloodied 'X' upon his back.

Puttick's mark.

I gazed silently upon the body. I had made the choice, all those months ago, to venture from the safety of the convent out into the world; to accept all that I found there as coming from the hand of the Lord, who would grant me the faith to accept my trials. If I had caught even a glimpse then of the things I would see during my journey, I would have turned my face from that open door, run to the purity of cloth and altar, never to stir forth again.

Yet I had seen, and there was no way to forget.

'Help me,' I called to Macclehorse, walking into the house.

The big man sniffed repeatedly and scrubbed his eyes upon his sleeve as we carried the old woman outside upon her table linen. My eyes remained dry as I arranged the bodies side by side. Levi found me some water in half a broken pail, and gently I wiped their faces clean of the blood and violence.

'God our Father,' I prayed, as the water ran across their lined skin, 'Your power brings us to birth, Your providence guides our lives, and by Your command we return to dust.'

'Amen,' Macclehorse choked. Levi said nothing, but I saw that he quietly kept a hold of the big man's coat, just a pinch of fabric between his thumb and forefinger.

'This land will burn,' Bird said. His voice was pitched low, hawk's eyes fixed upon the dead couple. 'And the fire will be our own doing. Smuttering black embers too cold or hot; the cold look on, afraid, and the hot ones eat up the world, 'til there is no hearth to hold the fire, no wall to hold the hearth.'

He looked into my eyes.

'There is no "amen" here.'

13

They are confounded,
because I have hoped

We set out after Puttick with renewed purpose, even though it was nearing night. It did not seem to matter if we rested or not, only that we pressed on, toward retribution.

Before we left the trading post, I gave up the Union uniform and unrolled my habit once more. It was time that I remembered who I was: a soldier not of governments or cities, but of the Lord.

My hands were blistered from the shovel I had wielded to dig the graves, and black with the mud I had pushed into them. We had all worked to offer the bodies some dignity and peace in their final resting. Macclehorse had found a strip of hide, used it to bind two sticks together into a crucifix, and I had whispered holy words as the dirt fell.

A moon like an inflated stomach heaved itself into the sky. Macclehorse called a halt. He had stared grimly ahead into the darkness those past hours, had not once complained of the lack of whiskey.

'How far you reckon we got to go?' he asked.

Bird rubbed at his beard. 'If the marshal reckoned Puttick's in the Saint Bois, I'll bet he's thinking of the cave, up by the bluff.' Bird's face was serious. 'I just hope to God you have a plan, Sister. As I've heard it, the most wanted men from here to the New Mexico Territory hide out there. No telling what we might find.'

'We find Puttick,' Macclehorse said savagely, 'an' we send him into justice in a California collar. Ain't that right, Sis?'

I nodded slowly. I had set out to find Abe, to deliver him from the life of sin into which he had found himself thrown, yet what if he too deserved justice? What if he sported a brand, a mark of

violence and corruption upon his chest? If it had been *his* knife
that had cut into the flesh of an old man's back?

I pulled out my pistol, checked that it was loaded. The men
followed suit. Macclehorse carried a rifle, battered and dented,
but powerful all the same. Levi loosened his clothing. I saw now
that he wore a knife at his ankle as well as at his waist. Bird pulled
out a shotgun, a brutal weapon with a sawn-off barrel. He smiled
grimly beneath my questioning gaze.

'Like I said, this is a lawless land.'

We rode all night. Near dawn, we came to a ravine, where
large rocks rose steeply on either side, as though a mountain had
been smashed to pieces.

'The cave's a way down there,' croaked Bird, indicating the
distant side.

I nodded, swaying the saddle. My eyes were prickling with
tiredness. Far below on the ravine floor, mist swirled in the light
of a day not yet broken.

'We should rest,' murmured Macclehorse, drawing up alongside me with a wan smile. 'Won't be no good if we're too played
out to take aim.'

I nodded and slid from the horse. We made our way into the
trees, found a secluded place to make camp.

'I'll take first watch,' offered Bird.

I was too tired to argue, to do anything but roll myself into a
blanket upon the ground. I had thought that sleep would claim
me as soon as I closed my eyes, yet instead I saw Abe, his teeth
bared in a savage grimace as he shoved an old man to the ground,
as he drew his knife and sent it plunging down.

I sat up, gasping for air. Cold sweat chilled my neck and I
grasped at the rosary. It was several minutes before my heart
ceased hammering, before the terrible feeling of dread released
its hold upon me.

The camp was quiet. Macclehorse lay upon his back, sleeping
too deeply even to snore. Levi was by his side as always, and
Dove stretched along the boy's length for warmth. The hound
looked up sleepily when I moved and thumped his tail twice.

I made my way through the trees. The sun was just risen, the horizon veiled with a haze. Birds wheeled beneath me as I reached an outcrop and gazed down over the rock-strewn land.

'Can't sleep?'

Mr Bird sat behind me, legs stretched along the ground. There was a knife in his hand, paused above a half-whittled object.

I admitted that I could not, and took a seat beside him to watch the day break.

'You're thinking on what you might find down there,' he said, scraping a few more shavings from the stick. 'And about Muir and his crimes.'

I ran the rosary beads through my fingers. 'Whatever I find,' my voice was rusty with weariness, 'whatever he may have done, I made him a promise. He trusted me with his hand once, and I will not let him fall.'

'You think you can save him from sin?' Bird's knife scraped away rhythmically.

I reached the rosary's cross and held it, thinking of the lives that had left their stain there. 'Sin leaves none of us untouched,' I said slowly. 'I cannot save Abe from that. But I can save him from himself, from the fire that waits in all of our chests; that would engulf us, if were we to let it.'

Bird looked up sharply at the reflection of his words. I gave him half a smile.

'What of Puttick?' he asked, hands still. 'What of a man like him? You believe that he can be saved?'

'I must,' I whispered.

After a moment I felt Bird's yellow eyes leave me, heard him sigh as he focused out over the horizon.

'Get some rest, Sister,' he said gently. 'You will find that faith tested soon enough.'

14

I change my face,
and am tormented

I did not dream, and must have slept deeply, for when I next opened my eyes the sun was shining through the leaves, noonday strong. My head was foggy, my thoughts a step behind my body as I rubbed at my eyes and looked around.

The camp was empty. Macclehorse's blanket lay in a furrow of leaves, and Levi's too. The horses stood drowsing nearby, but there was no sign of Dove. I walked toward the lookout point, wondering that I should have been left alone.

It too was empty. Only the few wood shavings that blew in a gentle breeze suggested that Bird had ever sat there. Unease prickled at me, and I hurried back to the camp for my weapons. I had slept with the pistol and knife beside my head, and they remained where I had left them. I slung them around my waist with relief.

It was only then I noticed a strange scuffling and thrashing and a low whine, like a creature in pain. I crept through the undergrowth, knife drawn.

It was Dove. He had been tied to a tree, jaws muzzled with a rope so short he could barely twist his neck. When he saw me, he went wild, straining and whimpering. I pulled at the knots with shaking fingers, then drew my knife. His fur was raw and bloody where he had fought against the ropes, while I had slept on, oblivious.

He licked at my face frantically as I cut the cord free from his neck. As soon as it was loose, he took off, shooting through the trees. I called his name, but he did not stop. Leaves and stones skidded underfoot as I raced after him, flashing past the camp

445

toward the steep path that ran down the treacherous side of the ravine.

I scraped myself upon rocks and branches as I staggered downhill, grit sliding beneath my boots. The dog was a flash of gray ahead of me. Just when I thought my lungs would burst I saw him snarl. He launched himself up another slope.

Above us, a dark mouth opened in the side of the cliff, surrounded by huge boulders and precarious trees, protected by a vertical drop. Smoke was streaming from the mouth of the cave, white as milk in the sunlight. I gritted my teeth. A signal. It would be visible for miles.

Dove was still ahead of me when an anguished cry split the air, rebounding again and again away into the ravine below. I clawed my way toward the cave, terrified of what I might find. The dog's growls reverberated as I hauled myself up the rock and stumbled into the dark space, blind from the daylight.

'Abe?' I called, grabbing for my pistol.

'Sister!' It was Macclehorse, his voice thick with pain. 'Don't—'

Too late I heard movement behind me, felt the cold kiss of metal against my neck.

'Call that beast off,' Bird hissed in my ear, 'or it dies.'

I shouted for Dove to stop, not knowing whether he would obey. After a moment I heard him whine, saw his shape ghost away into the cave as my eyes adjusted.

Macclehorse lay half fallen upon the floor, his beard and face wet with spittle and tears. I caught the smell of blood: it pooled around one of his legs, oozing from his thigh. In his lap he cradled Levi. The boy was lifeless and pale, arms flopping. There was blood upon his head, but I could not tell from where it came. The dog whimpered and pawed at the child.

'He has killed him,' Macclehorse wept.

Bird made a dismissive noise as he reached to drag the pistol and knife from my belt.

'The child isn't dead. At least, I don't believe so.'

He shoved me hard, sending me stumbling to my knees. I

watched as he loped to the mouth of the cave and flung my weapons into the valley below.

'There now,' he grinned, as the sunlight caught in his flat golden eyes. The neck of his shirt hung open, and for the first time I saw the scar, thick and furrowed in an 'X' across his chest.

'Puttick,' I said, my voice dark with anger.

15

Skin for skin,
and all that a man hath, he will give

The outlaw tilted his head in acknowledgement, and sneered down at Macclehorse, sharp-eyed and pleased.

'Doesn't pay to keep company with fools, Sister, does it?'

My heart was thundering in my ears, a hundred questions racing through my mind. The big man beside me strained forward with rage, only to fall back once more.

Resolutely, I turned away from Puttick. The outlaw made a disgusted sound in his throat.

'Where are you hurt?' I asked Macclehorse.

'Bastard shot me in the leg,' he said. 'So I couldn't do no runnin', but then he remembered the lad and dog.' His face crumpled again as he held the boy protectively. I stroked the red strands back from the wound on the boy's forehead, and felt for his pulse.

'His heart is strong. He will live,' I soothed.

'Well, I said so,' drawled Puttick. He lounged near the smoke signal and had taken up his whittling again. 'Now, Sister,' he smiled back at me, 'don't you want to know about Abraham?'

I gritted my teeth, trying to stay calm.

'Where is he?'

'You will see him soon enough,' he blew a splinter or two from the wooden object and threw it over to me. I made no move to catch it. A roughly hewn crucifix hit me softly and clattered to the cave floor. 'You might need that,' he pointed. 'I imagine you'll have some praying to do before you finally meet that maker of yours.'

Before I could reply, a distant shout echoed from outside, and he clambered to his feet.

'If that's his gang, we're good as dead.' whispered Macclehorse.

I leaned forward to listen. The shouts from outside had grown louder. I heard men issuing orders. Puttick stood on the lip of the outcrop, shotgun slung over his shoulder. Before long he dropped it into his hands to aim upwards, at something above the cave.

'Afternoon, marshal,' the outlaw called. 'Fine day for a scalp hunt.'

'Let's get this done, Puttick.'

I froze. The voice belonged to Reasoner.

'She there?' the marshal called.

Puttick glanced back into the cave at me.

'Surely is,' he winked, 'and all in one piece too, like I promised.'

'That was the deal,' the lawman replied stonily. 'Sister Thomas Josephine, are you there?'

I glared at Puttick's smiling face and could not help the snarl that twitched my lip.

'I am.'

'This makes us square now, Marshal?' said Puttick from behind his gun. 'They're worth a thousand dollars, Muir and Josephine, and I'll take a hundred for this other old crow. You swore I'd have amnesty for a spell, once they were taken.'

'We're square,' barked Reasoner from above. 'Now we're coming in. Don't do nothing rash.'

I heard boots scrambling upon rocks as Union soldiers began to climb into sight, weapons at the ready. The marshal clambered down after them, hands raised.

'Good to see you, Benjamin,' Puttick grinned, jiggling the shotgun. 'Won't you join us—'

Before he could say another word, Reasoner darted forward. He seized the outlaw's shotgun, then struck him hard around the back of the head with a cosh that he had hidden in his sleeve. Puttick crumpled like a doll.

The marshal sighed, staring down at the fallen man, and wiped his brow.

'Idiot,' he murmured, before looking me in the eye.

'Sister Thomas Josephine,' he announced, 'you are under arrest for seven counts of murder across the states of Nevada, California, Arkansas, and the New Mexico Territory . . .'

16

And they shall meet the darkness
in the day

The day was warm and bright, with all the fresh promise of the summer. The merciless swamp heat to come was as distant as heaven. I closed my eyes. The breeze brushed my eyelids, and for a moment I imagined myself to be back in the garden of the convent, watching the apple blossoms shiver, pale and perfect against the stone walls and blue sky.

I tried not to look upon the crowd gathered beneath my feet. At another time, I might have spread my arms to them, viewed them all – the young and callous and infirm – in the light of God's grace. Now they were little more than stuffed animals, their glassy eyes shining up at the spectacle before them.

Reasoner stood at the foot of the gallows. For a man who had apprehended three of the most wanted fugitives in the west, he did not seem content. He shifted from foot to foot and glanced up every so often, worrying at something in the pocket of his coat.

We had been taken back into Arkansas, to Fort Smith. There I learned that Puttick's men had dumped Abraham on the jail-house steps, bloodied and beaten, barely hours before our arrest. No doubt Puttick had believed that he would be carousing in some camp by now, kept safe by his deal with Reasoner. He should have known that the marshal would have no qualms about lying in order to make his arrests.

The four of us had been tried together: Macclehorse and I, Puttick and finally Abe. The whole procedure had been a sham. I had been shunted into the stand without ceremony, in the middle of the night, with a jury made up of drunks and those in the pay of the law. The judge had read out the crimes attributed to me, savoring each and adding a few fictional ones for good measure. It was over before it began, the sentence read and passed. There had been no one present to object as they dragged me away.

I watched a group of small birds, fluttering joyfully through the crowd, picking at the crumbs the spectators dropped. Levi stood, his red hair shining among the other bystanders. Dove sat beside him, panting gently in the heat. Even the death-hungry judges at Fort Smith had balked at hanging a child, and some good woman had spoken for him, had taken him away to raise up right. Perhaps she had brought him today, to teach him a lesson. Perhaps he had come on his own, to say goodbye. The boy's eyes were fixed, like mine, upon the steps of the gallows. I had been brought out first. Now they were leading the other doomed men to the hangman's structure.

My eyes lit on Macclehorse, his face swollen from weeping. Two lawmen half carried him, for he could not support his weight with his wounded leg. Puttick staggered after them, beaten to a pulp by his guards, but it was the third man I looked to: the only person who seemed real in this living nightmare, more so even than I. I watched him ascend the steps, heard the jingle of metal, the sound of a familiar boot upon wood as he approached, and finally looked up into his mahogany eyes.

'Abe,' I whispered.

He was barely a pace away, and had I been able to, I would have reached out to touch him. I contented myself with looking. His face was thinner than I remembered, discolored by bruises and lack of sleep. Yet I smiled, for there was that slanting jaw, that stubborn jut of chin, those eyes.

'It is good to see you,' I said.

Something like anguish overtook his face as he stared at me.

'Sister,' his voice trembled and broke upon the word. 'Sister,' he tried again, 'we are about to die.'

'I know, Abe. But still, it is good to see you.'

He flinched as the thick rope was tightened around his neck. I could hardly feel the chafing against my own skin.

'Why did you come?' He looked tortured. His gaze took in every inch of my face, to see all he could, while there was time. 'You was safe. Never thought you'd forgive me . . .'

The crowd began jeering as Puttick's noose was tightened.

'I promised that I would come for you,' I said firmly. 'What you did is long forgiven. You took your own justice from Carthy. I didn't understand then, but I do now.'

Muir was shaking his head at me.

'I did it for *you*,' he said. 'To save you. Carthy would've forced you to sin, one day, when his madness took him. My hands were already stained, Sister. Yours were clean. I were happy to die to keep them so.'

He leaned toward me, as far as his rope would allow. The magistrate standing on the steps of the gallows was calling out our names, the crimes we were guilty of. The crowd heckled and catcalled, but I felt my breathing slow, the noise fade, as I stared into Abe's face.

'Abraham C. Muir,' I smiled through my sorrow, 'sea like the wide ocean, not "c" for cat.'

His own smile was broken.

'Tell me one thing, Sister,' he whispered, as the hangman took his position. 'Tell me your name, your real one.'

I stared into those brown eyes that seemed to hold the world.

'My name,' I told him, as the crowd's screams became frenzied, 'my name was Lucy.'

The hangman pulled the lever.

Nunslinger: Book 10

Gospel Sharp

The True Tale of how Sister Thomas Josephine of St. Louis, Missouri, escaped the Hangman's Noose, Rode the Outlaw Trail and was Framed for Murder in the State of Colorado

I

And the tenth I will utter
to men with my tongue

My death met me with darkness and agony, as I had feared it would. A moment's gasp of terror and the rope snapped taut; my feet left the wood and a violent jolt snapped through my body, ripping soul from flesh, to bring me at last into the presence of my maker.

But heaven was not bliss, it was not peace eternal and freedom from a blemished human form. It was dirt and a bursting in my lungs. It hurt.

And pain is the lot of the living.

I opened my eyes. The gallows yawned open above me: a square of high blue framed by the platform through which I had fallen, the frayed end of a rope twisting uselessly. For one awful moment I gasped emptily, then air flooded my lungs, blessed air, and I drank it in.

The noise of the crowd filtered into my ears, slowly at first but building like a river, angry and white. Still wheezing, I rolled onto my knees. There was one thought that claimed me then, before prayer or Lord or questions: if I lived, what of him?

I spun around, terrified of what I might find. Abe lay six feet away. For a heartbeat he was still, then his chest was heaving with breath. A gunshot rang out and the dirt before me exploded.

The shouts of the crowd increased, boiling over into violence. I saw a soldier run forward, aiming at my chest, crouching low to fire his revolver beneath the scaffold. Before I could cry out he was tackled to the ground. Another man had come out of nowhere to smash the weapon from his grip.

It was Reasoner. For an instant, our eyes met across the distance, before the brawling crowd swallowed him up. Roped wrist

457

and neck, I could barely breathe, let alone move, but I crawled toward Abe through the dust and the noise and carnage. He was fighting his way to me, bruised and battered though he was. We came to a stop eye to eye, just as we had been barely a minute before, at what we thought would be our worlds' end. His smile was as wild as my own, unbelieving that we lived.

But the bullets were still flying, civilians screaming in panic, men still lunging to fire under the scaffold, and Abe yelped as a charge clipped the heel of his boot. He dragged me away, using his body to protect mine. A stack of lumber shielded the steps of the gallows. We crawled toward them on raw knees.

Macclehorse cowered there, white and gasping. I reached out to him when the broken noose about my throat was snapped taut. Someone had the rope in his hand; was dragging me backward. I kicked out, choking.

Puttick's face appeared above me, blood vessels spidering his eyes red and yellow. His face was savage as he fumbled with the rope, his bound hands clumsy. I finally managed one stifled cry for Abe.

Muir lunged forward but it was too late. Puttick released me, and I scrabbled away only to find myself pulled up short. The outlaw had tied the end of my noose to his own, roping us together like a pair of cattle.

'What have you done?' I cried, even as the bullets thudded into our shelter.

'Need the Lord on my side,' he yelled, baring his teeth behind bleeding gums. 'Or the devil, don't care which. You got the ear of both, ma'am. If you live, so do I.'

'Bastard!' spat Abe, but before he could move there was a great splintering: the stacks of lumber were being blasted away.

'We got to move!' Puttick yelled, but all I could see was Macclehorse, pale on the ground, his wounded leg thrust awkwardly before him.

'Go,' he told me, eyes swimming with pain.

Puttick heaved upon rope to drag me away, near cutting off my air. Rage took me, and I spun around, driving a knee into the outlaw's groin. He spluttered and retched at the end of the rope, but this time it was I who dragged him toward the old hunter.

'Mr Macclehorse,' I said savagely, 'I will not leave you behind.'

The old man looked as though he would object, but I grabbed his shirt in my roped hands and pulled, until he stood along with me.

Splinters were flying, the dust kicked up into chaos. The whole town seemed to have opened fire; it would only be a matter of time before those bullets caught us.

'There!'

Ten paces away stood the undertaker's cart, a pair of horses rearing and snorting in the harness. Four rough coffins rattled behind them, propped open and ready to receive our lifeless bodies.

'We'll never make it,' yelled Puttick, as a shot ricocheted past his head. 'Have a pound of lead in us before we even take a step!'

'We must try!' I was staggering under Macclehorse's weight. My head was reeling with prayers, but in my heart I feared that the outlaw was right. We had escaped one death only to land in the jaws of another.

'It's true,' said Macclehorse, sweat rolling from his brow, 'I'm all done in.' He turned his eyes to mine, wind-toughened skin crinkling at the corners. 'Never thought I'd bite the ground in the grace o' God, Sister. Guess he might forgive me after all.' He wrenched himself from my hold. 'Tell the boy!' he bellowed over his shoulder, and staggered out into the line of fire, roaring curses at the crowd.

I couldn't cry out, couldn't see anything save for the dust before me as we ran, four paces, five, while bullets whistled all around. Then Puttick was pushing me upward into the cart. I caught one glimpse of Abe, clawing himself into the driver's seat like a man possessed.

The cart shot forward, but too late. Pain slashed across my flesh, white hot and burning, sending me tumbling into the coffin that should have been my final resting place.

2

A threefold cord is not easily broken

'Sister!'

The air was dust and frenzy. Gunfire sounded, but it was distant, fading.

'Sister!' Abe called again. With great effort, I stilled the terror that coursed through my veins.

'Abe!' I gasped as well as I was able through my bruised throat. 'Ride!'

I heard him bellow to the horses, and our speed increased. Resolutely, I struggled up until I was sitting. My hands remained bound. I was scraped and bruised all over, jolted by the thundering cart. A burst of agony made me retch, and I risked a glance down at my sleeve. Dark liquid was blooming through the fabric of my upper arm.

The rope at my neck jerked sharply. Puttick was dragging himself up from the back ledge, his yellow eyes narrowed against the dust. Before I could open my mouth, the cart whipped sharply and he was hurled forward, the coffins sliding precariously. Two wheels lifted and thudded back onto the ground.

My head was spinning. I begged the Lord to give me strength, but the cart tilted again. Hard fingers closed upon my wounded flesh, and I screamed at the pain as I was dragged from the coffin. Not a moment later it slid from the cart, smashing into pieces on the road behind us.

'You live, I live,' Puttick said, grinning wildly. He let me go and his hands came away coated in blood.

His face went white, and he opened his mouth when Abe's shout was thrown back to us.

'Hold on!'

Puttick pulled me with him and made a grab for the edge of the cart.

We heard an outraged bellow and a huge cow rose up before us. I braced myself for the impact, but she bellowed again and bolted from our path. Another dashed after her, then another, until our tracks disappeared beneath the red-brown bodies, lowing in fear and scattering in our wake.

Ahead, I could see a stand of trees, and water beyond, the river at the edge of the town, churning and muddy. My head spun and there was little I could do but gasp until Muir brought the horses to a halt.

'Help me!' he commanded, diving from his seat. Puttick half pulled, half carried me from the back. Muir was releasing the horses from their harnesses. They shook and sweated, eyes rolling with terror.

Abe staggered to the back of the cart and set his shoulder to the wood. Puttick gritted his teeth and followed suit. Together, they shoved the cart with all their might. It slid down the hillside, slowly at first, but gathering momentum until it crashed over the side of the bank into the middle of the river.

Puttick surveyed the bubbling wreckage, sinking beneath the eddying water.

'Well, Muir,' he panted, 'looks like—'

Muir's fist slammed into Puttick's jaw, dropping him instantly. I fell with him, still joined by the rope.

'She's hurt, you fool,' Puttick snarled, but Abe was not listening. He was ripping at the knot that bound us together. It gave way. He grabbed at the noose around Puttick's throat and began to pull.

'Abe,' I croaked. 'Abe, leave him.'

'He would've seen us hanged,' Muir's voice was shaking, his eyes locked on Puttick. I could tell he was itching to pull the knot tighter, to leave the outlaw broken-veined and strangling on the ground. 'He would've watched us swing, an' laughed all the while, had Reasoner not tricked him.'

'Y'all get nowhere without me,' Puttick choked, 'she needs help. I know folk that can—'

'I *met* your folk,' Abe raged, dragging on the knot. 'They beat on me 'til I was half dead.' Puttick coughed up spittle, fighting to breathe.

'Abe,' I took his shirt in my lashed hands. My ears were roaring and I struggled to fix him with my gaze. 'I cannot let you do this.'

His eyes flickered, emotion shifting in their depths. Slowly, he looked down. Blood dripped from my wrist into the dust at his feet. His face turned white at the same moment my knees buckled.

3

Out of prison and chains

'There's a safehouse couple miles north of here, near Lee Creek,' Puttick drawled, picking rope fibers from the grazed skin of his neck. 'Or there was, recent enough.'

I was silent. Abe tore off another strip of his shirt and soaked it in the river. I accepted the saturated cloth and squeezed the water onto my parched tongue. He had already shredded the sleeves of his garment to bandage my arm. I had bled through the fabric in seconds.

I had awoken beneath an overhang. The sunlight was reflected upon the river, creating bright patterns against the rock face. Had we not been running for our lives, I might have called it idyllic, but as it was, every snap and rustle of leaves, every flurry of birds had us tensing like prairie dogs.

'We get food there,' Puttick continued, 'weapons, another horse too, if there ain't been any others past in a time.'

'Others?' I asked quietly.

'Other motherless sons of—' Abe snarled, before catching my eye. 'Others like him, is what he means.'

The outlaw rolled his shoulders and assumed a pious expression. 'I am not saying that those we find there will be lily-white and clean of hand,' he told me, 'but sure as hell they'll have no love for the law.' When I did not answer, his playful countenance dropped, as quickly as it had risen. 'She's bleeding out,' he said coldly. 'What other choices have you got?'

'You'll have a knife in our backs before we even shut eye,' Abe spat.

'It is true, you were ready to sell us to Reasoner just days ago,'

I interrupted, as Puttick tried to protest. 'Why should you help us now?'

'Can't a man repent him of his sins?' the outlaw asked. When I did not reply, he shifted, as though a barb prickled within his chest. 'Something ain't on the up and up about any of this. By all rights, we should be dead.'

'What do you mean?' I pressed. 'Was it not your men who—?'

'They had naught to do with the gallows,' Puttick snapped. 'I thought it were your man, Reasoner, but now I ain't so sure.'

I shook my head. 'The marshal is bound by the law. He did not like the trial, but I do not believe he would interfere with its resolution.'

'Then who?' Abe demanded. 'Because ain't like anyone with a knife would just waltz up an' saw through them ropes.'

'We should have half the fort hounding us,' the outlaw said, 'but there ain't nothing.'

'Your gang, keepin' them off?' asked Abe grudgingly.

'I told you, they had naught to do with it!' Puttick burst. His manner had changed wholesale, furtive and closed where before he had mocked. Self-consciously he rubbed at the scar upon his chest.

Abe's eyes widened in realization. 'They're out for you, ain't they?' he said slowly. 'You been caught one too many times an' now your men are thinkin' it's time for a change of leadership.' He shook his head with a laugh. 'An' I thought *I* were a dead man walking.'

Puttick lunged at Muir, who scrambled up to meet him.

'Enough!' I called. Both men fell still, an arm's length from each other. I struggled to my feet, though Abe held out a hand to stop me.

'Whatever passed today,' I murmured, 'whoever our savior, we have been given a second chance at life. Do you truly wish to squander it?'

I stood resolute amid their silence. All three of us had been disfigured by the world; marked body and soul by cruelty and greed, by swift deaths and swifter, brutal lives.

'I intend to live,' I told them fiercely.

They returned my stare for a long time. Finally, Puttick turned away, a wry smile on his face.

'Then the Lord grant we die doing just that.'

4

All rivers run into the sea

It was dusk by the time we smelled smoke through the trees. I was weak with blood-loss and hunger, barely able to lift my head above the horse's neck. Abe walked by my side, keeping me from slipping from the animal's bare back.

I peered around blearily when we stopped. Muir's head was raised to the breeze and Puttick's too, both of them wary, part-hunter, part-prey. Abe led the horses slow and quiet over the pine needles that cushioned the earth.

'Is this the place?' I asked Puttick through numb lips.

'It was, twelvemonth back,' he peered through the branches, 'and I have not heard anything to the contrary since.'

The safehouse looked to be little more than a hovel; weathered boards nailed together against the slant of the hill. We had come within twenty paces when the door flew open and an old man stumped out, a sawn-off shotgun leveled at us, a rifle on his back, yelling at us to raise our arms.

Puttick smiled, unperturbed.

'Uncle Bill!' he called. 'How's Aunt Sal?'

The old man blinked from beneath a grimy top hat, rubbed his gums together once or twice.

'She laid up,' he called back after a long while, 'bunions like the devil.' He narrowed his eyes at us. 'You brought supper?'

'Pair of chickens,' Puttick said, 'from the fort. Need eatin' soon, else they'll spoil, one in particular.'

Abe caught my gaze, bewildered, but had the good sense to remain silent until the bizarre transaction was done.

'So I see.' The old man was examining me, scratching his head with the mouth of the gun. 'Best bring 'em in, then. Tie your beasts up yonder.'

Abe insisted on carrying me into the house, taking care not to touch my wounded arm. As soon as we had crossed the threshold, the old man slammed and barred the door with surprising speed.

'Ain't seen no one today,' he told Puttick briskly, hesitation gone. 'S'not to say they won't come lookin', this close to the fort.' He kicked away some of the dirt that covered the floor and stooped to haul open a hatch. Beyond it, a tunnel widened into darkness.

'What's the damage?' he jerked his head toward me, already rummaging through a trunk.

'Bullet,' Puttick replied, dropping down into the hole. 'No more than a scratch, but she's bleeding pretty bad.'

The old man grunted, handed down an oil lamp.

'Thought you was a gonner, Colm,' he said. 'You got the Lord or the Old Man to thank for your hide?'

Puttick laughed, ducking out of sight. 'You'll have to ask her.'

'What the hell was all that?' Abe grumbled, as he helped me through the narrow earthen passage, 'about Aunt Sal an' bunions and a chicken?'

'Bandit code,' came the answer. 'Aunt Sal's the law, you two be the chickens.' I saw the glint of Puttick's eye in the darkness, amused. 'Tell anyone that an' I'll cut out your tongues.'

His voice was light, but abruptly I was standing back in the Indian Territory, staring down at the bodies of an old man and his wife, slaughtered senselessly.

'We should not be here,' I murmured to Abe.

His face was gaunt in the dim light.

'No,' he agreed, 'but it's all we got.'

We emerged into a long, low room. It had been dug into the hillside, the walls shored up with planks. Puttick's gas lantern illuminated six pallet beds, bare of blankets. Boxes and crates were stacked high in the corners. Puttick knelt at one and wrenched it open. Pale light gleamed through a crack in the

467

opposite wall. Beyond, I could see leaves, animals moving in a makeshift corral.

Abe lowered me onto one of the pallets, and I gulped at the stale air, fighting the dizziness that came upon me.

Puttick was swearing while he rooted through the crates.

'Where the hell's the rest?' he demanded angrily of the old man, who had followed us down. 'There's naught here but scraps and leavings.'

'It were your boys what took it,' the old man shrugged nonchalantly, evidently accustomed to such outbursts. 'They rode through, few weeks back, when they was out to grab that deserter, what's his name . . .' He trailed off, peering at Abe, then at me, in my habit.

'I'll be damned,' he said quietly.

'Stop your gawking,' Abe growled. 'Can't you see she needs help?'

Hurriedly, the old man tipped the contents of his pockets onto the bed.

'All I got,' he told me apologetically, 'I ain't patched a lady up before.'

'It is no different,' I told him, gritting my teeth as Abe began to loosen the sodden bandage.

The man's supplies consisted of liquor, a roll of linen and a few needles. After a moment's hesitation he produced a twist of paper, filled with a strange reddish powder.

'Cayenne pepper,' he mumbled. 'Burns like all hell, but it'll do to stem the bleeding.'

I closed my eyes, pushing my fear aside as I asked the Lord to send me strength, for I would need it.

'Boil some water,' I whispered, reaching for the liquor.

5

Dreams follow many cares

When they fed me, I could barely keep the food down and could not have told what I had eaten. My hands shook, so much so that Abe eventually took the spoon and offered the sustenance in small bites. I swallowed what I could.

My body was worn down to threads. Liquor had offered its lacklustre relief during my surgery but the pain had been great. Time and again, I thought of all the men I had stitched up, patched and sewn like empty clothes. Now, it was my body, my flesh pulled together and darned with cotton thread.

Night had long fallen. On the other side of the room Puttick was talking about provisions, about a spare horse, but I could listen no longer and lay back upon the bed. I longed for a cool hand to rest upon my forehead, for a calm voice to bring me rest, to pray me into peace. But who would look upon me with kindness now? The church, the law, they all condemned me. Yet everything I had done had been in His name.

In whose name? hissed the treacherous voice at the back of my mind.

I felt a blanket settling over me, scratchy and stale from use. I looked up to see Abe, smiling faintly as he smoothed it down. He sank onto the neighboring bed and lay back with a groan. I turned my head and for a moment, we only gazed at each other. I felt myself smiling like a fool, drunk with pain and liquor, and in that flickering light, Abe's mouth curved unconsciously in reply.

'What?' he asked.

'Mexico did not work out.'

He laughed, a bone-dry sound.

'No, it did not.' His eyes drooped closed. 'Damn stupid plan anyhow. Too hot, an' all them snakes. I'm for Canada now.'

'Canada?' I mumbled, my words a struggle. 'What could there be in Canada, Abe?'

There was a long silence. I smiled into the blanket and let my eyelids drift closed. Distantly, I heard the sound of footsteps, of the oil lamp being blown out.

'Freedom,' a voice whispered into the darkness.

6

As light differeth
from darkness

'Puttick's a devil.' Abe's voice broke the quiet of the afternoon.

We had slept until late, drained to our cores, and had woken to a beautiful spring day. I was weak still, the wound upon my arm was swollen and raw. I prayed against infection, and set about washing it, binding it with fresh bandage. Even that activity exhausted me. Puttick was minding the hovel upstairs, awaiting the old man's return, and Abe had insisted that I rest in the doorway of the shack while he told me of his journey from Mexico.

'Din't take me long,' he continued, 'to realize what sort of man Puttick were, after we escaped the chain gang. Before that he were different, made me trust him. You seen the way he is – changes, like he's pullin' off a mask. Only you never know which face is real. Course I'd heard rumors of what he'd done to folk, but . . .' he scrubbed at his eyes.

In that moment I remembered Chicken, his eyes bright as he told me grotesque stories of the outlaw's cruelty. I did not want to imagine what horrors Abe had witnessed as part of Puttick's company.

'Worst part is,' he told me wearily, 'he's sane as you or I. Now Carthy—' A jolt ran through me at the mention of that name. Abe too swallowed nervously. 'Carthy were out of his mind, but Puttick? I seen him toy with people, whittling away at them, 'til they don't know themselves.' His face was dark as he stared at his hands in his lap. 'You should've let me kill him.'

'No,' I sighed into the air. 'His soul belongs to the Lord, though it has been maimed almost past measure.'

'But not past salvation,' a voice interrupted. Abe and I leaped in our skins. Puttick had appeared from nowhere, his hawk eyes fixed upon us.

'What do you want?' Abe snapped.

'I was merely going to invite you to hear the news from down-river,' the outlaw said, hunkering down beside me. His face was serious. 'There's a posse on our trail, Reasoner and others beside. Whoever held them back at the fort, they're on the scent now. If we want to remain at liberty, we better be prepared to get.'

'Can't,' Abe crossed his arms. 'Sister ain't strong enough.'

Puttick raised his eyebrows. 'Shall we not ask her?'

We rode at sundown. I could barely hold the reins of my horse, yet there was no help for it. *Ride with the devil or die by the law*, Puttick had told us mockingly.

I had once fled into the desert with nothing but a rosary and a pair of pistols; the state of our provisions now was little better. Muir and I rode on the pair of old carthorses, Puttick on a third, rangy beast borrowed from the safehouse. We had a few pouches of salt pork, a twist of tobacco, a bundle of blankets, and little else to last us on our journey.

By unspoken agreement, we followed Puttick north, even when Muir made a vague suggestion that Mexico might be closer.

'We'd have to go through Texas,' Puttick dismissed him with a flick of his hand. 'The south is seething like a week-old corpse. We'd be run down by conscript hunters in a snap, and I would hate to ponder on your fate, ma'am.'

'It wouldn't be because your "boys" are riding the Red River down there?' Abe asked sarcastically. 'Stringin' up old ladies and butcherin' farmers for their worthless handfuls of graybacks?'

'What 'bout you, Muir?' Puttick retorted. 'Ain't you still wanted down there for murdering the Sister's Union lover?'

'Canada,' I broke in before either could begin a fight, 'is the other side of the country.' My face was burning, but I forced myself to remain calm. 'It is hundreds of miles away. How are we to travel? We would surely be apprehended.'

'It's a thousand miles, if it's a step,' Puttick corrected

snappishly. 'But there's a trail; runs up through Colorado, into the mountains and Montana Territory then clear 'cross the border. Law never found it as yet. We followed that, we'd be safe.'

'Safe from what?' muttered Abe darkly.

7

Of earth they were made

We rode for days without seeing a soul, although Muir was certain he felt Indian eyes on us. Despite my efforts, the wound in my arm was angry and inflamed. It made me feverish, yet there was little to be done, in the wilderness of Indian Territory.

Puttick did not make for the easiest traveling companion. At times, he taunted and prodded us so remorselessly that Abe was forced to ride far behind, or lose his temper entirely. At others, he was Mr Bird again, sharp-eyed and sagacious, leading us through that remote country on hidden paths, anticipating my exhaustion seemingly before I did.

What of the man who had sat beside me, I wondered, as dawn spilled over the Sans Bois mountains, who had asked me: *What of Puttick? What of a man like him? You believe that he can be saved?*

I asked the Lord to grant me wisdom, yet I was no closer to understanding when, three days later, we came upon the sign.

It had been driven into the ground at the edge of the trees, neat and whitewashed, wholly out of place in that ancient world. BEAR CREEK, it read, in thick, black letters, PRIVATE PROPERTY OF E. WINDROSE.

We gathered around it, staring down at those letters as if they spelled out an almighty puzzle.

'Thought you said these was Cherokee lands?' Abe said accusingly. 'Should be naught out here but Injuns and beasts.'

'These *are* Cherokee lands,' said Puttick. 'Something's not right here.'

A short ways downstream we smelled smoke from a cookfire. A cabin sat in shadow upon the bank, half hidden by the trees.

With the supplies almost gone, our longing for hot food and fresh news began to outweigh our caution.

'Do you think they are the ones who put the sign there?' I asked.

The outlaw grunted. 'Don't know. If it is a safehouse, I do not remember it.' His yellow eyes were fixed upon the plume of smoke that was rising from the cabin's roof.

'You're jus' worried there'll be friends of yours in wait,' Abe snorted.

'Unlikely,' he shot back, 'but it could be hostile Injuns. No telling.'

Abe sniffed at the air once or twice.

'You ever known Injuns cook army-issue pork an' beans?' he goaded, and clucked his horse out onto the bank.

As we approached, Puttick dismounted and picked up a large stick from the ground, yanking away a few twigs until he could hold it as if it were a shotgun.

'Watch my back,' he hissed, and crept forward. I followed, choosing my footing carefully, for the ground was littered with animal bones, some bleached and gnawed clean, others with scraps of flesh still clinging. I held my sleeve to my face as I passed a pile of offal, pulsing with blowflies.

'What is this place?' I whispered to Abe. He was no longer so confident, gazing at the gruesome debris. 'Trappers,' he swallowed hard. 'Least I hope so.'

At the threshold, Puttick looked over his shoulder and nodded once.

'Don't nobody move!' he roared, kicking open the shack's rickety door, 'we got arms and we'll damn well use them!'

Seven men stared back at us in astonishment. All of them held bowls and cups; one had frozen with a spoonful of beans near his mouth. As I watched, one of the beans dropped unctuously onto his lap. The interior of the shack was dingy, with no windows save for a gap in the sloping roof to let out the smoke. It stank of unwashed bodies and half-cured skins. The walls were thick with pelts, fox and beaver, jackrabbit and coyote all hanging limp from pegs and nails.

'We do not want trouble,' I announced as calmly as I was able, hoping to avoid violence, 'just food and some provisions and we shall be on our way.'

'It ain't never,' one of the men spoke up after an age, peering at us through the smoke. A wild beard covered his face almost to the eyes.

'No way it could be,' the bean-eating man replied, without moving. 'Not all away down here.'

'But lookee at that scar,' the first man protested, struggling to his feet. Despite the bright day outside, he was dressed in a bearskin coat. Puttick bristled and gripped his branch. The man did not seem perturbed, but held up a hand at the level of my face and squinted one eye. 'If it ain't her, then I'm a muskrat.'

'Stay back, Sister,' Abe hissed behind me. 'They're mad as goats.'

'Injun Abe!' another of the men burst excitedly, scrabbling to his feet. He was younger than the others, his beard wispy and sparse. 'It's him, Pa!'

'The one holdin' the branch?'

'Naw, the other! It's him, Pa! It's gotta be them!'

Before either of us could move, the bearded man surged forward. Puttick gaped as the old man pushed past him in order to grasp Abe's arm. He began propelling it up and down, as vigorously as one might a water pump.

'Injun Abe,' he gushed, eyes bright, 'here, in my place.' Muir's arm continued moving on its own for a few moments. He opened his mouth angrily, but not before the trapper had turned my way. He was shorter than me by a good five inches, but nevertheless he ducked his head, and lifted an invisible hat from his brow.

'The Six-Gun Sister,' he breathed, staring up at me. 'Ma'am, y'all are welcome.'

476

8

Laughter I counted error

The men, we learned, were indeed fur trappers. Most were from Kansas, but some mumbled so vaguely about their homes that I suspected they were deserters from one army or another. They scraped the remainder of their meals into three bowls to give to us and then sat, hunched together in that hot cabin, watching us eat.

The beans were chalky and slimy with animal fat, but they were warm, and after days of cold salt pork, very welcome indeed. I began to murmur a prayer of thanks before raising my spoon, only to realize that the men were glaring at Puttick and Abe, who were shovelling in the beans as if they would disappear.

'Wha'?' Abe demanded though a mouthful, then followed their glance to me. 'Oh for—' he began to curse, but threw his spoon down and waited while I said grace. An enthusiastic chorus of 'amen's followed.

'Is Uncle Bill home?' Puttick asked warily, 'or Aunt Sal? How're them bunions of hers?'

'P'shaw,' said the trapper, 'no need for that. We ain't seen any of your kind since Wild Bill rode through here nigh on two year back. I'm Burley,' he told me with a wide smile. 'Abner Burley. That there's my boy Timothy,' the young man tripped upright and half saluted, 'an' that's Cousin Dan, an' Ralph, an' Mr Peaman from Moberly in the hat, an' Young Asa, an' on the end is Coot.'

Coot still held his spoonful of beans, and on being addressed, flushed to the roots of his hair and hid them behind his back.

'What are y'all doin' down here?' Timothy gabbled as soon as

477

his father had finished speaking. 'Last we heard you was over the border! How'd you get down from Colorado agin so fast?'

Muir and I exchanged a glance. Puttick shrugged and stuffed in another mouthful of beans. I swallowed with some difficulty and wiped the grease from my lips.

'You must be mistaken,' I told the boy, 'we have been in the Territory, ever since Fort Smith.'

'Naw,' the boy insisted, 'cain't be. After God snatched you from the gallows, y'all swam clear up the Arkansas, stole a stage coach an' rode over the border.'

'That ain't how it happened,' interrupted Young Asa, who had to be sixty years old if he was a day. 'I heard that when the devil came t'collect Colm Puttick, he saw the Sister, an' he were so taken with her that he snapped the ropes hisself.'

Silence fell as they all stared at me, waiting for confirmation. I felt my cheeks growing hot.

'How the hell d'you know about us anyway?' Muir demanded crossly.

'*Everyone* knows 'bout you,' Timothy said, eyes glowing. 'Why, yesterday at the trade post, I saw a fight break out over a poster of y'all. They was selling it for near five dollars.'

'All over the newsheets, it is,' Burley nodded. 'No one can countenance how y'all escaped like that.'

'You got the papers?' Puttick barked, working at the grease left on the dish. 'Recent?'

The young man tripped off toward the back of the cabin.

'Is one of you Mr Windrose?' I asked. 'Mr Puttick reasoned that we were in Cherokee lands, but we saw a notice, upriver. '

'Aw, *that*,' Burley rubbed his hands uncomfortably, 'naw, that ain't nothin'.'

'Didn't look like nothing,' Puttick challenged, 'looked like someone laying claim to Injun land.'

'Now this creek's mine, I tell ya,' Burley flushed. 'I bought it fair an' square off a coupla Injuns for a barrel of whiskey an' a fine wolf pelt.'

'Pa's just loaning it out,' Timothy said, clutching a satchel full of newsprint to his chest. 'We was all outta money, an' some fella at the post said he'd heard of a man who paid good dollars for any bits o' land going, all over the place. Pa signed a paper an' they gave him that there sign.'

'What fool would want to buy this heap?' Puttick snorted. 'There ain't nothing for miles but forest and Injuns.'

'This here's a fine place,' protested Burley, 'on the Salt Fork, plenty of water, not far from Kansas. An' I never met the man hisself. Did all the dealings with an agent. He said Mr Windrose wanted it for fishing.'

'They do not send road agents out for fishing,' the outlaw muttered to me, before glaring up at Timothy. 'Those the papers?'

'Got most of 'em from the post yesterday,' the boy said, proudly handing them over, 'ain't had time to read them yet. I can't figure my words too fast.'

Puttick grunted and slumped down to pore over the pages. I remembered Mr Bird's habit of perusing whatever newspaper he could get hold of, cover to cover. He did not do it on a whim, I realized then; he was charting the country's movements, looking for news that would keep him alive.

He had not been at it for longer than a few minutes when I saw his eyes narrow, his back stiffen. After an agonising pause, he raised an eyebrow and tossed the paper my way.

The moment I saw the name of the publication, I had a great deal of trouble not to shriek and rip the whole thing into shreds.

GOSPEL SHARP! the headline screamed. *SIX-GUN SISTER CHAOS IN COLORADO! ONE DEAD IN HOTEL SHOOTOUT!*

Abe leaned in over my shoulder. His eyes traveled slowly over the letters.

'What the—?' he began.

'Templeton,' I said through gritted teeth.

9

Her heart was a net,
her hands were snares

*Snatched from the very jaws of death last week by some power
beyond mere human imagining, the Six-Gun Sister, otherwise
known as SISTER THOMAS JOSEPHINE, has made her
avenging force felt in Colorado.*

*Dedicated readers of The Californian – which as everyone
knows has the highest weekly circulation in all the Western
States and Territories – will also be aware of this humble writer's selfless quest to pursue, at great personal risk & peril, the
escapades of the Holy Sister, where'er she may roam.*

*From New York to San Francisco, the Sister has set the
country aflame. In every city, one finds young women peti-
tioning the novitiate of convents and purchasing firearms for
their reticules. Penny dreadful escapades of the Six-Gun Sister
are to be found well-thumbed in the pockets of adventure-hungry
children.*

*Despite the ever-increasing bounty on her head, the Sister
remains at large, and, having escaped from beneath the very
noses of the law, it seems Thomas Josephine has set out upon
a new and bloody spree.*

*"Regardless of the events at Fort Smith, there are crimes for
which Thomas Josephine must answer," Marshal Benjamin
Reasoner told the Californian. "We will bring her in, for her
own safety as well as the community's."*

*"She got wings like a bat, so I hear," Marshal Harry Burk
told me, outside the Colorado county jail, "given her as a gift
by a demon. She flies on 'em at night, that's why she can
travel so fast, an' she carries that Injun man an' the outlaw
Puttick around with her in a special sack."*

480

Being of close personal acquaint with the Sister, I can assure you, dear readers, that I never witnessed a pair of wings – infernal or otherwise – upon her person. But however she has traveled, by mortal means or magick, there is no denying that two days past, upon the stroke of midnight, the Six-Gun Sister stormed the parlor of the Fairway Hotel & Saloon in Colorado City, her face painted with a bloody crucifix, a pistol in her left hand and her right raised to God.

With her were a pair of fiendish men, disguised by dark masks, who were no doubt her fellow dead-men-walking "INJUN ABE" C. MUIR and the OUTLAW COLM PUTTICK.

"They was pushing everyone to the ground," said Frankie Curll, the barkeep at the Fairway, who sported marks from the violent scuffle. "Upturnin' tables an' smashing the place like they was possessed. I tried to stop them and got a chair to the head for my trouble. The Sister was there, shoutin' something 'bout judgment and hellfire and the wrath of the Almighty.

"Then she points at this man, Mr Tellman, who'd been playin' cards fine and quiet like, and asks him his name. When he answered, her men came forward, cool as you please, and shot him right in the face."

The Californian can exclusively report that Mr Linus Tellman was a prominent member of Colorado society, a financier of good standing and reputation. Why the Six-Gun Sister should wreak her holy vengeance upon him is as yet a mystery, but no doubt any answers we find shall be written in blood . . .

'That cur,' snarled Abe, when I told him what was written there. 'Falsehood from start to end, to line his pockets.'

Mr Peaman was shaking his head avidly. He wore a hat made from a whole coyote pelt, its paws hanging down to his shoulders like earflaps.

'Naw,' he told us, 'that Mr Tellman's dead, awright. Saw a likeness of him, sketched in his coffin, an' the bounty on y'all is close to five thousand dollars.'

'Not that we'd dream on the money, Sister,' Burley said hurriedly, eyeing Puttick's scowl. 'You're a hero to them what know best, foxin' the law an' the army, like you do.'

A shiver ran across my skin.

'This was not me,' I said quietly, and every gaze in the cabin fell upon my face. 'Whoever has committed this crime, they've used my name, but the Lord knows it was not I who shot Tellman.'

'It ain't her style,' Puttick said cynically.

'S'all wrong,' Abe agreed, 'they got her holdin' that pistol in her left hand. Everyone knows she's useless as a blind beggar unless it's in her right.'

'Well if this weren't you three,' said Burley, pulling on his lip, 'then who were it?'

482

All the days of thy unsteady life

We had no answers for the trappers, though their speculation was rife. Eventually, Abe saw that I was tiring and put an end to the matter by snapping that it was not the first time I had been falsely accused, and that if everyone kept their heads better, perhaps I would have more chance of living in peace.

The men looked abashed at that, and apologized for troubling me, but the harm was long done. Someone was murdering in my name. Darkly, I remembered the child in Little Rock, how his sisters played at being me, slaughtering sinners as a game. In that moment, all I wanted was to ride into the wilderness alone, to find some secluded place and stay there forever, beyond the reach of the world.

The trappers had other ideas. They were horrified and fascinated by my bullet wound, the hanging scar around my neck. I politely declined their offers of bear grease and river mud to help soothe my skin, and settled upon plain water from the creek. The wound was inflamed still, pulling at the stitches, but I gritted my teeth and cleaned it, determined that it should heal.

That evening, before we shared their meager food and swallows of whiskey, nothing would do for Timothy but that I demonstrate my legendary 'handiness' with his pistol. I obliged with my good arm, and put a hole in the lad's beaver hat, which he had balanced on a tree. He gazed at it in delight, told me that he would treasure it to the end of his days, and tell all his friends that it were the Six-Gun Sister who put it there for him.

They had little extra to spare, but the next day they stuck to the outlaw's code and outfitted us as well as they could. An ancient rifle and a pair of knives, worn thin as paper, were the only weapons they could offer. Puttick and Muir fought over the gun until it was settled by a coin toss. The outlaw won, leaving Abe to grumble about cheating.

Reluctantly, I once more gave up my habit. Coot was the smallest, and gifted me a pair of calico trousers – his best, he mumbled, and though they had been darned to within an inch of their life, I thanked him graciously. I was forced to hack what remained of my habit into a shirt. I hoped God would understand that, not for the first time, necessity outweighed sanctity. I used the strips that were left to wrap my brow and head, covering my hair beneath a wide-brimmed hat.

Finally, with great reverence, Burley unfolded a fine buckskin coat. He stroked the fringing and told me that it had 'belonged to Peter'. He did not say who Peter was, but from its size, it appeared that the coat had once been worn by a youth.

Abe and Puttick fared worse than me. Puttick's new wardrobe consisted of a crumpled leather duster, while Abe wore a jacket of mixed, hanging skins. His hair had grown long and tangled once more, threaded gold at the ends from the sun, and with his wind-browned face, he looked very wild indeed.

'Injun Abe,' I greeted him with a grin. He grimaced and surveyed my get-up.

'Whatever you wear,' he shook his head with amusement, 'it never takes. Y'always look like Thomas Josephine to me.'

His smile was warm, and for a moment I returned it. All at once I remembered that cliff top above San Diego, in the glory of the sunrise and the rush of freedom, standing so close to Abe that I could see the blood beating in his veins.

Thought it might make you smile . . .

'Hate to interrupt,' Puttick was smirking nearby and I turned away abruptly, squinting up at the sun as if its heat could force away my agitation. 'But we best be leaving, unless you wish to stay and await the law.'

Burley knew of the hidden outlaw trail, and gave us instruction on how to ride for its start across the Colorado border, two days hence. He promised to keep the law from our heels, if he could. I blessed him for his kindness and he held onto my hand until he was obliged to bustle away, claiming to have some grit beneath his eyelid.

Timothy handed me up to the saddle and I settled the reins in my good hand. The horse I rode was one we had liberated from Forth Smith, a bony, cowed creature, but it sniffed the air as if recalling distantly what it felt like to run after an eternity pulling coffins. I urged it into a gallop.

With the wind on my face, trousers on my legs and a knife at my waist, a strange rush of elation took me: not happiness exactly, but a fizzing through my bones, like the air a moment before a thunderclap.

We flashed through sun-dappled pines. I breathed deep their ancient resin. Why would the Lord have intended for me a life of seclusion, an unruly thought whispered, when I could ride, and run, and fight in His name?

That night, we reached the prairie. The trees dropped away, land yawning outward. In the evening air, endless grass rippled, like the spine of a great creature, bristling.

We spoke little, and only of practicalities. If there was an idea of life beyond the near tomorrows, it was too fragile to speak of.

The breeze pushed from the west, smelling of dust and grass and emptiness. I slept that night as well as I ever had on my hard bed in the convent: rolled in a blanket on the edge of a wasteland.

There is no remembrance
of former things

The prairie took no note of borders or distance. Switchgrass rose as tall as the horses' shoulders, on and on, until I thought I would go mad with it. It seemed possible to be lost forever in that labyrinth of stalks.

The wide spaces soothed Muir, and he was in a rare good mood. Once, I turned to find him gone, vanished so completely and silently into the tall grass that my heart leaped into panic.

Just as I called for Puttick, Abe reappeared, not ten feet away, grinning like a schoolboy who has played a great practical joke. I could not help but laugh. Puttick asked grudgingly where he had learned such a skill, and Abe told of his early years, tracking and hunting with the Sioux. The outlaw only grunted in reply, but I thought I saw a flicker of respect cross his sharp face.

The tall grass receded and we found ourselves within a narrow canyon. A constant wind howled down its length, and I missed the long, tickling stems that had kept some of the dust from our faces.

We camped beneath a stand of hackberry trees that jostled thirstily around a trickle of water. Prairie chickens scratched and waddled through the shrubs, their feathers kicked up like an Indian chief. The infection in my arm had abated enough that I could stalk one, the way Owl had taught me, and pluck and gut it.

I stared down at my hands as I worked. They were smeared with blood below the buckskin cuffs, wielding the knife with ease. A year ago, one Sister Thomas Josephine had followed a wagon train, helpless. She had been afraid: of death in the desert, of the dark stranger who had dragged her so thoughtlessly with him as 'insurance'. That woman was gone. Pieces of her had fallen away, in the snows of the Sierras and the sands of Mexico. I was not certain of what remained.

The next day brought a foreboding sight. Barren plains of withered grasses trembled constantly before the west wind. The weather had begun to turn its temper against us.

'Storm's coming,' Muir and Puttick observed in unison.

As we traveled, a squall picked up, until we were forced to wrap our faces and squint our eyes against it. The light grew sick and yellow, clouds roiling together before there was an almighty flash, scorching my vision. Muir pulled his shirt from his face to cry out, but his voice was taken by a huge rumbling. Puttick was raised up in his saddle, pale and staring across the distance.

A dust cloud hit us, grit scouring our hands, our faces. The horses screamed, dancing and tossing their heads at the wind's force. Puttick was shouting for us to ride, kicking his mount to make it run, but it was too late. The air exploded into a whirlwind of dirt and pain, and I was blind, my horse staggering sideways. I heard a cry below the chaos, before that too faded. Panic took me: I was alone, buffeted and choking in the storm.

A cry caught my attention, the sound snatched away in an instant. I forced one eye open. A dark shadow of man and horse was weaving back and forth before me, as if following an invisible current. I could not tell if it was Abe or Puttick, but the figure waved an arm, signaling me closer. I forced my horse onward. I had almost reached him, when a vicious blast nearly knocked me from the saddle, battering against my eyelids, screwed closed. I felt a tug, and realized that my bridle was in someone's hand, that they were leading my mount sideways, through the wind.

Finally, like a scream dying, the storm began to abate, the dust to drop. I could feel it, eddying down around me. I swiped at my eyes, clearing them of grit, and dragged the shirt from my face.

'Abe,' I began, squinting up.

The words died in my mouth. A stranger was staring back at me, a black scarf tied across his nose and mouth, a dark leather coat raised high about his neck. I opened my mouth to cry out, but said nothing as a gun was armed behind me.

'Tell your man to drop his rifle,' someone said.

12

Better is the end of a speech
than the beginning

'Ma'am, if you'd make this 'un to Sadie I'd be much obliged,' the young man asked me, clutching his hat to his chest as our horses plodded companionably. 'She's my gal up in town an' I know she'd be that pleased if she knew her name was being writ in your hand.'

I told him that I would, scrawling a message on the brown paper that asked the Lord to take Sadie into his grace. The youth rode off grinning, tucking the paper carefully into his jacket.

'Sadie is no doubt the biggest whore in Denver,' Puttick snapped, 'and if that cow-chaser can read, I'm a turkey.'

'Gobble,' said Abe, riding past with a grin.

I fought to keep my face straight as Puttick scowled.

The men had encircled us, their faces masked and weapons readied. Puttick had hung onto the rifle, even though the rusty gun would have been little use against the five men all armed to the teeth. When he refused to throw it down, I had summoned my courage and spoken out.

Once we assured them that our only interest was in traveling, those rough men lowered their weapons. Like us, they were headed north, and warily, we set out together across the desolate prairie. I signed autographs when they asked, and when one of them took it into his head to question loudly whether I was a real woman or no, the others hurriedly quieted him.

Up ahead, the dust storm was blowing itself out. We could see it, blurring the horizon like chalk.

'You ain't what I expected,' the leader told me after a time. I had felt him watching me, his eyes narrowed. 'For a moment back there, I thought we was all goners, the way you've been takin' folk out.'

My stomach lurched uncomfortably at the memory of Templeton's article.

'Mr Tellman was not—' I began, but the drifter was shaking his head.

'Naw, not him,' he dismissed, 'I mean them farmers in the New Mexico Territory. That's three ranches now that you burned t'cinders, according to rumor. Why'd you go after them?'

I gaped at him, trying to make sense of his words.

'You've heard wrong,' I stammered.

He made a noise in his throat. 'Maybe that's so. But y'all better have a care who you talk to. There's none here would get within spittin' distance of the law, but there'll be them that think otherwise. Beefing lawmen an' big bugs is one thing, but farmers who ain't never raised more than a plough . . .' he trailed off, shot a sidelong glance my way. 'Jus' have a care is all,' he said, as he rode away. 'Colorado's swarmin' with varmints.'

I was still in shock when Abe rode toward me. He was wholly at ease among the drifters, no doubt due to his youth spent wandering ranching towns. He had been sharing their whiskey, trading stories of the saddle, and now his cheeks were flushed with liquor. He winked at Puttick, who was sober as a judge.

'Say they're headin' up to a place called Hardesty,' he announced cheerfully, 'by all accounts, there ain't no law around unless you cross the border. What you reckon?' His face was hopeful. 'They say there's a saloon there that ain't half bad, an' I'll wager they wouldn't be too interested in our means to pay, once they knew who we was.' He laughed and kicked his horse into a gallop before I could call after him.

'Been hearing more rumors of your misdeeds?' asked Puttick, over my shoulder. His voice was quiet but his eyes tracked Abe as he rode away. 'You'll find it ever more so. Folk get a name on their tongue an' find they like the taste of it. Say it more and more, 'til you start hearing stories about yourself, 'bout things you never did.'

'At least mine are unfounded,' I said sharply.

Puttick only stared, his yellow eyes strangely bright beneath that heavy, gray sky.

'A name is a burden, Sister,' he told me eventually. 'Gathers weight with every lip it falls from, 'til you find it's too much to carry and remain yourself.'

'My name belongs to God,' I insisted, unnerved, but he only shook his head with a bitter smile and rode away.

We reached the town that evening, when dusk fell and the heat of the plains was sucked away into the sky. Hardesty lived up to its name. We heard it, smelled it before we were even within the limits. It was as if all of human life within a hundred miles had been drawn to that spot, where the river emerged grudgingly from beneath the earth.

Just before the buildings began, Puttick stopped dead upon the road. He was peering down at something in the gathering darkness. I rode back to see, even when Abe carried on ahead with the drifters, roaring for us to get moving, and that time was a-wasting.

Puttick was staring at a town sign. HARDESTY it proclaimed, POPULATION 153. A second line instructed all visitors to surrender their weapons to the town sheriff, but it had been hacked through until it was almost indecipherable. But below that:

'"Land property of E. Windrose,"' Puttick cursed. 'Who in God's name buys a whole town?'

'Someone with the good sense to know that a man needs a drink after a ride over them plains,' Abe yelled back. 'Pony up, will you?'

The town was a riot of angles; many buildings were little more than canvas, stretched over whatever wood could be got. Here on the plains, every branch was precious, haggled and hawked for three times its worth. Sod houses rose clumsily from the ground, the spaces between them churned up by boots and wheels. The few frame buildings there were slouched lazily upon each other for support.

491

Hastily painted signs posted here and there advertised livestock and land grants, gambling and dry goods. Although it was night, whoops and hollers filled the air like smoke. Women with paint on their faces shivered outside a large tent, calling for us to spend the shank of the evening with them, their skirts heavy with dust.

We followed the drifters toward the saloon, the Yellow Snake. It was one of the only wooden buildings in town, with a second story that looked ready to slide free at any moment. It did not seem wise to leave the horses hitched outside such a place, but Abe slid from the saddle and barreled through the door after our guides. Puttick followed, while I hesitated on the threshold.

The saloon was crowded from floor to rafters. A stale fug rose from countless tobacco pipes and cigarettes, from the turf fire burning in the hearth. Every face was scorched and creased, skin lined beyond its years by the fierce sun. I lingered in a corner while Abe fought his way toward the bar.

I listened warily. All around me, talk was of the war. General Lee had surrendered; Mosby's Raiders were next. In that wilderness it meant little. The people who lived here knew that the land was no man's but God's: they did not care which lawyer took the chair in Washington, so long as they made sure the money flowed west.

'Four dollar a day for able-bodied men, that's what I heard,' a man was bellowing across a table near me. 'Four dollar! Man must be richer than Croesus an' twice as dumb.'

'Windrose ain't no fool,' slurred his neighbour, 'but he is powerful rich. Bought up this whole place, din't he?'

'What's he want it all *for*?' a third man demanded. 'Ranching? I ain't working no cow farm.'

The second man was shaking his head. 'Naw, it ain't ranching. Think 'bout it, we got Texas t'the south, an' Kansas above, an' Colorado an' all them mines t'other way—'

'For four dollar a day I'd shovel shit for graybacks,' interrupted the drunk, 'that agent fella said Windrose was up near Denver, an' you can be sure as hell that's where I'm bound.'

I turned away, intending to tell Puttick what I had heard, when I caught my name.

'She is courted by the devil,' a bedraggled saloon girl was shouting over the noise to a group of men, 'an' he gives her all sortsa gifts to try and get her to be *his* bride 'stead of Christ's, but she just keeps on giving him the mitten.'

They all laughed, save for one man, who shook his head seriously.

'She ain't human at all,' he said through watering eyes. 'She's an angel, sent to clear the land of the godless. Those 'steaders she killed were living in sin. They coupled up with savages, and she has sent them to judgment.'

I turned away, my face burning with horror and shame. My fingers worked emptily, as if my rosary – long lost at Fort Smith – still hung between them. I began to slip toward the door, unable to remain still and silent in that unhappy place. A body stepped forward and blocked my path.

It was Puttick, his hat pulled low, jacket wrapped tight around his neck to hide the scars on throat and chest. He was staring at the bar.

'Hold onto your hat,' he murmured.

13

The crackling
of thorns burning

The drifters we had traveled with were lined up at the bar, in whispered conference with a red-faced man who looked to be the proprietor of the place. A quantity of empty whiskey glasses stood before them, and as I watched, Muir slugged back another measure.

'Is that a bluff or do you mean it for real play?' I heard a voice ask loudly.

'True as eggs is eggs,' said the lead drifter, helping himself to the liquor bottle, 'ain't that so, sir?'

He filled Muir's glass to the brim. Abe shrugged, grinning sheepishly, and dispatched the whiskey.

'Muir and Thomas Josephine!' roared the landlord, slapping the bar. 'The Six-Gun Sister? The Lord's avenging angel herself? Where is she?'

The crowd surged and jostled, as if a rat had gotten among them. To my horror, the men stepped aside, until thirty pairs of eyes looked upon me. The hoots started up then, the fingers thrust toward the scar upon my neck. Some men were coming forward to shake my hand, others tugging at my hat, to try and see beneath it.

Furious, I looked around for Muir, meaning to drag him from that place, but hands were grasping at my clothes, pulling me into the center of the room and shoving me down into a seat. I gripped the knife at my belt and I caught one glimpse of Puttick through the crowd, his arms crossed, lips upturned in a grim smile.

Then the landlord's red face was pushed level with mine, shining with grease and perspiration.

'All y'all fine folk know this one!' he announced to the room. From somewhere deep among the bodies, the note from an accordion started up, wheezing like an old dog. The man sang a note, loud and long.

'Sheeee came on west ridin' over the plain, straight from old Missoura, brought her a cross an' a borrowed name . . .'

'The Six-Gun Sister!' roared the crowd, joining in.

The man had a powerful voice, and his face grew purple as he sang, miming actions. The crowd were delighted, thumping their drinks and boots in time. They parted for an instant, and I saw Muir, doubled over by the bar, his palms on his thighs, howling with laughter.

'Sister!' he yelled when he saw me looking, 'Y'hear that verse 'bout you dancing with a demon?'

'She caught her a man from o'er the plain,' the man sang out, pointing to Abe, 'a killer and thief and traitor. Injun Abraham was his name . . .'

Muir looked astonished for a moment, then took up his laughing again, even as the crowd hollered out their chorus. As the man started his next verse, I saw a gap between the bodies and slithered through it, making my escape from the middle of that terrible charade. I was breathing hard, my ears ringing, face burning. Somehow, worst of all was Abe, his laughter battering at me over the din.

I stumbled outside and gulped in the night air, sickened to the core. I had started my journey west in order to work good; to spread the Lord's light into a corner of the world drowning in the darkness that flowed from the heart of man.

But that darkness was here, in vanity and death and its glorification. I had once feared that I would die in the desert, nothing left of me but white bones picked clean, and no one to mourn the body that had covered them. Now, such a fate seemed a blessing, if this was how the world would remember me.

A name is a burden. No wonder someone had taken mine and used it to kill. No wonder, when my identity had become twisted beyond all recognition.

'Sister!'

A hand grasped my shoulder and I spun, my good arm raised, ready to strike. Puttick caught my wrist in his hard fingers, held my gaze until I wrenched my wrist away.

'Don't touch me,' I hissed, all too aware of the tears that burned the edges of my vision.

He was Mr Bird then, calm in the face of my fury.

'There's a man you should speak to,' he said. 'He's mighty confused that you're here, for he told me he saw you this afternoon, not ten mile away to the north. Not only that, he's seen someone else 'round town asking questions. A woman. And she's looking for you.'

'You think—?'

Puttick raised an eyebrow. 'I do not know what to think. But one thing's for sure; *someone's* been on a killing spree, and it sure as hell ain't you.'

14

If the iron be blunt

I allowed the outlaw to guide me toward an old man who sat on a stool by the door of the saloon, staring glumly into the spittoon at his feet.

'Friend,' Puttick greeted, kneeling on his haunches beside the man and offering him a twist of tobacco from his pocket. 'Will you tell the Sister what you told me?'

The old man's eyes lit up when he saw the tobacco. He snatched it and chewed off a piece with his remaining teeth then tongued the chunk around his gums appraisingly. It must have passed the test, for he nodded.

'Aye,' he told me, whetting his lips with brown saliva. 'Saw you,' he peered at me with his beetled eyes, drawing them over my brow, the scars on my face and neck. 'Naw,' he said slowly, 'weren't you. She were different: not so fair; paint on her face.'

I pressed him to tell me what he had seen. Puttick sat by, quiet as a cat.

'It were out near Old Creek,' the man continued. 'She were there 'long with these two big fellas.' He chawed down on the tobacco, staring at me all the while. 'Thought they was gonna see me off, firin' at my mule, but the lady tells 'em there ain't no harm in my bein' there. She saw I got some soap see, on my wagon, and she were mighty desirous of havin' her a piece. So I gave her a bit and she gets on to washing this garment, jus' like what a black cap would wear, so I figured, she were you. But she weren't. Or you ain't.' He looked sideways at Puttick. 'You headed for the Patterson ranch an' all?'

'Ranch?'

'Only place on that trail for ten mile,' the old man said. 'Figured that's where y'all – she – were headed, out to collect more sinners.'

My mind was reeling, from the noise and the smoke and the old man's story. I pulled Puttick aside.

'How far is the place he spoke of?' I asked.

'You're thinking of going after them,' he accused. 'What good d'you think you can do there, with no weapons and no notion of what's waiting—'

'I must try!' I wrenched out of his grip. 'My name might be a burden, but it is my own. I will not lay it aside.'

I pushed back into the saloon, intent upon finding Muir, on leaving that place of inhumanity and greed. I pulled up short. Abe was leaning heavily on the bar, surrounded by a forest of upturned glasses.

'Say, Muir,' I heard a man next to him holler as I shoved my way forward, 'she ain't bad lookin'. You ever get any horizontal refreshment on the trail?'

'She's a *nun*, you sonofabitch!' Abe exploded, seizing the man by the neck. 'Last cur who thought otherwise got my bullet through his pretty blue eye!'

The man sneered and threw a punch, only for it to go wide. Roaring, Abe slammed his head into the man's skull, sending him flying back. He crashed into a table, overturning it. Within moments, the whole saloon was a mêlée. Glass flew and shattered, fists flailed out in all directions. I ducked as a man swung a chair, sending it flying over my head. Abe was being attacked; men hung from each arm as another drove a fist into his stomach.

Furious, I grabbed a whiskey bottle from a table and smashed it over one assailant's head. He went down in a mess of glass and liquor and blood. I pulled the knife from my belt and lunged at the second man, yelling for Abe to move. The blade tore through the sleeve of the man's jacket. He twisted away, ripping the handle from my sweating palm. I turned to grab it but someone booted me in the back of the knee and I went down, into the dirt and clogged sawdust. My wounded arm struck the leg of a table

498

and I cried out in pain, even as the attacker reached down to grab my collar, a savage grin upon his face.

But his hands froze a few inches away from me. I watched as his grin contorted into a rictus and he fell forward, blood pouring from the back of his neck, where a blade had been driven into his spine.

I tried to scramble away, even as I searched the ground desperately for anything that I could use as a weapon. The neck of a bottle was all that I found. I held it in front of me as a dark figure knelt to work the knife free of the man's twitching corpse. It emerged, crimson and dripping, and raven eyes looked into mine from beneath the brim of a hat.

'You are welcome, *Madre*,' a familiar voice said.

15

If the serpent bite in silence

Owl stared at me from across the campfire, gnawing on a piece of jerky.

'You owe me two,' she said dispassionately, through the tough meat. 'That is the second time I save your life.'

'What are you doing here?'

I had asked her the same question before, when she had pulled me from the fray. She had only looked at me with her endless, black eyes, tried to drag me from the saloon, but I had refused to leave without Abraham. She rescued him too, dispatching his three assailants with her knives, leaving them gurgling and groaning upon the floor.

Puttick had leaped out from nowhere to follow us, and had almost received a blade in his stomach for the trouble. Owl had only shrugged when I cried that he was with us, before leading the way through the back of the saloon and out into the night.

The drifters from the plain had found us upon the street and invited us to their camp, to make amends for jawing and starting trouble, they said. Abe was the worse for drink: in truth, I had never seen him in such a state. He slumped to the ground as soon as we stopped walking, and before long took up a wheezing snore. I turned my attention to the woman before me again.

She had not changed much; her skin was darker, her face thinner. She wore a long leather duster and men's clothes, and the shadows beneath her eyes spoke of hard living. I noticed that among the scars that ringed her wrists were two that looked newer, pale pink and shiny.

I told her that she had not answered my question.

'I am deciding, *Madre*,' she chewed, 'whether to kill you or no.'

'Who *is* this?' Puttick demanded, removing a rag from his mouth. He had bitten his tongue in the brawl, and his voice came out thick and awkward. 'She the one been killing farmers?'

'No,' Owl and I told him in unison and glanced at each other. 'At least, I do not believe so,' I finished.

'No farmers,' she shook her head, 'then it was not you, either?'

'Do you not remember Mexico?' I asked her bitterly, 'they found me guilty for *your* murders then. It is much the same now.'

Owl grunted, toying with one of her knives. Her hair hung down her back in its thick, dark braid.

'Then it is this other "Sister" that I need to kill,' she murmured, climbing to her feet. Puttick and I both surged up, to block her way. She looked from one stony face to another, and her jaw hardened.

'I have been tracking you,' she told me bluntly, 'the last weeks. I was in the New Mexico Territory. They took me there, after El Paso—' something flickered across her face, a wing of despair, of darkness, 'to the place where my people are imprisoned. I did not stay.'

She stared me in the face. 'There are ranches near there, on the Pecos River,' she said, 'farms. My people had homes at some of them, where they lived, married to white men. They were good people. They were kind to me when I escaped.'

'Were?' I asked. I did not want to know what she would tell me, but the answer came, nevertheless.

'Dead,' her eyes were blank, 'or scattered, only little ones left. They were sinners, I heard people say, and that is why you killed them, because they were redskin heathens mating with white.'

'It was not I,' my voice was soft with horror. 'The Lord knows it was not I.'

I sank to the ground before the fire, staring into the flames. The thought that good people had died, terrified, with my name upon their lips made me sick with rage.

'You said you had been tracking me,' I asked slowly, 'an old man said he saw me this afternoon, not ten miles away, on the way to a ranch.'

'The Patterson ranch.' Owl nodded. 'I hear this too.'

I was on my feet in an instant.

'Then what are we waiting for?'

'You are leaving?' Puttick demanded, as I gathered up my knife, began to ready my horse. 'What of Muir? He is in no state to ride.'

'Stay with him,' I ordered, cinching the straps, 'if he wakes do not let him come after me, not if he will just get himself killed.'

The outlaw hesitated. I could see him eyeing the ancient rifle that lay upon his packs.

'Stay with him, Puttick,' I told him harshly, as I pulled myself into the saddle. 'You owe me that much.'

I wheeled my horse around before he could argue, though I heard him calling out.

'Colm Puttick,' said Owl, riding up alongside me, 'he is not so fierce.' She shot me a look from beneath her hat. 'My friends are dead. Whoever this woman is, if I find her, I will kill her. You know this, *Madre*.'

'I do,' my voice was icy as I kicked my horse into a gallop, 'but not before I get some answers.'

A woman more bitter
than death

We raced through the dark night, barely speaking, only stopping for the shortest time to rest the horses. Above us the sky was clear; the North Star helped us to find our way west. I did not know what we would meet, out there, on that isolated ranch.

Finally, we saw a pinprick of light flutter through the darkness across the plain. Over that distance it traveled like a tiny beacon, calling for aid. We spurred our horses all the faster.

The ranch was large, spilling out into the limitless space, but a fence surrounded the house. We led the horses across the final distance, tethered them in the darkest corner.

I slid the knife from my belt as we crept forward. Our boots hissed across the yard, kicking up the scents of animals, of sun-baked earth into the midnight air.

The flickering light was that of an oil lamp; my stomach con-tracted with fear when I saw the front door standing wide open. We had almost reached the threshold when a gunshot rang out, appallingly loud in the silence. Owl pushed me aside, racing for the door.

The room beyond was in chaos. I could taste the blood in the air, and stared in horror at the shining pools of it that spattered the floor and walls. A woman was slumped in a chair at the table, her eyes wide and glassy, a gaping black hole over her heart. A youth sprawled further within the room, two bullet holes staining the rough cotton of his shirt. I felt tears burning my eyes.

I heard a gagging sound then, a wet gasping, and spun around. A man had fallen against the wall at the back of the room. He was looking up: the light glinted upon his open eyes, on the dark blood spilling from the wound in his chest. I ran to him and knelt, ripping the scarf from my neck and pressing it against his injury even though I knew it was useless. The cloth was soaked through in an instant, and as I watched he coughed, red sputtering from his lips to run into his beard.

'I'm sorry,' I whispered, frantic, unaware of the tears that were streaming down my face, 'forgive me, I am sorry.'

His eyes were wild, flitting over the scars beside my ear, upon my neck, as I choked out a prayer for his soul. Before he died, his eyes came to rest on something over my shoulder.

I followed his gaze. Three shadows were hurrying across the yard, two larger and one smaller, the latter wearing a loose garment. With a snarl I threw myself to my feet.

'Owl!' I cried.

She was already running. One of the figures raised a pistol, but she flung a knife, and someone swore as the gun was knocked to the ground. The attackers turned tail, making for a group of horses. Owl raced after them, hard on their heels. I was gaining upon the smaller figure; when only a few feet separated us, I gritted my teeth and lunged, snatching at the trailing fabric.

We crashed to the ground, both crying out from the impact. A woman's voice. She was thrashing and struggling, but I was stronger and shoved aside my pain. Her hand caught my face, nails scoring a trail and sending my hat flying, but I leaned down with all my weight, pinning her as I dragged the knife free from beneath my jacket.

She fell still, gasping at the sight of its sharp edge. The lamplight spilling from the doorway caught upon her face then and my blood froze.

She was a reflection of me, almost. Her eyes were pale blue, the color of forget-me-nots, where mine were gray, but she had scars upon her temple and neck, like mine, even a mole, high up upon her cheek, just as I did. Yet as I stared harder, I realized that the scars were smudged, the mole too perfect; it was all greasepaint.

'Who are you?' I demanded above the knife, my voice hoarse with panic, with shock.

'I'm Si— . . . Sister,' she stuttered, 'Sister Thomas Josephine.'

I pressed the knife closer.

'No, you are not.'

The woman's gaze went wide, terrified as she took in my face for the first time.

'You're her,' she gasped, 'oh God, you're her?'

She choked and began to cry, tears spilling onto the thick paint that adorned her face.

'Please,' she begged, 'I ain't killed anyone. I did not . . . I didn't know . . .'

'What about them?' I demanded, dragging the collar of her habit in the direction of the doorway. 'What of all the others – the ranchers, Tellman?'

'I only said some words,' she cried, as the blade touched the skin of her throat again. 'Buxton and Hayle, they did the killing, said they had it coming, those people.'

'Why?' I shook her, barely recognizing my own voice through the fury.

The woman was sobbing uncontrollably; her eyes squeezed shut as though I were a nightmare she could escape.

'I'm just an actress,' she wept, 'and he said that you'd hang anyway, said these were bad people and someone needed to get rid of them.'

'Who?'

'He'll kill me if I say, please—'

A gunshot sounded from the darkness and I jerked in surprise. The tip of the blade I was holding sliced into the woman's neck. She shrieked in terror.

In that moment, I saw myself reflected in her eyes: my teeth bared in a snarl of hatred, blood staining my sleeves. The knife fell from my hand. I pushed myself back onto my knees, shaking. Released from my grip, the woman curled into a ball, her fingers pressed to the thin rivulet of blood that ran from her neck.

'Get out of here,' I whispered, 'and may God forgive us both.'

She was on her feet in an instant, but hesitated, staring down at me. After a moment, she reached into her pocket and brought out a piece of paper, much folded and thumbed.

'Windrose,' she told me, eyes swollen and flower-blue in the dusty light, 'the man who paid, he was called Windrose. He sent me this.'

I reached out for it, even as I saw the shadows move behind her.

'Wait!' I cried, but it was too late. Owl's blade flashed in the lamplight, one stroke, slashing the woman's throat as if she was a lamb at slaughter. I screamed in horror as she fell, as her chest convulsed and blood bubbled from her lips and her gullet.

The life drained from the woman. Her arm was flung forward, the paper still in her hand, extended toward me. I crawled forward to grip her dying fingers, to plead the Lord to have mercy upon her.

Owl stood, watching impassively. When I had finished my prayer, she bent to clean her knife upon the dead woman's habit. Something in my gaze must have stopped her, for she froze, halfway to the ground, and wiped it on her own trousers instead.

I was trembling with rage, with grief as I took up the piece of paper. It was thick, its edges ragged, ripped from a notebook. I opened it. It was a drawing, a portrait, rendered with painstaking detail.

It showed me, looking over my shoulder. A habit covered my neck and face, a few wisps of hair breaking free from the edges of the veil. My lips were slightly open, as if in speech, my eyes sad. A shudder ran through me, for every flaw upon my face, every detail had been captured perfectly, as if the artist had studied at me for hours.

Someone had signed the bottom corner. When I read the name, my heart stopped.

T.F. Carthy.

Nunslinger: Book 11

Ninth-Hour at Noon

The True Tale of how the 'Six-Gun Sister' Thomas Josephine of St. Louis, Missouri, Rose from the Grave in order to Commit Murder

Eleven hundred pieces of silver

SIX-GUN SISTER DEAD IN FINAL, BLOODY CONFRONTATION

Murder begat murder here in the lawless west, when the SIX-GUN SISTER Thomas Josephine, formerly of St. Louis Missouri, was finally relieved of her life last week at a ranch on the border of the Colorado Territory.

The struggle that took place at the remote dwelling is believed to have been a fierce one, for reports have been returned to the Californian – the newspaper with the largest weekly circulation in all the Western Coast States and territories – of a grisly tableau. The Sister lay outside the house, leaving the bodies of her victims within. Her face a mask of sinner's blood, her throat slashed from ear to ear. Some believe this is proof that the Sister – overcome by the burdensome guilt of her heinous crimes – took her own life.

Purportedly, the sky grew black all around as her body was taken up, and the men there present feared that the wrath of the Lord would descend upon any that touched her. Several witnesses swore that they saw her soul being lifted, borne away by a winged demon and an angel both, toward judgment.

Sister Thomas Josephine – known as the most wanted woman in the west, whose exploits have been faithfully reported by your dedicated correspondent at the Californian – was held accountable for eight charges of murder across the states of Nevada, California, Arkansas, and the Colorado Territory. She is also believed to have been responsible for the recent slaughter of innocent citizens at smallholdings across the New Mexico Territory.

Her fellow partners in crime, the TRAITOR ABRAHAM C. MUIR and the vicious OUTLAW COLM PUTTICK remain at large.

The candle flame took the newspaper. Its bright fingers reached out, tasting the edges before consuming it whole. I watched it burn until nothing remained.

The rain fell like gravel, hissing off the roof to form muddy puddles outside. Someone started up coughing on the other side of the room, and I hunkered down a little further. The building was neither trading post nor saloon, but it was the only shelter for miles. The floor was littered with travelers, bedraggled and footsore, many hiding tell-tale Confederate gray beneath their blankets.

I had no money, but a pair of rabbits I had caught was enough to buy me a glass of whiskey and a few inches of floor space for the night. I took a sip of the cloudy, brown liquid. It burned my throat and I shuddered, but was grateful. I had barely eaten, barely slept for days, and that burning served to fill some of the hollowness in my stomach.

My head dropped to my knees. I saw again the woman's face as she fell. I had achieved what I had set out to do; I had stopped the killing of innocents, but at what cost? I took another large gulp of the whiskey, trying not to remember.

I had fled that ranch, leaving the dead where they had fallen. The sight of the portrait, signed by a dead man, had driven me into blind panic. I had ridden as though there were a demon upon my heels, out into the darkness.

I do not remember the journey, save for the thoughts that rolled incessantly through my mind: wherever Sister Thomas Josephine trod, she brought death. I saw them again, those who had perished along my path, Laverman, Falk, Chicken. I saw Carthy once more, his heaven-blue eyes upon me as he fell. I saw Muir, as he tumbled from a cliff with a bullet in his chest; as he stood, beaten but gentle upon the gallows; as he smiled at me sleepily in an outlaw's cave.

I bit back the sorrow that threatened to wrack my body. He would be better off without me, I told myself, it was the Lord's will. Here was my chance to break the cycle of death, to begin again, and do God's work.

Yet every time I tried to pray, Abe's face caught itself up in my litanies, his voice tangled around the holy words in my mind. And at every other moment, I heard again the final words upon a dead woman's lips.

Windrose. His name was Windrose.

2

How shall one alone be warmed?

I must have slept a little, for when I woke I heard the rumbling of voices beneath the rain. It was late. I peered up blearily, rubbing at my neck, my nose catching the scent of boiled meat.

A man was seated at the stacked crates that served as a bar. A long, leather duster hung like sodden wings down his back. I shifted to see better, and he turned my way, alerted by the noise. Yellow eyes flared in the firelight.

I caught my breath, ducking back into the shadows. It was Puttick.

'Got any soft tack?' he called to the proprietor.

The man shook his head morosely. 'There m'be flour, but it's a dollar a sack. You want some o' that?'

The outlaw shook his head, returned his attention to the meal. It was rabbit, I realized, the ones I had caught, stewed up by the bartend. Where Puttick had got money from I did not know, and did not want to know. I stared from the darkness, barely daring to breathe.

'Come west?' grunted the bartend, needlessly swiping a cloth at the top of the bar.

Puttick nodded.

'Heard there were a mighty set-to that way, near Hardesty,' the man continued slowly. 'They caught that crazed black-cap. Permanently ventilated her an' all.'

Puttick ate in meager bites, grease dripping down his wrists.

'Might want to be careful what you say, friend,' he said, 'else you and I might find ourselves at odds.'

'No disrespect,' the man replied humourlessly, uncorking the liquor bottle. 'My ma were a Catholic; guess that makes me one too, though I would not know a saint from a skunk egg.' He poured himself a measure of the brown liquid. 'To the dead,' he toasted Puttick. The outlaw nodded in agreement and sipped at his own glass, teeth still working on the meat.

'What about them what traveled with her?' the man pressed after a time. 'Heard plenty 'bout the shootout but not 'bout them. The Injun man and t'other, wa's his name? Bullock?'

'Puttick,' said Puttick, tearing at the meat with more ferocity than necessary, 'Colm Puttick. Don't know where he is, but last I heard, Injun Abe on the dodge near Hardesty still, blind-drunk.'

'He's a prime ass,' snorted the barman. 'If I were him, I'd be halfway to nowhere by now.'

Puttick twisted the glass before him in a circle. 'Aye.'

'Of all the things,' the bartend sneered, 't'fall in with a converted crow. Now, I hear me there were these whores in Denver, what would dress up like her in a habit an' all, they'd do things to a fella like you'd never believe—'

In an instant the bartend was strained across the bar, his arms flailing and his face growing pinker by the second. Puttick had the man's collar in his fist and was twisting.

'Muir *is* a prime ass,' he told the man as he struggled, 'but the devil knows he loved that woman. He would've stuck with her 'til they ripped the breath from his neck, and rightly too.'

He sighed and let the man go, losing heart in his torment. The bartend gaped for air, staring with bulging eyes as Puttick slurped up the remainder of the stew and grimaced.

'You got a necessary?' he asked.

The bartend pointed the way with a shaking finger. Puttick slouched off, grabbing one of the oil lamps and pulling the duster up over his head against the rain. As soon as he was from sight, the proprietor dragged a rusted old shotgun from beneath the bar, and began to load it.

I sank back against the wall, my head reeling.

He loved that woman, would have stuck with her 'til they ripped the breath from his neck.

Dread and longing and shame crashed together in my mind, until all I could do was fold my hands together so tightly that they ached and beg the Lord with one, clear prayer to show me His will.

If He was listening or watching, He chose to stay silent. Across the room there was a clatter. I heard the bartend swear as he stooped to gather a loose shotgun case from the floor. The weapon rested unattended.

When I stepped outside, the gun was heavy in my hand. Rain soaked me to the bone in an instant. The outhouse where Puttick must have gone was as rickety as the saloon. I saw the light of the lantern he'd taken needling through the cracks in the wood. I crept forward on silent feet and threw open the door.

'What the—' the outlaw swore. His trousers were around his legs, the duster gathered up to his waist like a skirt. He blanched when he saw the weapon in my hand but scowled in the same instant.

'Alright,' he snapped. 'If you're going to do it, get on with it. Damned cowardly way to beef a man, when he's seeing to business.'

He could not see my face, I realized. I was nothing but a silhouette with a gun to him. I hesitated, my voice lost. Muir might be in trouble, but for a brief moment, I was safe. The world believed that I was dead and gone. The moment I spoke would be the moment I came back to life.

And yet, I had to know.

'Where is he?' I asked, throat tight. 'Where is Abraham?'

3

The eyes of a wise man
are in his head

Slowly, Puttick smiled his predator's smile. 'Well,' he called out, 'grave too lonesome for you, Sister? Come to take Muir back, to be your companion in the afterlife?'

'Where is he, Puttick?' My voice was steady.

The outlaw peered into the darkness behind me, where a couple of saddlebags waited.

'Those my packs?' he asked.

'Not anymore.'

He nodded stoically. 'It were the other "Sister", then, who died?'

When I was silent, he gave a short laugh. 'Suspected as much. Told that to Muir too, not that he was listening.'

'What have you done with him?'

Puttick raised his eyebrows.

'*I've* not done a thing, other than leave him to his madness. Stayed with him as long as it was safe, but the town's startin' to crawl with lawmen.'

He stood, set about rearranging his trousers. I flushed and looked away.

'He wouldn't leave. Said he was waiting for you, that he would not believe anything 'til he saw your body, and damn the rest. There was no reasoning with the man. If he ain't caught now, he soon will be.'

I took a step back into the rain-shrouded night.

'It will kill him, you know,' Puttick's voice stopped me. He was trying to find me in the darkness. The oil lamp caught upon his eyes. There was no heartlessness in his face then, or cruelty, only the look of a man worn thin by his own duplicity. 'One of these days, his love for you will be the end of him.'

515

The tears were hot upon my rain-chilled skin as I rode through the night. I swiped them away with a muddy hand. I had to get back to Hardesty. The horse ate up the distance, swallowing the miles that I had traveled out into the wild.

When I finally reached the town, it was darker, quieter than I remembered. It was long after midnight and most were abed, the spirits of even the hardiest drinkers dampened. A few specks of light wavered through the raindrops. I left the horse at the edge of the buildings and crept my way through the churning mud of the streets.

The undertaker's, Puttick had said, that was where Abe would go. I remembered seeing it as we had ridden in. It was the smaller of the two frame buildings in the town, the other being the saloon. Death and liquor were the only sure things in such a place.

A lamp had been left burning in the smeared window. A smell rose as I drew close; damp and wax and new-shaved wood gone sodden. Offcuts from coffins.

From nearby I heard a muffled thump, staggering footsteps. The door to the building was ajar, a thin line of light at its edge. I pushed it wide.

The walls of the undertaker's were hung with dusty black crepe, an embroidered bible verse nailed to the desk. Three men lay fallen within. They must have been standing guard over the place. I knelt and touched the cheek of one, not more than a boy. A wound above his eyebrow bled heavily, but he was breathing. In the flickering light I saw that my fingers had left a muddy stain upon his skin.

A second door led deeper into the building. A shudder ran through me. It was the parlor where the dead would rest, waiting to be set into the ground. The scent of cheap cologne was over-powering, yet it did not mask the sweetness of decay that permeated the air.

Something was moving beyond the door that led to the next room, a strange rustling: a shifting of cloth, of labored breath. Despite every rational thought, I was afraid, my limbs trembling as I took step after step forward.

516

May God the Father be with me, I breathed as I drew ever closer, *may God the Son protect me, may God the Holy Ghost be by my side.*

I used the shotgun to push open the door.

In the dim light I saw a man, standing over a coffin that had been placed upon a table. His shoulders were drawn up to his ears, his head bowed to meet them. His hands gripped the coffin's lid, about to lift it off.

My voice was trapped in my throat.

'Abe?' I whispered, the sound thin and cracking.

I heard a snatched intake of breath as he froze. He had been sobbing, I realized, silently in his chest.

'Sister?'

'Abe,' I breathed, 'I am so sorry.'

He raised his face for a moment, listening. 'Thought I heard her,' he gulped to the air, 'thought she were speaking to me again.'

I could bear it no longer and stepped forward, reaching for his arm.

'Abe, I am here—'

He spun and lashed out. The edge of his fist caught me across the chin and I staggered back. His swollen eyes were wild as he stared at me.

'Who are you?' he choked, as I righted myself, 'what are you?'

'You know me, Abe,' I whispered.

'Don't believe you,' his face was twisted as he took half a step forward, 'you're that other one.'

'No,' I said softly, stepping close to look into his eyes. Slowly, his fingers descended to my face. I felt their warmth as he brushed the skin of my temple, tracing the purple scar left by his bullet. I caught them with my own.

'Do I seem dead to you, Abraham Muir?'

4

If the wheel be broken

I watched the coffee steam and bubble in its pot in the heart of the fire. Its scent filled the cold morning air and I breathed it in. *Life,* I had thought once. Whatever happened in the night, soon the morning would come and somewhere, coffee would be raised to weary lips.

I heard a stirring behind me and smiled, retrieving the cup from the fire.

'We have Mr Puttick to thank for the provisions,' I called out, as I poured cold water into the brew, 'although I doubt he intended them for our use.'

Unsmiling, Muir took the mug and stared down into it. His eyes were red still, whether from emotion or intoxication it was difficult to tell. He had been far gone in liquor the previous evening, and it had been all I could do to coax him away from the town while there was still time to make an escape. I had found his horse hitched behind the undertaker's and shoved him into the saddle.

We had ridden as far as we could, until the sky grew light and Muir began to slide from his horse. I had made camp then, told Abe to rest, but in truth I had not slept a wink. Instead, I had sat watch over him, as the rain ran itself out.

I busied myself in packing up the camp as he gazed into the coffee, but his silence followed me. I felt his mahogany eyes upon my back.

'If you do not drink that soon, it shall go cold,' I told him without turning.

'You were going to leave me.'

His voice stopped me in my tracks. I stared down at the ground, glistening with the tempest past.

'Why?' he asked when I did not answer, climbing to his feet. 'Do you think I have anything else, in this world?'

I picked up the shotgun, checked that it was loaded.

'I cannot ask you to come with me into danger,' I told him, struggling to keep my voice flat.

'You cannot prevent me from following, neither,' he snapped.

'Please, Abe,' I told him, avoiding his gaze, 'this is not your fight.'

'Weren't ever about that, and you know it.' His dark eyes locked with mine. 'Something's got you rattled,' he said softly. 'What is it?'

There was no hiding from him, not then. Trembling, I pulled the drawing from my pocket and held it out.

'The woman had it,' I said haltingly, 'she told me that Windrose gave it to her, when he paid.'

Abe's face turned bleak as he stared upon those lines, lovingly wrought in pencil, at that name. *Carthy*.

'It ain't possible.' He had to clear his throat. 'He's dead.' He thrust the picture back at me. 'It's old. Has to be.'

'By why should Windrose have it?' I felt something twist within me; hope, traitorous hope. 'What if . . .'

'I killed him, Sister,' Abe said savagely, 'you bear the proof, right there on your face. God help me, I would do it again.'

He was breathing heavily. I folded the drawing and returned it to my pocket.

'You ain't going after him.' Abe's voice was harsh.

'I am going after Windrose,' I told him, gathering up my packs, 'whatever that means.'

He grabbed my arm as I passed.

'You're hopin' *he* might be alive,' he accused. 'You're hopin' to find them pretty blue eyes still open.'

I yanked my arm free.

'Yes, I do wish it,' I said, my temper flaring. 'Because if he is alive then you are not a murderer, Abraham Muir.'

The silence stretched between us as we stood, hurt and hurting both. I clenched my hands inside my pockets, reaching instinctively for my rosary before I remembered it was gone.

'Well,' Abe said at last, the damage etched upon his face, 'like it or not, it's a murderer you've got watchin' your back, Sister.'

We rode for Denver. The tension crackled between us, yet we both knew that it would be impossible to turn our backs, to flee for Canada and obscurity, knowing what we did. The Lord had given me a choice, I knew, as we rode headlong across the plains of Colorado: run or hunt. I was tired of running.

How long wilst thou wander, my wayward daughter?

Even sore at each other, Muir and I fell back into our old rhythms as we traveled, faster than ever, and after four days, most of the bitterness had ebbed away.

'How many deaths have we faced, Sister?' Muir asked drowsily, as we rested at noon in the shade of a single tortured greasewood tree. 'I am startin' to believe we do not know how to die.'

'To live is the harder road,' I told him. The sun thundered down outside our shelter until even the flies fell still. 'You know that as well as I.'

'Is that what you'll do with this Windrose then? Let him live?'

The other name hung, glaring and unsaid between us.

'It has always been my way.'

Muir only grunted and shook his head. 'One day it'll go bad. You'll die for sparin' a life, an' you know it.'

'So be it, if that is the Lord's will.'

'Is it yours?'

'We should ride,' I told him abruptly, climbing to my feet, 'if we are to reach Denver by tomorrow.'

Denver City sprouted from the base of the mountains like fungus at the root of a tree. We kept our hats well lowered as we rode among the buildings, although in truth, there was little need. The town was too crowded to care about us. Like many such places, it had swelled from the ground, constructed itself out of ambition and impatience, rather than solid bricks and mortar.

Although it was yet spring, the heat battered us relentlessly, worse than on the plains, where the wide distance was open to the breeze. Shops boasted offers of silks and French perfume, the varnish of their signs blistered.

A few ladies were promenading up and down the boardwalk, the fabric of their parasols sagging like starved flesh in the burning sun. Men bustled from store to office in moleskin and beaver felt, pomade running in greasy rivulets down their collars.

And above it all rose the mountain peaks, tortured and beautiful all at once, the teeth of a magnificent beast, its mouth open in a snarl. The city beneath seemed doubly absurd, glaring up at those heights as if they were an inconvenience.

Further into town the streets became more crowded. The sun-bleached boardwalks were crammed with people, the babble of their voices loud and alarmed, all pushing toward something.

They were trying to reach a newsboy, I realized, his arms draped with paper sheets like drying laundry. He was bawling at the top of his voice while another lad shoved the editions into people's hands as fast as he could take their pennies.

A familiar apprehension gripped my stomach.

'I do not like this,' I murmured to Abe.

His face was pale beneath its tan, but he grasped the arm of a youth who was passing by, asked him what the commotion was for.

'Ain't you heard?' the boy said, wriggling free. 'It's Abe, Honest Abe. Lincoln's dead.'

5

And yet the sea does not overflow

'One hundred thousand dollars,' said Muir in disgust, taking a deep swig of his beer, 'one hundred thousand, for an *actor*. It ain't right.'

Across the street, a man was pasting posters to the wall of the courthouse. As we watched, he ripped an old one free to make room. My face, reproduced in black ink a foot high, was crumpled upon the ground, to be crushed beneath the boots of passers by. In its place he slapped the likeness of a man, pale and handsome, with dark curled hair and a fine moustache. *MURDERER STILL AT LARGE* screamed the letters.

'What kinda name is Wilkes Booth, anyhow,' grumbled Muir, draining his glass, 'an' who's goin' to pay up a hundred thousand dollars? Half the world an' his mother were after our heads for *five*.'

I made a non-committal noise and opened the newspaper upon the table. Muir and I had stabled the horses and taken refuge in a saloon to escape the frenzied streets and consider our position. The news of the president's murder had sent the country into uproar. Gone were the speculations of Muir's whereabouts, the fanciful reports of my death. The relief it brought came with a strange pang of resentment that we – of such infamy – should be so easily forgotten.

I read of Lincoln's death with not a little sadness. We had never taken sides at the convent; those who fought were all God's children, whether their uniforms were blue or gray. Yet the president had seemed a good man, amid so much destruction. I murmured a prayer for his soul.

'Twenty-five thousand *each* for these Surratt and Harold sons o' bitches,' Abe burst, throwing his newspaper across the table. 'I will not read a word more. There's soldiers marchin' two hundred miles on shank's pony, with rotten supplies, an' the bastards at the war office are givin' fifty thousand for a pair of goddam accomplices.'

He marched off toward the bar, fuming. I opened my mouth, to remind him that the coins we had found in Puttick's saddlebags were dwindling quickly, but a line in his discarded newspaper caught my eye.

It was a cheap publication, the *Denver Rancher*, thin and poorly printed. The story was barely three inches high, crammed on to the back page of the paper, alongside advertisements for canned beef and tonics.

SIX-GUN SISTER: DEAD OR ALIVE? began the article. *The Six-Gun Sister Thomas Josephine met her end these few days past, in the New Mexico Territory. However*, it continued, and that one word made me grip the paper so tightly it almost tore, *it has been reported that the US Marshal's office has suspended the remuneration of the Sister's bounty until her identity can be confirmed. US Marshal Benjamin Reasoner, who was tasked with the Sister's capture, is said to be traveling from Kansas for the purpose. With such doubt cast, this humble reporter cannot help but posit the question that no other journal has yet seen fit to ask: why, in the whole of the Western States – where every other man is a sinner – should the Six-Gun Sister have chosen not only a respected businessman, but a handful of innocent farmers as her victims?*

I jammed my hat onto my head. Abe was returning from the bar and cried out in protest as I snatched the beer from his hand and replaced it with the newspaper.

'We have a problem,' I said.

6

Learning, and errors and folly

The office of the *Denver Rancher* was a pigsty, quite literally. *Pyke & Sons, Hog Breeders*, a sign declared, beneath which the title of the newspaper had been hurriedly added. Abe and I watched as a huge old man wrestled a hog into a packing crate amid much squealing and squalling. When he was done, he looked up, shaking the sweat out of his beard.

'Want a hog?' he asked briskly.

'Naw,' replied Muir, pulling his eyes away from a huge, tusked beast, 'we're here 'bout the paper.'

The man grunted, not unlike the swine.

'Inside,' he waved his fist dismissively, 'go speak to himself.'

'Himself' transpired to be a young man with a huge drooping moustache. His face was every bit as florid as his father's.

'Norman Pyke,' he introduced himself eagerly as we entered. His office was a portioned-off area of barn, a hastily erected wall covered in advertisements and handwritten sheets. Behind him, a rickety printing press stood upon the straw. 'What can I do for you? A subscription perhaps?'

Abe snorted with laughter, which he struggled to turn into a cough as I shot him a glance. He unfolded the paper, saying that we were interested in the author.

'The Lincoln piece?' the young man said, eyes lighting up. 'I am proud to say that that particular story was the work of the editor, which is to say, myself.'

'This one here,' Abe interrupted, flattening the back page upon the desk. 'Who wrote this?'

'Ah,' the young man acknowledged with a sneer, 'I can only apologize for that, but we were short three inches, and there was nothing else.' He rummaged through a box filled with scraps of paper. 'Funny little man, in here every other day with some new tale of that lady nun turned bad. Old news, I told him, but you know these hacks,' he smiled up obsequiously, holding out a chit, 'once they get a story they are like a mongrel with a femur.'

Abe took the paper with a scowl. 'Sounds like fine news to me,' he snapped, 'better than all the accounts of this Booth fella.' He looked down at the paper and swore, thrusting it into my hand. 'Knew it. Where can we find him?' he demanded. 'This hack?'

'Where he always is,' the young man bristled at Muir's tone. 'Now if you do not want a subscription you will excuse me. I have a newspaper to run.'

We followed the young man's directions to a saloon at the other end of the town.

'You should be more careful,' I murmured, as we walked openly through the streets. 'We are not forgotten yet, and you still have a bounty upon your head.'

'A thousand bucks,' Muir dismissed, a little waspishly. 'Who's goin' to care 'bout a thousand when they could have a hundred times that?'

'Nevertheless,' I continued doggedly, 'you heard about Reasoner traveling here. It would be well for us to lay low.'

''Til we find your man, you mean.'

'Until we can discover who Windrose is, and what he wants, yes.' My cheeks were flushing, as I fought down a memory of Carthy as I had last seen him, lit by the fires of El Paso.

Muir grunted. I did not like his tone, but there was no time to argue, for we had reached the bar of the editor's description. It was a haphazard construction, half brick and half wood, a Union flag flying crookedly from its roof. The smell of stale beer and overflowing spittoons wafted from the door as we stepped inside.

For a moment I blinked in the dark interior, blinded by daylight. Gradually, the place took shape. Men rose out of the gloom, stooped over tables made from crates, nursing their drinks to swill. Several wore the rags and weather-ravaged faces of prospectors, drinking away their final hopes. Among the sagging heads I saw one in particular, hair dull from old pomade, a plum velvet waistcoat stretched threadbare across his back.

We made our way carefully across the floor.

'Bet you a shiny nickle he screams,' muttered Abe in my ear, as he clapped Franklin Templeton on the shoulder.

7

He that observeth the wind

I did not expect a man of Templeton's character to faint. We had a deal of trouble hauling him upright between us, and undue attention was the last thing we needed. Luckily, the clientele of that place took little notice, familiar as they were with the effects of the local rotgut.

Outside, Muir spotted a water trough and together we plunged the newspaperman's head beneath the surface. He came up spluttering.

Templeton seemed much the worse for wear since our previous encounter. His fine moustache was untrimmed, his shirt stained. Weight had fallen from his face, though his belly still tested the limits of his waistcoat's buttons.

'By all that's good and holy,' he gaped, 'I knew you were not dead.' To my astonishment he grasped my hand and pressed it to his heart. 'Bless you, ma'am, I never wished it to be true, the Good Lord knows I did not.' His face crumpled then, and he began to weep.

'He's roostered,' Abe swore in disgust, wrinkling his nose at the smell of raw liquor, 'won't talk no sense 'til we get some food in him.'

We dragged Templeton to an establishment that smelled no better than the saloon and ordered three plates of whatever they were serving. The resulting mess of meat and potato cost us nearly all of our money and was scarcely worth it, being dry and gluey with fat, but I managed to force some down. Templeton, in contrast, ate with the fervor of the starved.

'It's a daisy,' he breathed when he had finished, eyes still misty, 'just a daisy that you're alive, ma'am. But how did y'all find me?'

Muir fished a piece of gristle out of his teeth and shoved across the newspaper article.

'Still writin' lies, Templeton?'

The newspaperman waved his hand luxuriantly, despite his filth. 'It was the best I could do,' he sighed. 'That blatherskite at the hog farm paid me barely a dollar for it! Can you countenance that?'

'What about the *Californian*?' I asked. 'You were reporting my death with great embroidery, not so long ago.'

Templeton beamed.

'You mean to say you have read my work?'

Abe growled. The newspaperman held up his hands.

'It was before the facts, ma'am. *I* was determined to give your passing the honor it so deserved, but my employer had differing notions. Said I should be out east, covering the war.' He sniffed and attempted to coif his ailing whiskers. 'I told him that if all he required was a trained dog to fetch his stories, they had better send a penny hack.'

'You got the boot?' grinned Abe.

'We parted ways,' Templeton snapped, 'but I am currently engaged on a most ambitious project, a monograph that is sure to entice the nation, once I find a willing publisher. I am calling it, "The Six-Gun Sister: The True Tale of How Sister Thomas Josephine—"'

'Mr Templeton,' I interrupted, before he could infuriate Abe further, 'we are in need of your help.'

At that he fell silent, eyes large. I saw his fingers begin to twitch, desperate to be holding a pen. I braced myself.

'Have you ever heard of a man by the name of Windrose?'

The newspaperman's face dropped.

'My dear lady,' he told me in a tremulous hush, 'if you wish to mention that name, you best do so in private.'

8

When princes eat in the morning

Templeton took us to a tall, straggling brick building on the edge of town. It looked as though it had been abandoned halfway through construction; chinks in the walls were stopped up with rags, and one side of the roof was entirely unfinished.

'My present circumstances find me pecuniarily discomfited,' he gushed, as he waved us into a room at the very top of the house beneath the beams, 'but we shall be private, at least. The old woman downstairs has a cankerous leg, so she cannot climb up and intrude.'

The ceiling was little more than pasteboard nailed to the rafters. In some places, light showed through, and a family of pigeons cooed and gurgled in one corner. Templeton offered me the only seat, and proceeded to settle himself upon the pallet bed with great dignity, leaving Abe to huff and fend for himself.

'I think,' he told me, fumbling for a notebook and licking the tip of a pencil, 'you had best tell ol' Franklin everything, ma'am.'

Muir snarled and made a grab for the notebook.

'There is no harm in setting the record straight, Abe,' I told him. 'That is what I intend to do. Mr Templeton, is that understood? I shall tell the truth, and you shall record it faithfully.'

'Assuredly, assuredly,' said the newspaperman. 'Now may I suggest we begin with Fort Smith?'

I told Templeton all that had transpired since our escape from the fort. He began scratching notes in a strange scrawl he called shorthand, which Abe took an instant disliking to, on account of the fact it looked so different from the letters I had taught him. The newspaperman watched me closely all the while.

'But how did y'all *do* it?' he asked curiously, leaning forward over his belly. 'I heard someone say that the ropes had been sheared to a thread. One of Puttick's men, perhaps?' I saw his fingers twitching over the pencil. 'Come now, deed's done, no harm in telling the tale.'

'We have wondered over it ourselves,' I murmured to the floor. I could feel Abe's eyes upon me, and knew we were thinking the same thing, reciting that dreaded name over in our minds. 'The fact is, we do not know who our savior was, or why.'

Templeton did not seem worried by this fact. On the contrary, he wrote all the faster.

'A mystery! Why, I made my bread and butter on mysteries,' he muttered gleefully.

Evening fell as I talked; the sky sank to deep blue through the cracks in Templeton's roof. He lit a candle and hunched over its spitting flame. I wore my voice out telling him of Hardesty, of how Owl had tracked the imposter across New Mexico, how we had reached the ranch, too late. Of the woman and her final words.

I lapsed into silence. The portrait with Carthy's signature was in my pocket, but I did not have the words to share with this man, so intent upon scrawling down my life.

Templeton did not seem to notice my silence.

'Windrose,' he drew the name out, staring down at his notebook. 'So it has come to him.'

Then, like a sprite he leaped up, seizing a carpetbag and rummaging through it, pulling out sheaves of paper. 'I did conduct my own modest investigations, before I ran out of ready funds,' he told us, holding the pages to the light. 'I discovered that the Six-Gun Sister's murders were not so indiscriminate as I thought. Begging your pardon, ma'am.' He shook open a thick document and laid it on the ground. It was embossed with several heavy seals. 'Mr Linus Tellman,' Templeton traced the signature with one chubby finger, 'and here, Mr Edward Windrose. They were in business together.'

'What is it?' I peered down at the ornate, swirling letters that topped the lengthy certificate.

'It is an application for a land grant,' Templeton told me, eyes shining. 'I went to great pains to persuade the lawyer's clerk to look the other way while I liberated this copy. If granted, it will cede land worth eight hundred thousand dollars into the sole control of Mr Windrose, now that Mr Tellman is dead.'

Muir choked when he heard the figure. 'Eight hundred thousand?' he echoed incredulously. 'What the hell does eight hundred thousand dollars buy? Half of California?'

'It buys five hundred miles,' Templeton sniffed, rolling up the paper, 'from Boulder County clear to Fort Sumner.' He fixed me with his gaze, clear and calculating. 'Whatever the reason, Thomas Josephine, it would appear that you have come to the attention of the wrong man.'

9

And all things obey money

'You will find that searching for him is like ants at a picnic,' Templeton warned us, as we set out into town the next morning, 'once you begin looking, you spy them everywhere.'

So it was with Windrose. Every other venture in Denver City seemed to have his name attached. He was lord and master to those people, philanthropist and owner both, and his reach was vast.

'Why do you think I began taking my libations at this establishment, dear friends?' Templeton asked us, mid-way through a morning whiskey at the same, shabby bar where we had found him. 'It is almost the only place to where his fingers have not probed.' He knocked back the rest of the liquor and rapped upon the bar for another. 'I was being followed,' he hiccupped, 'before, when I began my investigations. Two scallywags picked up my trail like a pair of hounds. Only left off when I did.'

'You didn't think that were worth mentioning?' Abe snatched the whiskey out of the man's hand. 'While we was out there, jawin' the name out to all an' sundry?'

'The woman in Hardesty, she had two men with her,' I interrupted, before they could begin quarrelling. I strained to remember the frenzied exchange at the ranch. 'She called them Buxton and Hayle. They must have been the ones who were masquerading as Mr Puttick and you,' I told Abe.

'Bastards,' swore Muir, and tossed back Templeton's whiskey.

'I will wager that Windrose has an army of such men in his employ,' the newspaperman sighed, eyeing his empty glass sadly. 'All I could garner is that he has a ranch, out west a ways.

Fine place, so the gossip goes. There is some sort of construction site up north too, but I was never able to find out much else.'

'What about the man himself?' I pressed. Abe shot me a look, hearing the eagerness in my voice. 'How do we see him?'

'You do not,' Templeton shrugged, 'for no one does. The talk in town is that his health is bad, that he never leaves the ranch. He has a legal man to see to his affairs.'

A chill ran through me as I remembered Carthy's ruined form, racked by disease and by the wound I had inflicted that would never heal. I told myself that it was impossible. Windrose could not be Carthy; Carthy was dead.

How many times have you escaped your reckoning? a voice in my mind hissed. *Why should it be different for him?*

'What I cannot fathom,' Templeton was saying, knocking upon the bar for more whiskey, 'is why he has involved you in this masquerade.'

My hand crept to my pocket. I felt the brush of Abe's fingers as he tried to stop me, but I pulled the drawing free, my heart thudding.

'The woman who was dressed like me, she had this,' I swallowed. 'She told me that Windrose had sent it to her – for use as a likeness, I suppose.'

I watched Templeton's eyes widen as they traveled over the lines and shading, finally coming to rest upon the signature at the bottom.

'This was drawn by Lieutenant Carthy?' He gaped at us. 'But he is deceased! Mr Muir here saw to that.'

'The man is gone,' Abe snapped, 'an' anyone who believes otherwise is soft in the head.'

'But that does not explain how Windrose came to have the drawing,' I countered, the blood hot in my cheeks.

'You believe they are connected?' Templeton said, fumbling for his notebook once again.

I shook my head in frustration. My thoughts were in chaos. 'I do not know. I just know that I have to see him.'

Templeton spread his hands helplessly, yet after a moment his eyes took on a glazed expression that had nothing to do with the whiskey. 'Oh now,' he murmured, 'oh now, wait just a dandy minute.'

'I do not like that thinking look upon his face,' grumbled Abe into my ear. I waved for him to be silent, so that we might hear Templeton.

'I believe,' he was saying slowly, 'that there is a woman at the ranch, a Miss Windrose. I am uncertain of their relation, but I've heard that she does some charity work here in the town.'

'And?' Muir said crossly, 'you intend to smuggle us up to his ranch under her canary cage?'

An expansive smile was growing upon the newspaperman's face. 'Might it not be easier to gain the trust of a young lady?' he said eagerly. 'I seem to recall you looking mighty fine in a bonnet, Sister.'

My smile was undone as Muir slammed the glass down onto the bar. He was furious, I realized.

'This is madness.' His dark eyes searched mine, like a hand reaching through thorns. 'You are throwin' yourself after danger, Thomas Josephine.'

I returned his gaze, my heart in turmoil. The softness at the edge of his words made my heart leap, even as it angered me.

'Where there are wrongs, I must try to right them,' I said, a little too forcefully. 'You know that. I swore an oath to the Lord.'

'An oath,' he scoffed, lips white, 'you'd rather mark your virtue by the dead than risk your heart upon the living.'

Abruptly, he fell silent, mouth open in the wake of his words. I clenched my hands to stop them trembling and raised my chin. Muir eyed my hard expression.

'I'll have no part in this,' he whispered, 'damned if I stand by an' watch you chase your death.'

Then he was gone, stalking from the bar. I stared into the air where he had stood a moment before, his words sinking into my soul.

'Mr Templeton,' I said after an age, 'there is a way to get at Mr Windrose, and we are going to find it.'

And vows are to be paid

I soon discovered that the editor of the *Denver Rancher* was right: once Templeton took an idea into his mind, he was not to be dissuaded. Reluctantly – for it seemed the most promising way to gain access to Windrose – I agreed to his plan. I would abandon my rough trousers and buckskin for a gown and bonnet.

The newspaperman offered his credit to pay for my clothes; an apology he said, for the falsehoods he had written about me. I did not know from where he had obtained the funds, and I feared their source was less than honest.

If Muir had been there, he would have snorted with laughter and told me to bide myself; that such things as unsavory sources of money were upon Templeton's own neck. I had not seen Abe for more than a day, not since our quarrel at the bar. His absence troubled me.

Meanwhile, Templeton had procured the garments I needed, arguing that he had greater experience of a lady's wardrobe than I. I allowed him to choose what he would, so long as it was modest.

When the time came, I shed my shabby clothes. The calico and hide from the plains had become my habit, I realized; they had shielded me, sustained me. The new garments felt like a costume. When I first donned them and turned to the looking glass, I did not recognize myself.

A demure blue dress with voluminous sleeves covered me from ankle to wrist to my neck, there secured by a silk scarf to conceal the scar that circled my throat. There was a bonnet, decorated with pink false flowers, and Mr Templeton had instructed me to comb out my short blonde curls so that they fell upon my temples and hid the scar there too. Lastly, he had helped me into a pair of lace gloves and dusted my face liberally with a pot of powder, tutting that I was 'too sunburned for a lady'.

He was delighted with his efforts, and once he was satisfied he began scribbling in his notebook, glancing up at me from time to time, telling me that he always suspected I was a great beauty, until I was forced to ask him to refrain from speaking. He too had made himself presentable, his whiskers finely trimmed and waxed once again, a new shirt beneath the old plum waistcoat.

'We shall take a turn about the town,' Templeton reassured me, setting his arm beneath my gloved hand, 'so that you might accustom yourself to your costume, ma'am.'

As we descended the stairs, my feet, encased within tight, buttoned boots, were unsteady. The scent of the powder he had applied was overpowering, until I thought that I would not be able to breathe through it.

Templeton dragged upon my arm as we walked, chiding me for striding so boldly, telling me I should not stare about me so, as though I was being hunted.

'It is a difficult custom to break,' I muttered, as we crossed the thoroughfare.

'Templeton!' a voice shouted, and my heart began thudding. It was Abe. I did not know what to do with my hands as I heard his familiar steps approach. 'Templeton!' he said again, bounding up onto the sidewalk, 'I have been askin' about, and have found—'

He stopped dead at the sight of me. I struggled to meet his eyes.

'Mr Muir,' Templeton hissed, glancing about him, 'if we are to speak in public then I must insist you greet the Sister as one might a lady. We cannot know who is watching.'

With a black look, Muir inclined his head stiffly.

'I found them two hard cases,' he said to Templeton, 'Buxton and Hayle, what the Sister said were at the ranch. Saw them loiterin' around Main Street, by this fancy-lookin' carriage. The man in the stables were indisposed to let on who they were, but I persuaded him some.'

There was a graze upon his cheekbone, I noticed, and his knuckles were swollen. He tried to hide them behind his back as he surveyed me. 'Thought we might've taken them on 'stead of prettying up, but I see I am too late.'

'Was it Miss Windrose's carriage?' I demanded, flushing at his tone.

Muir nodded. 'That's what the man said. But I don't see—'

Before he could finish, I ducked away from Templeton and hurried out onto the street. My heart was loud in my ears as I stumbled past horses and barrows, hampered by the dust and my skirts. Upon the next street, a fine four-wheeled carriage stood near the sidewalk, pulled by a pair of sleek bay horses, its black lacquer shining beneath a sprinkling of dust.

A woman was emerging from a building, her hands busy with a pocketbook. She was immeasurably elegant, a dark blue bonnet and veil shading her face, a silk dress that rustled as she stepped onto the running board of the coach. I felt a strange surge of envy as I looked upon her. The two men Abe had mentioned were already in position, one perched upon the back, the other in the driver's seat.

With a deep breath I tripped up to the window of the carriage, dragging a handkerchief from my pocket at the same moment.

'Miss Windrose?' I announced. 'I believe you dropped this.'

11

The daughters of song
shall grow deaf

The woman looked up. Her face was pale, despite the beating sun of the plains; her dark, heavy brows raised in surprise. For a long moment, she surveyed me, still as stone, before her cheeks rounded.

'My goodness,' she smiled, 'thank you.' She took the handkerchief gently in her lace-gloved hand and examined it. 'But I do not believe that this is mine. Might you be mistaken?'

Her accent was impeccable, from somewhere back east, and abruptly I felt that she would see through my disguise in a moment, so awkward was I in my attire. I turned away when her voice stopped me.

'Miss?' She was leaning upon the windowsill of the carriage, her head tilted curiously. 'Would it be impolite to ask how it is you know my name?'

There was amusement in her voice, and I tried my best to smile back, though my heart was racing.

'I have heard of your charity work,' I stuttered, 'from some other ladies. They described your carriage perfectly.'

'That I can well believe,' she said, with a quirk of her lip, 'although I am surprised it was my charitable works that recommended me. Most of the women here are not forthcoming with their approval.'

'Nevertheless,' I murmured quietly, 'I am pleased to make your acquaint, for I should like to fill my time serviceably, if you ever have need of a volunteer.'

She gave me her gracious smile again.

'But you have not yet made my acquaint, Miss . . .?'

'Templeton,' the name was out of my mouth before I could think twice upon it. 'Mary Templeton.'

539

The others were not where I had left them. I searched the surrounding streets, in case they had strayed, and had to stop myself from pursuing my investigation into a nearby saloon, remembering that respectable women did not do such things. The evening was drawing and the light fading rapidly, bringing out a character of the town that I had no wish to witness, unarmed as I was and wearing skirts.

I slipped back across town and took the steps of Templeton's lodgings two at a time, tripping and cursing the useless yards of fabric. The handkerchief was still clenched in my hand as I elbowed through the door to our rooms.

'We meet tomorrow,' I said breathlessly to the dark interior. 'She is attending to benevolent works and has asked me to—'

The scene before me was gruesome in the dying light. Templeton lay whimpering upon the floor, his hands before his face. They were streaked with drying blood, running through his fingers and onto the cuffs of his fine new shirt. Muir stood over him, my shotgun in one hand, flexing his swollen knuckles like a prizefighter.

He took advantage of my silence and threw a newspaper at me. It was a copy of the *Denver Rancher*.

'Page three,' he barked, before turning the gun upon Templeton. 'Don't you even think of speakin' to her.'

The newspaperman only moaned as I tore open the sheets.

BLUNDER AT UNDERTAKER'S: the black letters proclaimed. *SIX-GUN SISTER ALIVE IN COLORADO.*

'He sold us out,' Abe spat.

12

Who knoweth not to forsee

'If we leave at dawn, we can get into the mountains,' said Muir briskly, pacing Templeton's room. 'Puttick said the trail were north through the Rockies, an' clear into Canada. Once we're among the peaks, there's no way they'll find us.'

'I am not leaving,' I said, wetting a rag in the pitcher of water. 'I told you, I am meeting Miss Windrose tomorrow. She is our best way onto the ranch, to get to Windrose.'

Abe kneaded his eyebrows. 'Reasoner and half the US Marshals east of Kentucky will be on us in four days, perhaps less if they've a mind,' he said wildly.

'Then we must get onto the ranch *soon*.'

I passed the wet rag down to Templeton, who peered at me through swimming eyes and dabbed at his nose. It looked broken.

Abe caught my arm. Through the cracked roof, a gibbous moon bulged.

'We could have run,' he said, close, 'if it weren't for that damned picture, we could've been halfway to freedom by now.'

I was silent, for at that moment I did not know how to answer him.

The shadow that lived beneath Muir's skin flickered as he turned away, back to Templeton. The rotund man yelped and cringed against the wall.

'Who did you tell?' Muir demanded, knocking the rag away. 'Who and how much?'

'Nothing, nothing truly,' Templeton stammered, 'that is to say, I may have suggested in not so few words that y'all were alive and well and somewhere in Colorado, but beyond that—'

Muir seized the collar of the velvet waistcoat and pulled.

'What did you say of Carthy?'

'Not a thing,' Templeton gasped, 'nor of Windrose. It would be more than my life is worth, and they were interested only in Thomas Josephine.'

'Who?'

'The correspondent!' yelped Templeton, as one of the waistcoat's buttons pinged off in Muir's fist. 'Whoever it was did not give a name, only sent that awful boy at the *Rancher* a hundred dollars and asked me to write twenty lines with news of the Sister. He could not help but publish me after that. Whoever wrote, I believe they already knew you were alive.'

He panted, looking frantically back and forth between us. 'Where did you think my credit came from? That money bought the clothes you are wearing, ma'am.'

'Fool,' Abe cursed, and threw him back, temper abating. He shook his head. I could see his thoughts racing.

'If this is Windrose's doing,' he said, 'then sure as hell he's got somethin' bad planned for us.' He pursed his lips and seized Templeton's satchel from the ground.

'You,' he barked, tossing it to the newspaperman, 'time to earn your absolution.'

'Where are we going?' gulped Templeton, getting to his feet and slinging the bag over his body. 'Sister, please do not leave me alone with him, he shall kill me for sure.'

'Abraham, do you intend to murder Mr Templeton?' I sighed.

'Not if he makes himself agreeable,' Abe sneered. 'Franklin an' I are goin' to pay a visit to Mr Windrose's lawyer, see if we can get a handle once an' for all on who he is and what he's playin' at. Then perhaps we can get outta here.'

'Impossible,' Templeton hiccupped, 'they shall surely be closed at this hour.'

Abe cast about the room, and seized the large stone that was weighing down Templeton's papers upon the desk.

'Then we shall just have to let ourselves in.'

'I am coming with you,' I announced, hunting around for my ordinary clothes. 'You have no talent for breaking windows.'

Muir pushed Templeton toward the door.

'No you ain't,' he said firmly. 'You need your sleep, Sister. Got an appointment to keep in the morning.'

As Templeton clattered down the stairs, Muir lingered in the doorway.

'What I said, before,' his dark brows were wrinkled in a frown. 'I cannot take it back, but I am sorry if my words caused you pain.'

I smiled at his apology.

'"For now we see through a glass, darkly; but then face to face,"' I told him quietly. 'Corinthians,' I laughed, when he looked puzzled. 'Go.'

13

I made me singing men

I waited for Miss Windrose in the hallway of the town's infirmary, a 'Hotel for Invalids' according to the sign nailed next to
the door. It looked as though it had been a townhouse: dark wood
paneling sagged away from the walls and a once-rich carpet was
sandy with dust. There was a likeness in a frame upon a table. I
picked it up in trepidation, afraid of what I would see.

It showed Miss Windrose, some years younger, upon the arm
of an older man, bull-necked and stocky, with a bald head and
an impressive moustache. He glowered out from the
photograph.

'My father,' a light voice said behind me, and I turned. Miss
Windrose had appeared. Her auburn hair was braided and coiled
about her head, sleeves pinned neatly to the elbow, a pristine
apron fastened over her gown. She moved beside me to view the
photograph and I caught a waft of lavender, of soap and of linen
dried in sunlight. The scents jolted me, unfamiliar after months
of sweat and dust and smoke.

'He is much changed,' she said sadly, gazing into the glass.
'He helped to fund this hospital, before the war, yet now, one
might even think him a different man.' She trailed off and smiled
away the melancholy in her voice.

'But we are not here to talk about him. Thank you for coming,
Miss Templeton, although I am terribly afraid that you will find
the experience tedious.'

She led the way back into the building. We emerged into a
walled yard, where several weak plants and vines were struggling
beneath the sun. A group of children were playing there; not
playing, I realized after a second glance, and not wholly children

either. They were waiting, placid or restless. Some scraped at the ground repeatedly, another threw pebbles at the wall with all the ferocity he could muster.

All of them looked half starved, their faces thin and sunburned. They were not yet fully grown, but they already bore the stain of experience. Even the smallest there surveyed us with guarded eyes and I was reminded of Nettie, insolent and frightened, and of another girl, long ago, with matted blonde curls and the mud of the St. Louis docks upon her shoeless feet . . .

Nearby, one of the large men from the carriage leaned in the shade, a cigarette jammed between his lips. Wordlessly, he took a ledger out from under his arm and handed it to Miss Windrose.

'Hayle, this is Miss Templeton,' she introduced, 'she has come to help me with my work.'

Hayle said nothing, only nodded, but I could not shake the feeling that his eyes were fixed upon me from beneath the shadow of his hat. I ducked my head. How much had he seen, back at the Patterson ranch?

'John Luther?' the woman called, and one of the boys blinked up through the sunlight, emerging from his melancholic contemplation of the ground. She smiled. 'Come here, child.'

The boy shuffled closer. I noticed that his hands were bandaged, as though he were wearing mittens.

Miss Windrose smiled. 'How do you fare today?'

The boy rubbed at his cheek with one bandaged hand.

'I got tooth pain bad,' he mumbled, 'but a quart of whiskey'd sort it straight off.'

'No liquor for you, John,' she said, making a note in the ledger. 'I shall ask the doctor to bring you some medicine.' She knelt down before him, her silk dress rustling. I saw his eyes widen as she looked into his face. 'Where are your family?' she asked him gently.

Muttering, he shook his head.

'Do you have a father? Is he in the mines?'

'He were.' The boy scuffed at the ground. His boots were mismatched, full of holes. 'Then he coughed up blood 'til he died.'

'I see.' With a sigh, Miss Windrose reached forward and took the boy's bandaged hand, filthy as it was. For a moment, fear contorted his face and I thought he would lash out, but he only gazed down at her gloved fingers in awe.

'How old are you, John?' she asked.

'Twelve'm,' he stuttered, cheeks flushing beneath the dirt.

'And should you like to live on a ranch for a time? Eat well and grow strong?'

'Can't pay,' the boy murmured in shame, 'got no money, an' they said I'm too small for the army.'

'Do not concern yourself about that,' Miss Windrose smiled. 'Once you are strong, you will work for us. We will pay you four dollars a day and give you food and a place to sleep. How does that sound?'

The boy was near sobbing with relief as a porter arrived. He was dispatched, to be bathed and to have his head shaved.

'His hands were blistered from digging,' Miss Windrose said to me in a hushed voice, as we watched him go, 'they were so badly infected he could barely use them, but we will make him well.'

Each child was called; they listed their ailments when asked, everything from boils to stomach pains. Miss Windrose calmly listened and made a note of each.

'I do hope this does not upset you, Miss Templeton?' she asked after a time.

I assured her that it did not, and was curious to know where the children came from, what disaster had befallen them.

'Oh dear.' Her eyes were the color of almonds, and were wide with dismay. 'I thought you knew, from the way you spoke. I fear you will not want to remain here, when I tell you.'

'Miss Windrose,' I smiled, 'I am not feeble of heart or spirit. If that were true, I should not have come.'

She sighed. 'All of their families came, bitten by silver fever. Many children are forgotten or abandoned among the mines.

Those that we find, we bring here. I have been chided many times for championing their needs over those of our soldiers. There are hundreds of women willing to shred their linen into bandages for the Union, yet few who will open their hearts to these poor wretches. They are the victims of our progress.'

Despite everything, my heart ached for the children, with their lives so similar to mine, and I could not restrain a rush of admiration for this woman and her concern. So I might have acted, once, had my path upon the world been different. Abruptly, I remembered what I was, what I intended for this woman's father. I forced the feelings down and summoned a smile to my face.

'It is a noble aim, Miss Windrose, and I am happy to aid you, if I can.'

'I am so relieved, Miss Templeton. It is rare indeed that I find someone who shares my sentiments.'

We set to work then. She found me another pencil, and together we bent over the ledger, tallying the figures and costs of medicine into neat columns. Before long, we returned inside. The children who were waiting for their baths ducked their heads respectfully as we passed.

'What will happen to them?' I asked, as I followed Miss Windrose onto the parched street. 'From my experience, it is difficult to find an establishment that will care for such children, to stop them from falling into their old ways.'

Her look was quick and sharp.

'You are quite the surprise, Miss Templeton. I had thought you would be disgusted, but here you are, an expert on abandoned children.'

I smiled politely, hoping it would suffice.

'As you heard, my father will offer them work,' she told me, 'they are young, but with nourishment, they will be strong. With so many maimed by the war, the able-bodied will be hard to come by, and we shall have need of them.'

Rather than explain further, Miss Windrose insisted that I take tea with her at a parlor nearby. I readily accepted: my determination to discover a way to the ranch far outweighed my trepidation. It was sweltering indoors, but my companion only dabbed gracefully at her perspiring temples.

'It has just occurred to me that I have been exceedingly rude, Miss Templeton, for I have not asked you a word about yourself. I shall speak no more until I know.'

She dropped a lump of sugar into her tea and settled back expectantly.

I took a sip to cover my anxiety.

'There is nothing interesting in the least to tell,' I demurred, praying that God would forgive the lie, 'I am from Missouri, and am in town with my uncle.'

'Templeton,' she frowned, 'I have heard the name. Your uncle is not a correspondent, for a newspaper?'

'Yes, I am afraid so,' I stammered, thoughts racing, 'I do not know him well at all, in truth, but he is the only family I have.'

'I am sorry for your loss,' Miss Windrose told me tactfully. 'My own mother died long ago, before we came west.'

'How did your father come to be in this place?' I asked quickly. 'It is rather on the edge of civilization,' I finished, to cover my eagerness.

The woman gazed through the limp gauze at the windows. I wondered at her age then. She looked to be two or three years older than I. Most women her age were long married, especially with a fortune behind them. She could have been entertaining in some drawing room in Boston or Chicago; but instead she was here, living on a secluded ranch, with a frontier town her only hope of society.

'My father had grand plans,' she murmured after a time. Her voice had a strange edge to it, pensive and almost scornful. 'He looked west and saw something other than wilderness. He saw life, sleeping beneath the surface. All it needed was an artery to feed it, he said, and we should see it burst out into being. This war, it has made his business ... difficult. But soon all shall be well. Where there is land, iron and men are all that are needed.'

She shut her mouth quickly, and melted into her same generous smile.

'You see how starved I am for company, Miss Templeton, I am talking pure nonsense.'

At that, the door of the parlor opened with a clack. Hayle stepped in from the blinding street, and stood passively, blocking the light.

'I have kept you too long,' she said, placing a few coins from her pocketbook onto the table. She took my extended hand firmly when I stumbled up, and looked into my eyes. 'I cannot tell you how pleased I am to have met you.'

'And I you, Miss Windrose,' I murmured, taken aback by her seriousness.

'Call me Elizabeth, please,' she gathered the ledger and the pocketbook beneath her arm.

Before I could speak further, she had gone, sweeping from the door before Hayle, who followed like a shadow.

It had all been for nothing, I fumed. I had lied, made myself ridiculous in masquerade, and I knew no more than when I had begun. Frustrated, I strode outside after they had gone, too exasperated to care that a proper lady did not stalk the streets as if she wore trousers and a gun belt. Muir was right; it was madness to think that this was the way to get at Windrose. Was his daughter so naïve, that she knew nothing of what he had done? What was he hiding, out there, at his ranch? Who was he hiding?

War has made his business difficult, Miss Windrose had said, as if she understood. *Where there is land, iron and men are all that are needed.*

The words froze me in my tracks, their meaning suddenly as clear as if the Lord had shone a light upon them. I took off for Templeton's rooms at a run. He and Muir had been asleep when I left, having returned at dawn from their night raid upon the lawyer's office. I had not yet asked them what they had found there, but – if I was correct – Windrose's motives were no longer a mystery.

I clattered up the stairs, the skirts hitched to my shins. The door was ajar.

'It is a railroad!' I cried, as I half fell into the room, the bonnet tumbling over my face. I pushed it back.

The place was empty. Papers littered the floor, the table was upturned, its legs smashed to pieces. The shotgun was missing. I forced myself to be calm and hunted through the chaos. My old clothes were trampled in a corner. I retrieved the knife from the pocket of the buckskin jacket and hid it within my sleeve. I braced myself against the wall until I was able to breathe without gasping, and raced for the stairs.

The old woman with the canker was peering around her door, one eye glistening from a rime of filth.

'What happened here?' I demanded of her.

She shrank back, baring her gums.

'Gone, your fancy men are,' she said. 'Shameless harlot.'

In one move I shoved open the door and grabbed the front of her soiled nightgown.

'Where are they?'

'Who are you?' she whimpered. 'You ain't no lady—'

I tightened my hold.

'They said they were marshals,' she squawked, 'but I never saw no badge on them. They were with them big fellas from the Windrose ranch, the ones what are always stalking 'round the place, scaring folk witless ...'

I shoved her back inside her door and ran onto the street, praying that I would not be too late.

14

Who know not what evil they do

I do not recall how I reached the stable, but by the time I collapsed against the doors I was breathless from panic and heat.

'Why, you look all aflutter, little lady.'

A man in a huge hat was leaning over the porch of the saloon, a grin twitching his beard. 'Why don't you come and rest your pretty self awhile? Ol' Sue here will buy you a sarsaparilla.'

His holster was unbuckled and swung loose upon his shoulder. I could see a pistol clipped within it, heavy and solid.

Feebly, I waved my hand before my face.

'My horse,' I murmured, 'I must get to my horse.'

I tripped away into the stable and ducked into the shadows. Sure enough, a moment later there was a rumbling of voices and the thud of boots in the dirt.

'Lil' lady?' the man called, strolling into the stable. A pair of gleaming new spurs jangled upon his boots. 'Pardon my sayin', but you don't seem in any state to be riding.'

He stopped dead as the knifepoint pressed into his neck.

'The gun,' I told him quietly, the breath whistling in and out of my lungs. 'Do not make me hurt you.' I pressed the blade closer as he tried to strain away.

'Aw, heck,' he swore, reaching for the buckle.

I spun away as soon as it was free, arming the gun in one movement and shoving the knife into the top of my boot. I kept the weapon trained up at him as I backed away toward my horse.

'If you'd be so kind,' I told him, gesturing toward the tack.

Blanching, he prepared my mount, glancing my way all the while. When he was done, I made him back up.

'How do women ride in these things,' I muttered, as I swung

my leg over the saddle, and the fabric of the dress bunched and caught. I shoved the bonnet back from my face.

'Where is the Windrose ranch?' I asked the man, aiming true upon him again.

'Criminy,' he gaped, eyes upon the scar at my temple, 'are you . . . ?'

'The ranch?'

'Due west outta town,' he gulped, 'past the gulch, below the pass. Jus' follow the wagon tracks.'

I kicked back my heels and bolted out of the stable. It was afternoon, and the streets were quiet, folk heavy from the heat and the noontime meal. I sped for the edge of Denver, toward the mountains that raised saw-like teeth to the blistering sky.

I did not have to look hard to find the trail. The ground was recently disturbed by tracks, a wagon, horses. The brittle grass was bent and pitted from their passing. Above me, a buzzard wheeled, questing the landscape for death in lazy circles. Dread filled my chest as I watched its ragged wings and I spurred the horse ever faster.

My lips moved in rapid prayer, in time with the drumming of hooves beneath me. The land began to rise, bristling with fist-sized rocks and brown stalks. An hour slipped by and my horse began to tire, but I urged it on, sending it scrambling upward, toward a summit.

When we topped the peak, the beast staggered to a halt, sweat gleaming on its neck. Below, the foothills dipped away into a shallow valley, improbably green and lush, a wide pasture with a fringe of trees that climbed the base of the mountain.

At one end stood a grand house, stolid and imposing, its architecture at odds with the roar of nature above. The afternoon was golden, and all was quiet, peaceful, save for the blood that resounded through my veins, for the pistol that thudded against my hip through the pocket of my dress. I urged the horse forward.

I did not know what I was going to do as I rode up to the house. I only knew that somewhere nearby, Abe was in danger.

I was within shouting distance of the walls when the dogs began barking.

I kicked my tired horse on, trying to clear the trees, but it was too late. The hounds streamed from behind the house to surround me, snapping and snarling, their muscular bodies tense. One leaped, its jaws closing upon the trailing fabric of my dress. I screamed as it nearly dragged me from the saddle, shaking its head, teeth ripping into the garment.

The horse was shying in fright even as it tried to run. Through the noise I heard a voice calling out. I pulled the knife from my boot, but the horse reared and I was thrown, slamming into the ground among a frenzy of jaws and teeth.

15

In fruitless solicitude
of the mind

I smelled soap and lavender, felt a throbbing pain at the back of my skull. I opened my eyes. I could see the sky beyond lace curtains, slashed orange and crimson by the sunset. My hands sank into something soft and yielding as I pulled myself upright: cushions. I rolled onto my side, taking deep breaths to fight off the nausea.

My bonnet was gone, I realized with a tremor of unease. In its place was a damp handkerchief, another upon my forehead. I peeled them off. Gingerly, I ran my fingertips over my scalp. Through the short curls I felt a lump, the size of an egg, tender and hot.

There was a noise behind me, and instinct sent my hand flying for the pistol in my pocket. It was still there. I gripped it through the fabric in relief.

'Oh, thank goodness,' a voice rang out and I released the weapon. Miss Windrose stood in the doorway, a tray in her hands. Her face was pale as she hurried into the room to kneel beside me.

'My dear Miss Templeton, whatever could have possessed you to ride out here alone?' she chided, pouring a measure of brandy from a decanter. 'I am so dreadfully sorry. The dogs are never loose on the grounds if we are expecting visitors.'

I pushed myself away from her.

'Where is he?' I demanded. 'What have you done to him?'

The woman's dark brows slanted in consternation.

'Who? My father? He is upstairs, in his study.' She mistook my noise of disbelief as she tried to press me back into the cushions. 'Please do not concern yourself. It is true, he dislikes visitors, but—'

'Abraham,' I said, staying her hand as she tried to feel my forehead. 'Templeton. Where are they?'

Her quick brown eyes were bewildered.

'You do not know,' I whispered. 'How is it that you do not know?'

'You have been hurt worse than I feared,' she said soothingly, and eased a pillow behind my back. 'Drink this, it will help.'

I took the glass from her and drank the brandy down in one swallow. Her eyes were wide as she watched.

'That blow to your head has made you insensible,' she said. 'Please, do not move. I must send to town for the doctor.'

'I am not . . .' I cried, but she was gone, hurrying from the door, hands clasped in her skirts.

The brandy was hot in my throat and lent me the strength to examine my surroundings. The room was spacious and graceful, delicate furniture and a piano in one corner. I flung the handkerchief aside and tried to lever myself from the sofa. I managed it on the second attempt, though my vision blurred and my stomach heaved dreadfully.

Concussion, I cursed inwardly, breaking into a sweat. *I am growing tired of concussion.*

I staggered over to the door. A hallway opened beyond, the floor polished and carpeted with thick rugs. The house was finer than anything I had ever seen, but I could not appreciate it. I blinked to clear the snow from my vision and stumbled toward a wide staircase.

Upstairs, she had said, in his study. Was Windrose sitting quietly with his business even as Abe was tortured? Did someone else sit with him? I set my teeth and began to climb. I could hear Elizabeth's voice issuing orders distantly, but I gripped the banister, placed one foot before the other.

Dizziness overcame me at the top, and I clung to an ornate pillar, praying to the Lord for strength until the spell had passed. I dragged the pistol free and armed it. The clicking of the mechanism was loud as a thunderclap in the hushed building.

I shook my head, trying to listen through my ringing ears.

From somewhere came a clinking: like coins upon a table, being scraped together. I crept forward, one hand to the wall, the pistol heavy as lead in my grip.

At the end of the corridor, a door stood open. The sound of coins came from within. Every muscle in my body was taut as I raised the gun and stepped over the threshold.

The room was a library walled with books, floor to ceiling. An imposing desk stood facing the door, a small table at its side, lit by a large oil lamp. In the chair before it was a man, the one I had seen from the photographs. He looked thinner now, a good deal older. He sat, shoulders hunched, head lowered over a pile of coins, spilling golden upon the polished surface. His hands had paused.

'Where are they?' My voice cracked and I took a step forward, thrusting the pistol out before me. 'Where are Abe and Templeton? Where is Carthy? Tell me, Windrose.'

The man looked up. His eyes were bleary and vacant, gummed and flaky in the corners. His lips hung open. I watched, horrified, as a string of drool trickled down his chin.

'I'm afraid he cannot tell you anything,' a voice behind me said.

16

But time and chance in all

Miss Windrose walked past me into the room, as if the pistol in my hand was as harmless as a flower. Her father looked down again and began to scrape at the gold, piling it higher and higher until he could grasp it in his hands and let it run through his fingers.

'It is the only thing that calms him, now,' she stood behind his shoulder as he began the ritual again, pity and disdain upon her face. 'Driven by greed even at the end.'

She took a seat at the desk and smiled at me sadly.

'Please lower the gun, Thomas Josephine.'

I gripped it all the firmer, despite my confusion.

'Where is Muir?' I demanded, though my voice trembled. 'What have you done to him?'

'Please, sit with me.' When I stood my ground, she sighed, her cold frown returning. 'He will not have been harmed, unless through struggle. If you sit, I will tell you. You may keep the pistol, if you wish; it does not trouble me.'

Reluctantly, I approached the desk and lowered myself into the chair. Miss Windrose held my gaze solemnly, as the noise of rattling coins continued beside her.

'I was not lying, when I said how pleased I was to have met you,' she said after a time. 'I have followed your journey for a long while, Sister.'

She reached into the desk drawer beside her and took out a bundle of letters, tied with blue ribbon. Carefully, she removed one from the bottom.

'"I apologize for my long silence, dear Elizabeth,"' she read softly, '"but there was trouble outside of the fort: a wagon train, attacked by savages, once again. Yet all is not unpleasantness here, for I have met a most singular woman. Her name is Sister Thomas Josephine."'

She lowered the page. 'These are all from Theodore,' she murmured. 'Letters while he was away at war. Do you know how many of them make mention of you, Sister?'

I shook my head, nauseated by the realization that was creeping upon me.

'Every one,' she said, eyes fixed upon mine. 'From the first day he met you to the day he died, your name does not go unwritten.'

'Theodore . . .' I whispered.

'Theodore Carthy,' she pushed the letters across to me, 'my handsome soldier. You made a widow of me, Sister, before I was even a wife.'

I gaped emptily at her, words lost within my mind. This elegant, silk-dressed woman had held Carthy's hand in hers before he had ever raised it against me, before he had hounded me across the country, toward his own ending. I recalled then, the daguerreotype in his room at Fort Laramie, of a young woman. I bent over in the chair, and put my spinning head in my hands.

The woman at the desk watched me impassively.

'You saw the portrait he drew?' she asked. 'He sent that to me with a letter. I did not even know he could draw, before that. Any fool would have realised how he felt. How often I stared at your face, and how I hated you.'

I raised burning eyes to hers as she continued.

'In his correspondence, it was "Thomas Josephine" again and again. At first it was your purity, your spirit, so unlike any other woman he had met. He was sure we would be friends, he said.' Her fingers lingered over the pages. 'But then the letters changed. He squandered whole pages upon you, lamenting your obsession with Muir, your blindness. And then came this.'

She held up a page. The writing veered clumsily across the paper.

'Thanks to you, a proud soldier was reduced to a man who

could barely fire a gun,' she said with a bitter smile, 'or hold a sword, or even write a letter.'

There was a clatter from the table beside her, and both of us jumped in alarm. The old man wheezed and began to pile his coins together again.

'His deterioration was fast,' she told me, eyes upon her father's progress. 'He never realized what became of his fine future son-in-law. I suppose I should be grateful for that. I did not know what I should do, at first, without either of them, but the speed with which father lost himself forced me to see that action must be taken.'

I could barely focus. 'Tellman,' I said, my voice hoarse. 'And all the others. The farmers in the New Mexico Territory. You killed them. You sent Buxton and Hayle and that woman out there and you murdered in my name. All those people, dead, and you see that as *action*?'

She nodded distantly. 'There was no help for it. Mr Tellman and father bought the land together. They were to bring their railroad out west, straight through some of the best land in the country. But father's share of the grant would have been forfeit had Tellman discovered his ailment.' She looked at me calmly. 'Eight hundred thousand dollars, that land cost us. His legacy and my entire future is tied to it. I couldn't lose it.'

The money clicked and slithered through her silence, the noise strangely hypnotic. The concussion was pressing heavily. I blinked hard to focus. Miss Windrose was staring fixedly at me.

'Do you understand?' she asked, 'the grant will give me five hundred square miles, from the mines of Colorado to the deserts of New Mexico. And I will fill it. I will bring the railroad through it, and it will become *my* legacy. I will plumb this country and bring forth humanity. Those children, abandoned by society, are just the start. Can't you feel it, Sister?' There was something in her gaze that begged me to understand. 'You too ran for the west. Didn't you see the ground at your heels turning to track?'

'I saw God's work to be done,' I stuttered, speech more difficult with every passing moment, 'I saw souls to be saved.'

'You saved *me*, Thomas Josephine,' her eyes were bright, 'I am not naïve any longer. I read Theodore's medical report, what the army doctors wrote there about him. Had he not followed you, he would have returned here, and I would have married a shell of a man, consumed by disease. And in time, I too would have succumbed . . .'

She broke off, swallowing hard. 'But your life, what you have done, it made me see there is another way in this wild land, if I only have the strength to take it.'

She reached into a drawer by her side and drew out a bundle, wrapped in dark silk. Reverently, she folded back the cloth. Inside was a pistol. I stared in disbelief. It was one of Muir's. She placed it upon the desk, and gathered something else from beneath it, something that clicked and rattled like bone.

I could not move for shock as she came to kneel upon the floor by my side. Her hands were warm and dry as she pressed my rosary into my palm, bone and blood, wood and stains familiar against my skin.

'You saved me from Theodore, from a life that would have destroyed me,' she whispered, brushing the scarf away from my neck to reveal the scar from the hangman's noose, 'and so I saved you.'

I stared, sickened, at my savior. Had she smiled thus as she bribed the hangman to weaken the ropes, to stand back and watch as the weight of our bodies snapped the nooses that were intended to kill? Panic flared within me; the zeal I heard in her voice was an echo of Carthy, of the madness that had taken him.

She stepped back.

'You have not saved me,' I said. 'You have used me. And it ends here.' Each word was a struggle. I dragged the pistol from my pocket, shaking all over though I was, and leveled it at her head. 'Where is Abraham Muir?'

She stared me down.

'Gone.'

'Where?'

When she did not answer, I forced my muscles to aim over

her shoulder and fire the weapon. A dull click filled the room as the hammer landed on an empty chamber.

'I told you it would not trouble me,' Miss Windrose said impatiently, 'and I am not lying to you, Thomas Josephine. I will never lie to you. I am ten thousand dollars poorer, and Abraham Muir has gone. I offered him a choice, just as I will offer you a choice.'

My legs buckled under me at her words. Through the fog in my head, I pleaded with God to show me the truth, but all I felt was a terrible stirring of doubt, a memory of Abe's words in that dark saloon.

Damned if I'll stand by and watch you chase your death . . .

'A choice, Thomas Josephine,' Miss Windrose was saying. The tips of her fingers were white from where she braced herself against the desk. 'Stay with me here. I do not want to be alone. Be my companion; help me build this new territory. I could keep you free from the law, from those who hunt you.'

My lips trembled into a snarl.

'Or?'

Slowly, she reached forward for Muir's pistol and armed it.

'Or it continues,' she was pale as stone, 'your life, always hunted, always afraid, with death on your heels. You knew it would be thus.'

'So be it,' I whispered.

Her lips hung open for a moment as she took in every inch of my face.

'Then I am sorry,' she said.

She swung round and fired the pistol. Gunshot thundered through the house, and with it the sliding of coins, raining to floor as the old man slumped forward and died.

'Sister,' I heard Miss Windrose cry, as I staggered into a run, fleeing that place in horror, 'why did you have to murder my father?'

Nunslinger: Book 12

West of Absolution

The True Tale of how Sister Thomas Josephine came to Meet her Fate

I

When evening comes,
it cometh with the twelfth

The clouds scudded across the graveyard, dimming the ground in patches, as if God's hand passed across a lamp. In their absence, the sun flared, and the group of black-clothed figures shivered and sweated in turn, their perspiration whipped away by the wind of the plains.

I watched them from the shadows of a half-built mausoleum, far enough away that I felt sure they could not see me. It had been abandoned, a rough-hewn wooden shack staring up at the roofless sky. In this land of dust and distance, no one wasted stone upon the dead.

The first shovel of earth was swept away by the wind before it could fall. Miss Windrose's dress was tugged with it, a long, gauze veil snapping wildly. There was a handkerchief in her hand. Did she truly grieve? I wondered; had she grieved thus when the news finally reached her of Carthy's death, crying herself pale, and cursing me in her prayers?

Windrose. The name was now forever linked with mine in the eyes of the law, along with Carthy's: both victims of the Six-Gun Sister. They did not concern themselves with motive any longer. I was crazed, they shrugged, hunting sinners where I found them.

The mourners drifted off and the gravediggers began their work. A huge plinth stood empty at the head of the grave, waiting to receive a statue. Miss Windrose turned away and I tensed in the shadows. It had not been easy to get close to her. By the time I had found my way back to the city from the ranch, sick in body and soul, the whole of Denver was in uproar over the news of Mr Windrose's murder. Elizabeth had worked fast.

I heard my name on countless lips, some weeping, others threatening punishments that chilled me with their brutality. Luckily, the gown I wore offered some disguise, but still I was forced to skulk like a thief in the shadows, while all around my face was plastered in duplicate, triplicate on every building. I had heard talk of the burial, and had crept out of the city before dawn, taking up my hiding place and waiting until the grand funeral procession arrived.

I pulled the blanket I wore like a cloak further over my head and slipped out of the shade. Miss Windrose waited patiently at the gate, staring down upon the mourning figures that snaked down the hillside.

'We both know that pistol is empty,' she said, without looking around.

I halted, six feet away. After a moment, I armed the gun.

Beneath the shadow of her veil I saw one eyebrow raised.

'You are more resourceful than I thought, Thomas Josephine.'

Her eyes were swollen from weeping, her face pale and slack above the heavy gown. Anyone else would pity her, having lost fiancé and father both. Had I been anyone else, I might have reached out to comfort her, but as it was, I only kept the weapon steady.

'Where is he, Elizabeth?'

My voice came out as a croak, worn from lack of sustenance, lack of sleep. The woman before me only shook her head.

'I told you.'

'You lied.'

'We all have our price, Sister,' she shot me a sidelong glance. 'I understand better than you think. I know what it is to lose the man you love when you realize the truth about him—'

'Muir is different,' I said. 'He would not leave me.'

'Do you know that for certain?' When I was silent, she sighed. 'He was tired. I could see it in his face.' She folded her handkerchief neatly. 'You should be grateful. His life will be the easier. He will fade back into the world and live peacefully. Ten thousand dollars can buy a man freedom, Thomas Josephine.'

'Abe would never take your money.'

Miss Windrose smiled sadly.

'He can do no wrong in your eyes, can he? I can see why you frustrated Theodore so. Part of me wishes you were right.'

A cloud of dust and clattering hooves announced the arrival of her carriage.

'You are sure you will not join me?' she asked seriously.

'Whatever your plan, I will not be a part of it,' I said, my voice low with anger.

'You will, Sister,' she said calmly, as she walked to her carriage and climbed inside. 'You yourself decided that.'

2

My name is as oil poured out

As I waited in the darkness of the shabby corridor, I found myself haunted by Elizabeth Windrose's claim that Abe had chosen to leave without me. I had but one charge for the pistol and a ragged blanket, stolen from a drunk who had fallen over in the gutter before me. I moved only at night, when it was too dark for people to see my face. I should have left the city, taken to the wilderness where I might be safe, yet I could not. Not without Abe.

Keep the way of the Lord, do judgment and justice, for Abraham's sake . . .

His life would be easier, she had said. Was she right? From the first day we met he had been running. Had it not been for me, he might have escaped, been living simply somewhere now. He might have returned home to his livestock town, found the red-haired girl of his youth and raised children on a homestead.

Tears burned at my eyes, and I turned my face into the peeling wallpaper. Had I robbed him of his freedom?

Feet upon the stairs shook me from my thoughts. I swiped my sleeve across my face and armed the gun. Steps crossed the hallway, slow and weary. In the sick, flickering light of a single candle, a man cast about him furtively, opening his door.

I stepped forward and pressed the mouth of the gun into his fleshy neck.

'Hello, Franklin,' I whispered.

He had not been difficult to find. A man of his description cut a figure in Denver, even peopled as it was with outcasts and oddities.

The newspaperman's hotel room was in darkness, but even so, I could see the discoloration on his face, bruises growing old beneath both eyes, a scab where his lip had been split. He moved stiffly and with care: I did not doubt that his body was as battered as his face.

'You should not be here,' he told me, drawing away from the window.

'I could not leave,' I told him. 'You know that.'

'It is pandemonium out there,' he said, pulling a bottle of brandy from behind a cupboard. The rim clattered against the glass as he poured out a measure and handed it to me. 'I am in great demand, as the country's premier authority on the habits of the Six-Gun Sister.' He swigged from the bottle, wincing as the liquor touched his swollen lip. 'Habits,' he half laughed, and sank onto the bed.

'Muir was right,' he continued wearily. 'Every bounty hunter and marshal this side of the Missouri River is in town, or heading toward it. Windrose was a saint to these people. He was to bring the future with his railroad.'

'*Her* railroad,' I said, and drank the brandy down. 'It is Miss Windrose's now.'

Templeton nodded, took another swig.

'Muir and I discovered as much, at the lawyer's place. Miss Windrose gained power of attorney over the entire estate, a few weeks ago.'

'She killed him,' my voice was cold. 'Her own father.'

'I knew it was not you who did the deed,' Templeton's cracked lip trembled. 'Yet so I wrote it, like they asked.'

'Who?'

'Miss Windrose's tame apes,' he sniffed, 'Buxton and Hayle. They came for Muir and I. Abraham put up a mighty struggle and knocked a couple of Buxton's teeth clean out of his head,' he laughed weakly. 'It did not amount to anything. They are vicious men, Sister; had the pair of us spitting up blood before we even reached the road.'

'Where—?' I scrambled to my feet.

Templeton's face crumpled. 'Do not ask me where Muir is. I swear on the Virgin's head I do not know. I have told as much to every tracker and lawman who has asked, though some asked less amiably than others.'

He retrieved the bottle and sloshed another measure into my glass, spilling half over my sleeve.

'We were separated,' he told me, when the next swallow had found its way down his gullet. 'They tossed Muir in a wagon with a group of brutes to hold him and drove off before he could as much as holler. Hayle and a few others went to work upon me in an alleyway. He warned me of what would happen, were I to refuse the task of reporting certain stories.'

'They took Abe to the ranch, I am sure of it,' I sipped the second brandy. 'Miss Windrose said she offered him a choice. Ten thousand dollars, for his freedom. She told me that he took it.' My hands clenched about the glass. 'I know she is lying.'

Templeton was shaking his head slowly.

'Whatever the case, no one has seen hide nor hair of him in town.'

'He has not left me,' I shut my eyes to the room, to the savagery that waited outside those thin, frame walls. 'I know it.'

I felt a touch upon my hand. Templeton's fingers were hovering above my own.

'If you stay, you will be caught,' he said, 'in days, hours even, Sister. You should run, as far and as fast as you can.'

'"Where could such a one as I flee?"' I said with a bitter laugh. 'They have Abraham captive and I will find him.'

For a long moment the newspaperman gripped my hand, before heading for the door.

'Are you going to turn me in?' I asked tiredly.

Templeton smiled at me over his shoulder.

'No, ma'am. You asked me for my help once, and I swear, so long as you are at liberty, you will have a friend in Franklin Templeton.'

3

We will make thee chains of gold

When I awoke, the room was empty. Templeton had insisted that I take the bed, settling for the cover of his coat upon the bare boards, and I had not objected. I listened closely to the stillness around me, hand poised over the pistol. Outside, the sun was low on the horizon. I had slept for a whole day.

I found a jug of water and scrubbed at my skin. The bullet wound from Fort Smith was tender still. It had healed clumsily, skin puckered like a rosette, but it no longer gave me so much pain.

Templeton had kept my men's clothes, and I shed the hateful dress in favor of old calico and leather. Gently, I placed Muir's rosary about my neck where it hung against the livid hanging scar. I gazed down at it. It looked right, and real.

I was in such a daze that I almost missed the bundle that had been placed at the foot of the bed. I could scarcely believe what I found inside. Cornbread, cold bacon, even a cake made with raisins and sugar. I ate like a savage, kneeling on the floor and chewing with such haste that I almost choked. I muttered a prayer through the crumbs. The sustenance filled me, but more than that: I knew it had been offered in kindness, and that humble gesture was a salve to my troubled soul.

By the time Templeton returned I was pacing the room. His fingers were stained with ink, I noticed, and he stank of the saloons.

'I did not want to do it,' he told me before I could speak, and grabbed at the brandy, 'but there was no help for it. They stood over me like demons until the last word was done.'

He drained the bottle to its dregs and stood, gasping, the alcohol glistening on his moustache.

'Ask me then,' he said, eyes bright. 'Ask me what I have done.'

'You have helped me,' I said, taking the bottle from his hand and setting it upon the table. 'There is no one else in this town whom I could have turned to—'

'"Six-Gun Sister strikes terror in Boulder County,"' he interrupted. '"Ranch destroyed as Papist Murderess burns home of philistines to the ground."' He slumped into the chair. 'I did not have a choice,' he said. His voice had the air of confession. 'They were waiting for me, Buxton, Hayle; dragged me to that godforsaken hog farm and told me that if I did not turn in my copy with the news . . .'

'What news?'

The newspaperman swallowed emptily.

'Another ranch attacked, upcountry,' he whispered, 'a family killed, place burned down to the ground. Not a stick left.'

My stomach began to writhe.

'They are saying it was me,' my voice was strangely flat. 'You wrote that it was me?'

'There was no help for it!' His face was gray as old meat. 'They said they would kill me, if I did not cooperate.'

'Why are they doing this?' I demanded. 'Innocent people are dying, and what for?'

'I do not know!'

I pressed my knuckles into my eyes, trying to think.

Where there is land, iron and men are all that are needed.

'The land grant application,' I said abruptly, 'where is it?'

Templeton slid from the chair, dragging the carpetbag from beneath the bed. Papers spilled from it. 'Here,' he nearly ripped the document in his haste to unfold it upon the blankets.

I glanced down at the neat script, the heavy ink, the government seals.

'"Now know ye,"' I read rapidly, '"that the General Land Office of the United States of America, will give and grant unto the parties, the tract of five hundred miles, formerly detailed, for

572

the sum of eight hundred thousand dollars, *if* it is suitably cleared
for the aforementioned enterprise.'"

"'Suitably cleared'?' I said. 'Of what?'

Templeton met my eyes, horrified. 'Of people.'

Templeton

4

Because of fears in the night

The wood cracked, splintering around the flimsy lock. The noise rebounded through the street. Templeton was yelling for me to stop, but I didn't care. I kicked the door hard again and again, putting my full weight behind my boot.

It flew open and I stalked into the building. Rage roared through my body. It drove me remorselessly, coal within an engine, stoked to blazing.

'What are you doing?' Templeton's voice was high with terror.

I ignored him and strode into the office. It was dimly lit, stuffy and dry, a dark wood bureau piled high with papers. A man with neatly parted graying hair had half risen from the desk, a pair of eyeglasses in his hand.

'What the—?' he said angrily.

'Good evening,' I greeted from behind the pistol.

I watched his face drop a spectrum in color.

'Oh God,' his eyes bulged, flitting to the door and back. 'What are you doing? You should not be here.'

Before I could answer he lunged for a drawer, hand out-stretched. Instinctively, I fired. He screamed, falling back, blood pulsing from a ruined fingertip, spattering the papers before him.

Briskly, I reached into the drawer. A revolver: fine, and loaded. Evidently, the man's business was a dangerous one. I armed it and stepped back, dropping the pistol into my pocket.

Sweat poured down his face, blood running onto his cuff.

'Templeton,' I said slowly, 'is this the man?'

The newspaperman looked as though he would vomit.

'Yes,' Templeton nodded, 'that is he. Mr Windrose's lawyer.'

'*Miss* Windrose's lawyer,' I corrected. 'Is not that so?'

'Yes,' the man was panting wildly, 'what do you want? I do not know anything, I swear it.'

'That I do not believe.' I cast my eyes about the room. A silk scarf was hanging upon the coat stand. 'There,' I told Templeton. 'Take that. Tie his arms.'

He did so, flinching as he pulled the lawyer's arms behind his back and fixed them at the wrists.

'Sister, he is bleeding rather freely,' he murmured.

'He will continue to do so until he talks,' I said coldly. 'Now, where is Abraham Muir?'

'How should I know?' the lawyer snarled.

I wedged the mouth of the pistol beneath his chin. He yelped at its touch. 'I swear,' he said, 'I had nothing to do with it.'

'Tell him,' I told Templeton fiercely, 'tell him of Miss Windrose's latest success.'

The newspaperman wrung his hands anxiously. For a moment there was silence, save for the lawyer's ragged breathing, the steady drip, drip of blood onto the floorboards.

'Another family of homesteaders dead,' Templeton's voice was hoarse, 'a farmer and his wife. They died trying to save their children, but the fire had spread too far . . .'

I leaned down until my eyes were level with the lawyer's.

'I did not know what they would do,' he whined. 'Miss Windrose, she owns this town. If I hadn't done as she asked I would never have worked again—'

'Will your business give you comfort?' my voice was trembling with fury. 'Will it ease your guilt when you remember the names of those who have been slaughtered?' I felt his breath upon my face, sour with fear. 'You will be damned for your ignorance,' I promised, 'by your own conscience, if not by the Lord.'

'Sister,' Templeton interrupted. He was staring down at the desk. Stretched upon its surface was a map, weighted down at the corners. Through the glistening bloodstains I saw a line drawn in black ink, running from the mines in the mountains to the desert of the south.

Small dots had been marked in blue chalk, each with a neatly written surname, stretching along the entire length of the trail. Four had been struck through. I knew then that each of those markings was a home, wrestled from the forbidding land by years of labor, by sacrifice and hope. My lips moved silently, tallying the number of lives that Miss Windrose intended to take. The lawyer had turned pale, watching me.

'Which one?' I demanded. 'Which one is next?'

'The Hopkins ranch!' he said. 'But it is too late . . .'

I seized the map from the desk.

'You forget, sir,' I told him, 'I have the Lord on my side.'

5

The watchmen who keep the city

I fled through the dark streets, the scent of smoke clinging to my clothes, my hands sullied with blood and ash. The bright streaks of flame still burned behind my eyes. I saw again the oil lamp leaving my hand to shatter upon the desk, the fire guzzling the statutes and documents, the paper foundation upon which Miss Windrose's empire rested. A minor inconvenience for her, perhaps, but for me, it was the first blow.

The streets around me were crowded, but no one paid me any mind in their rush toward the conflagration. I looked over my shoulder. An orange glow was blooming above the rooftops from the lawyer's office, smoke roiling into the air. In a wooden-walled town like Denver, fire spread faster than a man could spit.

The rosary clicked and tangled about my neck as I came into sight of the town jail. I should have been afraid, but there was no room left for fear within me, only the resolution to do what must be done.

My own face watched me from the posters nailed outside the jailhouse; I hung back in the shadows as three marshals clattered down the steps and loped off into the night, spurs rattling, swearing about the fire.

The door swung closed upon its hinges as I crept forward. A single chair stood outside, next to a spittoon. Quietly, I wedged it beneath the door handle. Along the wall, one filthy window was open a crack. I peered through the glass. I could see prison bars, could make out the shapes of a few inmates, lying upon benches. Not six feet away sat a man at a desk, a newspaper spread before him. I pulled out the revolver and rapped upon the glass.

Reasoner glanced up in alarm. I watched his face change as we locked eyes. For a moment I surveyed him, as I had done during his first visits to the convent.

Then he stood, and came close to the window.

'Thomas Josephine,' he said softly.

'I know,' I interrupted, 'I am wanted for ten counts of murder across the states of Nevada, California, Arkansas, the New Mexico and Colorado Territories . . .'

He had removed his pistol from the holster, I saw, and was holding it an inch below the sill.

'Do you surrender?' he asked.

A breath of laughter escaped me.

'I am afraid not, Marshal. I have the Lord's work to do.' My strength wavered for a moment, but I held my voice steady. 'Have you had news of Abraham Muir?'

Reasoner's eyebrows twitched in surprise.

'He is not with you?'

'Would I be asking if he were?'

After a pause he shook his head minutely.

'We have had no word of Muir.'

I tried to keep my face blank, but he must have seen something of the despair that assailed me.

'You cannot keep running,' he told me, 'if you were to turn yourself in—'

'I would be hanged,' I replied, 'for crimes I did not commit.'

He scowled at that. 'I have a great many questions.'

'Perhaps this will answer some of them.' I pulled the land grant application from beneath my jacket and slid it through the gap between the sill and the frame.

He took it with his free hand and shook it open.

'Windrose?' he frowned.

'Sister!'

The cry sent us both leaping from our skins. A pair of horses came bolting out of the night, my own and Templeton's, the newspaperman clinging to the reins of both.

'Sister!' he gasped again. 'We must ride! They are on our trail!'

For an instant nobody moved. Then Reasoner dropped away from the window. I swung the revolver up at the glass, firing once, twice.

Shards exploded into the room. I saw the marshal, cowering beneath their force. The prisoners had surged to their feet, bellowing in fright.

'Thomas Josephine!' shouted Reasoner, staggering to his feet. 'Do not do this!'

I hauled myself into the saddle.

'Follow Windrose!' I cried, before racing away into the night.

6

In the broad ways, I will seek him

Our flight from Denver was frenzied. We rode hell for leather, knowing that within the hour every lawman and bounty hunter who could prise himself from a saloon stool would be tracking us.

'Where are we going?' Templeton called, as we cantered wildly.

I did not answer, only sent my horse snaking back and forth to confuse our tracks. The clouds blew across the moon, plunging the land into darkness, and it was not until my horse set a foot wrong and nearly tumbled into a gulch that I was forced to call a halt.

Gasping, I looked back. I could no longer see Denver, only a faint orange glow, a few pinpricks in the darkness, on the horizon.

'We shall have to wait for dawn,' I told Templeton, dismounting, 'I cannot see the way.'

'The way to where?' He slid to the ground with a groan.

'To help. Of a sort.'

We passed that endless night in shivering at the base of a hill. I stared fixedly toward the east, willing on the coming day. Templeton slept, aided by the brandy in his hip flask, his head nestled upon a rock. Finally, when the false light of dawn made the sky pallid, I walked away, found a place to kneel in the loose dirt.

I had once said my morning devotions upon a Sioux altar, watched the sun rise across a barren plain not so different to this one. Then, I had been innocent, and would never have dreamed that one day I would risk everything for the strange, dark man who had dragged me so precipitously from the course of my life.

I prayed, trying to see my way back to that woman, with her unblemished faith and her handful of broken beads.

I felt the rising sun begin to pull itself up my clothes an inch at a time, and looked out through my lashes. In that hazy light, the land wore its old face, vast and wild and solemn. It was changing, I knew. I had seen it happening, in the streets of San Francisco and the wreckage of Arkansas: becoming a country of hungry mouths and hot iron rails.

'Glory be to the Father, and to the Son and to the Holy Spirit,' I whispered, 'as it was in the beginning, is now and ever shall be, world without end.'

'Amen,' a voice behind me said, low with amusement.

My eyelids flared open.

'Abe?'

I was on my feet in a moment, ready to fly forward in joy. Livid yellow irises stopped me in my tracks.

'Wrong man, Sister,' said Puttick.

... yet I found him not

'You two left a trail like a pair of blind mules,' Puttick chided, leading us down into the mouth of a gulch. 'Took me all of no time to find you, once there was light enough.'

'We were in a hurry,' I said curtly, as my horse picked its way across the loose stones. Part of me stung still from the hope that had accosted me for one, brief moment.

'So I hear tell,' the outlaw smirked and clucked his horse over a difficult piece of ground. 'I was travelin' north anyhow, after a setback or two.' He sniffed and shot me a hard look. 'Would've bypassed the city altogether, had I not read a surprisin' account in one of my newspapers.' He glanced over his shoulder. '"The Savage Murder of Denver Philanthropist Edward Windrose."'

'Why, that was mine!' Templeton cried excitedly from the back of his ailing horse. It was a low creature, short of leg and temper. Puttick watched the newspaperman dig his heels into the horse's flanks to no avail.

'Was it indeed?' he said, before turning to me. 'You reckon it was wise to bring him in tow?'

'I had no choice. Mr Templeton would have been arrested had he stayed behind. And we shall need all the help we can get.'

'"We"?'

'I came to seek you out, Mr Puttick.' For a moment, the stories of the bushwhackers came back to me, their sordid fascination with the notorious Colm Puttick. I would never have believed then that such a man could be anything but an enemy.

'I need your assistance,' I said quietly. 'It is about Windrose. And Abe.'

The outlaw grunted and rode down onto the floor of the gulch. High walls of rocky ground rose above us, casting a chill shade and turning the sky into a bright strip of blue.

'Can't see this place from the plain,' Puttick informed me, dismounting. 'We can rest here a while. Give you time to explain why you're so desirous of keeping my company all a'sudden.'

Templeton lurched from his saddle to join us, holding out a hand.

'The outlaw Colm Puttick,' he gushed, 'I cannot tell you how gratified I am to make your acquaint—'

He looked down at the knife pressed under his nose.

'Newspaperman,' the outlaw said, clear and low, 'you ain't seen me, you will not remember me, you will not write even the first letter of my name. Or I will hunt you down and cut off your hands. That understood?'

Templeton nodded, staring cross-eyed at the blade.

'Assuredly, assuredly, Mr Puttick, any friend of the Sister's, etcetera.'

'I don't believe she would count me a friend.' He removed the blade. 'And I'd ask you to forget that name. I'm going by Bird, now.' His eyes flicked toward me. 'I prefer his company.'

In the hour that followed, I told Puttick everything that had passed in Denver, of Miss Windrose and her father, of her plan for the railroad that would burn its way south from the mines, that would give her the power of a gateway to the west. That all she had to do was clear the land of settlers.

'She has Abe,' I told him, as calmly as I could, 'I am certain of it. She knows that I will—'

'She knows that you'll ride through purgatory to find him,' said Puttick.

I stared down at my hands.

'I need your help,' I forced myself to say. 'Besides everything else, they plan to attack another ranch, and I cannot take them on alone. Miss Windrose has a great deal of might behind her.'

'And we have nothing but the hangman's noose behind us,' the outlaw laughed. 'That is the kind of hand I have been dealt all my life.' He shook his head. 'Goddamit, I'm going north anyhow. Show me this map of yours.'

8

Who is she that cometh
from the desert?

We rode like hunted wolves, following Puttick through trails in the fissured land, watching from the peaks for movement or the merest hint of smoke upon the horizon. Our caution was rewarded; we saw not a soul, save for the eagles that climbed the sky above our heads.

According to the lawyer's map, the Hopkins ranch lay in a valley among the wild foothills of the Rocky Mountains. It was two days' journey away, Puttick guessed. Every step we took from civilization was a step that sent my heart alternately racing and plummeting: were we drawing closer to Abe, or further away? Was he even now being tortured, while I rode free? Sometimes I wanted desperately to turn back, yet I knew I could not fail the Lord again. I had sworn to protect innocent souls in the west, but now, more than ever, I was forced to do so with weapons as much as faith.

We traveled near thirty miles that first day. Unused to such journeys, Templeton fell asleep as soon as he had wolfed down his handful of hardtack and pork. The outlaw and I sat up for a time, waiting for moonrise. By the pale shimmer I checked the state of my weapons: a knife, a pistol and a revolver, enough ammunition for both, shared by Puttick.

I began to clean the guns, murmuring a prayer as I loaded bullets into the chamber.

"'Love your enemies; pray for those who persecute you.'" Puttick was watching my movements. 'Wasn't that always your creed, Sister?'

'And what of yours, "Mr Bird"?' I asked quietly, setting to work on the revolver. 'Did Colm Puttick finally grow tired of his brutality?'

585

Rather than biting back, Puttick only looked out at the night.

'Every man grows tired,' he said eventually, 'and he starts to wonder if there ain't another way to live; a way where the ground beneath his feet does not bleed with every step.'

I felt his yellow eyes on my face.

'I am up to my knees in blood, Sister. Reckon if there's anyone to help me walk out of it, it's you.'

I clenched my jaw. His words brought doubt and shame to my heart, made the guns heavy in my hands, but I continued to work at them, resolute.

'Will you truly run through hell, to save your man?' he asked after a time. 'For you may well need to.'

'I would do so for any man,' I said stiffly. 'I promised that much to the Lord.'

The outlaw moved his head from side to side; had I not known better, I might have said that there was pity upon his face.

'But none more so than him. If you don't open your eyes to that, you will not see the end until it is too late.'

'I walk by faith and not by sight,' I retorted, snapping the chamber closed.

He smiled sadly. 'Then, Sister, you are doubly blind.'

9

The new and the old,
I have kept for thee

The sun lingered in the sky, old gold on bloodless blue. All around I smelled resin from the pine and juniper clinging to the slopes of the foothills. We had made good time following an old wagon trail, and had come across the ranch just as the day was waning.

'I do not have a weapon,' said Templeton anxiously, as he watched us check ours for ammunition.

'That is because you do not know how to use one,' said Puttick tartly, sorting through a handful of percussion caps.

'I do not like this,' the newspaperman was uneasy. 'Should we not wait for darkness proper?'

'You ever tried shooting a man in the dark, sir?' Puttick snorted. 'Go be useful and watch the trail. Whistle if all's well.'

For once, the older man did not object, but trotted back to lurk at the edge of the treeline.

My heart was hammering even as I secured the weapons within my belt. We had ridden close to the little farmstead beneath the cover of the trees, moving like hunters, slow through the undergrowth.

I peered out through the branches. Beyond a dark swathe of grass and a corral was a house, long and low, light from a couple of oil lamps flickering in the twilight. A whistle from Templeton told us that all was clear upon the track. Puttick and I crept forward through the trees, until we could slip into the corral and run quietly through the shadows, trying not to disturb the shifting horses.

A water trough provided some cover. We dropped down behind it, side by side in the gathering gloom. My muscles were twitching with apprehension as I armed the pistol and revolver and Puttick readied his rifle. The click of the hammer being drawn back sounded like a deathwatch beetle in the night. I stared grimly at the cold sheen of the barrel.

'How old are you, Thomas Josephine?' the outlaw whispered suddenly.

The question gave me pause. The years of my life were so distant, so scattered, they did not seem to belong to the same woman.

'Twenty-seven, I believe. But I have never known for certain.'

Puttick gave a brief laugh and rested his forehead against the rifle.

'I have ten years on you. That's three decades' worth of sin. Not six months ago I would've raided a place like this. Would've killed folk like these, maybe remembered enough to let the little ones live, but maybe not. What has me chargin' into their lives now, acting their savior?'

He cast me a thoughtful look in the gathering dark.

'No wonder it drove Carthy mad ...'

A gunshot blasted across the evening, echoing harsh as a handclap against the trees. I had no time to consider Puttick's words, for a cry followed the weapon's retort, a man's voice shrieking in pain. In an instant we were on our feet, vaulting the fence, sprinting headlong across the yard. I gripped the pistol hard as I threw myself through the open door.

Had I not been holding the weapon tightly, it would have fallen from my hand. Four figures stood, weapons drawn, surrounding two men who were slumped in the center of the room. A stocky old man, who I took to be the farmer, held a rifle, an older woman wielded a makeshift pike, while a young girl grappled with an ancient musket, smoking at the end. The fourth figure turned to stare at us, a knife in each hand, blood-soaked from wrist to elbow.

As I watched, she tossed something small and flesh-colored on to the floor in front of the two men. One of them cried out as it landed with a small thud. It was Buxton, I realized then, and the other was Hayle; they were covered with gore and one was missing an ear.

Owl lowered her knives.

'You are late,' she said.

10

Besides what is hid within

'Matthew Hopkins,' the farmer told me, coming forward to shake my hand. 'That there's my wife Susan, and our girl Kitty.'

I reached out to take the proffered hand, only to find that I still held the pistol. Flushing to the roots of my hair, I shoved it back into my waistband and clasped his hand with my own. It was strong, despite his age, and rough with calluses.

'What the hell is going on here?' Puttick exploded, glaring about the room. He held the rifle before him. 'Where did *she* come from?'

'Hello, Colm Puttick,' Owl greeted calmly, blood still dripping off her knives. 'I thought you did not like him?' she asked me.

I leaned around to look at the pair of men they had captured. Hayle was groaning and cursing, blood coursing from the side of his head. Buxton glowered, his teeth gritted. There was a ragged hole in his upper thigh, surrounded by scorch marks and leaking gore.

'I did not think it would fire,' Kitty told me shakily, hefting the old musket. 'It were my granddaddy's. I packed it with buck-shot . . .' she leaped back as Hayle lunged. Hopkins struck him with the butt of the rifle.

Puttick and I kept the pair in the sight of our weapons while Owl and the others set about tying them, hand and foot. When they were finally secured, Puttick swore, lowering his gun.

'*Now* will someone tell me what in Sam Hill is going on?'

'Better fetch Templeton,' I sighed.

By the time darkness fell, we sat comfortably within the farm-house. Outside, a cold breeze rolled down from the mountains, making the stars shiver. The family shared what they had, and we drank tea, ate bread and lard before the hearth. It would have been cosy, were it not for the loaded weapons beside each plate; the pair of wounded ruffians tied in a corner, letting out a curse or a groan every so often.

'I followed them,' Owl chewed, gesturing to Buxton and Hayle with her spoon, 'after the Patterson ranch. You run off, back to town but these two I follow. It was not difficult. They are lazy. All the way to that big house in the mountains, I watched them. Like a hawk,' she grinned, and Hayle snarled, thrashing in his ropes. He fell still when three weapons were leveled at him.

'Many times, I could have killed them when they slept,' she told me, 'but I thought, they will go after others. And when they do . . .' she shrugged.

'What she is not saying,' Hopkins said matter-of-factly, 'is that she rode ahead of them, when they stopped at noon. Damn near flogged her horse to death doin' it, damn near got a bullet in her gut as well, 'til she took off her hat. We was expecting *you* to attack, see,' he said to me, and I felt my face begin to burn with anger, 'but she warned us, told us what was what. That it weren't you coming, but these two.'

'Mr Windrose made an offer for our land,' Susan told me, 'a few month back. It were generous enough, but this is our home. Matthew worked ten year to get enough money for these acres, an' near another ten farming them. We ain't leaving. We told him as much.'

'Then came the stories, 'bout other settling folk gettin' killed down south, but we never thought—'

'That they had refused to sell too,' my head sank to my hands. 'Five hundred miles of land to be cleared of homesteaders, and only one person in the country who could kill so many without motive.' In the silence I listened to my heartbeat, to the shifting of ash in the grate. I raised my head to look at Miss Windrose's men. 'All to be certain of her claim. She will not stop, will she?'

Hayle only sneered at me and spat.

I was on my feet, had the gun to his head before I even knew what I was doing. I stared at him, pale and bloody beyond the pistol's length. All the fragile cheer of the hearthside was gone as I barked out that one question which plagued me, drove me.

'Where is Muir?'

Hayle's lips lifted into a smile.

'You won't do nothing,' he said. Confidence oozed from him as he settled back against the wall, blood stained as he was. 'You never killed a man in your life.'

'I asked you a question.'

Hayle only snorted up a ball of mucus and spat again.

I raised my eyebrow.

'Owl,' I called over my shoulder, 'did you cut off his ear?'

Stony faced, the woman nodded, brushing strands of black hair back from her face. 'You want me to cut off the other one?'

I opened my mouth to respond when a force struck my shins, sending me tumbling to the floor. The pistol flew out of my grip, and in an instant, Hayle attacked, pinning me to the boards with his body as his bound hands grappled for me, thumbs plunging toward my eyes.

A flash of silver, a dark shadow above and warm blood exploded onto my face. Hayle's body went limp as he opened and closed his mouth emptily, life flooding from the sundered arteries of his neck.

Hands grasped my shoulders, and Puttick dragged me free from under the body. I swiped the blood from my eyes. Templeton and the Hopkins family looked on, grim-faced. Susan offered me a rag.

'Did you have to kill him?' I asked Owl, scrubbing at my face.

The dark-haired woman pursed her lips and began to clean her knife.

'We need only one of them to tell us where to go.'

Every pair of eyes turned toward Buxton, who was gazing in alarm at Hayle's lifeless corpse.

'North,' he blurted, 'up near Stout. I do not know if Muir is there,' his eyes were fixed upon Owl's knife, 'but that is where *she* will be. It is the start of the railroad.'

11

The sons of my mother have fought against me

The road stretched ahead of us, if it could be called a road. It was more akin to a dust farm, banked up at the sides and rutted by the passing of wheels. Puttick spat down and tramped back toward us.

'Reckon this is the stage route,' he called, around a mouthful of tobacco. 'We'd do well to keep clear of it, *if* we knew where the hell we are s'posed to be going.'

Buxton looked harassed. He was tied to the saddle and grimacing from the pain in his leg. Puttick and I had roped his horse to ours, in case he should try to escape. I had done my duty and bound the injury, but nothing more.

'I told you, this were the way,' he insisted.

'If this is a trick—' Puttick growled.

'I believe we are on the right track,' Templeton interrupted, squinting at the crumpled map in his hands. 'There is something marked here, just south of Camp Collins, though I cannot make out what it is.'

'Then we do not need him?' Owl asked, reaching for her knife.

I looked into Buxton's perspiring face and sighed.

'Leave him be. He may be of use yet.'

We had set off at dawn, reasoning that if we rode hard, we would reach the railroad camp by nightfall. As the sun began its slow descent into the mountains, a restless tension fell upon us all. Had we been hounds, our hackles would have bristled. Puttick especially was silent and seething.

'Tell me, Sister,' he said abruptly after a time, 'what will happen if your dear Abraham is *not* Miss Windrose's captive?'

593

His voice was innocent, but my stomach tightened, for I knew his tone, knew that these were Puttick's twisting and taunting words, not those of the more measured Mr Bird.

'What,' he continued caustically, 'if your man has taken that ten thousand dollars and high-tailed it to the nearest cat-house?' Before I could answer, he wheeled around. 'I know! You shall say, "Abraham Muir is a good man", but any man would be good if he were around you, Sister, he could not help it.' His eyes were livid. 'Here we are, killers and castaways all, galloping off into danger and near certain death with the Six-Gun Sister.' He drew up beside me again.

'But it's Muir, goddam drifter Muir from Arkansas who's got you at his back,' he said. 'You doubted him once, when you thought he rode with me, and you doubt him now, in your heart, but still you follow.'

I stared him out, watched as the fury drained from his face, as the mania ebbed back into the pool within him. Then I pulled my horse to a stop upon the road. The others followed suit. Buxton was staring at us.

'A life for a life.' My voice was hard and clear as glass. 'That is how it has always been between Abe and me. That is how it will always be.' My horse kicked up puffs of dirt as it shifted. 'I cannot ask any of you to come with me.'

Puttick dropped his chin to his scarred chest.

'Damn you,' he laughed emptily, 'it is too late for that. You got me.'

'And I,' said Templeton, 'although I do not know what help I shall be.'

Owl looked at our expectant faces.

'I have nowhere better to be,' she shrugged.

'I would leave, but I am tied to a horse,' Buxton said, but shut his mouth abruptly as Owl glanced his way.

I felt a smile playing around my lips for the first time in many days.

'And Corinthians would have us believe that evil companions corrupt good morals,' I said.

'What about Proverbs,' Puttick countered loftily, 'Twenty-seven, seventeen?'

'Indeed. "Iron sharpens iron,"' I grinned.

12

The daughter of the multitude

We raided the first trading post we found. I sent up a brief prayer for God to forgive me as I loaded my pockets with ammunition. The proprietor lay tied upon the floor of his shack, staring up at us in bewilderment. I pitied him, for a more rag-tag group of thieves there never were.

We rode into the foothills, loaded down with bullets and knives. Here the stony ridges were accordion-sharp, green with spiny shrubs that bothered the horses and caught at our clothing. The sun was golden, in the hinterland between afternoon and evening. We pushed hard. Just as the heat of the day began to wane, we crested a ridge and saw it.

The work camp spread out along the floor of a valley. Every tree had been hewn down, as far as the eye could see; even the drought-stunted cottonwoods had been hauled into the camp, where they waited to be stripped of their branches like fowl. Coal dust caked the eastern ridge. A huge, black pile of the stuff rose against the hill, as high as a two-story house.

Two long, low buildings framed the camp, and as we watched, figures poured from their doors. Even from a distance I realized who they were: the older children whom Miss Windrose had saved from the Denver streets, from the mines. They were rushing toward something, a hundred, two hundred of them.

'She has built an army,' Templeton swore softly, following their progress as they hurried into the road where a carriage was pulling to a stop. In its wake rode a company of Union soldiers, their buckles flashing in the evening light.

'She knew you would come,' Buxton sneered. 'You'll have t'get through half the cavalry to get at her.'

'Stop his tongue,' Puttick growled.

'Not literally,' I warned Owl.

Rolling her eyes, she ripped a length of rag from a bundle on her saddle and stuffed it into Buxton's mouth.

'This is madness,' hissed Templeton, watching as Miss Windrose stepped from the carriage to greet the soldiers. 'Sister, this is surely suicide. There are forty armed men down there—'

'Forty-four,' Puttick dismissed, 'bluebellies all. Look, they hold their rifles like they're mopping a parlor.'

'We are but *four*,' Templeton pleaded. 'How are we to take them on?'

I was not listening to him, for my eyes had strayed into the corner of the camp nearest to us, where a number of crates had been stacked, away from all else. I turned back with a twisted smile.

'Follow me.'

13

Put me as a seal upon thy heart,
a seal upon thy arm

Puttick sat quietly beside me. I could smell the sweat and the dust of the road upon him, the sour tang of gorse crushed beneath our boots. Night was falling upon the camp. I peered along the steep slope. Owl was a shadow, standing perfectly still, her boot resting upon a small keg.

A barrel shifted on the loose ground beneath my own foot. I pressed down a little more firmly. My hands were shaking as I armed the pistol. Puttick armed his rifle with a click, and loosed a shallow breath.

'What will you do?' he asked in a whisper. 'You and Abraham? After all this?'

'What we have always done.' I gave him a half-smile, grasped the rosary with my free hand. 'Try to live.'

He laughed soundlessly.

'Amen, Sister.'

I opened my mouth to reply when a gunshot thundered from above. A man's cry followed, and the drumming of hooves. Buxton shot from the ridge behind us, a cloud of grit spraying up as he rode for the camp, bellowing all the way.

'Templeton,' Puttick swore, surging upright.

The next moment, the air was full of death, bullets skimming past our heads and ears with their terrifying whine. I dragged Puttick down even as charges thudded into the hillside around us, sending leaves and dirt flying.

I glanced over my shoulder. Owl too was cowering from the bullets, and all the while, the barrels rested at our feet.

'Now!' I yelled.

I kicked the barrel from under me. Puttick sent his own

spinning into the darkness a moment later. I leaped to my feet, sighted the pistol and murmured one, desperate prayer to the Lord as I fired.

Puttick's rifle discharged at the same time, a tongue of flame and smoke. Along the ridge I heard a shot from Owl too, rebounding down the valley sides. For a breathless instant, we stared at each other. Then an almighty force flung us backward, flame blasting up into the sky like a demon, as the nitroglycerine exploded and exploded again.

My ears were ringing, my eyes blinded by the dust, but Puttick was dragging me to my feet.

'Go!' he yelled, pulling the shotgun from his back. 'Find Muir!'

I threw myself down the hillside, toward the smoke and flames. The heat seared my face and I let out a wordless cry as another explosion rattled the ground, sending me sprawling.

I did not know where the bullets were coming from. The very air was smoldering as I choked some of it into my lungs. I staggered to my feet, only to fall again, tripping over a dark shape that lay upon the rock-strewn ground. Fingers gripped my leg and I screamed, kicking out. A man was grappling along my body, a Union soldier, reaching for the guns in my hands. His face was a mess of gore from the blast.

Furiously, I rolled, pinning him to the ground beneath my knee. His pupils were dark wells within the whites of his eyes.

'Where is he?' I yelled down at him. 'Where is Muir?'

The man only gurgled, his mouth flooding with blood. His eyes flickered over my shoulder, staring at something behind me. I threw myself to one side just as the butt of the rifle came slamming downward.

It caught my bad arm and I yelled in pain, dropping one of the guns. A figure was looming above. It was Buxton, raising the rifle to shoot me.

Crimson exploded from his chest and sent him staggering. Above, silhouetted by the flames, I saw Puttick lowering his own rifle. His teeth shone like a coyote's in the night.

But then his face convulsed. I followed his shocked eyes down to his chest, where a dark stain was spreading on his shirt. I heard myself crying out, even as a second bullet thudded into him, and a third. Then he was gone.

In that moment I felt nothing and everything: there was a high-pitched whine in my ears, the smell of burning rock and hot iron, spilling from weapons and bodies.

Will you truly run through hell to find your man?

The rosary beads dug into my hand. At their end was the cross, that small wooden token that had drunk the whole of America into its grain. Blood and snow, sand and sweat, carved for me by a man who I would not allow to die.

My eyes were clear as I strode toward the buildings. A soldier came running from the shadows, crouched low. My bullet struck him in the leg. Another fired from behind a stack of lumber. I shot the rope that held the logs and sent them tumbling down.

Ahead was the doorway, corn-yellow oil light spilling though the smoke. I threw myself up the steps and into the building.

'Abe!' I cried, surging forward.

The click of a gun sounded and I spun, pistol raised. Miss Windrose stood behind me. She was breathing heavily, a revolver in her hand. The sleeve of her dress was torn and her neck and face peppered with blood from the explosions.

We were aiming dead at each other's chests.

'It did not have to be this way.' Her voice shook with anger. 'All this violence.' She blinked away tears fiercely. 'I am trying to *help* people, Thomas Josephine, I am trying to give the hopeless of this country a future.'

'One built upon death and deceit.' My voice was scorched. 'What sort of a future is that?'

'The one we must take up,' she said. 'The one my father believed in, that Theodore went to fight for.'

A grim laugh broke from me.

'Carthy knew he had been wrong,' I said. 'He begged me for salvation and I told him that it was not too late. It is not too late for you, either.'

'I do not want salvation,' Miss Windrose raged, tears streaking her face. 'I want freedom!'

A violent blast shook the walls.

'Where is Abe?' I shouted, for the world was breaking around us.

Before she could answer, there was a noise from the doorway. Metal sparked at the corner of my eye; the barrel of a gun, taking me in its sight. I spun and fired, the pistol shuddering in my grip. Beyond the smoke, I saw a figure lurch, and my heart stopped.

The boy fell forward into the light. John, his name came to me in a flash, John Luther, from the hospital. A rifle, too big for him to wield, clattered down beside him. The sounds of fighting faded as I watched the ribbon of blood unfurl from the corner of his mouth.

Miss Windrose's scream broke upon my ears. I knew then that I was damned.

14

Till the day break and the shadows retire

I did not move. Not when the cry went up and horses thundered into the valley, bearing soldiers and lawmen, commanding everyone there to lay down their arms.

I did not move, not when the child was taken up from the floor, when Miss Windrose was prised away from his small body. Not even when I saw Templeton creeping forward, a pencil and paper trembling in his grubby hands.

I only stared at that spot on the ground, at that small pool of innocent blood that contained barely a palmful of bright years, a palmful of summers upon this earth. God had not guided my hand. *I* in my defiance and desire, doubly blind, had wrought this.

They had taken me somewhere. I did not know where and did not ask, for it was of no consequence. At one point, the hands that pushed me to and fro grew gentler, and I looked up to find myself cuffed to Marshal Reasoner. There was no triumph in his face as we swayed with the movement of a jail coach, no victory. He did not speak to me, only of me, as if I was cargo, and for that at least, I was grateful.

Days had passed since then in a parade of emptiness. Prayers shriveled and died upon my tongue. I had no right to utter them. They had left me my rosary, but I could not use it. I could only hold the beads against my palm, worn smooth by the years against Muir's neck.

My traitor senses pulled me back to consciousness when no self-recrimination could. I smelled pomade, sweet, greasy and familiar, and raised my eyes to the grill in the door of the cell.

Templeton stood there, his mouth trembling at the corners. After a moment the door swung open, and he was admitted. He kept his distance, though there was no need. I was chained to a rough brick wall. I had not noticed before. It looked strangely familiar.

'Sis . . .' Templeton's voice sputtered and died as I met his eyes.

'He was never there, was he?'

My voice rasped, like that of an old woman.

Templeton looked as though he had been drained of blood. He stared at one of his fingernails as he shook his head.

'No. He never was.'

I sought his face desperately. I had one hope. It was a single, golden thread in the darkness, fine as a spider's web.

'Miss Windrose did not lie,' the newspaperman cleared his throat. 'For all her failings, she did not dissemble on that point. Muir took the money.'

Templeton shifted, evidently unnerved by my silence.

'I never thought—' he began, and stopped miserably. 'I have debts, Sister. Miss Windrose holds a great many cards, and I do not have the constitution for resistance. Muir made a wise decision. The war is all but finished now, and people like her, they will hold the power, they . . .' he trailed off.

'The boy?' I asked, though it took every last ounce of my strength.

'He might live,' Templeton murmured.

I watched the guilt contort his face. He gripped at his chest beneath the waistcoat.

'You believe in redemption, don't you, Sister? Might I be saved from this?'

His face was flushed with unshed tears, red with remorse. I knew we were seeing the same image then, that small figure upon the ground, my bullet in his chest.

'Come here, Mr Templeton.'

He almost tripped over his feet in his haste to kneel before me. I leaned forward.

'Ask the dead,' I whispered into his face, 'ask the innocent who were killed. They will tell you where to find your salvation.'

I did not watch him leave. The emptiness that roared around me was too great. I could do nothing more than close my hands about my knees, weighed down by the passing minutes.

Eventually, there was a noise outside. Reasoner's face appeared at the door.

'Is it time?' I asked.

We will run after thee

The marshal stayed a step behind me as we walked, one arm raised, as if I might bolt at any moment. He wore two pistols, I saw, loosely holstered. Evidently, I was considered dangerous.

A door was swung open before me and I stepped into blinding sunlight. The heat of noon blazed down, until I was forced to close my watering eyes. Wind whipped against my face, carrying dust and a smell that I remembered from another life. I opened my eyes.

I began laughing then, a terrible dry sound that wracked my throat. I laughed until I doubled over the shackles upon my wrists, until the parade ground before me swam and blurred. I heard Reasoner's alarmed voice, issuing orders, felt him take my arm and drag me into the shade of another building.

A chair was pushed under me. The laughter ran itself ragged, leaving me weak and gasping. I found a tin cup in my hands, and drank the sun-stale liquid in greedy gulps.

'Even the water tastes the same,' I croaked up at Reasoner.

He was glowering down at me. I dragged the cuffs upward in order to wipe my eyes upon my sleeve.

'"Toward the south, and again to the north: the wind returneth upon her circuits."' I looked into his face. 'We are at Fort Laramie.'

He shifted his feet to and fro.

'It was the closest place a court could assemble.'

'If I did not know better, I would think the Lord was mocking me,' I murmured, looking about.

We were in a small room, wooden walled. Apart from the stool on which I sat, there was a table, a bowl of water and beside it, a bundle of brown cloth. Reasoner stepped forward to shake it out. Bile caught in my throat. It was a habit.

'They will not see you, dressed as you are,' the marshal told me. 'You're to wash and wear this.'

My hands, so still before, began to shake.

'I cannot,' I told him, trying to hold my chin firm, 'it would be an insult.'

Reasoner rubbed at his brow as if it pained him.

'The general will have it so, whether you will or not. I'd rather they did not ask me to use force.'

I sighed and held out my wrists. Cautiously, he freed them from the cuffs.

'Do not concern yourself, Marshal,' I told him, as I picked up the washcloth. 'We both of us know that I am not leaving this place.'

He kept his back carefully turned as I scrubbed the dirt from my face and neck, from beneath my nails as best I could. Twice, I thought I might lose control again, to sob or laugh as I remembered washing thus, sluicing away the dust of the plains, cutting the curls from my head, not knowing that Lieutenant Carthy would claim one as his own. That he would write back to the fiancée whose likeness I had seen, with news of his talks, his suppers with me.

I have met a most singular woman . . .

I shuddered as the loose garment dropped over my head, as I pulled the veil over my hair. The habit, which had once given me such comfort, only now brought sorrow. Finally, I hung the rosary around my neck.

'There,' I said, holding my wrists out to Reasoner. 'Will this suit them well enough?'

He stared at me for a long moment, before grunting and securing the shackles. Outside, the sun glinted from one window in particular. As the glass flashed, I thought I saw a face looking back, eyes as blue as the sky above.

Reasoner took me to a tiny chamber, somewhere between a hallway and an anteroom. Voices, firm and resolute, were filtering through the walls. A soldier outside the door broke off his study of me to disappear inside.

'They will prepare for you,' the marshal said.

I nodded. My mind was racing, yet I could not make it settle upon any one thought.

'They will hang me, will they not?' I asked vaguely.

'I cannot say.'

Reasoner was unhappy, I realized. Before, he had been dour, resolute, but never uncertain in his work.

'You know,' I whispered, 'about Windrose? You know it was not I who killed all those homesteaders?'

His eyes were troubled.

'Whatever the case,' he said, 'there are crimes that must be answered for.'

'What of Puttick? And Owl?' I demanded.

Reasoner frowned at me.

'Owl? Are you well, Sister?'

I stared in silence and he shook himself, as if to loosen the bothersome emotions that hung between us. 'Puttick hasn't been seen since the night we caught you. We'll find him in the end.' He scowled, for I was gaping at him like a fool. 'Why should you ask?'

'For no reason,' I managed, and folded my hands. 'I am happy that he might live, if you can countenance that.'

The silence lengthened to one heartbeat, then another. I felt my lips part, to form that name, the one I was most afraid to say.

'And what of—'

The door swung open.

'They are ready for you,' someone called.

Reasoner took hold of my shoulder and pushed me forward. I began shaking then, as I was jostled into a room that was hot and close. Benches lined the space, crammed with soldiers, with civilians, all hungry to see justice dispensed. At the front a man in a general's uniform sat perspiring at a desk. Below him in a makeshift witness' stand stood another man, his wrists manacled.

Reasoner caught me as my knees collapsed.

It was Muir.

16

For love is strong as death
and hard as hell

'Abe!'

The cry broke from me and I ran forward, forgetting everything except his face, raised to mine. I was jerked back by the chain of my cuffs.

'Court will now hear the full testimony of Abraham C. Muir, formerly of the 3rd Colorado Infantry, wanted for desertion and two counts of murder, including that of Captain Theodore F. Carthy.'

Muttering swept the room. Abe stood, silent and stony-faced beneath the accusations. I opened my mouth to cry again, but Reasoner seized my arm with hard fingers.

'Silence,' he hissed. 'You will do him no favors.'

For a moment Abe's eyes traveled over me. Then he turned to face the court, chest raised. A slim man in a city suit stood up beside him and opened a document.

'I, Abraham Muir,' he read out in a monotone, 'being of sound mind, do hereby confess myself guilty of all the misdeeds leveled against me.' A shiver of excitement ran through the spectators. 'What is more,' the city-man raised his voice above the noise, 'I do confess that I knowingly, and with bad intent, seduced one Sister Thomas Josephine, of St. Louis, Missouri. I did this with the sole purpose of exploiting her to conceal my further crimes, which amount to numerous murders across the states of California, Arkansas, the Colorado and New Mexico Territories . . .'

'No!' I burst, straining forward again.

'If she cannot be silent she will have to be removed,' the general snapped at Reasoner. 'Continue.'

The suited man nodded up at him.

'Mr Muir, that was your full and true testimony?' he asked. Muir stared straight ahead.

'It was.'

'You accept and acknowledge that all crimes attributed to the "Six-Gun Sister" Thomas Josephine are in fact your own?'

'I do,' Muir said stiffly. 'Thomas Josephine was my unwilling captive, as any man from Lieutenant Carthy's regiment can testify. Later, I deceived her into believin' she were in love with me. She is innocent in all this.'

'No,' I begged, 'Abraham, please!'

'You see?' Abe turned to the general, before he could utter a reprimand, 'even now she would die for me.'

'Enough!' the general looked thoroughly displeased as he consulted a piece of paper. 'Court will now hear the testimony of the Reverend James O'Beirne of the Vicariate Apostolic of the Nebraska Territory.'

The room fairly exploded as a priest stood up and made his way forward. His black robes and sash were travel-stained. I thought my heart would thunder out of my chest as the man of God turned and looked upon me with sharp, dark eyes. Shame and anger crashed together as I returned his gaze.

'Father O'Beirne,' the suited man said forcefully, to quell the chatter, 'in the absence of a diocese across the Western States, you represent the jurisdiction of Pope Pius IX. Is that true?'

'It is.'

The man's voice was soft, Irish. I continued to stare in horror as the suited man produced a second document, with the look of a letter.

'You have provided us here with an article of correspondence from Sister Beatrice Clement, the Mother Superior of Thomas Josephine's Visitandine Order in St. Louis. It informs us that the Sister in question has always been infirm of mind. Do you acknowledge this to be the case?'

'I do.'

O'Beirne's eyes were fixed upon mine. I read their warning there clear enough and said nothing.

'I acknowledge,' he told the general, 'that Thomas Josephine has been naïve and easily deceived. But whatever her sins or failings, she is of the Church.' He took a sealed document from within his cassock and handed it to the suited man. 'Sister Thomas Josephine has been granted a pardon from the Archdiocese. The Archbishop requests that she be returned immediately to her convent in Missouri, where she can be kept from further sin.'

The lawyer handed the pardon up to the general, who looked at it with irritation.

'Are there any further testimonies?' he asked, shifting impatiently in his seat.

'No, sir.'

'Well then.' He pulled himself up within his uniform.

'In light of the evidence given here today, I find Sister Thomas Josephine not guilty of the crimes of which she has been accused. She is to be returned immediately to the custody of the Church, where she shall be confined for her own safety.'

Muir sagged visibly with relief. I stared at him in shock. My mind had slowed to a crawl, unable to decipher what was taking place. All I could see was Abe, as he turned his head to give me his broken smile.

'In conclusion,' the general was barking, 'Abraham C. Muir, I find you guilty of the crime of desertion, as well as sixteen counts of murder, all of which carry the penalty of death. I hereby sentence you to death by firing squad, applicable immediately.'

A silent roar filled my ears, the world disconnecting around me. Arms caught my elbows as I half fainted, but I fought to keep my eyes open, to keep them on upon Abe. Tears were beginning to coat his cheeks as he likewise fought to keep me in his gaze through the crowd. He was pushed from the judge's bench, toward the door that led to the parade ground and death.

I felt the shackles drop from my wrists. Another hand gripped my shoulder, strong and fierce. Reverend O'Beirne was beside me, propelling me in the opposite direction. Reasoner too, his face grim.

'No!' I struggled.

'Keep walking and stay quiet, you foolish woman,' the Reverend Father hissed.

I saw it then, the path my life would take: the long, cold days at the convent. Watched always, whispered about, drugged and spoon-fed when the pain within my soul became too great. Never again the wide, open plains, the thrill of a horse cantering beneath me and the scent of woodsmoke, of gunpowder, of liquor in my nose. Never again that smile, lifted crookedly to greet me, those eyes, deeper than the ancient trees of the western forests; those scarred hands, closed upon mine.

'Thought it might make you smile . . .' I whispered.

Reasoner turned in alarm at my words, too late. I slammed my head backward, my skull smashing into the face of the priest, and lunged. For one, endless moment, the marshal hesitated, his eyes wide. Then I was shoving him away and the pistols at his waist were in my hands, their wooden grips singing against my palms. I armed them in one movement and ran.

A soldier leaped at me from the aisle only to trip sprawling over Templeton's outstretched leg. I had one chance. Gritting my teeth, I sighted both weapons and pulled the triggers.

The two soldiers escorting Muir cried out and fell, each struck in the shoulder. I threw myself at Abe, dragging him into the tiny anteroom. It was barely more than four paces wide from wall to wall, and completely empty.

'Quickly!' I screamed, lunging to bolt the outside door, as men pounded across the distance toward us.

White-faced and shackled though he was, Abe slammed the courtroom door shut and leaned his full weight against it. The crash of limbs exploded from the other side as I ran to him.

I sobbed his name over and over, my forehead pressed to his. His manacled hands were holding my head, eyes taking in every inch of my face.

'What the hell are you doin'?' he demanded, half laughing, half crying. 'Sister, you were *free*.'

The inner door shuddered as people threw their shoulders

against it. I could hear weapons being armed, ready to blast through the thin wood.

'Ten thousand dollars, you cost me,' Abe was whispering into my face, 'ten thousand in bribes to the law and the damn Church so you could *live*.'

'Not without you,' I told him fiercely, 'never without you.'

The crashing came again, and I flung my weight beside him, to hold them back.

'No good,' he yelled, as the hinges began to tear away from the doorframe. 'We're clean outta luck.'

I thrust one of the pistols into his hands.

'Just as well, Abraham, I was starting to think we did not know how to die.'

The gunshots started then, from both sides, blasting around us, filling the air with splinters.

'What you said, Sister, you still think it's true?' Abe shouted, as the panel cracked behind us. 'That no man is beyond salvation?'

Shoulder to shoulder we stood, each with a pistol raised. I reached out and gripped his hand.

'I do not know, Abe.' In the last moment before the door gave way, I raised his fingers to my lips. 'But I have found mine.'

EPILOGUE

British Columbia, Canada, 1866
Who is and was and is to come?

The morning was bright, the sun squandering the last of its warmth before the chill of winter set in. The man inside the trade post turned his face to the breeze as it rustled the posters and bills of sale tacked to the walls, and then went back inside to make the coffee.

When its bitter scent had filled the room, he carried his tin mug over to the counter where a quantity of newspapers lay. Contentedly, he began to turn the pages, his eyes traveling over each and every line. The gold rushes were bringing more and more prospectors north. There was even talk of turning the colony into a province, nice and proper.

A noise from outside sent his head jerking up, but he soon lowered it again. A thickset man dressed in trapper's furs stumped in through the door.

'Mornin', Bird,' the trapper mumbled, slow and ponderous.

'Help yourself to some coffee, Oscar,' the man at the counter said, without looking up.

Gratefully, the trapper unhooked a second mug from the shelf and poured himself a steaming cupful. He stood quietly, taking the scalding liquid in small sips.

'What is it, Bird?' he asked, for the man at the counter had stiffened. His yellow eyes were fixed upon a single line of text, far down upon the page. After a time, his lips drew back over his teeth in a manner that could only be described as wolfish. The trapper shifted uneasily.

'Bird?'

'Nothing, Oscar. Some folk starting up a mission over Alexandria way, is all. A nun and a priest, says here.'

'A nun?' snorted the trapper into his coffee. 'What sorta nun would be crazy enough t'go venturin' up the Fraser River in the middle of gold fever?'

'Can't think,' replied Bird with a slow grin. 'Now, shall we to business?'

ACKNOWLEDGEMENTS

Gosh darn, the folk I need to thank deserve more than a green-horn like me could ever conjure up. First, I guess, I gotta thank Ma and Pa, for the stories, the patience and the love: a barrelful of each. Lucy too, my oldest pard and partner in crime. Wouldn't be writing this if not for my agent, "Wily" Ed Wilson, who dragged me off the slush pile, gussied me up and slapped my rump out there. Same goes for Editor (Anne) Perry; hands-down, pistols-up the best there is, and the only soul in this country who would've said yes to a nun with a gun in the west. All of my readers this past year, y'all have kept a first time writer warm. Friends who've listened to my ramblings number the fine Misses Gordes, Geussens, Cheshire, Preston & Mayling. A bow to Charlton Mackrell (Patron of the Arts), Timorous Beastie and the Brothers Hill. Salutes to Grandma Iris for the gin, and the Coppells for bailing a body out more than once. R (1992 - 2003) I promised you this mention a long time ago. And finally, imper-atively, Nicholas: my help, hearth and hope.